Friedrich H.K. La Motte-Froquè

The Magic Ring

A knightly romance

Friedrich H.K. La Motte-Froquè

The Magic Ring
A knightly romance

ISBN/EAN: 9783337310233

Printed in Europe, USA, Canada, Australia, Japan

Cover: Foto ©Andreas Hilbeck / pixelio.de

More available books at **www.hansebooks.com**

THE MAGIC RING

A Knightly Romance

BY

DE LA MOTTE FOUQUÉ

ILLUSTRATED

London and New York:
GEORGE ROUTLEDGE AND SONS
1876

To

The Gentle Reader.

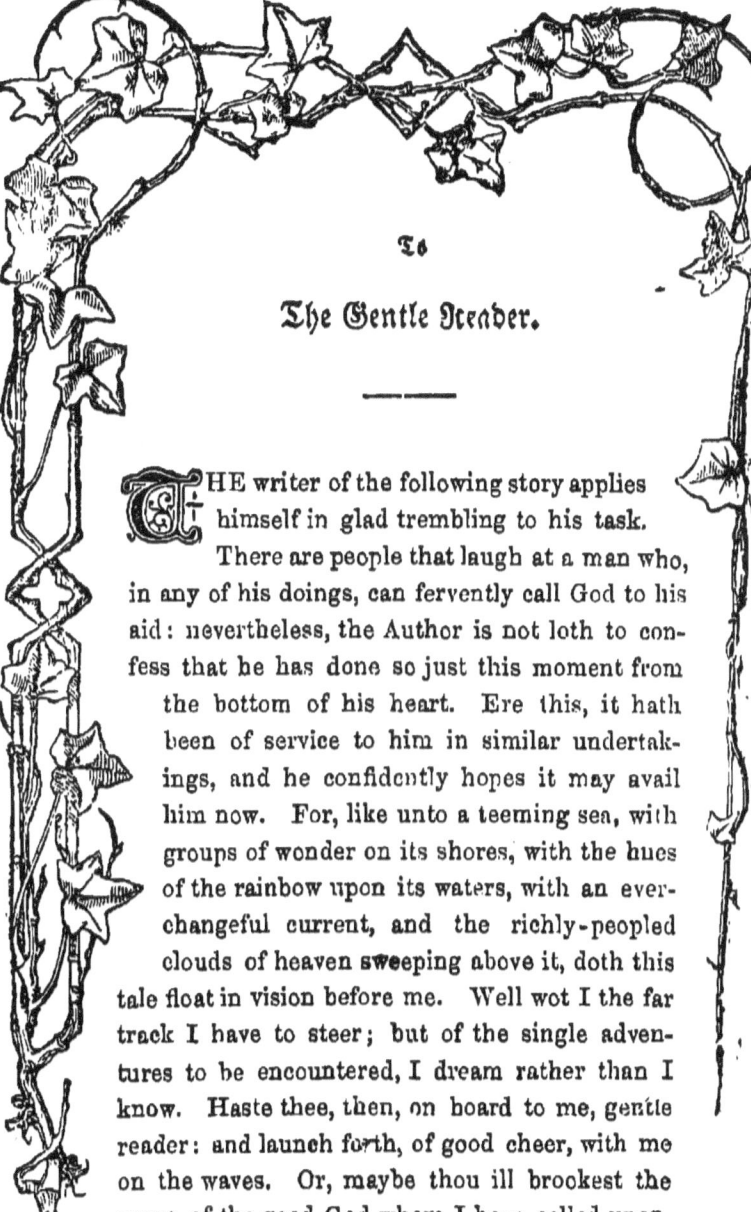

THE writer of the following story applies himself in glad trembling to his task. There are people that laugh at a man who, in any of his doings, can fervently call God to his aid: nevertheless, the Author is not loth to confess that he has done so just this moment from the bottom of his heart. Ere this, it hath been of service to him in similar undertakings, and he confidently hopes it may avail him now. For, like unto a teeming sea, with groups of wonder on its shores, with the hues of the rainbow upon its waters, with an ever-changeful current, and the richly-peopled clouds of heaven sweeping above it, doth this tale float in vision before me. Well wot I the far track I have to steer; but of the single adventures to be encountered, I dream rather than I know. Haste thee, then, on board to me, gentle reader: and launch forth, of good cheer, with me on the waves. Or, maybe thou ill brookest the name of the good God whom I have called upon, or thou mightest well be content, I ween, with that which I shall give thee, with all that hath suggested or still may suggest itself. Know only, that what pleases thee best is not my own; but that it is a certain sweet gift from above, which only becomes mine when I myself am better than lies usually within the compass of my degenerate nature. Albeit, in the following leaves, I give thee the very best that I can achieve; and in so saying, I tender thee the pure truth, for which my word of honour stands pledged. To mead, then, and to grove, to fight and to festival, to day of woe or of wedding, as they hereafter shall unfold themselves, I welcome thee from the bottom of my soul!

The Magic Ring.

CHAPTER I.

IN the favoured land of the Suabians, hard by the banks of the Danube, lies a beautiful mead; and there, one month of May, just as the last rays of the sun were taking leave of the flowers, strolled a young scion of knighthood, named Otto von Trautwangen. From the castle of his father, Sir Hugh von Trautwangen, that stood not far off, on a lofty hill, he used often to repair to this pleasant scene; now amusing himself with the baited hook in the stream, and now shooting his cross-bow-bolts at mock dragons, witches, and cobolds, which he fashioned for himself in many an uncouth form, painting them in gaudy colours, and then setting them up on the green plain, where he was sure of not injuring any one unawares. But to-day, bow and bolt lay by him on the grass, while he let his hook wanton gently over the smooth mirror of the waters, less, it would seem, for the sake of fishing, than in the listless play of thought. There was not perhaps even a worm upon it. Then Bertha von Lichtenried came that way; she was his father's niece, and had been brought up with him from his earliest childhood in the castle. She sat down beside him on the sward, and asked him, half teasingly, yet in a tone of kind interest, what he might then so sweetly be dreaming of. He scarcely knew himself, and still less could he say, since her pretty little face had been smiling on him from the water. It looked all too beautiful from out the flood; and haply she thought the same of him, for she still kept smiling on his counterpart; and thus did the two beauteous children hold parley, as it were, in the mirror with each other. When Otto had bethought himself for a time, he remembered that a pilgrim in a red-cross mantle, passing on the other side of the river, had first made him so thoughtful. He told the maiden of this, and how very solemn it had seemed to him, that the palmer should ever keep his eye steadfastly before him, looking neither to the right nor to the left, as if hurried on by some irrepressible longing; so that one could not even guess whether it was age or meekness, or fervent eagerness to reach his goal, that thus bowed down his head. Then he began saying, how fine and glorious a thing it was to travel far over land and stream and sea; how endlessly dear above every thing this must be to one; and how, in such wanderings, travel itself was not so much a burden as that dreary resting all alone.

"But you are not thinking of wandering thus?" said the maiden, with a trusting smile.

"Heaven forbid!" answered the youth. "These low lands here are all my goal, or rather my magic ring; but only take care that *you* never leave them, my wondrously fair little cousin."

Bertha blushed so brightly, that it looked as if a tiny star had kindled in the water, while she said to her young kinsman: "Since you are so *very* sure, then, we may venture a joke about parting. Let us sing that little farewell ditty that old Master Walther rhymed. We feel more at ease, you know, and all the happier after it, for not really needing to leave each other."

And Otto began to sing as follows:

"Sweet home of our childhood,
Dear place to us,
I greet thee, but greet thee
Bitterly thus.
Bitterly thus, for oh! adieu!
How mournfully it knelleth!
And that thou art no more in view
My tearful eyelid telleth."

Bertha answered:

"Thou naughty distance,
So smooth and so fair,
How gladly I'd track thee!
How little I dare!

For ah! the word's adieu! adieu!
Maiden must wait so lonely,
And with her weeping eye bestrew
The garden flow'rets only."

They ceased their song; for so large a train of pilgrims passed by on the other side of the stream, and in such motley guise too, that the young people turned their whole attention that way. In the centre of the throng were beautiful women, conspicuous on costly-arrayed mules; while a guard of warriors, with huge halberts, walked close at their side. Then, again, some there were who, in spite of the gray garb and the cockle-hat, might at once be said to come from court, their noble grace and seemly air matching so oddly with that of the burly peasantry that pressed around or jostled through them. Yet honest burghers too might be seen in their numbers, of staid and goodly bearing, and limners and minstrels, as shown by the furniture of their craft, with which, far beyond the seas, on the very spot of His Passion, they hoped to serve God and their Saviour. At last, too, came knights on beauteous chargers, in full suits of burnished mail, the red cross on whose shoulders was their only token of pilgrimage. And just as the train arrived opposite the youth and the maiden, the ladies began singing the following strain:

"The East! the East! oh! eastward hie,
Leave care beneath the sable western sky;
The East is all of spangles set:
There, sweetly telleth many a flower
Of hallowed crypt and relique bower;
There, singeth Cedron's rivulet,
And in its father's arms the flock doth lie;
There, holy zeal and prowess meet.
And die we? oh! such death is sweet.
Then eastward, sisters, brothers, eastward hie!"

They sang so sweetly and joyously, that the sun seemed as if he would rise again through his bright night-veil of crimson, and, wooed by the sound of their enthusiast lay, turn evening into morning for their sakes. And now, when the fairy tones had died slowly and solemnly on the ear, the knights threw in their merry war-strain. The halberdier-escort of the ladies took part, and a mounted trumpeter in the rear of the knights mingled many a fitful blast with the song. The warrior words ran nearly thus:

"Saracen, thy toil waste not
O'er thy weapon store;
Speed thee, Saracen, or taste not
Home's endearments more.

Hence thy banner soon must fly:
Though afar 'neath Asia's sky
New award of land be given thee,
From the promised one we've driven thee.

Knightly Richard, lion-hearted,
    Many an oath hath ta'en,
Winging there, where Christ departed:—
    Fruitful hurricane!
On that holy spot
Will the war be hot,
He who falls, hath Gloria,
He who lives, Victoria."

The train had passed, the youth and maiden still kept silence, till Otto, at length, with glowing cheek, began to speak. "It is true," said he, "King Richard of England, whom they call Lion-heart, from his bravery and generosity, hath vowed a crusade. My father and Master Walther were talking only the evening before last about it. Heavens! what a glorious war that will be!"

"If you *will* always begin," said Bertha, with a sigh, "to talk so rapturously of war and marching as soon as the least thing goes by, I scarcely have heart to go on with the ditty about parting."

"Ah, you little silly child!" said the stripling, smiling; "there has not been a word said yet about any thing of the sort. Give heed prettily to your voice now; you know we sing the next rhymes together."

But it seemed fated to-day that they should never bring their song to an end; for just as they were going to begin the next stanza, a noise, as of many horses, sounded behind them on the mead, and they turned their eyes quickly that way.

CHAPTER II.

A TROOP of richly-clad squires leaped anon from their steeds, and began pitching gay and costly tents on the turf; whilst a lady of wondrous beauty came riding towards them, with a retinue of noble damsels, and was reverentially handed from her white palfrey by an armed cavalier. A pretty sight it was to see the dame and the knight strolling side by side over the greensward: the lady's vesture of azure velvet, with sweeping verge of gold embroidery; the mail of the knight, of bright deep black, inlaid with many a cunning emblem of shining silver. His whole array was almost odd to look upon, for the plates of his armour were quaintly set in curious quirk and curve; but his port was grand and noble withal; while his unhelmed head told of the merry grace of youth. The loiterers passed not far from the spot where Otto and Bertha were standing, who modestly greeted the distinguished strangers. The lady as kindly returned their salute, and tarried with a look of pleasure by the tender pair, towering up tall and slim in their Teuton stature, yet with faces of childlike beauty. She at length beckoned them to her, and a pleasant conversation ensued, in which Otto and Bertha's life of unbroken union and homely joy lay soon unfolded before her. Their story was short, and its in every way simple and ordinary features were expressed in few and equally simple words. Then the lady-stranger looked on her companion with a pensive smile: "Count Archimbald," said she, "if we had to tell our story, should we have done so soon?—And yet," continued she, turning to Otto and Bertha, "I feel as if I owed you, dear childreu, the wondrous story of my wanderiogs. You will be pleased with it, and I can almost fancy that your graceful modesty only keeps you from questioning me. It is but fair that I should be frank to those who have been so trusting and open-hearted to me." Thereupon, as her tent had been raised in the meanwhile, she led both the young folks within it, their hearts burning with childlike curiosity to hear the singular tale; and whilst Sir Archimbald went out to order the little camp, she sank upon a tasteful couch, beckoned Otto and Bertha to her side, and began as follows:

"My name is Gabriele, and I am sprung from the ancient and noble race of the Portamours. Being left an orphan at an early age, I often heard from my guardians that I might be one of the richest and grandest ladies in France, if I had but a certain ring, which a Norman dame of the family of Montfaucon had managed to appropriate to herself by unlawful wiles, and which her daughter, of the same age with myself, now possessed as an heirloom. This ring was always held up to me as Paradise is to other children, or at least made of the same importance, and the same sweet object of hope. So then it turned out that all my dreams, waking and sleeping, centred on this wonderful gem, without my knowing any more about it than that it gave a right to certain large domains, and—what seemed of infinitely greater weight—made its owner familiar with many magic secrets, and means of swaying the realm of spirits. Think, then, what I felt when, one evening, at the court of the king, where I was present for the very first time, I was presented to a noble maiden, Blancheflour de Montfaucon name, on whose fairy hand, mirror as she was of every charm and grace, I at once, by the description that had been given me, descried the magic ring. To become mistress of it for the first time was very easy to me; for we were shown into the same chamber for the night, and Blancheflour drew her ring so carelessly from her hand, that in her very first slumber I achieved the capture of my property; and so adroitly too, that the next morning she scarcely noticed her loss, but after a little fruitless searching, as if nothing had happened, skipped away to the tourney that was just then beginning. But now a handsome knight dashed up to her, whom I found, upon inquiry, to be Sir Folko de Montfaucon, her brother, and whose bright falcon-eye had descried from afar both the absence of the ring from her hand and its appearance on mine. After exchanging a few words with his sister, he rode gallantly but very gravely up to me, lowered his lance, and, 'Lady,' said he 'wilt thou choose thee a champion, that I may win from him that ring of my Blancheflour's that glistens on thy fair little hand?' I did as he craved, and chose for me one of the most famous lancemen of France, who, alas, was thrown so speedily and helplessly on the sand, that my only choice was to fulfil the settled laws of the combat, and, amid a flood of the bitterest tears, to restore the conqueror, for his sister Blancheflour, the birthright jewel which I had so lately recovered.

"In pensive mood I sought my room, heedless of the games to which the other noble damsels had, for that evening, bidden me; and I gave my handmaid a pettish rebuff, on her bringing me a beautiful fishing-rod, inlaid with mother-of-pearl, with a long line of gold, and a silver hook. I had meant to make use of this at an approaching water-party of the court; but what was all that to me, now that I had lost my ring? So the sullen waiting-maid set the fishing-rod against the window-sill, and left me alone with my tears. Towards evening, I had cried myself tired; and the laughing of my companions, who were playing at ball on the lawn of the garden, enticed me to look at least through the window-panes. At that instant I noticed Blancheflour draw my ring from her finger, that she might play more at ease, lay it upon a mossy bank beneath my window, and thoughtlessly run back again to the game. With anxious haste and beating heart I threw open the lattice, and in doing so, the fishing-rod, as if tendering its aid, fell on my arm; in a trice I held it out, and found that the golden thread reached down with ease to the ring. On the very first trial it was swinging on the little silver hook; and drawing it quickly up, I covered it with a thousand kisses. But what did the brief triumph avail me? No sooner had the childlike Blancheflour poured forth her new plaint to her brother, and no sooner had he espied the ring on my finger,—for I was too proud not to show my newly-regained property in public,—than he again begged me to choose a champion from whom he might wrest it. And oh! how could such a one abide Folko's valiant arm? He soon lay stretched on the sand, while Blancheflour gave her brother my ring to take care off, and little store of hope remained of my ever winning it again. Still I never ceased to keep the dear token in view; and one day, while we were resting from the chase. at the foot of a nearly branchless tree, and something was said about its being almost impossible to climb it, I teasingly called on Folko to try his fortune. Just as I had hoped, his love of enterprise and knightly feats blinded him to all beside. The ring, which by no other chance he ever took from his finger, was now laid upon the turf, as being a hindrance to him in getting up, and the venturous task was begun. When, as I afterwards learned, after many fruitless endeavours, he at last reached the top, I was off and away with my gem, and travelling towards England; where, in the court of Richard the Lion-hearted, I might seek a champion to battle for my right with the victorious Folko. The great Richard gave me welcome, as beseemed that mirror of knighthood; and on my craving his choice of a champion for me from his garden of heroes, leading his favourite knight before me, he bid him kneel, and sue for the grace of consecrating to me the last drop of his blood. How proud was I now! with what an eye of unconcern did I behold Folko's appearance at court to renew the combat for the ring! Ah! my hopes were all in vain! I ought to have known that the knights of the Frank country were mostly superior to the English in the skill of the tourney. My brave champion, it is true, was aware of this, and had settled that the joust alone should not carry the day, but that the unhorsed combatant should be free to grasp his trusty falchion; this, however, only made Folko's victory more toilsome and more glorious, but not the less sure. With three deep sword-wounds, my knight was borne swooning from the lists; while Folko kneeled to me, and with comely modesty craved back the prize. The noble Richard would have persuaded him to solace himself with his newly-won right, and leave the guerdon itself to the fair lady, who parted with it in such bitter tears. 'Great king, and noble chief of all Christian knighthood,' said Folko, 'fain, for my part, would I leave to this enchanting lady the free ownership of the ring, and hold my life, moreover, forfeited to her, in that I am guilty of the tears that trickle from those beauteous eyes; but as it is, the jewel falls to Blancheflour de Montfaucon, my sister, and in naught dare a true knight be remiss to his lady, as your knightly majesty best may tell.' To this the king of the Lion-heart could make no demur; and once more despoiled of my ring, I withdrew, in deep sorrow, from court. Still I lingered in the neighbourhood, hoping that as knightly trial of arms had always favoured Sir Folko, so fortune and cunning might remain favourable to me. Things were thus, when I heard that Sir Folko was bent upon a journey into the land of Wales, to see with his own eyes the old places and ruins where King Arthur of the Round Table had fought and dwelt with his knights. Resolved to venture my utmost, I hastened before him into the mazy mountain-ranges, and disguised in a rusty armour of ancient fabric and well-closed helmet, I waited for him in a lonely valley, through which he would be obliged to ride. He came, and in a nicely feigned voice, which my vizor happily served to render still more hollow, I challenged him to deadly fight. He demanded my reason, and my name. These I refused to give, and made as if I fancied that he wished to escape me. Down then he sprang from his horse (since I was on foot), his heavy arms glittering and crashing so, that I was nearly swooning away with fright. But I kept my stand, vowing that I never would fight with him till he should take off his wizard-ring; it was well enough known that that was what made him invincible, and that he otherwise was weak and timid as a child. With an angry cry he tore the iron gauntlet from his hand, and threw the ring on the grass. In a twinkling I had seized it. Loosing my casque and throwing it from me, 'It is to be hoped now that Sir Folko,' said I, 'recognises Gabriele de Portamour, and is too nobly favoured to spoil a defenceless lady of her ring, or even to thwart her journey.' He bowed in silence: 'But I hope to have the honour,' said he at length, 'of meeting you on peopled spots, where you never can lack a champion.'—I then vanished from before him, and, on horses purposely held in readiness, with an arrow's swiftness I gained the sea. Favourable winds wafted me across to the Saxon land, which I had fixed upon from hearing that it was the true resort of honour for gallant souls and trusty knighthood. And, sooth to say, the noble Count Archimbald von Walbek has pledged himself to me for death or for life; and I am free from care with so renowned a warrior at my side, who never yet was vanquished by mortal foe. While relying on him, I wear the blue and gold blazon of the house of Montfaucon, to foreshow the right which the ring gives me to their domains; though gladly will I leave them these, if I may but keep my dear and wondrous ring. Perhaps, too, the puissant Folko has long ago given it up and forgotten it; for, since leaving England, I hear not a word of him any where; so that I well may rejoice in my happy wile, and look forward to that peaceful repose which may acquaint me with the secret virtues of my gem, of which I as yet know scarcely any more than a few unfathomed riddles."

Otto and Bertha thanked the fair Gabriele for her tale, in words of the fairest courtesy.

"What a beautiful ring it must be!" whispered Bertha.

"I will gladly show it to you, sweet child," said the smiling Gabriele, and drew it on its golden chain from her snow-white bosom. Two serpents of virgin gold, in mingled coil, bore jewelled crowns on heads of blood-red hue; these were set round with signs, like some which Otto well remembered to have seen on strange weapons in his father's armory; they called them Runic rhymes, and had told him that they came a great way out of the north. Surmounting the serpent-coronets was a bright green gem, that almost looked like the tide of the Danube. But Gabriele said that its hues were the very colour of the sea.

Whilst youth and maiden were thus gazing at the gem, Bertha admiring the uncouth symbols, and Otto, with flushed cheek, stealthily breathing on it a kiss, the curtains of the tent, now brilliant with many a taper, were thrown aside, and Sir Archimbald stepped in. Another knight followed him.

CHAPTER III.

"HEAVENS!" cried Otto and Bertha with one voice, as the stranger drew near, "it is the mighty knight Folko de Montfaucon himself!" As it often happens, they both of them, during Gabriele's story, had formed an inward picture of the victorious hero; and the new-comer answered to it in a most wonderful way. That they were not wrong was plain enough from Gabriele's turning so pale, and from the gallant address of the cavalier, who bowed reverentially to her, and asked her if she recognised the knight by whose favour he had been introduced as the one from whom he might challenge, by brunt of arms, the jewelled ring. Gabriele nodded assent, and Sir Archimbald spoke thus: "Warrior unknown, it befitteth me, then, to unfold to thee that I am the Count von Walbek. Thou wilt have heard of me, and it resteth with thee whether thou wilt tilt with me for the prize, or wave thy claim to it in peace."

A bright flush mantled on the knightly Montfaucon's cheek, and his dark eyes sparkled like the far flash of the lightning-cloud; yet he bent in courtesy, and, in a gentle voice, "I know not, Sir Count," quoth he, "if it seem worth while to thee to vanquish Baron Folko de Montfaucon; but this I know, that the pride of fighting with the renowned Archimbald von Walbek would alone awake in me the desire for combat, had I no other cause to battle."

"Shall we to the lists this evening?" asked Archimbald.

"This noble lady must give the word," replied Folko: "it may perhaps be unwelcome to her, after the fatigue of travel, to witness our tourney."

"Rather to-day than to-morrow," said Gabriele, in eager alarm. Upon this, Archimbald went out to arrange the scene of fight; the knights first agreeing that he who left the ring marked out, under whatsoever plea, should be held defeated, and have no further part in the fray. Moreover, the encounter with the keen falchion might follow the running with the lance, as had been the law of fight in the knightly school of the King of the Lion-heart. Whilst, then, Sir Archimbald was without, making preparations for this solemn trial of skill, Folko had taken up Gabriele's lute, and sinking down at her feet in elegant ease, was gracefully toying with the strings. Splendidly he looked in his mail of deep-blue steel, and its rich setting and chasing of costly gold, with his dark-brown hair, and finely-turned mustachio, beneath which the rosy lip smiled so winningly forth, displaying two rows of teeth of pearly whiteness. Gabriele, but ill at ease, fixed her gaze in mute impatience before her. He who had seen them both sitting there, in like array of azure and gemmed with gold, would scarcely have guessed that theirs was the converse of foes, but rather that the lady had presented the knight with the beautiful blue scarf, inwoven with gold, that swept from his sinewy shoulders adown his slender girth, and that he now sought to tender his thanks in the softly-wooing sounds of the guitar. Things, however, did not long remain so peaceful; Archimbald quickly appeared at the portal of the tent in fearful array; for he had already donned and locked his helm, the quaint vizor of which formed the head of an eagle, with a huge silver beak, and matched so oddly with the rest of his grotesque armour, that he might easily have been deemed the denizen of some fabled land of wonder. "All is ready," said he; and Folko bounded, light as a feather, on his feet, laid the lute with the most courteous care on the cushioned floor, and, with fair greeting, left the tent. Then Count Archimbald tendered the lady his arm, and led her into the open air. Otto and Bertha followed, with glowing and astonished looks, as though they had been transported in a dream to the fairy world of their often-read and often-sung legends.

Without the tent, a bright glitter shone dazzlingly from amid the olden darkness of night. A wide circle, roomy enough for two steeds to charge and manœuvre in, was encompassed with a festive garland of blazing torches, which spired up in red cloudlets of flame to the pitchy firmament, shrouding the space beyond the ring in the deepest and most shapeless black, but lighting up every floweret in the dread arena with almost more than noontide brilliancy. Archimbald led Gabriele to a seat, prettily fashioned of turf, and spread with the most costly coverlets ; it was so placed that she sat exactly opposite the centre of the challenge-ground, where the knights would encounter the shock. Round her stood the rich retinue of herself and Archimbald,—Otto and Bertha were at her side,—whilst on the opposite barrier, through the red blaze of the torches, a medley of foreign and richly-arrayed forms might be seen, who, no doubt, belonged to the serving-train of the Baron de Montfaucon. Now, whilst Archimbald, craving leave of the lady, turned to the right, towards his war-horse, Folko was descried on the left, issuing forth on his swan-necked nimble steed of silver-gray, with helmet donned, and already closed, of the most tasteful fashion, and all of gold. As his antagonist was not yet addrest to the fight, he trotted in playful manœuvre over the lawn, swaying his willing steed, it seemed, more with words than with the rein. As soon as it came near the spot where Gabriele sat, as if at the beck of its master, it bent its fore-legs, then started again with a mighty caracole in air; and with such light bounds that it almost seemed to fly,—the gold bells jingling pleasantly on saddle and head-gear,—it sped back to its place. There it stood submissively still, a caparisoned statue ; then beneath the rich coverlets, bending its pliant neck towards its lord, it seemed to fawn upon him, and to ask him if it had done every thing aright; while he drew off his gauntlet of steel, and kindly patted the neck of his charger.

A strange contrast to this was Archimbald's coal-black steed, spotted white with foam, rearing and plunging, and threatening to rive the chain-rein by which two horsemen strove with might and main to hold him; and then to see Archimbald, with one bold bound, spring deftly on the restive creature's back, urging him with the keenly punishing spur to still wilder gambols; swaying him many times hither and thither, and plying rein and limb with amazing power and dexterity, till at last the charger owned his lord, and stood rooted to the spot at his pleasure. But the eyes of the black steed flashed so fierily, that they might well be likened to torch-brands; while he dashed his right fore-hoof with violence to the ground, as though hollowing a grave for the foe of his stalwart rider.

Now both knights, in token that they were waiting the fray, bent low to Gabriele, till their tall waving helm-plumes almost touched the ground; and then, with lances couched they again sat erect and still.

Gabriele's white kerchief flew upward in the darkness of night, shrill trumpet-blasts sounded, and the combatants rushed with such lightning-speed at each other, that their encounter was scarcely seen before the ear caught the crash of the splintered lances, and the loud rattling of the mail pieces after the gigantic shock. But the combatants had sped past, without swerving in the saddle; and bringing round their steeds at the reverse corners of the course, they now stood still, each astonished, as it seemed, to see his antagonist in his seat.

"Fresh tilting-spears!" cried Archimbald; and squires ran up, leaving their masters the choice among a variety of powerful weapons. When they had chosen and poised their new arms: "Two lances more, knight of Montfaucon," cried Archimbald; "is it not so? And if that do not finish it, we will fight it out with the naked sword-blade."

"I am a guest here," said Folko, politely bending, "and honour every cup in which my noble host pledges me."

Again the trumpets sounded, and again the two knights flew to the shock; this time, however, with such impetuous violence, that both the chargers sank back on the crupper, till, hotly spurred by their riders, they again sprang up, and sped past each other to their posts. Folko's lance was shivered in a thousand pieces on his antagonist's breastplate; Archimbald's spear was simply snapped. At this, both Walbek's serving-train and Montfaucon's shouted for joy; for each saw in it a happy omen: the latter vowing that their master must have given the firmer thrust, and that the count's lance had only glinted off. The knights were armed anew; the third trumpet-call was wound, and as they closed with burning fury, Folko's silver-gray was seen to rear on high, and totter from the violence of the shock; while its rider, skilfully bending to the saddle-bow, plied his golden spurs, and urged his charger to bound lightly forward; Archimbald's black steed, on the other hand, plunged and fell: then, no longer curbed by the hand that now hovered lifelessly over it, it gathered itself up in its rage, and,—itself and its quaintly harnessed rider looking like two evil spirits,—scoured in mad fury over the lists, dashed out of the circle amid the blazing torches, and vanished. The rattle of the falling mail, in the gloom of night beyond, told that Archimbald was on the ground. For some time Folko remained quietly in his bounds; he then alighted, stroked the mane of his silver-gray, cast the broken lance-helve from him, and, with drawn sword flashing amid the gleam of the torches, stepped into the middle of the circle. No one advanced to meet him; and outside in the darkness was heard the hollow murmur of the horsemen and squires, hasting to and fro, about their prostrate master. Then cried Folko at length: "Sir Count von Walbek, your black charger bore you from the lists against your will. That shall not be reckoned; be it free to you, with the bright falchion, to repair your disaster: I stand and await you."

For a long time all was silence. At last, "My lord has fainted," cried a squire; "He can fight no more," cried another voice; "We must away with him to the next convent, to the monks," said a third; and in a moment after, the train was heard tramping slowly and mournfully over the mead.

Then Sir Folko returned his shining sword to its scabbard, and moving, with raised vizor, to the spot where Gabriele was seated, he begged her, on his knees, for the guerdon of fight. The beautiful damsel, amid a warm flood of tears, pulled a little thread of gold, and drew forth the ring from her tender bosom: how differently had she done so a short time before, when she showed it in triumph to the youthful strangers! Still was it unloosed from the thread, when Otto, stepping up before the knight of Montfaucon: "Let a suit of armour, noble sir, be given me, with horse, falchion, and lance; and I will fight with you for the jewel, in the name of this noble lady, if she deem me not unworthy of the honour." A ray of glad hope mantled faintly on Gabriele's countenance. At once she thought of the numberless old legends, in which youthful heroes, ere boyhood was scarcely over, had worsted renowned champions and mighty giants in defence of hapless damsels. Folko was again on his feet, and keenly eyeing his unlooked-for adversary. Of a sudden, however, he turned away with a smile; and looking back upon Otto: "Young squire, young squire," said he, "where hast thou thy golden spurs? Dost thou think it already time for thee to battle with knights? Three sword-strokes, and a night-watch over thy arms: and then hie thee to me again, and right gladly will I meet thee." Thereupon he again kneeled before Gabriele, and craved the ring: and scarcely had it in his hand than, courteously bending, he was again upon his silver-gray charger, and dashing away with his service-band.

In a bitter flood of tears Gabriele turned to her train: for immediately, on the unfortunate issue of the tourney, having begun, at her wish, to strike the tents, and load the sumpter-horses with the baggage, they had now brought that business to an end. Not an hour longer, said the weeping maiden, would she tarry on so ill-starred a spot; and without giving the least heed to what Otto said, or to his offers of aid, she turned sharply away from him, as from a silly, forward child, and rode off into the gloom Otto called after her: "God help me, noble lady; but I will never rest till I am a knight, and can lay your ring at your beautiful feet." But this protestation, too, she seemed not to notice. And soon in the far distance he could hear the light tramp of her palfrey over the moor.

Alone and deserted stood Otto and Bertha on the eventful spot. All seemed like a dream. The half-burned torches, the scorched and trodden grass, alone vouched for the truth of those strange apparitions. Neither found aught to say to the other; but they silently turned their steps homeward through the deep gloom of night; sadly changed to what they were when, a few hours before, they tripped down to the green. Once or twice only said Otto on the way, "Are you crying, dear Bertha?" But she always answered, "No," and wound her kerchief closer round her head; so that Otto thought he had been deceived, and had taken his own involuntary sighs for Bertha's weeping.

CHAPTER IV.

In the vaulted hall of his ancient castle sat Sir Hugh von Trautwangen. There were hung the warlike accoutrements of himself and forefathers, and there too he had been used to pass the greater part of his day, since age had debarred him from the hunt, the tilting-ring, the tourney, or the fray. But now the two tapers that lit up the large round table from their sconces of massive silver were almost burned to the socket; and son and niece, quite contrary to custom, still let him wait for them in vain. As often as a footstep sounded on the winding staircase, the old man thought the two young people were coming, and, in kindly longing, glanced towards the door; but when a page entered, to see perhaps that his master still had light, and wine enough by him in the large flagon, which had been cast from silver medals, Sir Hugh would look as if he had not at all been expecting any thing, and this or that expression of uneasiness on the part of the servant would meet with no answer; or at most it would be, "Young blood—merry hearts! What is there to mind about? All will come right."

But the clock in the castle-tower struck nine!—ten! and neither son nor niece stepped forth from the deep darkness without into the hall of their home. From his bald head the old man took the little green-velvet cap, held it in his folded hands, and fervently he prayed that God might not reckon to the innocent children the many sins of his youth, but lead them back of His eternal goodness, guiltless and safe, into the castle.

Still he prayed, when the large oaken door opposite him flew open, and the two whom he longed for stood before him in the hall, their faces glowing with all the freshness of youth. For that once he had heard no one on the stairs, and the fulfilment of his prayer broke quite unexpectedly upon him; as the right sort of fulfilments usually do, coming sweetly and suddenly upon us whilst we ask for them. The young pair felt quite touched and sorrow-stricken when they saw the hoary old man sitting bare-headed in the opposite arm-chair, with folded hands; pale with many years and with the anxiety that but just then was over, and still paler from the low-burnt tapers between him and them. They felt keenly for whom he had been praying, and they at once raised their hands in the same thankful gesture on high, imploring pardon. But Sir Hugh had recovered his accustomed mien; he replaced his cap, and motioning them to him, he asked them, in a grave but kindly air, what they could have been doing that kept them out so long.

"Father," said young Otto von Trautwangen, "if we had but stayed just a very little longer, we should all of us, as seems to me, feel better and more light-hearted than we do, and the beautiful lady with the ring too; for then the fray would be settled already, aud triumphantly for us, it is to be hoped; but, as it is, Heaven knows how long I shall have to trudge through the world after my vow—and that all comes of your not earlier having dubbed me knight."

Sir Hugh gazed with amazement on the face of the bold boy, not only on accouut of the strange words that he had uttered, but still more so because his look was so altered, as if in a few hours he had become quite another creature. But Bertha, without any disguise, began bitterly crying, perhaps still more bitterly than Gabriele had before done for her ring.

At this Otto looked round quite astonished, and observing that his favourite's eyes were red and dim with many an earlier tear, "Ah, dear Bertha," said he, "then you were crying though on our way back! Why, then, did you always say 'No' when I asked you? And why do you cry at all?" Bertha answered him only with a mingled smile of kindness and of pain; then begging leave of the old man to go to rest for the night, and hiding her face with her hands, she passed out of the hall.

Otto would have stayed her, but a stern look from Sir Hugh held him spell-bound to the table; and when Bertha was gone, "Young lad," said he, "you have either been dreaming and raving, and in that case to-morrow will make all right of itself, or you are really in earnest with your vow and your knightly journey, and then a tear or two in your little cousin's eyes are of less account. Seat yourself opposite to me, and tell me plainly and advisedly what has happened to you, and then we will soon set matters straight together."

When now the boy began to tell his tale, and got further and further in it, the old man too began to grow very grave, and so markedly so towards the end of the story, that he could not take his eyes off a huge sword that hung not far from them on the wall, and peeped half-shown from its sheath.

When the adventure of the mead was ended, "Sooth," said Sir Hugh to the old sword, "thou hast anon had something to object against being hidden, and hast never quite been willing to sheathe thyself, oft as I have tried to lay thee in peace and repose. Now I see thou wast not altogether so wrong. Out with thee, then, old comrade; and, Otto, reach me him down without more ado."

With a shudder of awe, the stripling turned to the object of his father's address. He felt as if it might almost be some suddenly risen spectre, or other thing of fear. But it was only the well-known weapon that flashed on his eye, though glittering with unwonted brightness in the flicker of the struggling taper. So he joyfully grasped the golden hilt, and, unheeding the rattling fall of the massively-mounted scabbard, he bore the naked falchion to his father. "Ha! the joyful sight," cried he; "not more cheerily sparkled the knight of Montfaucon's blade in the circle of torches!"

"Of the knight of Montfaucon's blade much might be said," rejoined the old man, as he poised the huge weapon in his hands, "and still more might be said of hasty vows and suchlike; but of this by and by, or not at all perhaps; for vows must be kept, and you have given yours to Gabriele. But if you ever chance upon a jeweller, who once had a costly stone that he would in no wise part with, but in whose diamond-flash he sought to refresh and strengthen his aged eyes till death, till some wandering princess bore off his gem in spite of vow and prayer; or a gardener, who, in stilly joy, cherished some little flower in the snuggest corner of his nursery, till a wanton dove came darting downward, and, tearing it up, root and stem, winged away with it over the sea;—oh! if you ever see this, or the like of it, then guess what old Sir Hugh must feel now." Two big drops, bright as crystal, started in his age-sunk eyes, as he strode firmly into the middle of the hall; and when Otto, humbled and touched to the heart, would have embraced him: "Young warrior," said he, "this is too serious and solemn an hour to allow of aught that might be branded as soft-hearted foolery. Kneel, young Sir Otto von Trautwangen. Our business now is to dub thee knight."

Otto, with folded hands, devoutly bent the knee. He almost

looked like one of those monumental statues that we often find at young men's tombs—pious, simple, and expectant of a happy resurrection. Sir Hugh took the huge sword, and thrice touching the shoulders of his son with the flat of the blade: "Bear that from me now," said he, "but never again from another." Then placing himself in front of the youthful knight, he said, "Sir Otto of Trautwangen, in virtue of my power as knight and banneret, I have devolved to thee the sacred dignity of knighthood. Acquit thee worthily of thy charge, to the succour of the fair, of widows, and of orphans, but, above all, to the glory of our most holy Redeemer Jesus Christ. Rise, then, and come to my arms, and let us be boon comrades together."

So hearty and fond an embrace had father and son never known till that solemn moment, when, over and above every other tie that bound them, they had become brethren too, and companions in arms. Thereupon Sir Hugh, with the old sword in his hand, strode towards a large shield of golden brightness that hung immediately over his chair. Thrice he struck violently upon it, at measured intervals, till the high halls rung again, and the saloon became full of armed menials.

"This is Sir Otto of Trautwangen," said he to them, holding his son by the hand; "and now must this dear young warrior hold his night-watch over his arms. Carry, then, the silver-bright mail down into the chapel, for *his* shall it be now; and he who means well to the house of Trautwangen and its youngest blossom, let him abide wakeful to-night, and pray God that these solemn hours may bear lively fruit for time and for eternity. Amen."

And they bent their way down the winding staircase to the chapel, which jutted far out eastward from the foremost walls, and formed, as it were, a bulwark of the castle. Then the squires-at-arms laid the shining furniture of war down before the altar. Sir Hugh blessed his knightly son, placed the old sword in his hand, and left the hallowed spot with his serving-men; whilst the youth, with noble grace and drawn sword, planted himself like the watch of paradise before the silver-bright war-suit.

CHAPTER V.

Far aloft in the heights of the chapel burned a single lamp; and so wondrously did it light up the vaulted roof with its rich span of arches, entwining each other, and towering up like organ-notes from the taper shaft, that the eye wandered, as it were, through forest-boughs to the open sky; whilst the under part of the building lay sunk in dubious darkness, as earth and her fantasies mostly do to the simple ken of mortals. Pious thoughts at first kept hold of the young knight, to the exclusion of all others. He bent the knee, folded his hands on his sword-blade, and raising the golden hilt as a crucifix aloft, he fixed his gaze devoutly on the brightness of the roof above him. He thought on his sainted mother, of whom his only remembrance was, that she had died on a journey in the open forest, and, smiling sweetly on him, her weeping boy, had pointed up anon to the clear blue sky of spring; for then she could speak no more. Other memories crowded closely on that of his mother's death, till the fancy of the stripling, step by step, was led onward to the present hour. Then it occurred to him, that till that day the chapel had been an unknown and forbidden spot to him, and with mingled curiosity and awe he sprang to his feet. Picture on picture became visible on the neighbouring walls, some stepping out in such bold relief, that the twilight, with its varying light and shade, moulded them almost to living forms; others again, lightly painted on the flat surface, seemed but shadows among other shadows thrown upon them by the flickering lamp. He felt as though all this pictured array must form part of his father's life, of which he had learnt little else than he now knew of the walls of the chapel: certain configurations were clear to him, others were scarcely guessed at, and the chain of the whole was ill understood, and veiled in misty obscurity. Thus much he could plainly see, that, on one hand, tombs were there, with their solemn adornments; on the other, weapons won in fight, and suits of mail of wondrous fashion; for far and wide Sir Hugh had roamed, both into the holy Orient and Europe's blooming West; and again to the northern land, where there is more winter than summer, and where the sun remains unseen for many weeks together. From all these distant regions some effigy or memorial seemed to have found its way hither, betokening in narrow bounds, as it were, the richly-chequered life of the veteran knight, now on the verge of a still narrower limit. Large banners and Mahometan horse-tails waved in the night-breeze, and crooked sabres with richly jewelled hilts hung sparkling by rusty swords and battle-axes of olden date; corslets burnished as for the fight were there, and the sternly chiselled visages of aged men, or the gentle faces of women with pale, moonlike hue, shone beside them from the walls. Ah! one among these there was that riveted his eye with the sweetest witchery he had ever known. Some gloomy armour almost intercepted the view of it; and yet, he thought, it could be no other than his departed mother. It was just as if she raised her hand on high, and beckoned him to her. And he would have stepped to her at once, but he knew not whether it befitted his rank of knight to stray so far from the arms he had to watch; for the painting was quite at the other end of the chapel. Then arose a strange struggle within him that banished peace; his mother seemed still to beckon to him, and at last he thought he could even hear the sweet voice that from his early childhood had so often sounded in his dreams. "Ah, my darling boy," it seemed to say; "ah, one, one moment only! Think how long I have been dead, and away from thee. Ah, one moment only! God will guard thine arms." Well might the young knight assure himself that his outward ear heard none of all this; yet it struck too touchingly on his heart: so bending before the white marble effigy of the crucified Saviour that surmounted the altar, "O God-Man," spake he in prayer, "Thou too so lovedst Thy mother. Be guardian, then, over my arms, whilst I go to see if yonder figure be the image of mine." And therewith he walked courageously to the wished-for spot.

And it *was* his own dear mother: she was portrayed as in the thick shade of a forest, her arms stretched towards the clouds, and as he had only seen one of them before, it had appeared that she was beckoning him to her. Now he plainly saw that they were directed to none but God; for her light-brown eyes were uplifted to a golden triangle, that became visible in the deep-blue vault above her. What the picture wanted in the freshness and reality of life, the moist eye of the young knight easily transfused into it. He quite felt as though he again saw the clear spring-sky before him, to which his mother had pointed in that well-remembered hour, and the shady bright-green forest, that so winningly encircled them. And the colour, too, on his mother's cheek, so nearly blanched and faded, was unspeakably touching. He kissed it reverently, and said, "Thanks to thee, dear, good limner, that thou paintedst her when lifeless and cold; for my father and the rest would not let me see the beauteous corpse. But now it has just happened as I wished." Here he paused musingly, and pondered whether this could be her grave. Too gladly would he have thought so, and here poured forth his silent prayer by the dear remains; but he could not at all call to mind that a coffin had come with them into the castle, or any solemn obsequies been held there.

At this moment a current of air swept through the vaulted hall. The door rattled at the lock, an old banner above the young knight's head began to rustle, till he started up surprised from the depths of his musings, and looked hastily round to his arms. Then it seemed that a gigantic figure stretched forth its long black arm between them and him, and made a snatch at his confided treasure. Like ready wrestler, he sprang upon the dark apparition, and as he seized it, its helmet and other equipments fell rattling to the ground, and from behind the cloud of dust, which the rusty furniture threw up, a fleshless death's head grinned jeeringly at him from the trunk of his foe. In mad dismay he made a blow at it with his sword, and death's head, armour, and all, fell clattering at his feet. Then only he saw that no goblin mocked him, or other godless tenant of the grave; but that he had taken one of the figures along the walls to be hostilely moving, and had hewn it to the earth. It was a strange task to set up the old trappings in their places again; but, above all, to repoise the death's head on the shoulders of the mailed block, and to lodge the rusty casque on the top of it. Thus engaged, it looked to him as though he had hewn a deep cleft in the skull, which now, therefore, grinned on him in pain. This fancy quite got the better of his senses; and when all was in order again, he tore off the helmet once more, to convince himself of the truth. He beheld many wounds of various depth on the whitened bone, and was well aware that he had made but one blow: yet one of these, he was sure, was *his* doing; and he made haste to cover up the ghastly head again. Then stepping to his arms, he bowed before the crucifix, and implored forgiveness: "Lord, I have sinned," said he, "in that I have swerved from my post. Thou art almighty, and the best guardian of all things; but to me, and not to Thee, was the watch committed." Then it appeared to him as though his crucified Lord looked kindly on him; and he again felt undaunted. Often as thoughts of horror would rise, at his having held his first knightly encounter with a helpless corpse, yet he fancied anon that his mother whispered rhymes of solace in his ear, out of a song of old Master Walther's, which he had so often heard.

"Night flies away before the sun,
And fear doth into transport run,
And grim death into life."

So boldly and blithely he paced up and down before his arms; and when he again fancied that the beauteous face was signing to him, he would only give it a friendly nod, and gallantly saluting it with his naked falchion, would say, "I cannot leave now, dear mother, for I am on the watch of honour."

At last the morning, with its dear fresh blush and fragrant breath, came peeping through the lofty windows; the key turned in the lock, and Sir Hugh entered the chapel.

CHAPTER VI.

SIRE and son, with a sober gravity, and love that told of sorrow, exchanged their greeting: then Sir Hugh strode toward the altar, took the arms from the steps, and began to brace them on his boy. The latter could scarcely bear to receive the service of such venerable hands; but knowing the laws of knighthood, he stood still whilst the old man arrayed him in cuirass, gorget, and thigh-piece, placed the helmet on his head, and at last, kneeling down, buckled on his golden spurs. But father and son were equally astonished withal, that the huge sword, the sheath of which the old knight had brought with him, should now slide obediently into its hiding-place; for till then it would scarcely enter more than half-way. "It seems almost," said Sir Hugh, "as if this strange old fellow had got a notch more or less over-night." Otto shuddered almost, when he thought of the blow that he had inflicted on the death's head; and as they passed, on their way out, the suit of mail that shrouded it, a shy, involuntary glance escaped his eye.

"What," said Sir Hugh, drawing up, "did *he* disturb you? I should scarce wonder at that; for it was quite his way in his lifetime." Otto made no reply. But by the clear daylight he was still more astounded at the unwonted mould of the armour; and, above all, at two monstrous vulture-wings, of raised gold-work, that jutted out from the helmet, and which he had taken in the night-time for two mighty horns.

In this form they were almost more hideous to look at; and the young knight could not help thinking of several strange and fearful legends which his father had formerly told him, about a dreadful man with vulture-wings like these on his helm.

But how quickly was skull, and vulture-pinion, and all else in the world forgotten! For close by, the dear heavenly countenance of his mother, so yearning and so pale, looked forth from the pictured wall. "Ah, good father," said Otto, "can this be the grave-spot of the beauteous departed one who bore me?" In solemn silence Sir Hugh only shook his hoary head. "Do, then, I pray you," continued Otto, "lead me to the spot where the dear remains repose, that there I may pray once more before I set forth into the world. These live-long years, in my childish ignorance, I have failed to do so."

"This is no time for thinking on graves!" cried Sir Hugh, and drew the young knight briskly and almost angrily from the chapel. They stepped forward to the castle-rampart in the fresh and crimson glow of morning. Before them lay the Danube, mead, wood, and distant mountain-range, all dotted and garlanded with wavy light and glistening dew. "Not so soft-hearted, I pray thee, young knight of Trautwangen," said Sir Hugh, stoutly shaking the hand of his son; "there is time enough for weeping and sighing when thou art as old as thy father, and even then one must not let it be seen. Wait here and bathe eye and heart in the cool freshness of the morning; and when every thing is ready for thy journey, I will call thee away." So saying, the old warrior strode down from the rampart to the castle. The young knight remained above, thrilling with joy at the words and bearing of his father, and lighting up still gayer hopes after the rich span of country that lay in the distance before him, ringing with the warble of the lark and the song of the shepherd.

As he paced in this wise up and down, pleased with the jingle of his silver trappings, that chimed in so merrily with the gay scene around, his hardy foot struck against something in the high grass that gave forth a tone, mournful and plaintive, as if from undeserved wrong. Stooping down, he beheld Bertha's lute; and in truly deep thought must she have quitted the spot, to have left her favourite playmate in the damp moss and chilly dew. He bent over the poor lorn warbler, clasped it in his arms, and sitting down on the grass, he drew off his brazen gauntlet, to fondle the more tenderly and solace the forsaken one. It sounded so sweetly, and even joyfully, as he ran over the chords; and, in a clear, high note, he sang the following song:

"To the May-breeze, every where
Fair
Spring awakes in beauteous seeming,
And beside
Mirror floods of arrowy tide
All is loving, hoping, dreaming;
Speed then out,
Cull the leaves
That sweet spring weaves
About
Court and pleasance-ground and garden gleaming.

Though in boyhood's easy glee
We
Feel our childish hearts grow fonder,
Well we may,
While we knit the band in play,
Or through scenes of home so meekly wander.
But when light

Of sunnier sheen
Tells of keen
Delight,
Little ties like those are burst asunder.

Then they stir their burning flood—
Blood,
Heart, and soul, and sense, contendent,
Soon as pride
Calls to high-born lady's side,
And coy love turns heroine resplendent.
Maiden shy,
By garden stream
Of others dream;
But I
Must win my way where favour smiles attendant."

"Is this, then, in real earnest, your parting with me?" said Bertha, who, in the meanwhile, had stolen unseen to Otto's side, and was now gazing on him, if not with such bright eyes, yet with brighter tears than before.

For a moment Otto remained in silent thought, then—"Dear Bertha," said he, at last, "the song has betrayed almost more of me than I myself was aware of. At first I only wished to frame a carol to spring, and then the stream of my whole inner fountain came gushing out in truthful flow. But listen to me, dear cousin; we cannot, after all, deny that it is just as my song would have it. The strange lady, with her grandeur and her distress, has quite fired my heart; and this is the very thing that noble minstrels call knighthood's love. Our little playful doings were only child's sport. Come, now, smile and be merry; some wondrous stranger-knight will be sure to come, and make you quite forget your simple, childish Otto."

"He will not come," said Bertha slowly. "And as for the fine lady's distress, I too—" She blushed and paused.

"But ah!" cried Otto, in a fit of enthusiasm, "if *you* were ever to be in distress, my life, my all I have, were yours."

"But I will not at all be saved by thee, Sir Otto von Trautwaugen," rejoined Bertha, with haughty coldness. "Believe me, had the pagans bound me to the stake, as we often read in fine old legends about noble ladies, and the torches were flaming and hissing round the arid brushwood, and thou wert to come galloping up, in all the armed splendour that now clothes you so gloriously, and offeredst to fight for me, I would say, 'Avaunt! my champion thou shalt never be! More fire! more fire!' would be my cry. Ah! and then, I ween, my own poor tears should stifle it. And yet too warm are they for that."

And herewith she sank, bitterly weeping, on the grass. In the conflict of feeling, Otto pulled at the strings of the lute. One of them sprang in twain with a loud and plaintive cry. Bertha rose at the sound. "See," said she, "how you deal with every thing that belongs to me. Why, then, did you draw off your iron glove just now? With that you might still quicker have snapt the poor thing asunder. My lute! Sir Otto von Trautwangen, that at least is mine." And she tore the instrument from him, and walked away. He called after her in vain; she cradled the fondling in her arm like a wounded child, lured forth its softest and most soothing tones, and, without looking back, vanished with it behind the chapel.

At this moment Sir Hugh called to his son from the court-yard of the castle. "All is ready, all is ready!" he repeatedly cried: "to horse, young sir." And the youth hastened below, where he found a number of serving-men in readiness, and one of the squires held a light-bay steed with gilded bridle, which till then he had never dared to approach.

He stepped forth; and Sir Hugh said, with a painful smile, "Partings like these give pain, young soldier. Well, to horse at once, and try how so noble a creature can suit himself to your sway."

And the young knight guided the charger this way and that with powerful supremacy, till the squires were astounded, and felt that the noble steed must recognise his real master, and that the power of the latter over him must be of peculiar and unheard-of import. Dismount again, my dear son," cried his old father, with outstretched arms, "that I may once more press thee in fond fervour to my heart." And with clattering weapons the son swung himself from his horse, and flew to his father's embrace. The charger snorted wildly on the squires that caught at his rein, plunged out at them till he had cleared his way, and then trotting up to his young lord, he stood still at his side, and laid his head fawningly on his shoulder, whilst he caressed his aged father.

"Now, my son, God speed thee!" said Sir Hugh, softly withdrawing from that embrace of love; "thy train attends."

"My father, thou wilt not deny me one boon," said Otto; "it may be the last I crave, for I am setting out on a far journey, and haply have many a tough encounter before me."

"My son," rejoined Sir Hugh, "every word of evil import we must shun. Misfortune is quick to entangle us, and finds an easy ascent by means of those things which to our wishes are insurmountable precipices. So say nothing about last requests, but tell me rather thy boon itself; and little, I ween, shall I deny it."

"Dearest father," said Otto, "as far as I have read or heard of true-born heroes, they always ride alone on their first adventures. So did the great Seyfried, and thus have the best knights ever done. But you talk to me about a train, and here I see a whole band of serving-men standing around us. Do not send me out like a spoiled child, but as a stalwart fellow, whose merry heart and ready hand carry his own weal, and that of many others, along with it."

Whereupon Sir Hugh bid the horseman and squires, one and all, lay aside their riding-gear, and tarry at home. "For," said he, "my son has begged of me in such guise, that it were a great sin to answer him with a rebuff. And on thy part, young knight, speed thee quickly forth, or at last thy aged father's heart will soften. Thus much only I say to thee: deal as sparingly with the noble Baron de Montfaucon as thy vow permits; for he is not so very wrong about the ring, after all."

Then the young warrior flew to horse, and sped out of the castle; while old Sir Hugh, in bitter tears, went back to his hall, with the stamp of such venerable sorrow, that not one of his people had courage to look him directly in the face.

Whilst now Sir Otto trotted lightly over the mead, Bertha and the old minstrel, Walther, were sitting on the rampart, watching him in sorrow; for the old man had just come on a visit to the castle, and the maiden had confided to him her whole tale of woe. She was just beginning to weep anew, but, "Song stayeth sorrow," said Walther; "let us warble the young knight a lay for his pilgrimage." And he began as follows:

"The old man's strength is sapped and shaken,
    His wanderings past away;
But thou thy youthful course hast taken
    To many a distant fray.
For there's the fray of young lips meeting,
    The fray of spear with spear;
How soft and sweet that hurried greeting,
    How bitter that, and drear!"

Then Bertha sang:

"But thou shalt share the sweet ones only—
    The bitterer all unknown—
Though sorrow wring this bosom lonely,
    And death soon claim its own.
Though in some bower of love thou lay thee,
    The grave my couch shall be;
Then cull anon, I will not stay thee,
    The lily cull for me."

Walther was intent on continuing the song; but Bertha signed to him to stop, for she could not bear it any longer, and buried her face in her veil. By this time the soft sound, wafted on the morning breezes, had wound its way to Otto. He quickened his pace and lowered his vizor, that he might hear no more. As it was the first time that he had worn a closed helmet, the world looked quite strange through its open intervals, as though seen through some beautifying optic-glass; and in the fresh light of morning, all seemed to swim in a burning red more than any other hue; so that the young warrior could not refrain from sending a loud cry of jubilee into the wondrous scene before him; and forgetting every thought of pain, he flew, like the young bird of May, over mead, and heath, and field.

CHAPTER VII.

Where the stream of the Maine winds its silver streak of glassy blue towards the old imperial town of Frankfort, and villas, and fruit-fields, and shining villages beckon across to each other from its smooth and genial shores, a delightful life awaits one. He, especially, who in the beginning of spring may draw a breath there, and who, in all the full, vague hope of a youthful warrior, is riding out in quest of his first adventure, tastes such a cup of joy and gladness as in after-life will not often be raised to his lips. Something of this sort has he experienced who now is writing, and much he wishes his readers had known it too; both for their own sakes, and because they would then be the better able to realise that merry sense of delight which wove, as it were, a net of gold round the young knight Otto, in that beautiful country, and round every object that met his view. He could not tell which was the more delightful to him,—the spring or his journey; the blossoming fruit-trees and softly-undulating hill and vale, or the happy beings who peopled them.

In such a train of thought he reached a hostelry, not far from the banks of the stream, the eaves of which, entwined with vine and jasmine leaves, gave the young traveller a friendly invitation to his noon-tide rest. His noble charger was soon led into the stable, and fodder shaken into the rack. All this the knight had to do himself; for, true to his wonted pride, the noble steed would let none else come so near him; and now Sir Otto sat beneath the shady eaves,—with flagon and cup before him, and the noble Rhine wine,—glittering with a deeper gold, from the depth of the dark cool green that embowered him.

At this moment a man emerged from the doorway, not much older than Otto in appearance, but with grave and sunburnt visage; armed as a knight, but with equipments so soiled with rust and dirt, that he seemed to have come from some far journey. His armour, too, was wholly without adornment: the buckles and straps that held it together were unconcealed, and fitted to it just as it could best be managed, without any care for arrangement; so that he must have contrasted oddly enough with the young silver-clad drinker at the table. The stranger paid his salute with a certain blunt and hearty courtesy that was almost tinctured with moroseness; he then seated himself opposite to the young knight, and ordered wine for himself.

At first Otto was not quite pleased with his drinking comrade; he thought the pleasant images that, borne upon the sap-green foliage and the sunny sky, had cradled themselves on his senses would fly at the sight of this man, without leaving any thing better in their stead. But it soon appeared that the stranger belonged to a class of people whom we may meet with even nowadays in our good Germany; sharp-cornered, unpromising pebbles on the outside, though on the lightest touch beautiful and brilliant sparks fly out of them; and he who can test their interior with true alchymistic spirit, is likely to find a vein of costly gold beyond compare. The stranger had travelled far and wide in the world, and yet had always remained a good stanch German, or rather he had thereby become one; for the contrast it was that clearly proved to him how dearly his old fatherland should be prized. The two young knights became quite pleased with each other, and felt still more at ease on a third person joining them. He was a young merchant from Frankfort, Tebaldo by name, and had been sent to Germany for a few years, he said, by his Italian relations, to familiarise himself with the trade and traffic, the noble genius of the imperial towns, and their great commercial affairs. In the course of their varied conversation, the strange knight told the following story, which Otto and Tebaldo listened to with the greatest attention.

"In the distant northern land of our German brothers, the Swedes, there are people still held in the meshes of heathenism and horrid witchcraft, and more than all towards the frontier of Finland, because their wicked neighbours there have nothing better to do than to call up ghosts and genii, or, by dint of ugly charms, to work their enemies all manner of mischief in body, lands, or household. Just on the Finland boundary-line lies a circular mountain, overgrown on the Swedish side with dark brushwood, on the other with pine-trees, so wondrously close together, that the smallest bird could not find its way through the tangled trellis-work of the branches. Below it, at the foot of the brushwood, stands a chapel, with an image of St. George, who has been planted in the desert there as border-guardian against the dragons and other monsters of paganism. On the other side, and skirting the firm-set pine-grove, are said to stand the cottages of certain hideous sorcerers; while a deep, deep chasm reaches down into the mountain, and even forms the junction-line with the yawning gulf of hell. The few Swedish Christians who live so far up in those parts thought, besides the good saint, to provide another doughty guard against their evil neighbours; and they therefore chose for this special service a renowned old warrior, who had turned monk in his old age, and made him tenant of the chapel-hermitage. On his removal thither, the son of his earlier wedlock would never leave him, but became his servant, in prayer or penance standing dutifully at his side, with as little thought of quitting his father as he ever had in former times in the tumult of battle. A very edifying life it was these pious sons of knighthood led.

"Once upon a time, the young liegeman of God went out in quest of wood. He carried a sharp axe on his shoulder, and was girt, moreover, with a ponderous sword; for as there are so many savage beasts and wicked men thereabouts, the pious hermits had a dispensation to wear the arms of knighthood. Now as the good young man was rambling about in the thickest part of the copse, and could already see the pointed pines towering over the brushwood,—so near had he approached the Finland boundary-line,—a huge white she-wolf came springing on him from the thickest of the bushes, so that he only had time to slip on one side, and, being unable to seize his sword, to dash his hatchet at the foe. The throw was so well aimed, that, with shattered fore-foot and a painful howl, the wolf fled back into the forest. 'But,' thought the young hermit-warrior, 'it is not enough that I am saved: I must take care that no other man henceforth be either harmed or even frightened by the monster.' And in a moment he sprang nimbly after her through the thicket, and levelled such a heavy blow on her head, that she fell moaning to the earth. Then, all at once, a strange feeling of pity for the animal came over him. Instead of killing it outright, he raised it up, bound up its wounds with moss and limber withes, and at last bore it to his hut, in fervent hope that it might, after all, be granted him to heal his fallen foe, and tame it at last by fostering gentleness. He did not find his father at home, and in the height of his anxiety he laid his wondrous capture on his own bed of moss, over which he had drawn the figure of St. George; and then turning to the hearth of the little cottage, he sought to prepare a healing salve for the poor animal's wounds. But, in the midst of his task, the moaning, plaintive accents of a human voice seemed to issue from the mossy pallet. And what must he have felt when, on turning round, he beheld a wondrously beautiful damsel in the place of the wolf; the blood gushing through her gold-bright hair from the wound which he had dealt her, and the right arm, which his hatchet had shattered, hanging motionless, in all its delicacy and whiteness!

"'I pray thee,' said she as he turned towards her, 'do not kill me quite. The little drop of life which is left me gives me pain, indeed, and perhaps it will not last long; but yet I am sure it is ten thousand times better than this fearful dying.'

"Then the young man kneeled down, weeping, beside her; and she told him how she was the daughter of one of the wizard-men who lived on the other verge of the mountain, and how he had sent her out in that charmed form to gather herbs, and she had only rushed out so in fright and fear. 'But you broke my arm in twain at once,' continued she, in piteous strain, 'and I really did not mean so ill by you.' How she had been so suddenly transformed, she could not at all understand; but the young man saw very clearly that the neighbourhood of St. George's picture must have released this poor victim of witchery from the spell that bound her.

"Whilst now the hermit's son was thus kneeling at her side in tears, and trying to soothe her, the pious old man came home, and soon saw how matters stood; that the heathen girl, forsooth, had been disenchanted and freed from her wolf-like garb, and the youth become doubly bewitched by the sweet sway of love and virgin beauty. From that moment all his care was to heal her spiritually, just as the son was intent on the bodily cure; and as their united endeavours met with the best success, it was commonly agreed upon, as the stripling had made no vow, that the lovers should marry and return into the world.

"The beautiful girl was now quite well again, the day of her solemn baptism and consequent marriage was fixed, when, one fine summer evening, the two betrothed ones went for a walk together in the wood. The sun was still high in heaven, shining so warmly on the green earth through the spreading beeches, that they never grew tired of rambling, but dived deeper and deeper into the forest. The bride told tales of her former life withal, and sang the sweet-sounding songs which she had learned as a child. Idolatrous and impious as many of them seemed to the bridegroom, yet he could not check his dearest maid in her singing; first because he loved her above every thing, and then again she warbled with so sweet and clear a note, that the whole forest seemed gladdened by it. But at last he caught sight of the pointed pine-tops once more, and would have turned round, to avoid approaching the accursed Finland boundary. But the bride said, 'Why should we not go farther? I should so like to see the place where you wounded me on the head and arm, and took me captive, that you might afterwards heal me so delightfully in body and soul. It must be close by here.'

"They searched about this way and that, and it grew quite dark in the wood the while; the sun went down, the moon rose, and of a sudden the betrothed pair stood on the Finland frontier, or perhaps a little beyond it; for the bridegroom started with fright as a pine-branch swept his cap from his head.

"Then a strange scene of life encircled them; a large number of owls, cobolds, wizards, cave-sprites, and hags of the mist,—for the stripling learned these and stranger names he knew not how,—were dancing in hideous whirl; and the bride, after watching them for a time, burst into a wild excess of laughter, and at last joined madly in the dance with them. In vain might the bridegroom cry and entreat—she heeded him not; and she at last changed to so unheard-of a form, that he could no longer distinguish her in the frantic band before him. Yes; once, as he sought to drag her away with him, he found, instead of her, a woman of the mist in his grasp, who at once enwound him in her wide gray veil of woe, and would not let him free again; whilst cave-sprites were tugging at his legs, seeking to drag him down to the coal-black pits beneath. Happily at this crisis he signed the sign of the cross and spoke the Saviour's name; when these hideous mockeries set up a piteous howl, dashed wildly asunder, while the youth fled away to the Swedish frontier, and took refuge beneath the shady brushwood. But his bride had disappeared with them, and no endeavour of his could bring her back again. Often as he came to the boundary-line, and begged and shouted and wept, yet she would never return. Now and then he might see her, perhaps, glancing through the pine-shades, as if bent on the chase, but always in the company of hideous creatures, and quite savage and disfigured. For the most part she did not notice him; but when she did catch sight of him, she laughed at him with the most unchastened and revolting merriment, till he signed before her, in terror, the sign of the cross, and then she would fly howling away. In this manner he grew more and more silent day by day; went out no more in quest of his bride; and at last his only answer when spoken to was, 'Ah, she is gone over the mountain!' Naught did he know of any earthly object but the lost one. At last he pined to death. His father made him a grave, as he had once requested, on the spot where his beloved had been found, and lost again; and much fighting did the work entail upon him,—

now with the crucifix against evil spirits, and now with his veteran sword against wild-beasts, which the sorcerers and wizards must needs have set about his ears. However, he accomplished it at last; and now it seemed as though the faithless bride bewailed her lover's death; for ever and anon a sad moaning was heard at the grave. It is very like the cry of a wolf, indeed, but human sounds may be clearly distinguished in it; and I have many a time heard it there myself in the long nights of winter."

They sat for some time after this in earnest thought; till at last Tebaldo began to speak as follows: "The pains of truant love, the sighs we send to looks that once allured and now repel us, the wounds received from a hand more dear than every other,—these are the fellest witch-tokens of the fearful beldame who holds us one and all in her adamantine toils, and whom we are wont to call Nature. They say, too, that she generally bestows on mortals this better after-taste of her richest sweets, as contrariwise kind mothers give their children some delicious dainty after the bitter draught that heals them. I know a story of similar purport, and am ready to tell it, if it will give my noble comrades any pleasure."

The two knights begged to hear his tale, and he began:

"It must be five-and-twenty years ago or more, that, in my famous birthplace Milan, there lived as beautiful and lovely a girl as noble artist ever dreamed of, or skilful limner's pencil ever wrought. And with all this she was modest, discreet, and gentle-minded, and, despite her strict seclusion,—for the diamond sparkles from the closest bower,—she was honoured by the whole town with the name of the beautiful Lisberta. This Maylike flower of lovely Mayland (you Germans give our Milano a far prettier name than we do) was one day entreated to array herself in bright apparel, and to walk in the procession on the festival of one of the saints, that her lustrous beauty might enhance the brilliancy of the pageant. Remembering that God had granted her this luxuriant grace, she deemed it a pious duty to let it beam forth in honour of the Giver. She decked herself, therefore, in the loveliest guise, with flowers, jewels, rings and chains, and bright vesture; in short, with all that deserves the name of adornment; and as, long before the pageant began, her graceful task was at an end, she was lured by the sunny rays of spring on her lattice to stroll a while in the splendid garden laid out by her father, the richest merchant in the town. Wandering along the embowering avenues, among odorous plants and trees of golden fruitage, she at last reached the clear mirror of a shady fountain, that peeped up from the pretty garden's embrace like an enamoured eye, the sworn vassal of beauty. Ensnared and enchanted by the magic of its spell, she too, on her part, gazed adown into its depths, and beheld there so lustrously beautiful an image, that it almost fared with her as with the fabled Narcissus, who forgot the whole world for his fair semblance in the stream. Anxiously did she turn her gaze on the things around her, to save herself from that perilous spell-work of the waters, and at last was surprised by a wondrous shining, resembling flashes of gold and silver, in the grass. Flying from the glassy flood, she hastened up to the singular floweret, and found it to be a splendid sword, with golden hilt, silver-mounted scabbard, and faultless beauty of form. She took it up like a toy, shy as she otherwise was of such formidable implements; she even drew it half-way from the sheath, and wondered to see her face look still more beautiful on the polished steel than when reflected from the flood; though she felt far less afraid of this mirror of her loveliness. Ah! poor Lisberta, the real danger was at hand, that, like a merciless sickle, was to cut off the sweet flower of thy life! What though the bright blade spare thee, —yet not so he who wore it!

"For now, from forth the blooming thicket, stepped a lofty knightly form, no longer young, and yet not old, and with such heroic grace of air, that the fair Lisberta almost bent the knee to him in involuntary homage. 'Wound not thyself, lady,' said the knight, 'with that sharp toy. Rather would I see my heart's best blood gush forth in triple stream, than that a drop of the soft purple that courses through thy veins should come trickling from thy pearly fingers.' Thereupon, with well-bred air, he took the weapon from her hand, hung it in the sword-belt at his side; and before he could say another word, servants came calling for Lisberta, as the festal pageant had already begun. The timid girl made a sign to the noble knight, and, reverentially bowing, he vanished behind the green barrier of the garden. How utterly the glittering train, the song of the choir, and the huzzas of the multitude, were lost on poor Lisberta, I can scarce describe to you, noble knights. My heart bleeds to think how the beautiful victim waned, and too gladly have I dwelt on the happier tissue of her life, in the consciousness of the sad future that was coming. Allow me, then, from this crisis in her history, to pass more hastily to its end.

"On the evening of that scarcely appreciated festival, while the fair girl was sitting at her flower-wreathed lattice, rapt in delicious reverie, the parting sun shining brightly on her face, she could not help noticing that one of the high, wavy plants, which wound their tendrils round the higher trees of her garden, had freed itself from its fastenings, and instead of clambering up its guardian stem, was trailing down from the window-sill to the terrace below. Rising to bind up the branch again, she beheld a figure flit by beneath her, in whom she too surely recognised the cavalier of the glittering sword. Hastily she stepped back, quickly drew in the tendril, and behold, on its just now drooping point, a little note, fastened to it by the dread yet handsome wanderer, was drawn with it into the room. On opening and reading the letter, she quickly learned from the knightly stranger's love-suit that he was a warrior from distant lands, who in Milan was called Signor Uguccione. He was greatly honoured for his chivalrous and social virtues, and months before she too had heard of him, in many a tale of peerless wonder. Her wounded heart, then, was all the sooner won. Anon was the blooming creeper released from its fastenings, sinking with its pretty errand, like a gentle carrier-dove, to the terrace below, and soon drawn up again on the same service, with Uguccione's answer to his lovely mistress. In this pretty way were greeting and response wafted up and down many times together; and at last even Lisberta herself flitted down the secret stairs that led from her chamber into the garden, where, beneath the shadow of night, she might converse undisturbedly with her beloved Uguccione.

"But in course of time, though Lisberta's letters glided down on the limber plant, yet no one went by to release them from its tresses. On drawing it up again, she found only the seal of her own disconsolate woe—her own unopened letter upon it. At last she began to inquire about Uguccione; and learned that many days before, he had disappeared from Milan in an incomprehensible manner. Still the poor thing never ceased to loosen the plant day by day from its fastening, and let it down to the terrace; and then when she drew it up without the wished-for letter, she would weep bitterly; and she did this so long, that at length, in excess of sorrow, she died of a broken heart. A friend had the blooming creeper planted on her grave, and I have often seen its leaves and flowers shedding umbrage and fragrance on that lonely spot."

CHAPTER VIII.

Deeper and deeper the shade of woe had gathered on Tebaldo's cheerful countenance during the recital of his story, so that he seemed quite changed at the close of it. The merry toper of the moment before now looked the funeral guest, whose heart was lying in the dark grave with the buried one. After a few moments' pause he recovered himself, and said, "You must not be displeased with me, noble knights, if I have spread a dark pall, as it were, over your cheerful banquet and golden wine-cups. I am at other times a light-sped youth, and take glad part in boon-carousal and merry meeting; yet the story I have just told often thrusts itself betwixt me and my pleasures, and till, at such times, I have disburdened my heart of it, it never lets me rest in peace. This all comes of kinsmen and kinswomen taking me so often to Lisberta's grave, and telling me there of her loveliness and truth, and of Uguccione's treachery: the tale has pretty well grown up with me, and taken root in me. Signor Uguccione may look to his life if he ever should fall in my way. I can scarcely think of any greater pleasure than to plunge his gold-bright sword into his heart, shouting in his ear the while, Lisberta! Lisberta!"

His glowing eyeballs here flashed like the murderous fire of war, that flames out over an exasperated land in the dark hours of night. But Otto gave little heed either to this or to his last words of menace. His whole soul was rapt in the story, and in the doleful thought of forsaken love. At last confiding melancholy took the seal from his lips, and he began to tell his comrades (though without mentioning family names) what had befallen him,—how happily he had lived on the banks of the Danube, from his childhood upwards, with his innocent affection for his little kinswoman Bertha; how, at last, lured away by powerful yearning, he had broken that early lovely tie in sunder; and how the pain of lost affection, which the two stories had told of, had made the sorrows of his beauteous little cousin weigh heavily on his heart; and he at length finished his half-childish, half-manly talk, by asking whether his two comrades thought that Bertha too might die, like the hermit-knight and the beautiful girl of Milan.

On this the strange knight looked him keenly in the face, and with an icy coldness, which seemed to mantle over his whole countenance and frame with hostile and petrifying power, "As ye have so much to say," said he, "about the Danube and Bertha, may your name be Otto von Trautwangen, and your fair little kinswoman's, Bertha von Lichtenried?" Scarcely had Otto answered both questions with a "yes," when the stranger rose, and donning the heavy helm which he had brought out under his arm and laid down at his side, "It is well that we are met here," rejoined he; "for I am Sir Heerdegen von Lichtenried, Bertha's brother. After a long course of roaming, I am bent on a visit to my little sister, now budding into womanhood, and have just come in the nick of time to take vengeance for her on a conceited and light-headed chatterer like you."

His concluding words stifled in Otto's heart every thought of reconciliation, however much he might have been inclined to it at first, and with ringing mail he started up to grasp his casque and sword. But on the Italian's endeavouring to throw in a soothing word or two, whilst Otto was buckling on his weapon, "Trouble not yourself, I pray you," cried Heerdegen; "if the young silver-bright coxcomb has spoken the truth, the thing calls for vengeance; if he has childishly lied, chastisement is quite in place."

By this time Otto was standing at the entrance of the bower, and beckoning his foe towards a thick line of bushes, that wound for some distance along the banks of the river. Heerdegen closed his helmet with a clash, and strode forth at his adversary's side; whilst Tebaldo, with a great show of merriment, kept pace with these men of steel, or strolled on a little in advance of them.

"Pardon me, noble sirs," said he, on their way thither, "if you see me so merry over this solemn affair of yours. Never, my whole life long, have I wished for aught more racy and refreshing than to witness a fight for life or for death betwixt two heavy-armed knights like yourselves. Yes; I should have been glad enough to enter upon this grave diversion at my own peril; as it is, I have at most managed a single bout with cowardly, light-armed banditti. And if people really will fight with each other by way of sport, it is the most foolishly courteous farce that can be imagined. Praise and blessing, then, on my good fortune, for helping me to so dread and glorious an eye-feast to-day; for I know of a surety, ye will bear yourselves like heroes!"

Where the bushes entwined their dark branches in the closest embrace, a clear lawn opened its verdant barrier to the angry knights. Without more ado, they at once came to a stand, and straightway unsheathing their swords, they fell on each other with impetuous fury; while, at a short distance from them, Tebaldo leaned against the trunk of a lofty lime-tree. The sword-blades went whirring and hissing through the air; not a blow fell flat; but each skilfully caught on the ringing shield, or, recoiling from the plumed crests of their helmets, besprinkled the green turf with the down of feathers, rather than with blood. Sir Heerdegen shouted the while from his rusty vizor, in the choking voice of anger, "Bertha, Bertha!" and Otto seemed to stagger at the fearful cry, little as the foeman's steel could make him cower. Now Lichtenried's blows fell more hotly and crashingly; young Sir Otto began simply to guard, without further thought, it seemed, about offensive onset, and half his shield flew in shivers from his hand. Then he suddenly rushed on, like a wounded lion; a lightning flame seemed to have shot through his soul, revealing the very hue and fashion of its brightness; for the young warrior, wildly hurling the shivered buckler behind him, and grasping his glaive with both hands at once, shouted, "Gabriele! Gabriele!" as though his silver helm had found a silver tongue. Shrill rang his resistless blows on his foeman's casque, and mail, and shield. Anon gushed a red rivulet from Heerdegen's vizor; and when, retreating from the crimson shower, the young Trautwangen stayed his sword, Lichtenried sank down effortless and powerless, and, with clattering arms, fell tottering on the grass.

Tebaldo and Otto kneeled down beside the lifeless one The helmet, almost shivered by that blow of fury, was soon unloosed, and the seething blood lay like a purple coverlet on Heerdegen's visage. As soon as Otto, who, by the custom of knighthood, was skilled in the art of healing, had stanched the stream as might least give pain, and washed the clotted gore away, they found the wound to begin at the left temple, passing between the eyebrows far down the right cheek. The bandage soon lay firm and aptly fixed; but the knight too lay in his deep still swoon, as motionless as a corpse. Thus pale and blanched, and suffused with a soft expression of languor, the resemblance to Bertha spoke touchingly in his features. Otto bent over the fallen one, and shed a bitter flood of tears. An old legend now broke on his recollection, which Bertha and he had heard a long time before from the lips of old Sir Hugh. It was about a knight who had unwittingly slain his mistress disguised in hostile mail; and now it seemed to him as though he had given the final death-blow to his poor Bertha. "Yes, the final death-blow!" said he aloud, "that is the real truth of it. For the first death-thrust was my heartless farewell, and with her brother's loss I shall have killed her quite."

The young merchant now reminded him that it was time to get the wounded man back to the hostelry; "for evening gathers," said he, "and rest in bed and under cover is necessary above every thing." They therefore raised their pale and rigid burden on their shoulders, no longer the merry carouser of the morning, placing him so that Tebaldo should support his head; "for," said Otto mournfully, "should he wake up on the way, he would much rather see your face so near his than mine. And besides, I might fancy it was Bertha's corpse, and let him fall in the mad terror of the thought."

In the hostelry Lichtenried again came to himself. Two serving-men, who were in attendance on him, applied themselves to nurse him; but when the sick man remarked that Otto was bent on tarrying longer, and even awaiting his recovery, "Sir Otto von Trautwangen," said he, "if ye are minded to do me a favour, ride hence this evening—nay, this very hour; for the sight of you has grown so hateful to me, that I should die, beyond a doubt, were ye much longer to force the nauseous drug upon me." Otto, therefore, sorrowfully mounted his horse, and with the stars faintly glimmering above him, and the sweet scents of evening around him, he rode along the highway with Tebaldo.

CHAPTER IX.

Two ill-matched horsemen they were, who now trotted on together beneath the night-sky of spring. Otto's soul seemed to have drunk in the whole darkness of the hour, but Tebaldo, on the contrary, the fragrance, the serene quiet around him, and the twinkling lustre of the stars. He tried to pour a portion of this happy humour into his companion's bosom; and his efforts failing, he sang all kinds of love-songs, in the sweet language of his country, as they passed on beneath the cool blue shade of night. Nor did Otto feel himself at all annoyed by this. From his understanding little or nothing of the words, he could the better fancy that one of the nightingales from neighbouring copse or lawn kept fluttering on at his side, with one unbroken chaunt; and it soothed him to be able to mould the pretty tones into that sense which chimed in most welcomely with the feelings of his heart.

In this way they at last surmounted a grassy eminence, and the great free imperial town of Frankfort, with its countless lights, shone upon them from either bank of the Maine. Otto reined in his steed in amazement. Such an array of beaming windows the knightly scion of the lonely castle had never yet beheld; and the farther the houses stretched out into the darkness, the more convinced he felt that one of the most skilful and festive illuminations was before him that had ever been seen on earth. Tebaldo regaled himself for a time on his noble comrade's astonishment. "Yes, sir knight," said he at last, "this is the far-famed city of Frankfort; and if you are minded to ride in with me, and to honour my house so far as to become my guest, you may happen to see things still more wondrous and delightful."

Whereupon they rode on past pretty gardens and pleasure-houses, situated outside the gates. Most of the buildings were amply lighted; and the sound of the lute and the song, and the clang of the ringing pledge-cup, came pealing on the ear; while, sparkling through the pretty tissue of leafy green, from many a high arcade and bower came the golden gleam of the tapers, and still more cheerily sounded the huzza of the merry revellers within. Otto thought he had been long ago in the town, when, at Tebaldo's challenge, the ponderous gates swung slowly apart, and they rode through the arched and echoing barbacan, as into a castled fortress, which the young knight at first really took it to be. But when he gazed, from the other side, down the long illuminated street, he understood that the city itself formed one gigantic burgh, whose burghers, perhaps, were not altogether so wrong about the pride which he had now and then heard old Sir Hugh charge them with.

At this moment his charger started at a dazzling stream of light, which the bright windows of a stately mansion shed from two large bays on the street below.

"Here we are, my noble guest!" said Tebaldo; and from the illuminated hall, a host of gaily-apparelled servants hastened up to take their master's steed, and, at his bidding, to attend to that of the knight. With a noble air Otto vaulted lightly from the saddle, and when the menials caught at his charger's rein, "Gently, sirs," said he, "that is no such easy task; I must lead him to the stable myself, unsaddle, unbridle, tie him up, and even give him his fodder; for he won't suffer this at other hands." The charger's flaming eye and pawing foreleg showed it to be as his master had said, and the servants therefore lit the way to a splendid stable, where a store of noble horses were standing at handsomely-finished racks. But these all shrank back in affright when the light-brown steed, led by his mailed lord, paced neighing and stamping through the vaulted stalls, and the knight's earnest bidding alone hindered him from here or there testing his strength against his fear-struck and panting companions. The grooms looked about for halter-chains, to fetter the spirited guest with. "It is all of no use, good sirs," said Otto; "he snaps such things in a moment; but when I tell him, he remains quiet.—Still, my good fellow!" cried he; and the charger stood quiet as a lamb, and peacefully snuffled at the corn that his master threw into the manger. Whereupon Otto went up into the saloon with Tebaldo, who had been waiting for his knightly visitor at the entrance of the stables.

Gay and many-coloured, and teeming with varied splendour, was the scene that opened to them between those lustrous walls; for a vast concourse of people moved, wave upon wave, beneath the high span of the roof; and in the background there seemed, as it were, a raised platform, where figures still gayer, more strange, and more brilliant, were plying their sport. One might at once perceive that Tebaldo was the king of the festival, for the less-honoured among the company made way for him with deferential obeisance; whilst the grandees of the feast, ladies as well as men,—and among the latter, many with the golden chains of councilmen,—thronged to salute him, and accepted their host's apologies for his late appearance as tokens of favour. The performance on the stage in the background of the hall was hushed, and seemed patiently to await a sign from the lord of the festival as to whether it should continue or cease, till Tebaldo, having seated himself, with his guest, quite in front, on an ottoman of purple, decided, by a friendly nod, for the continuance of the play.

Now might be seen in the centre of the scene a richly-dressed, gorgeous looking man, sitting in a raised arm-chair, with a number of little bags of gold in his hand, and wearing in golden letters on his breast the name of Plutus, as the god of wealth was called by the olden pagans of Rome. All manner of different figures drew near to this man from every side,—priests, courtiers, men of learning, singers, pilgrims, judges, and so on,—and with the lowliest gestures sought his protection. Then Plutus threw to them, from his gold bags, little or much, at pleasure, and they took leave of him as they had come, each with some short and significant rhyme. At last, too, there came a corsleted warrior, who bent most obsequiously before Sir Plutus, and said:

"Silver for bruises, for blood give gold!
Give, master, thy gift, and my blows shall be bold!"

Sir Plutus was just about to tender a well-timed answer, when Sir Otto von Trautwangen sprang angrily to his feet, struck the hilt of his sword, and cried out, "That fellow there disgraces his mail, and I will prove this to him on his head-piece, if he has heart enough to stand to me!"

Half smiling, yet half alarmed, the company cast their eyes on the indignant youth; whilst Tebaldo, in great choler, drove the mountebanks apart, upbraided them with the baseness of their infamous sentiments, and forbade the terrified players, once for all, to enter his house again. Then reddening with shame, he returned to Otto, and begged him, in the choicest and politest guise, not to ascribe the blame to him, if that rabble crew had been pert enough to honour the sons of trade by so offensive a comparison with knighthood. At this soft speech, Otto recovered his gentleness and good humour, and craved pardon for having spoken so rashly and unbecomingly on his part; whereupon they one and all repaired with great glee to a banquet which had been prepared with princely magnificence in another saloon.

But, brightly as the lustres sparkled, fragrant as was the odour of the viands, and refreshing the glow of the circling cup—yet Otto could not banish the remembrance of those two hateful rhymes. Not that he in any way felt indignant with his generous host, or his guests; but he could not help feeling that he was being so magnificently entertained for the blood that he had smitten from the brow of the noble Heerdegen von Lichtenried, and was here receiving "gold for blood;" for whether it were wine-gold or metal-gold, that was all one at bottom. Besides, there was an eternal buzz throughout the assembly about money and lands, and profit and loss; nay, even when Tebaldo (in noble indignation, as it appeared) tried to turn the conversation to the crusade which King Richard of the Lion-heart was soon about to begin, a new computation was straightway set on foot, as to whether the Genoese or the Venetians would gain most by it. Then Otto felt as though the red wine were gushing into the cups from the veins of Christian knights, and as though they were drinking it with zest, as a well-flavoured medicine. Yes, even for him, he thought, Heerdegen was brimming the golden goblet, and his hollow voice murmuring from his shivered vizor in his ear, "Hast thou opened thee a wine-cellar, then, in the depth of my wound? hast thou prepared thee here thy downy couch, after laying me down on my bed of pain? maybe it will prove my death-bed yet."

Here Otto could bear it no longer; all seemed to eddy around him as if in frenzy. So he started up, and begged Tebaldo, in a whisper, to allow him to depart;—that night he must sleep in his hostelry, he said; the reason of this he would tell him on the morrow.

"You need not tell me," answered Tebaldo, in deep dejection, "for I know already. But, for heaven's sake, come again to-morrow, or else I shall think you despise me too."

Therewith they kissed each other; and escorted by one of Tebaldo's household, Otto aroused his spirited steed from sleep, and led him through the dark streets to a neighbouring inn.

CHAPTER X.

Now morning began to break brightly in at the windows, and the noise of carriages, coachmen, and criers broke rudely on the tissue of Otto's dreams. Waking up at the sound, he hastily drew on his apparel and flew to the window; for he thought something extraordinary must be going on without. But he soon became aware that the gay tumult, which appeared so singular to him, was nothing but the every-day run of things there, at which no one was astonished; but, on the contrary, every one would assuredly start with alarm if things were suddenly to be quiet, as a miller would at the unlooked-for stopping of his mill. And he easily understood that so many large houses, most of which might compete in size with the lordly mansion of his father, must contain a vast multitude of inmates, with wrangling or peace in their hearts, and the accents of anger or of love on their lips. Had not much of this sort of thing been rife in the lonely stronghold of Trautwangen since its erection, and of a surety was at work there at that very moment? In that city there might be many a Bertha weeping, and many a Walther singing, and many an old Sir Hugh asking for his distant son.

In the midst of thoughts like these, the young knight was interrupted by one of Tebaldo's servants, who, by the merchant's orders, brought his well-cleaned and burnished accoutrements into his chamber, and offered to gird them on. He understood such matters, he said. Whilst Otto looked round with complacency on his shining equipments, "I crave your pardon, noble sir," said the servant, "for having left a small spot on the cuirass, just above the pit of the heart. It may be from blood that has but lately spirted upon it, at least it looks so to me; but as it was neglected at first, it turned to rust, which most likely will not stir so long as the splendid armour itself exists. But sooth, noble knight, it is not my fault."

"No, my good friend, it is not thy fault," repeated Otto slowly and sorrowfully, as he riveted his gaze on the cuirass; for too well he recognised Heerdegen von Lichtenried's blood, which must have spirted on him when he bent over him to bandage up the wound. Now the whole suit of mail displeased him; he had no inclination at all to put it on again; so he dismissed the servant with a word of courtesy to Tebaldo; he already had some one, he added, to array him, and would soon follow in person.

But girding on his arms was out of the question. When left alone, he paced his room in heated mood, passing his armour like a timid steed; and if he ever *did* approach it, it was only to conjure up every possible device for rubbing out blood-spots that he had learnt of his father's old squires and serving-men, and thereby to convince himself more and more how utterly vain was his every endeavour. "It will not stir," said he with a sigh; and then strode along more ruffled and disheartened than before.

At length a loud talking in the next apartment caught his ear, a fuming and execrating, to which he was quickly alive; for a service of armour was the matter in hand, which ill-suited the owner, and would not at all let him brace it on.

Wishing to escape from his troubled thoughts, and the painful throbbings of his heart, he pulled the door violently open. A half-accoutred knight stepped forward with equal impetuosity, and asked what he wanted. But they both stood stock-still with astonishment; for Otto at once saw that he had the late adversary of Folko de Montfaucon, Count Archimbald von Walbek, before him, who, in his turn, seemed to recognise in the stripling the witness of his disastrous conflict. Matters were soon explained.

"I am not vain enough," said Archimbald, "to wish you to bear me company in my fall before the arms of the Frankish baron. Much rather should I rejoice from the bottom of my heart, if you were again to win the fair Gabriele her ring; and albeit, to speak the truth, there is little likelihood of this, yet no one knows what awaits him, either in evil or in good. Good speed, then, to your enterprise. All may turn out as you wish. But now, by the by, just hear how cross things go with me. Exasperated by that ill-starred evening, I had sworn never to wear my black-and-silver eagle-mail again, and vowed, once for all, to go without any sort of armour till I should sheathe myself in a suit which, without cuirass or thigh-piece, I had won from some other knight. In this I have at length succeeded. But, see now, what cursed spider-shanks of limbs my antagonist had. I can neither thrust myself into arm or thigh-piece; in very vexation, I have just thrown the puny chain gauntlets through the window-panes, and nowhere will back or breastplate meet."

And at that very moment, while the knight stood there with his armour half braced on, some of the buckles snapped with his vehement gesticulations; and on two squires stepping up to repair the damage, Archimbald ordered them indignantly back.

"There is nothing to be made of it," said he; "give yourselves no further trouble; and as for taking the wretched stuff off me, I alone am man enough for that."

So saying, he tore buckle and strap clean away, and hurled the plates so violently to the ground, that nail and rivet flew rattling out. Pensively then he turned his gaze on the black-and-silver mail in the corner, which Otto easily recognised by the eagle-helm: "When I wore ye," said he, "I was still a man; but now, I ween, I shall never find furniture that fits my limbs aright."

On hearing this, Otto was reminded of the shyness with which he had but lately eyed his silver suit; "Sir Count," quoth he to Archimbald, "it strikes me that we are well met, and may easily help each other out of our distress. If you have sworn never to wear your armour again, I too have a suit in my room there which I do not like to put on any more, for reasons that I am equally loth to tell you; but, on my honour, they are not such as would do the mail discredit."

"You do not look as if it would, young warrior," replied Archimbald, with a friendly smile.

"Well, so be it," cried Otto; "then let us change."

"Done," said Archimbald; "I think the metal will suit us, for we are both of us of the high old Teuton stature."

The silver mail was quickly brought in. One of Archimbald's squires waited on each of the knights, and they soon stood fronting each other in transformed array; Archimbald's mien of defiance lowering from beneath the softened sheen of the silver helm, and Otto's blooming, almost maiden-like features from under the menacing eagle vizor. Then they stalked up and down with ringing step to the reverse ends of the chamber, to try how the new storm-attire suited them. And when they both were pleased with the exchange, each shook the other's gauntleted hand, and closed the bargain; Archimbald rejoicing with all his heart to think that the eagle-mail might, after all, give the dainty Folko de Montfaucon a warming: "For," said he, "a warming you will be sure to give him, Sir Otto; your stalwart hand, and your noble, martial mien, stand pledged for that."

Thus they parted the best of friends; Archimbald to make ready his horses for departure, Otto to gladden the young merchant with his promised visit.

In his spacious and richly-stocked wareroom stood the wealthy Tebaldo, surrounded by a host of clerks and servants, and a multitude of carriers, and purchasers besides. Curious it was to see how he ruled like a mighty prince the whole business of the place; settling this matter, or by a single wink distributing that, and yet never disdaining to lend a hand where it was needed; nay, even sometimes grasping the ell himself to measure off pieces of costly cloth. He was in the very act of doing this when his eye fell on Otto, though without happening to recognise him; for although the young knight had been looking on a long time at the entrance, yet the silver-black eagle-mail entirely transformed him, and his vizor, moreover, was closed. Despite of this, Tebaldo flew to him with devotion, as the iron is wont to do to the magnet; for all knightly accoutrements were a magnet to the iron of the young merchant's heart.

"Can I serve you with any thing, high and warlike sir?" said he; "you shall be waited upon before every one else."

Whereupon Sir Otto threw up his vizor; and, "Good heavens!" cried Tebaldo, starting half terrified back, "how much more glorious you look than even yesterday! and must I then stand by you with the ell in my hand?"

So saying, he dashed the slender trade-wand against a pillar, and shivered it in pieces. As it was composed of gold and ivory, all the servants thought that he could only have done it against his will. Most of them ran up, picked up the shattered bits, gathered the loose pieces of inlaid work together, and assiduously sought to comfort their master, by assuring him that the costly implement might be again set right. He, however, heard nothing that they said, but hastily drew the knight with him up the stairs of his mansion.

On himself and guest reaching an elegant and retired apartment, Tebaldo grasped both his hands in his own, and bending over them with a glowing countenance, "For heaven's sake, noble knight of Trautwangen," said he softly, "refuse not to take me as your squire, steedholder, or what you will; only let me go forth with you into the world, armed at all points, and ready for the fight!"

Otto looked at him in utter amazement, and reminded him, in a friendly tone, of his warerooms and his brilliant mansion; and hinting that the stars had pointed out to him quite another path to that which he was intent upon striking into.

"Say not so," rejoined the young merchant with vehemence; "I am a Milanese by birth, and many a Teuton shield, nay, imperial mail itself, has shown that our burgher swords are skilled in cleaving. There is something of the old Roman in us, good sir knight. Yes, you should scarcely judge of your mates at yesternight's banquet by their callous speeches and random chatter. I was vexed at them myself, as you saw; but more so because you misunderstood them, than because it was possible for me to mistake them."

"Not so," replied Otto; "but as there was so much said about prices and goods, it struck my heated fancy that festival and night-couch too were only wares, and the price thereof Heerdegen's blood; so I was forced to go. I tell you all this thus bluntly at once, because I am now grown cleverer, dear Tebaldo, and know very well that you will pardon me the mad delusion. I have no fault to find with any of them now."

"And you would be wrong to do so," replied the merchant. "See, in how varied vesture God clothes the trees, and grass, and flowers; and yet they all are at peace with each other, and deck the wood in concord. And, in truth, those people adorn most worthily the great forest of Christendom. Not only do they spread a refreshing shade over hill and vale, but stand manfully and firmly before the lightning, when time requires it. The only difference between them and you is, that *their* words put on the jerkin of the trader or seaman, and *yours* the burnished mail-suit. But the true craitsman disengages, with easy zest, the excellent and characteristic thoughts of each. Then spurn not trading folk, I pray you, and still less *me*, who am bent on a full transfer of myself from them to you."

"Dear Tebaldo," said Otto, "enough of that. You are older, and cleverer, I ween, than I. How, then, should I become your knightly leader, and make up to you, in the world, for all the wealth that you leave behind you here?"

"Well, if I am the cleverer," said Tebaldo smiling, "deliberation will rest with me."

"Besides," resumed Otto, "I am very fond of you; and it would cut me to the heart if you were to suffer harm. But harmed you certainly will be, for you can have had little store of sharp-edged weapons in your hand, to say nothing of your not knowing how to wield them."

Tebaldo glanced at him with a smile of good-natured irony; then turning round, he opened a door, and displayed a chamber full of the choicest corslets, morions, cross-bows, targets, and battle-axes. "These are the accoutrements of serving-men, and not of knights," said Tebaldo; "but I know the use of them."

Herewith he took a beautiful crossbow from the wall, strung it with power, fitted in the shaft, and pointed through the open casement into his garden. "Now for the knot in the old oak-tree there," said he; and after scarce a moment's aim, twang went the string, and away flew the shaft into the distant target, quivering with the shock, and the gay feathers alone peeping forth from the stem. A moment after, Tebaldo stood with battle-axe in hand, which he brought so doughtily down upon a well-braced corslet, that its jarring, sundered rings fell rattling on the floor.

"Will you take me with you?" said he, in cheerful confidence.

"Ah, with all my heart," replied the young knight; "I see you are ready of arm, and cheery of tongue; so where could I find a better comrade, were I to search the whole world over? But, Tebaldo, my dearest Tebaldo, how about the golden spurs, and your lack of knightly blood: for if you never want to rise to knighthood, what need have you to be my squire?"

"Let me only just pass for your serving-man," said Tebaldo, with a gloomier air: "it is not quite as you take it to be. Young cavaliers ride forth for golden spurs, but burgher-lads for burgher-wreaths and victory. When I shall have gleaned at your side the experience of war, and Milan's banner follows me for pleasure or for gain, before all the princes and dukes of Italy, the golden spurs will easily be forgotten."

"I sought not to affront you," said Otto in confusion; and at once the dark fire in Tebaldo's eyes passed away, and a very May-sky of frolic and kindliness came smiling forth from them. He now led his knightly friend down to a sumptuous morning repast; and from first to last the day was spent in carousal and festivity. However, the merchant was now and then called away to important business, which he appeared to transact with the greatest diligence, till Otto almost began to think his riding forth as serving-man could only be a wanton and frolicsome piece of rigmarole. But in the evening, when Tebaldo led him to his magnificent sleeping-room (for he had been obliged to promise him in the morning to pass the night under his roof), he whispered in his ear, "To-morrow before sunrise, Sir Otto! A trustee for my property I have already appointed."

And at early dawn, as Otto stood by his charger, saddling and bitting him, a dainty serving-man was quickly at hand, whom, only when he threw himself on his cream-coloured jennet, he recognised to be Tebaldo. With a cordial laugh, they pressed hand in hand, and trotted cheerily out at the gates; whilst, fresh and merry as the young hearts of the travellers, the sun began to beam forth on the green bosom of earth.

CHAPTER XI.

Otto and his companion were now riding farther and farther into scenes all new to them, flying over the borders of their German fatherland, conversing in the Frankish tongue with the people, and encountering, in gay alternation, many a merry or solemn adventure. But, meanwhile, things looked quite otherwise in the old castle of Trautwangen, on the banks of the Danube. Besides Sir Hugh and Bertha, a third inmate had now installed himself there: but he only gave a deeper cast of sadness to the scene; for he was Sir Heerdegen von Lichtenried, who, despite his wound, had hastened on to reach his sister, and from excess of exertion had fallen into a deeper and more feverish state of exhaustion. Not far from the old corsleted hall, where Sir Hugh was wont to pass his day, lay the suffering Sir Heerdegen, that Bertha might be enabled to attend to his wants without quite neglecting her aged uncle. Sir Hugh and Bertha stood equally in need of each other's consolation, for Heerdegen, in the sad frenzy of fever, had revealed every thing; both at whose hand he had received the wound, and why it was given. This often made the bright tears trickle down Bertha's blushing cheek, till it almost looked like the crimson morning in the shower of May. Sir Hugh, on the contrary, gazed gloomily on vacancy; and from his son's first fray being of so hapless a cast, he augured all kinds of sad results: yet he mostly changed to a serene smile, that spoke of trust in God, and showed that the gloom which darkled over his features was never meant to pass the barrier of his lips. And when the smile broke out, he was wont to repeat aloud a solacing rhyme of Master Walther's:

"Night flies away before the sun,
And fear doth into transport run,
And grim death into life."

It was the same that Otto had aforetime mingled with his prayer in the chapel. Sir Hugh dared not go near the sufferer; for in the false light of the glowing fever he appeared, in the eyes of the latter, to grow young again, and to take the form of his son; so that Heerdegen would accost him roughly, revile him, and bid him be off, or threaten to throw the whole burning temple-wound at his head, with all its fire and flame. At such times he would furiously clutch at the bandage, and old Sir Hugh would draw a deep sigh, shake his head, and return to the lonely hall, through whose huge oaken door the two sweet children, Bertha and Otto, could now never enter together.

But when the beauteous girl sat all alone by her wounded brother's couch, and a single lamp shed its soft light from a far corner of the chamber, he was still and peaceable; and at times he would even tell her some little story or other; and among these was the following one:

"Far up on the shores of the Baltic lies a land which they call East Friesland. In this country there reigns an unquenchable feud between chieftains and their vassals; for the former want to manage every thing by right of will, while the latter think themselves equally empowered to order matters in the way that seems best to them. So the land is kept in continual din and turmoil by these hateful disagreements, as my head is just now, my pretty sister. But then a glimmering cresset, too, sheds its calm and moonlike halo among them, as when you are sitting at the head of my couch, and I am rocking as in a cradle; shadow here, and light there; or here light, and there shade again. This comes from a high still tower, called the Felsenburg, lying open to the moon, and embathed in her hallowing beams. There there lives one of the daughters of the olden Drudas, who, moreover, is our kinswoman—our wondrous and, time out of mind, mighty kinswoman, sister dear. She is called the Lady Minnetrost,* and every day she boils up a great many herbs in one single caldron, which is made of nothing else but the purest gold.

"One evening I had lost my road, and I stopped unawares in front of the steep castle-hill, which looks far away over the whole level of the land. And tired as I was, and much as I needed refreshment, it seemed to me as though something had planted itself in my way as I tried to ride up the stilly unknown height. Just because it was so still, and so wholly unknown to me, I durst not move on for very fear of myself. Whilst I was thus halting, and taking counsel what to do, something came trotting fleetly and airily over the dew-bespangled meadow. A knight it was, with a fair slender maiden in his arms, who clung to him alike bashfully and fondly, and half sang to him, half said to him:

'Spur, dearest, spur thy palfrey light!
We near the stilly Druda's height.'

While he rejoined:

'For stilly Druda what care we?
Am I not wedded mate to thee?'

But they soon had to cease their love-rhymes, for a host of feudal vassals sprang forward from a number of little bushes, where they had been in ambush; and whilst a tall slim stripling seized the knight's bridle, crying, 'Holloa, you, where are you off to with my sister?' the others formed round him in a circle with uplifted halberds. But in a moment the knight had his flashing falchion out of its sheath. 'Thou wilt not get her back so easily,' said he. 'She chooses me, and I choose her. What hast thou to say to it, if thy chieftain claims thy sister? Seest thou not that I am the knight of Edekon?' 'In a few moments you will be the ghost of him,' cried the vassal, 'if you give not my sister back.' Whereupon the knight struck at him, and a wild combat ensued. As I could see very plainly that the maiden would fain stay by the cavalier, I dashed up to his aid, and made my blows tell on the peasantry. Manfully as they stood to it, we should nevertheless soon have done for them, but all at once (and God only knows how it happened), in the midst of our rancorous cleaving and thrusting, we heard the light clash of a casement, that was thrown open on the steep castle-height, and we were obliged to pause and look up to see what it was. And, lo and behold, the full moon shone brightly on the window, and the Druda stood before it, in her long white robe: menacingly she held up the fore-finger of her right hand,

* Minne, *love*; trost, *consolation*.

and pointed to the clear and starry sky. A thrill ran through us to our very marrow. We stood still a long time, and so did she. At length, 'You are very wrong indeed, all of you,' said she. 'One of you is a stranger, and his name is Heerdegen von Lichtenried. He is my nephew, and he must take the maiden gently on his horse, and bring her up to me into my castle. The rest of you go home in peace, and in three days' time brother and bridegroom may come and ask further about matters.' All was done as she had bidden: bitterly as the maiden wept, savagely as knight and bridegroom gnashed their teeth, and fearful as companionship with the castellan appeared, yet it seemed as if it could not be otherwise. In the deepest silence the combatants parted, and in silence as deep I took the truant girl into the castle.

"How things looked here, my dear little sister, I can ill find words to tell you, and it would be of little use if I could; for no description will open our minds to a sense of things so very wonderful. But look now at the peaceful glimmer of our cresset, look in the mirror at those pensive dew-laden eyes, and your lovely little face and air, and only think that a soft beam, the very softest you can find there, was shed over Lady Minnetrost and her castle. I was not allowed to enter, but she bid me tarry beneath a jutty at the gate. 'You will find it pleasant,' said she, 'to stay the time half in the open air, for very bad weather we never have here. What now and then falls in the way of rain is only a gentle, pleasant sprinkling, that refreshes the earth without bruising the blade.—And so shall thy weeping be, with a glad sunrise at its close,' said she, turning to the girl; and at that very moment she almost ceased crying, as she looked on the kindly Druda's countenance, all golden in the moonlight. Then they both went into the castle, and the delicious music of flutes and dulcimers began to steal forth from the inner chambers. I could distinctly hear how sweetly the maiden was being lulled to sleep. Afterwards the Druda came out again, bringing me a large golden goblet of wine, and savoury food on silver patens. She sat down, too, beside me, and told me of her kinship with our sainted mother, and how certain secret, pious lore had, since the memory of man, been the gift of her race; and how she now lived there, and deemed herself chosen to be the soothing genius of the savage land. Her stories were long and of wondrous sort, and lasted the whole night through, as she sat in the moonlight. Often I felt a shudder of awe creep over me; and then again I had the sweetest sensations, just as though our dear mother were folding me in her arms, and telling me some pretty fairy-tale. Ere morning broke, the Druda left me. 'You will gladly wait the event of all this here, I ween,' said she; 'and you may do so without danger.'—

So I fell cheerfully asleep, as when under the safe shelter of home.

"The next day or two I sometimes saw the Lady and the abducted one sauntering on the castle-wall, among tall white flowers that breathed the sweetest perfume, and, like spell-bound flames, stood peeping over the battlements. Often would the maiden begin bitterly to cry, and to call for her lover. And then the Druda would neither have recourse to words of solace nor to promises, but she would only look kindly at the mourner with her crystal, moonlike eyes, or break off a flower and coolly fan her with it, or sing her, perhaps, some plain old song. So the weeper would grow calm, and even smile, at times, with wonderful cheerfulness. And the Druda did just the same when the brother and the lover came, every three days, to ask after the truant one, if they began to be impatient, or give signs of menace and violence. She only had to smile, and the angry words floated from their lips like a sigh, or changed to kind entreaties, full of hope and solace. After thrice three days, they all had grown quite good and gentle. So the Druda gave them back the smiling girl. The bride walked to the altar between brother and lover, and chieftain and vassal remained good friends and kinsmen their whole life long.

"Many a like tale do folks tell of our kinswoman's doings, and rightly they call her Minnetrost, partly because she often solaces and heals a love-sick heart, and partly because her comfort is always loving and kind, and never haughty nor violent."

CHAPTER XII.

As Sir Heerdegen's stories took a gentler and holier tone (and since the above-mentioned one, they were almost all about the good Druda), his mind, and body too, and indeed his whole man, grew more peaceful and subdued. Then he began to ask after Sir Hugh, and to behave becomingly and reverently when the old man entered, and to crave pardon, in case the height of the fever had made him say or do any thing unseemly. Now Sir Hugh would often sit at his bedside; but this was soon unnecessary, for when once Heerdegen had begun to get the better of his illness, he soon succeeded in shaking it off entirely, sped cheerily to the chase over wood and plain, and at noon and eventide sat by the brimming goblet with Sir Hugh.

Bertha, on the other hand, as her brother grew hale and blooming again, was paler and sadder every day. It was easy to see that nothing had borne her up but anxiety for his recovery and the solace of old Sir Hugh. Now that the two warriors quaffed and chatted, and old Master Walther, with his merry hero-lays, was often summoned to the castle, the pretty floweret kept quite alone, as such forsaken flowers are wont to do: in woful songs and sighs and dreams she breathed forth the pure fragrance of her life into the stillness of Nature, and soon, perhaps, would have faded and pined away, like the pilgrim on the Finland border, or Lisberta in Milan. But her brother knew those stories too, and he took his stand by his little sister, like the straight staff of the garden-bed by the tender blossom. Most trustingly of all would she cling to him when he told her about Lady Minnetrost; and it was a keen source of joy to her that the pious Druda had not merely been a shadowy creation of fever in her sick brother's dreams, but that such a wonderful mistress of peace and comfort really did live in the north of East Friesland, and, more than this, was her own kinswoman.

Yet, in spite of this, Bertha's paleness and silent habit increased; and when Heerdegen questioned her about it, she would answer, "The real Lady Minnetrost here below, brother, I shall never see, I ween, face to face. But on the other side of that pit, which is so deep that men often call it *the* grave, there is nothing else but solace for love; and he who carries us over does it always when we are asleep; so think now what a light hand he must have."

Such speeches as these Heerdegen would report to old Sir Hugh, adding, that if Bertha were not speedily and bodily taken to her kinswoman Lady Minnetrost, she would in a few months be seeking her like, as she said, beyond that deep grave. Whereupon Sir Hugh mustered all his nerve, sent for his niece, and solemnly bade her set out, ere long, to East Friesland, with her brother, to visit her kinswoman, whom the people there called Lady Minnetrost. Doubtingly did Bertha look in the old man's face, who had now long since been deserted by his son. Whereat Sir Hugh bursting into a laugh, "Does such a little silly May-bird think," said he, "that a hale old tower, like me, must fall to pieces if it does not come flying round about it as usual?" and with a loud laugh he entered his chamber, and locked the door after him; then two big tears rolled down his beard.

However, on making his appearance again, he made hasty arrangements for their departure; and the blush of the second morning beheld, in the outer court, the sumpter-horses, two horsemen as escort, and Heerdegen's caparisoned charger. Sir Hugh came down the high stair-way with the travellers, humming a jocund lay of olden days. He kissed them both, and bid them make good speed to get out of the courtyard. Then at old Walther's side, whom he had invited to while away that and the next day over the goblet, he walked to the rampart and looked on, as Heerdegen and his sister trotted farther and farther over the glistening mead. And old Walther remembered the while how he had sat on that spot with Bertha when the young Sir Otto spurred his light-brown steed across that self-same meadow, and without meaning any thing by it, he again began to sing, as aforetime,

"The old man's strength is sapped and shaken,
His wanderings past away—"

Then old Sir Hugh seized the shoulder of the minstrel in fury. With the anger of a lion in his eye, and its strength in his arm, he roared aloud, "I will dash thee down the rampart, if thou thinkest to jeer at me! The old hoar man feels strength enough for that."

Walther was already tottering on the slippery verge, yet he boldly confronted the strong man in his rage. "If ye can forget yourself towards a singer, and a guest to boot, so do then! You are accountable, not I, and the reckoning is at hand."

Old Sir Hugh quivered as he loosened his hold: "For God's sake, forgive me," said he; "fell spirits, you know, have held sway over me in my lifetime, and when I felt so quiet, and perceived that this first taste of loneliness was the beginning of my penance, your song struck on mine ear as that of an utter stranger to me, who was bent on jeering at me in my powerless old age. He it was that I sought to hurl down the rampart."

"And a pretty penance *that* would have been," rejoined Walther. Sir Hugh stood a while suffused with shame, an unwonted state for him to be seen in; then, "I know not," he began, "whether you have heart or inclination now to go in with me and taste the wine-cup?"

"Why not?" replied Walther; "minstrels know pretty well how to manage with noble, impetuous creatures."

So saying, he followed his stern host into the castle.

CHAPTER XIII.

During many a day Heerdegen and Bertha travelled on, and the higher they ascended towards the northern shores, the maiden grew inwardly more cheerful and the young warrior more discontented. She once asked him the reason of this. "It is no better," said he, "or at least very little, than if I were leading you to the cloisters. For when the stilly dame once has you with her, she will certainly not let you go again so soon; and from what I know of you, and your little pensive flower-like heart, you will scarcely sigh to leave the moonlit walls again."

"Well, dear brother," rejoined Bertha, "then all will be just as I like, aud I am sure you are fond of seeing that."

"The world is to be pitied, though," murmured Heerdegen; "I should have liked to have led you to the altar."

"Why," said Bertha, "in our good kinswoman's house we shall certainly find all that is needful for the service of God,—chapel, oratory, crucifix, and altar."

"But I meant something quite different by the altar," rejoined Heerdegen, and looked poutingly down at his horse's hoofs; whilst Bertha, with half closed eyes and reddening cheek, glanced downwards on the other side, among the flowers and grass.

And when after suchlike parley she sought to cheer her brother, pointing out to him how subdued and peaceful the landscape was growing, with its softly-swelling, grass-covered hills, and its tire of verdant hedge-rows, "That is all very pretty in the height of summer," he would say; "but only let winter draw on with the hollow whistle of the storm among the hills, and the snow-drift, burying road and hedge-row beneath its cold unstable coverlet, and then see how the solitary, dingy dwellings lie scattered over the pathless waste, far less like houses than heathen tombs, with the dim smoke of the funeral pile reeking through the russet air,—then you will soon cease to praise the soft beauty of the landscape."

"But up there with the Druda," Bertha would say, "there is no snow or noisy blast, you know."

"Yes, yes, so they say," was Heerdegen's testy reply; "but I have never been there in winter days, for my part."

And then he would go silently on his way; and the more sullen he looked, the more ardently did Bertha's little heart long for her gentle, mysterious kinswoman, and her rich store of charity and love.

One day her brother's countenance grew far more thoughtful than ever; and Bertha fancied from this that they must be very near the end of their journey. Her young heart was beating with dreamy expectation; whilst Heerdegen, as evening fell, looked round, almost anxiously, for a hostelry, without, however, discovering any thing but the lonely moss-covered peasant-cots. He sent both his serving-men out this way and that to explore; and when a long time had elapsed without their returning, he bid the leader of the sumpter-horses wait for him at the spot where they had halted, and rode out with Bertha in another direction, in quest of shelter. But in the mazy round of hedge-rows and tiny dells they soon quite lost their way; and the stars were mantling the sky with their spangles of gold without the travellers falling in with any shelter for the night, or even knowing how to find their way back to the appointed rendezvous. But all at once they stopped before a steep acclivity. "Good heavens!" cried Heerdegen, "do I deceive myself, or are we really earlier at our goal than I had wished for? Fain would I, dear Bertha, not have given you up till to-morrow. But do look up at the dark mountain there, and tell me, if you can, whether there really is a castle at the top of it."

And at that very moment the full moon rose, all golden, over the hills, and the windows of the castle shone festively in her radiance, bright crosses shot glistening up to heaven from its towers, and sweet sounds came stealing over copse and lawn, whilst the yearning Bertha stretched forth her arms to the gentle beauty of the scene, and her brother sullenly struck his gauntleted hand on his corslet.

Then from behind a knot of birch-trees stepped forth a woman-like form, all white and slender as the birch-stems themselves, and with just their lucid veil of green in pendent flow over her shoulders. Bertha thought at once it must be the Lady Minnetrost; and when the veil flew back, and from a countenance so kind and thoughtful two gentle light-brown eyes beamed forth with the soft innocence of the roe, she felt quite sure of it then; and, weeping for joy, she sank down on the grass from her palfrey before that stately form. Even Heerdegen forgot all his sullenness. He alighted gallantly from his steed, and bending reverentially to the lady, he was on the point of preferring Bertha's request. But "I know all about it," said she; "joyfully we go forth to meet the guests whom we love to see. As far as the castle, good Heerdegen, you may go with us."

So saying, she extended each of them her hand, advising them to let their horses graze just where they were; for they were in very safe keeping. Thus all three went hand in hand up the castle-hill; and Lady Minnetrost sang, on their way thither, with the most sweetly-thrilling voice:

"What hath the Druda by her?
Oh! all that heart can crave or covet;
Sweet rest, and sport, and festal show;
The fairest buds of all that blow,
The flower of peace, the balm of woe,—
How man doth love it!

Then come, the Druda follow,
If these sweet things thou covet;
And thus on all thou hast below

The little flower of peace shall grow;—
The angels bright in heaven know
How heaven doth love it!"

They reached the castle; and Heerdegen, without a shadow of sullenness or reluctance, took a kind leave of his sister. It was just as if his whole being had never once had a taint of rudeness or violence. They cheerfully arranged the days on which he was to come to the castle-gate to see Bertha. So waving his farewell, he hied him down the height, and the maiden went with her smiling kinswoman to her home.

As the portal closed behind them, a clear lake unfolded itself to their view; and on their entering a shallop, which wafted them of its own self to the solemn pile on the other side, the full moon stood high in heaven, streaming up from the waters almost brighter than before, with her golden flock of sparkling star-drops around her. And on the surrounding battlements the tall white flowers waved and whispered in the night-wind, which Bertha had formerly heard her brother tell of on his bed of sickness. Now, for the first time, she really saw what his words had meant, as she floated on the still blue mirror of the lake, with the perfume of the pale flowers circling, like some sweetly-wreathed dance, round her temples.

The clang of the cymbal and the whisper of the harp sent their greeting from the storied pile; and when they left the bark, and wandered through the vaulted halls, the sweet sounds fell clearer and clearer on the ear. A soft, chastened light suffused every thing in the castle; for from the full moon alone it came streaming down, and, caught up in many a varied prism and cunningly-contrived mirror, spread a snow-white vesture of glory on every object around. Passing on into a costly saloon, where arch wreathed its light span over arch, Bertha could now see whence the fairy music came, for here it swept along in unfettered undulation. Rings of pure gold were pendent on the high vault above her, running through or over each other, touching and commingling in beautiful melody; now striking on the silver cymbals that hung from them, now chafing the harp-strings that enwove their golden net between the pillars. Here too Bertha understood how the fugitive bride must have felt when lulled into soft slumber by this minstrelsy of heaven; and recumbent on the velvet-strewn floor, she too was wafted away into the glad land of enchantment. Then raising her eyelids in her half-wakeful sleep, she beheld the golden circlets weaving their fleet dance on high, and the eyes of the Druda, with their moonlike radiance, watching beauteously over her.

CHAPTER XIV.

Bertha led a life in the castle that varied betwixt childish frolic and wisdom's higher lore. She stood as it were on a threshold, and yet could rest upon it in sweet composure, fanned by the light breezes of a twofold world. The mystic arts of her kinswoman were ever at hand for her to toy with, and yet they pointed anon to unheard-of mysteries in the distance. When her brother came to the castle-gate, she was fond of telling him from the flowery battlements how pleasantly it fared with her, and what wondrous things she saw. He, on his part, was delighted to see her fairy face peep forth every time more rosy from the snow-white flowers; and so they always parted in content and gladness.

More than every other pastime Bertha loved a wonderful mirror that was fitted into the wall of a retired apartment, and encircled with a number of secret symbols. On the Druda showing her this for the first time and drawing aside the curtain, "There, look a little at the pictures, child," said she; "I have something very particular to do."

And when Bertha stood alone before the glass, she at first could not at all make out how she was to do about the pictures; but she soon found out; for the mirror began to grow alive of itself, with a manifold variety of countries, animals, men, and buildings. Now she saw a vast sea before her, and ships coursing over it, to and fro, engaged in traffic or in war, beneath soft sunny skies, or scowling storms. Then, again, spacious churches opened on her view, with men that bent the knee in prayer; or large market-places, and lists and tilting knights. But Bertha was less pleased at seeing these, for they reminded her of the combat between the Baron de Montfaucon and Count von Walbek, and how much that had cost her. Again the mirror changed its configurations to the interior of a gorgeous palatinate, where a great king sat on his throne, with beautiful dames and knights around him. Moorish towns too were shown there, with their strangely attired inhabitants in the streets, in rich and flowing raiment. But what Bertha feasted her gaze upon with the keenest delight was a lonely and seemingly far northern country, full of wondrous groups of rocks, on one of the highest of which was an old moss-grown watch-tower. Through the windows of the watch-tower glimmered a tiny light, quite faintly and coyly trembling, and yet the maiden thought a wondrous store of quiet happiness must be found there. And she made no secret of this to her kinswoman, who would often say to her, "What pleases you so well, child, lies far, very far away from here, high up in chilly

Swedeland. I am soon going on a journey, too, to that lonely watch-tower; but, alas, I cannot take you with me."

This way of talking made Bertha all the fonder of the craggy country in the north; and never did she smile a sweeter smile of content than when the old tower showed itself on the lonely crag as she looked at the pictures in the mirror.

Late one evening the kind Druda had gone up with her fondling to one of the high towers of the castle, where there was nothing above them but the starry sky, and where the balmy airs of a summer's night came freely curling around tree and building, and swathing them about like the ocean calm. Then the Druda fixed her glance changelessly on the gold-bespangled firmament, and it seemed as though she not only saw, but heard also, things of glory coming down from above. Bertha, at last, with a light whisper, broke the long interval of silence.

"Ah, sweet lady," said she, "you almost listen as though you could hear the circling hooplets of gold in your halls, and yet every thing is still."

"Do I not, then, catch the sound of the circling hooplets?" rejoined the Druda, with a pitying smile; "to thee only, my poor untaught girl, all is still. For as the golden circlets are wont to revolve in the hall below, so here too, in the brilliant hall of heaven above us, the blessed circlets, called the stars, are endlessly whirling and ringing with a sound so passing lovely, that every other note must hush its noisy jar, be it the sweetest that earth can boast of. He whose ear is wedded to the starry choir, he only hears it. Others must content themselves with dumb amazement; or if their nerves are sorely strung, a blessed dream takes pity on them, and wafts them the sweet chimes whilst they sleep."

The maiden here cast a speaking look at her kinswoman; for she had a long time felt more yearning than fear about her mystic and magical arts, and she was on the point of entreating the Druda to initiate her in all the wonderful spell-work that surrounded her. But the Lady Minuetrost cast on Bertha a far stranger glance, that quite frightened her, and at once brought on a return of every fearful and untoward sensation that those magical appearances had formerly awoke in her. And gazing on her in the meanwhile with a still sterner and more piercing look, "Child, child," said she at length, "why wilt thou ask this of me? Thinkest thou, then, because it is allowed thee to play with those wonderful secrets, that they are nothing else but pretty toys? He to whom God has revealed them must bear the dire burden because he is appointed to it. But let not another stretch forth his hand thither. Pain, great pain, this burden often gives. Ah, child, dost thou fancy I have always lived here? so lonely always, and so little understood? Never called by a name like other mortals? Ah, no, no! A happy life I once led; and my secret lore dissolved the charm, though, sooth, without my being in fault. Now people call me Minnetrost, and store of comfort I have for the love of many; but for that which sweetened my own life, now I have none."

So saying, she began meltingly to weep, and laid her head, as if weighed down with tears, on the maiden's bosom. Sorrowfully, yet sweetly, it pierced Bertha to the heart; for she had always seen her wondrous kinswoman serene and cheerful, like the beaming moon; and now she, for the first time, became sure that she too was a mortal being, susceptible of joy and sorrow; and she could not help pressing her with the fondest affection to her bosom, and weeping with her, and saying to her, "Ah, my good, good aunt, how dearly, how very dearly I love you!"

But the Druda drew herself up in grave yet kindly guise. "If you love me then so much," said she, "you must take care and manage cleverly how we may still live together. List to me; I am going away for a very long time, to that far northern watch-tower in the Swedish country, which you are so fond of seeing among the pictures. To be sure, I travel quicker than other mortal children are wont to do; but still the journey is a very great one, the errand very weighty, and our parting must be for long. So keep quite still and snug at home the while; and do not look out of the windows, and still less from the battlements, if you will be advised by me. Your brother will never come to the gates while I am gone; I have sent him word by a messenger. Yet you shall have a pleasant time of it: the picture-glass will show you pretty things, the golden circles will ring sweetly round you; and the flowers, the lake, and every thing, will yield you service, as though I myself were here. But, dear child, draw not aside the curtain over the mirror with your hand; put not, with your hand, the golden hooplets in motion, and touch not my flowers. If you ever stand in need of any thing, sing a song to your lute, or just play upon it only, and it will come. Patience, my dear child, and gentleness and obedience. Then we shall remain together, and all will soon be unspeakably delightful!"

So saying, she kissed the astonished maiden, and repaired in silence to her chamber. The next morning Bertha sought all over the castle for her kinswoman, but in vain.

CHAPTER XV.

PEACE and stillness shed their soothing influence over Bertha's lonely days. The wonderful chimes and images sported with her most delightfully; and though she took upon herself the whole management of garden, household, and kitchen, yet invisible favour made all this so easy to her, that it seemed less like toil than a part of her own pretty pastimes. Now, one afternoon she sat rocking herself in the shallop on the deep-blue lake, and the summer breeze played refreshingly round the cheek and brow of the beautiful sailor. Little cloudlets, with the sun flashing through them, seemed to speed their airy dance in heaven; flocks of birds came fluttering about the battlements of the castle, or peeping in among the pale flowers, and then went winging away, with clear pipe and carol, through the bright blue of day, as though inebriate with joyance and liberty. It seemed as if all this sought to tell her something about things without, and to encourage her to take just one single peep at the merry world outside.

"And what harm can it be, after all?" said she to herself. "I question whether I quite understood my aunt, and her warnings. To look forth on the earth for which God created me, no one can possibly wish to forbid."

And almost as promptly as the thought was conceived, Bertha had turned the gold-bright shallop to the shore; and as it was to be far worse for her to look from the battlements than from the windows, she behaved, as she thought, very obediently, passing by the tempting white beacons of the flowers, and entered a chamber, from which she remembered often to have seen her kinswoman look out, while she spoke with her brother from the battlements. The little room, for that matter, contained nothing that was to be secret; and Bertha in a moment had the gaily-painted lattice open, and stood gazing on the far green land.

Here a delightful view unfolded itself, over fruitful vale and mead, as far as the neighbouring sea, on whose breathless mirror the sunbeams sped their radiant play, enwreathing a bushy islet near the shore with a halo of golden blue. Bertha felt herself filled with a deep yearning for the islet; she fancied (and without knowing why) that Otto must be living there; that he had built himself a blooming hermitage beneath its shades, in utter forgetfulness of the magnificent Gabriele, and was peacefully waiting there and hoping for his lost first love. This grew more and more in her mind into a matter of truth and necessity: she fancied she could already tell how the open glades among the copsewood were blooming brightly and fragrantly under Otto's care, and how tastefully-contrived paths were winding their white way through the plantation.

Soon after this a boat flitted towards her, rocking in the sunshine between the island and the shore, and the figure of her brother in it became every moment more distinguishable by his stature and gesture, and the cut and colour of his dress. "Good heavens!" thought she, "can he have found Otto on the island, and made it all up with him, and now is coming to row me across to him?" Thus thinking, it seemed quite plain to her that Heerdegen was beckoning her with his white handkerchief; but when she seized her own to return the signal, she started at the temptation, and quickly shut the lattice to. In deep dejection, she thought of her kind Druda, and how loving and sorrowful she had been on the eve of her departure; and bitterly she wept, to think that she could for a moment have been untrue to her counsel and entreaties. Yet—so weak are we poor mortals under temptation!—her yearning for the island and the little boat in no way declined, and to place a sure guard against her own self, she would often say aloud, "Stupid nonsense! Thank Heaven! I have not even got the keys of the castle-gate." Then all at once the thought flashed upon her, that she knew very well where they lay; and her alarm rose to such a pitch, that she was soon quite at a loss how to advise or to help herself.

Anxiously seeking to dissipate her thoughts, and hastily flying from the way they led her, she ran to the chamber where the mirror with the pictures was set up. On her way thither, she brushed past a chair on which her lute was lying, and the kindly strings sounded at the touch, as if to call her to them: "Oh, *do* take us with you!" they seemed to say; "you were to let our voice sound, you know, when you wanted any of those pretty, wondrous things." But Bertha's heated fancy was now quite deaf to light parley of this sort; she rushed breathlessly into the chamber, and awfully as the blood-red curtain threw its heavy folds over the mirror, she seized it in mad forgetfulness, and tore it violently aside from the magic plane.

And there was a waving and darkling on the mysterious surface, like the boiling of a mighty sea; a creation, stirring in its earliest travail, and suddenly reft of every tempering veil; when it shrinks with horror from the light into which it has been rudely hurried, and sweltering from the writhing mass come the misgotten monsters of the deep. Bertha would fain have screened it with the curtain again; but as surely as she raised her trembling hand, the rolling and whirling began its doubly frantic play, and, awe-stricken and hesitating, she stood riveted to the spot. At length a human form stepped forward on the mirror, pale and distorted with the wildest rage; and, try as Bertha would to deceive herself, she was forced to recognise in it her brother Heerdegen. On his head rested something with two huge gold-coloured vulture-wings: did he wear a helmet of so strange a device? or was it a real vulture, that perhaps had pecked him so pale with her sharp-pointed beak? Whilst she pondered over this, a womanly figure appeared on the shadowy glass: it was dappled with blood; and looking more closely, she shrieked in ghastly horror, "Great God! it is I myself!" Scared from the picture, and goaded on by the echo of her own mad cry, with bristling hair she rushed from the chamber into the saloon where the hooplets were hanging. Rigid and motionless, there they hung, as if held by invisible hands, without the least breath of sound; and Bertha would now for worlds have craved their loudest peal; for in the adjoining room there was a strange commotion, as though the pictures had freed themselves from the glass; and the hooplets might have overpowered that horrible din, and soothed the fearful anguish of her bosom. Just then, she happened to remember that she was to summon what enchantments she required by the sound of the lute or the song. But song seemed frozen up in her, from very fright and fear; and her lute lay far on the other side of that ill-starred mirror-room. In the height of terror, she raised her thoughtless hand to one of the nearest hooplets, and they began turning and sounding, though with the din of the storm-wind and the thunder, and hoarsely bellowing and roaring like savage beasts. The hissing and clashing of swords were heard, and a woful wail, like that of sinners in dying torment. Presently the hooplets flew round quicker and quicker, the howling noises became more hideous than before, a fiendish laughter broke upon the din, Bertha's head began to throb and go round, and then came a knock at the door of the mirror-room.

Bertha thought she could not keep from calling out, "Who's there?" and then her own voice would answer, "I myself!" and then she would see her own self enter through that fearful door, all writhing and bloody, and run grinning towards her with open arms. Nearly raving mad, she rushed from the mansion, sped swift as an arrow along the banks of the lake, across the courtyard of the castle, to the gates. The waters of the pool went boiling and hissing up to heaven, and every thing looked wasted and disordered; amongst other things, most of the flowers had turned blood-red, waving like mighty flames from the battlements, and bursting in fury on the fugitive. But what was her dismay, when she approached the outlet of the castle, and remembered that she had forgotten the keys! Was she to make her way back for them through all these motley things of horror? She felt that that would never do, for the effort would have crazed her. So she kept running on towards the gateway, calling in anguish for her brother, though she knew very well he could not come to help her over those high walls. But, lo and behold, the gates stood open, wide open, though they quaked most fearfully, and threatened every moment to fall together with a crash, and to crush beneath their ponderous bulk all that had ventured between them. Nevertheless the maiden took heart, and ran through them at the top of her speed. Scarcely was she past them, when the brazen valves fell to pieces with a deafening crash, so that, terrified by so narrow an escape from imminent death, she fled still more swiftly down the hill, and fell lifeless with exhaustion at its foot. Yet she still could hear all around her the wild clashing of weapons, and could remark, when she at times came to herself again, that her brother was carrying her in his arms, and saying to himself, as it were, "We must be quick and get to the shallop, and then off to the island. The people here are quite crazed with the spirit-doings at the castle." Then, mindful of her former presentiments, Bertha would whisper softly, "Oh! to the island; oh, yes, to the dear island!" and then as quickly would close her weary eyelids.

CHAPTER XVI.

On awaking, she found herself lying on the turf, with her brother kneeling at her side, and anxiously busied in reviving her. Still, a wild, confused hubbub sounded on her ear. She drew herself up, and saw that there was a dusty din and a flashing of arms on the neighbouring shore, from which she was severed by an inlet of the sea. The shallop was swinging at its moorings, at her feet.

"God be praised that we are on the island!" said she to her brother.

"Yes, indeed, that is lucky," replied Heerdegen; "for the whole land is up in arms about the thundering and storming at the moon-castle, partly to save the Druda, whom they suppose to be in jeopardy, partly to vent their own fury more freely on one another, since such uproar is wafted from the very dwelling of peace. Well, that is no place for tender damsels to live in now, and we must try what we can do to get away again."

"Why, then, away?" said Bertha; "why, then, leave this little island? Here peace and love and kindness are ever in bloom, with all that one can wish for on earth. Only just follow me; I know what to do." So saying, she strode on into the deep-green shade of the bushes, fully convinced, in the light-sped delusiveness of her former wishes, which she used to confound with the prophet imagery of the mirror, that she would find her Otto and his hermitage. Perhaps Heerdegen fancied she had really brought some mystic benevolent lore with her from the castle, as he followed her in wonderment into the mazes of the unhabitable forest.

But there they saw nothing like level walks, nothing like tenderly-nursed and tastefully-arranged flowers,—nothing, in fact, that told of the heart or hand of lonesome, yearning love. Bertha pressed forward in hotter zeal; she was almost on the point of shouting for Otto, but shame and the fear of her brother stayed her tongue. In the meanwhile, the branches of the trees became more darkly intertwined, their roots ran more lawlessly over the damper ground, snakes and other vermin, startled by the footsteps of man, went shyly rustling through the tall rank grass. Then the sea glimmered through again from the other side, and hastening along its strand, Bertha found only a still wilder region, where the parting rays of the sun played mournfully on many an old Runic stone and grave-mound, and mournfully the sea-breeze whispered in the moss that sprung from those gray memorials. Bertha sunk weeping on one of the weather-beaten stones, and in painful desolation she cried, "Then, was it naught else but a grave?" And the more her brother pressed her with questions, the more vehemently she wept, oppressed with bitter grief both for the shame of her premature hope and her disappointment.

In his concern and uncertainty about his sister's tears, Heerdegen began to upbraid the Druda, who surely, thought he, with her mad witcheries had so strangely crazed the poor maiden's brain. At this remembrance, a more painful fount was opened to Bertha's tears. In all her solemn gentleness, and the weeping woe of that last evening, with all her tender importunate warnings, rose the Lady before the mind's eye of the maiden; till, in remorse for her broken promise, and regret for the lost happiness which the Druda had signified to be instant on her return, poor Bertha quite melted into melancholy, and made her brother every moment more impatient.

Now all at once, close by them, they heard the clear and lovely voice of a woman, singing such words as the following:

> "Berries blood-red, leaflets green,
> Brew the darkling hero-draught."

And looking up, they beheld a tall slim figure sauntering along the shore, sometimes stooping to the grass, or stripping the branches of their leaves, and gathering all into a shining beaker that she carried under her arm, and which resembled a large golden horn. Rich flaxen tresses floated over the neck and shoulders of the loiterer and veiled her visage, as she plied her search on the ground. A richly-embroidered vesture, such as only noble ladies wear, though carelessly girded and gathered up as for a journey, curled wavingly round her tender limbs; from her waist hung a beautiful flashing sword; and bow and quiver were swinging at her back. She still kept on searching and singing the while, till the brother and sister forgot their own sorrow and vexation to watch the beautiful apparition, and to listen to the quaint words of her lay. It flowed in quite an uncommon strain, and told of a witch-draught that made heroes fierce for the fight, and unconquerable by any but charmed weapons; but at its every close the sounds grew soft and slow, and passed into a tenderer key. One was:

"But with caution drink, my quaffer;
Charmed mead is fierce. Oh, heed thee!"

Just as she was again bending towards the grass, "Heavens! how fair must her face be!" cried Heerdegen involuntarily. Then, quick as an arrow, she sprung to her full height, like some young fir-tree that has been bent over by force, when, suddenly riving its bonds, it shoots up anew to the blue of heaven; and, sunlike, the wondrous beauty of her features beamed through the surrounding gloom: yet anger soon flashed from those large blue eyes. Menacingly she shot her glance at the youth and maiden: "Ye have disturbed me!" she cried; "for what now this favouring evening? for what the rich bloom of these beautiful witch-herbs?" And angrily she shook the golden horn, till its fragrant store flew in a shower over the grass. Heerdegen would fain have approached her to make excuse for himself. But straightway the bright blade glittered in her beautiful hand. She waved him back with it, and stalked in grandeur to a skiff, which had probably just brought her over; then, with practised oar and rapid stroke, she urged it over the wide plane of the waters, and soon after vanished behind a wooded upland.

The youth and maiden gazed after her in astonishment; and in a very little while, just as they were beginning to talk about the strange apparition, Bertha started up with surprise: "Ho, brother," cried she, "what strange masts are those in the wood there?" Looking the way she pointed, Heerdegen, instead of masts, beheld enormous halberts, towering over the less stately grass. A moment after, many of the men who bore them stepped forth from the dark umbrage of the forest; gigantic forms they were, with loud-rattling, massive breastplates, and huge brazen bucklers on their left shoulders. Heerdegen sprang to his feet, and, with hand on his sword-hilt, he turned a searching glance the other way, whence the like frightful host of armed men were approaching. A handsome young warrior, in gold-coloured mail, with two large gold-embossed vulture-wings shooting from his lofty helmet, stepped forward from the mingled troop to the spot where they stood, and pointing to the young pair, with the mighty javelin in his sword hand, "Away with them to our ships!" said he.

"What will ye with free-born people?" cried Heerdegen; and the sword he grasped flashed upon the stranger. "Step behind me, Bertha! And he of *you* who first dares to near us forfeits his life."

Then a host of brawny bands levelled their darts at the stripling; but, "Hold!" cried their leader; "I will have them alive."

The javelins fell, but the bucklers locked themselves together, like a cleverly-contrived moving parapet, and closer and closer wound the brazen toils round Heerdegen and Bertha.

"Fie on this abuse of strength!" cried the menaced youth. "If thou of the gold mail hadst a bold heart, and wert a knight like me, the fray would soon put on another face."

"Halt!" cried the young chief; and the advancing giants of brass stood as if reft of motion. Then, stepping into the ring himself, he took his stand in front of Heerdegen, and leaning on the hilt of his ponderous sword, "What then," quoth he, "didst thou mean to say thou wert a knight? Thou hast not a single plate of mail on."

"Was I roving in quest of combat?" retorted Heerdegen. "I rowed over with my sister, at eventide, from the shore. Who would have thought of a surprisal?"

"But ye ought to have thought of it," replied the stranger. "If ye have shunned payment of my rent, I take from your strand just what pleases me, in passing; and ye both happen to please me, though thou, in thy jerkin and baret-cap, hast no such costly equipment as you chieftains usually have."

"I belong not to the chieftains of the land," said Heerdegen; "I am a stranger knight, and care naught for gay attire and trappings."

"So I see," answered the other, with a jeering laugh; "and who is to say how it stands with this knighthood of thine? Seize him, my men!"

The brazen wall, with slow advance, again narrowed its barrier.

"Halt!" shouted Heerdegen, with so thrilling a voice, that the adamantine figures again stood still, as at their lord's behest. "I know you to be Normans," continued he, "by your tongue, stature, and attire. Normans are brave warriors, prompt to single fight, and each high and venturesome emprise. I challenge thee, thou leader of this troop here, to try with me thy prowess in arms. The conqueror may decide on the fate of my sister and me."

"Ah! that's another thing," said the stranger. "Here we shall have a proper holm-bout, as we are used to call the solemn courses that we fight single-handed on our islands. Peace there, ye warriors; stake out the rounds for the combat; for now I see clear enough we have a true-born knight before us. But thou, stranger warrior, canst thou wield the weapons of our people? That is the chief point, for I have no others with me."

"Dost thou take me for a boy?" quoth Heerdegen. "An errant knight who hath roved over the north so long as I, will surely have learned its way of war above every thing, and know how to wave your ponderous shields, and hurl your mighty spears."

So the stranger chief at once gave orders that beautiful mail-suits, and helmets, and shields should be brought, and the very best javelins too, leaving his antagonist the choice among them. "Swords," said he, "I have not sent for for thee, because, sooth, thy own hangs at thy side; and such a one, to us warriors, is ever our best and trustiest friend."

Whilst thus Heerdegen was arming himself with the help of the Norman hero, "Art thou now satisfied that I am an honourable knight?" said the latter. "I was not quite so sure, at first, whether *I* had *my* equal before me in birth and prowess. Or else, if thou hast travelled much in northern lands, it cannot be strange to thee, that we sea-champions are not only skilled to conquer the foeman, but to spare him and honour him too."

"That I know," replied Heerdegen; "and fully trusting to it, I challenged thee to the fight. But now, tell me, above every thing, comrade, whether the beautiful damsel with the golden horn and knightly sword hath sent thee to avenge her, because I disturbed her while gathering her herbs, and berries, and leaves?"

"I know not what thou meanest by the beautiful damsel," answered the sea-knight. "Save the fair trembling image there, that thou callest thy sister, I know of no beautiful damsel far or near. So thou hadst better tell me at once what thou meanest."

And scarcely had Heerdegen told of the wonderful apparition, when the Norman turned to some of his fightiug-mates near him: "Think only," he cried, "Gerda has been here, and within the very last half-hour, seeking for witch-herbs! What can that betoken?"

Ill-pleased and silent, the warriors shook their heads, and

were hindered in giving their opinion by a young champion who came dashing up to them.

"What boots it now," said he, "to query or to scruple? Let him who will fight by the last lingering sunbeams make haste about it, and trifle no more. If he be left alive, he will have time enough afterwards for weighing matters; and if he fall, curiosity will be no longer in place."

And now Heerdegen being fully equipped, and having chosen his javelin and shield, the two combatants marched into the ring, which the deftest among the warriors had carefully measured and marked out with hazel-twigs. A hoary hero led each of them to his place, and, with a pressure of the hand, saying, "Bear thee bravely!" left them confronting each other alone. With spears uplifted, and shields held as a bulwark to their breasts, they wound their circle round each other at one unvaried distance and a slow and measured pace, each sweeping the barriers of the ring, and watching an opening for the throw. Bertha noticed with trembling alarm that her brother was unused to those strange implements of war, that he moved more awkwardly than his opponent beneath the giant weight of the shield, and managed only with labouring uncertainty to poise the ponderous javelin; whilst the sea-knight swung his lance lightly in his casting hand, like some dainty little wand. But well-tempered hardihood, and the joy of fight, flashed with equal lustre from the eyes of both. Could their flaming looks have been arrows, they must both have sunk pierced upon the turf. Anon one of them would brandish his spear, seemingly for the fatal throw, but it would only be a feint to lure his antagonist to some ill-advised cast, or some incautious adjustment of his shield; and then waiting what should follow, firmly as rocks, they would renew the solemn death-dance round each other. Now Heerdegen's spear whistled suddenly through the air, and at the same moment the Northman turned his gigantic shield, that flashed like a whirling moon, caught the missile on the firm boss of the guardian orb, and thus dashed it back, in an accelerated curve, on the caster. And at the same moment his lance went hissing forth, passing with such a shivering shock through the rim of Heerdegen's shield, that just as the astounded combatant was about to take to his sword, it bore him to the earth with it, and staved the targe in the turfy ground. Ere the fallen warrior could release himself, the sea-knight sprang, like some winged dragon, upon his neck, with an able grasp pinned both arms to his back, and instantly seizing the knob of his sword with the hand that was still free, he tore it from the scabbard, and hurled it away over the barriers. Yet in the midst of the struggle, he chanted in a loud and gladsome tone:

"Heigh! the mighty holm-bout
Hotly fought the Northman;
Well nigh reft of motion
The stranger warrior kneeleth!"

But Bertha, with increasing alarm, beheld her brother prostrate, and the golden vulture-wings on the conqueror's helm waving over the pale and raging visage of Heerdegen. Then remembering the vision in the mirror, now so hideously fulfilled; "O vulture, mighty vulture," she cried, "spare the noble quarry!"

The sea-knight looked up with a friendly smile: "Fear not that I shall harm him," said he. Then bending anew over Heerdegen, "Thou art weaponless," he continued; "yield only, and thou wilt find that thou hast dealings with an honourable foe."

Heerdegen hung his head in mingled shame and rancour. The Northman therefore loosed his hold, and approaching Bertha with a smile, "Let neither of you repent," said he, "being bound to bear me company a while on my journeyings through the briny flood. I have won you with good grace, and it is no more for you or him than if you had found another brother. To be sure he is the eldest, or at least passes for such, and so you must be good and do his bidding."

With this he turned to his retinue: "Boat, ho! and sails spread," cried he; "we must make many a mile to-night by starlight."

And scarcely was the sun set in the waves ere the brother and sister were off with the sea-knight's fleet; three fast-sailing, oddly-built crafts, in the same one of which they and the sea-knight were together. But Bertha stood on deck, and wept bitterly, as the evening mist curled along the lessening shore, and seemed stretching forth its white arms, as it were to clasp her, like an envoy from the lorn and kindly Druda. "Gladly would I come, right gladly would I come," said she softly, with the tears trickling down her cheek; "I never can get back again."

A white dove flew cooing over her, and the shore was lost behind the dark night-veil of the ocean.

CHAPTER XVII.

Some time after the last-named events had taken place on the North-sea strand, Otto and Tebaldo were sitting on a softly undulating lawn, in the midst of the beautiful land of France. A dark forest spread its deep shade above them; the sun stood high in the cloudless heaven; and without taking from the coolness of the air, little sportive flashes would stream through the spring-green foliage. The horses of the errant pair were grazing peacefully together; for the knight's light-brown charger had made up an acquaintance with the cream-coloured jennet, as well as its master, and now offered neither of them any further harm. Thus whilst Otto, in graver thought, was leaning back, and gazing through the leafy green on the blue sky above, Tebaldo took up a pretty mandolin, which he always had by him, tuned it, and as he ran over the chords, sang in a sweetly-flowing voice the following words:

"The far shores fly, and Travel plumes her wing,
In giddy glee we whistle through the air,
Still finding pleasance new, still unconfined!
Farewell, ye seas and mountains vanishing;
Hail, distant climes, that waft your odours rare,
And round to-day to-morrow's halo wind!
O Change, gay child, of fairest, tend'rest birth,
Speed ever thus the merry dance of earth!"

"No! I cannot sing your song after you," cried Otto, as he started from his reverie.

"Who asks that of you?" replied Tebaldo, with a smile; "sing another. Very few people sing the same songs, or even like to hear them; and that is just why there are, and must be, so many bards and minstrels."

"I care not to sing," said Otto. "Longing, in my breast, hath overflown that comely height at which it is wont to gush forth, a sounding sea of song. Speak, Tebaldo, is it not passing wonder, that we must thus push on in vain after two such brilliant personages as Folko and Gabriele, two names with which all Frankland is echoing, so long and so zealous as we are in our search?"

"It is just the very number of the mirrors that reflect their fair semblances," answered Tebaldo, laughing, "and the countless echoes ringing with their names, that lead us astray, and bring our endeavours to naught. Are they not, in fact, become like to returning spirits of old legendary days, of whose wondrous doings every one recounts all that appears most wondrous to him, and thinks himself justified to add to the score every lie that he can possibly conjure up? They are in some sort deified while still on earth, and for that very reason are less easy to find."

"You seek to make me laugh," said Otto; "but give me the mandolin: I would rather sing a song than that."

"Do you see how it is now?" said Tebaldo, handing him the instrument. Ah, well; sing, good knight, sing. Song is, sooth, the purest angel that wings its way into this world of ours."

Otto ran over the chords, and sang as follows:

" Little birds in lucid air,
Winging hither,
Tell me whither
Leads my way to lady fair!
Ah! while flitting thus about
In and out,
Ye have failed, I ween, to find it;
E'en in you,
Little feather-glistening crew,
Pleasure leaves a pang behind it."

"It is strange," said the Italian, as Otto paused, "that when you speak German, and somewhat earnestly withal, the trees, grass, and waters seem no little astonished, nay, even frightened; but the moment you sing, all is right again, and they look on us quite kindly the while. And just look what wondrous and beautiful guerdon they are now bent on sending you."

Raising his eyes, Otto beheld a young man on a spare white steed, riding towards them through the shades of the grove. He wore the green plaited garment of a minstrel, and over it a costly chain of gold, from which the polished zittar depended on his breast. He played upon it as he rode, for his beautiful well-trained palfrey sought skilfully to clear the low-drooping branches, that his master might not be disturbed in his graceful handiwork.

"Was it you?" asked the stranger, on reaching the travellers, "who were singing so enchantingly just now?"

And on Otto's courteous answer to that effect, he alighted.

"Allow me, then," said he, "to take a seat beside you; fellow will fain mate with fellow."

So saying, he took off his horse's head-gear, and left him free to stray through the fresh forest-glade. Straightway Otto's charger was at hand, challenging his strange pasture-fellow to the fight, and with such display of vehemence that the gentle animal was affrighted, and trotted back to his master for shelter. But Otto called out in a stern voice to the mettlesome light-brown, and it at once returned peaceably to the jennet; whereat the little steed of the minstrel again took courage, and sported in many a pretty gambol over the sward.

"We are perhaps bound the same way," said the friendly stranger; "nay, I fain would hope so. For now, wheresoever I behold a mailed knight, I can never bring myself, by any chance, to think otherwise than that he is travelling eastward to the Holy Land."

"Unhappily that is not the case with me," quoth Otto, with a passing blush; "but neither is it my fault. My promised word drives me anon to the West, sorely as my heart throbs for the refreshing sun of the Orient."

"Pity on it," said the minstrel; "it would have been nice travelling, I wot, in your company. But as matters are, you are every way in the right. A promised word is a holy pledge, and an ill tender of homage to God it would be, to serve the Holy One by leaving what is holiest undone. But will you not sing me a passing song now?"

"I know not how it is," said Otto, "but with the thought of the East you have quite saddened my heart. I could sing nothing fitting just now, or at least nothing of gladsome sort. I would much rather hear a song from you."

"Well!" quoth the stranger, "though, alack, I can sing of naught but the East. List ye, then, if ye will hear me."

Whereupon he struck the chords, and with a voice of wondrous sweetness sang the following words:

"What quivers through the greenwood ever?
  What rustles through the blue of air?
Ye trees, what tell ye one another?
  What news, sweet perfume, dost thou bear?

There comes from far a sound of wailing,
  As when deep sighs the bosom thrill;
Yet like a bride on bed of ailing,
  With all its pain, we love it still.

Ah, God! who could mistake the token
  Whose heart still warms at Christian strife,
How there each hallowed tie is broken,
  Where buried lay the Lord of life?

Of old, they slew the loved of Heaven,
  And now they revel round His grave;
To those our shrilly wail be given,
  To these our chastening lance and glaive.

Though there the cry of pain be sounding,
  Oh, list ye here the clarion dread;
And see, upon his charger bounding,
  The mailed knight with cross of red.

See billow still on billow throwing
  Its steely sheen athwart the sod!
See, what a wood the spears are growing,
  And every branch is waved to God!

Though long we tarried, still before us
We kept the path, and loved it well;
But none unfurled his banner o'er us,
And lone and blind, our spirit fell.

Now every breast hath ceased its sighing,
And every tongue is loosed to sing;
We see the fearless banner flying—
'Tis Richard Lion-heart the king."

Otto's cheeks glowed. He would have given worlds to have joined himself to the wonderful singer, and to have followed the royal banner of the Cross into the East; nay, he was just opening his lips to ask the stranger if he had not chanced to hear that the Baron Folko de Montfaucon was bound along with them to the Holy Sepulchre, for then every private feud would have been set at rest till after the pilgrimage, and their common journeying and fighting would have been the most glorious and happiest thing on earth. But before he could ask a question, a troop of warriors came at a trot through the forest, spoke reverentially to the minstrel, and rebridled the little white steed at his bidding; whereupon, waving a friendly farewell to Otto and Tebaldo, he rode off with them through the merry greenwood.

"Who was that?" said Otto to a trooper, who had lingered behind the rest.

"Heigh!" quoth the man, "it is the famous Master Blondel, the finest minstrel in all the English country, and King Richard of the Lion-heart's bosom friend, wherefore he too is on his way to the Holy Land with this great host of ours. The king has allotted us to him as an escort, so often as he chooses to strike off hither and thither on the road in friendly quest of something new, as is the merry wont of noble minstrels. Fare ye well, good sirs!"

So saying, he dashed after the gladsome rout, that might still be heard in the distance, as with jest and song they sped on through the forest.

"Doth it not seem to you," said Otto, after a long silence, to Tebaldo, "as though the best pleasures and powers of life only looked us jeeringly in the face, without ever deigning to show us the way to real enjoyment? Or, as you look so ill pleased at what I say, let me change my mode of talking rather, and, in lieu of *us*, say me. It is really, though, like the spiteful play of sorcery, that this very day I should behold, and quite near me too, that which seemeth to me the most beautiful and most glorious thing on the face of the earth, and that yet, for all that, a strange pulling at the chain of my sacred word so unceasingly drags me downwards."

"In real truth, I should have more to complain of than you," rejoined Tebaldo, in a somewhat peevish tone. "For just look now, noble sir, if you have made foolish promises, I made them not with you, so far as I know, and yet I should very gladly have set forth to Jerusalem."

"Go on, then, and leave me," said Otto, softening; "too much have I forsaken, and must therefore be well used to the like."

Then Tebaldo looked kindly on him, and speaking in a tone of tenderness, "No," said he; "may God forbid that I should do so! But away with wailing now, and look up once more to the blue of heaven. See how cloud, and branch, and flitting bird are mingling their pastime. Methinks, a balm for every earthly woe must shower down from among that gladsome throng."

Otto gazed on high. "You are right," said he; "nothing does away so well with all my silly fretting as a glance at the restless sun-blue vault above us."

When the youths had been thus lying, for some length of time, stretched upon the turf, with their glances riveted on the clear blue robe of heaven, behold, a falcon-gentil, of wondrous beauty, rose cheerily over their heads, and, like a fast sailer in a sea of clouds, shot up to such a height that the sun soon stood beneath him, enkindling in the brightest crimson glow the under-part of his wings and body. Joyfully did Otto start up, and call the lordly creature many times with the sportsman's lure. But the falcon swept not down to his hand. It was easy to see that he heard the call, and owned the voice of a noble huntsman; for he wound his airy path delightedly round the stripling; but on another call farther off in the forest, he struck his wings cheerily together, and with the swiftness of an arrow darted off that way. He had heard the lure of his rightful master.

"I am glad he is gone," said Tebaldo. "Nothing is more hateful to me, heart and soul, than a plundering fellow like that, with his crooked hook-like beak, his hideously sparkling eyes, and the knavish finger-claws on his legs. How can you possibly take any pleasure in him?"

"In the way you talk," replied Otto, "one might take a disgust to every animal. But I love all little creatures dearly, and a falcon like that more than all. So clever and so trusty!"

"So is the devil clever," said Tebaldo; "and if you call that trustiness, hooking itself on every where with its pointed talons, why, he can do that too."

"You, I ween, never rode out on falcon-sport?" said Otto.

"It is one of the sorry fancies of knighthood," rejoined Tebaldo, "to call such things delightful."

"Nay, say not so," cried Otto. "It is like living in heaven and earth at once—over us the winged hunter, under us a courser swift as the wind; away we go whirling through the meadows green, the cloud tent of heaven running dizzily round as we fly, with the glad rustling of the breeze in our hair, and the cheery halloo of our comrades around us,—then at last the wizard-bird holds his foe in ban, waving, and hovering, and flashing over him, and now—and now—"

Twang went Tebaldo's bow. Roused from his discourse, Otto looked round; and with a reeling flight, a shaft in his wing, and almost lifeless from the copious flow of blood, the falcon-gentil was seen making off to the other side of the wood.

"Who bid thee harm what pleases me?" cried the young knight, with a look of flame.

"Was it your falcon, then?" asked Tebaldo. "If you love every little animal so dearly as you just now said, you ought to rejoice that my shaft hath saved a poor timid fowl, that had just hid itself in yonder bushes, from the arrogant robber."

"No one hath made thee judge over the eagle's realm," said Otto sullenly.

"But just as much so," rejoined Tebaldo, "as you or any other have been made keeper and ranger there."

But the young men were interrupted, at the outset of their quarrel, by a third person's arrival.

CHAPTER XVIII.

On a spare steed of silver gray, and arrayed in costly hunting-gear, with a bright silver bugle at his girth, a noble forester stood unexpectedly before them. Like them, he was young, and his mien and bearing handsome. The very moment that Otto espied the bleeding falcon nestling in the stranger's breast, the latter perceived the fatal weapon in Tebaldo's hand; and striving hard, as one could easily see, to stifle the fire of his wrath, he turned away from the squire to the knight. "Gentle sir," said he, in the most courteous tone, "if it be thy pleasure to let thy people speed the chase in my forest, thou drawest not more largely on my hospitality than it would fain lay itself out in favour of every noble traveller; but I must beseech you, for the future, to spare so noble a creature as this." So saying, he tenderly stroked the wounded bird, throwing in many a winning word of solace, and thereby failing to hear Otto's excuses, which, forsooth, flurried as the young knight was by the beautiful falcon's wound and Tebaldo's unaccountable bearing, were not of the very richest order. But the quarrel with his comrade, and their unfinished wrangle, had only made the squire more dogged. Stepping boldly up to the stranger huntsman, "No one shot the bird," said he, "but I; and no one else has to answer for the deed."

"Back, Tebaldo," cried Otto. "You seem not to know what you have done,—trespassing on the forest-law of a noble gentleman, and, more than that, wounding so beautiful a creature."

"Oh, I know, I know very well," replied the hot Italian; "knights and princes have parted off the earth for themselves into little pieces, which are to belong solely to them, and on which every other mortal is to bid adieu to the rights which God has given him to the beasts of the field, and to many another sacred heirloom;—*is* to bid adieu, proud sirs, do ye mark me, but not always *does* bid adieu. For where my equals come together, there is no such great ado about your sorry law-faddle; and what Milan as a whole does, any and every single Milanese may do too; maintaining his inborn rightful liberty, despite emperor and king, or duke and earl. So now I shall just go and shoot me another fowl or so." And therewith he righted his cross-bow anew.

"Thou hast an odd sort of squire there, gentle sir," said the noble from the Frank country. But Otto, whose knightly feelings had been harrowed to the core, had, with sudden violence, already wrested the cross-bow from Tebaldo's hand, snapping it and stamping it to pieces, and scattering the fragments this way and that over the meadow.

"Well I wot, in plain language, that means a downright adieu," said the enraged Tebaldo; and on the knight turning sullenly away from him, he went to saddle and bridle his jennet. The charger, too, trotted up to him with a gladsome neigh, but Tebaldo drove him off. "Yes," said he, "thou, perhaps, wouldst fain have me still; but thy master willeth it no longer, and so thou mayest go thy own gait now."

The deeply-insulted Otto whistled to his charger, braced on his riding-gear, mounted him, and with great good-will accepted the noble sportsman's bidding to his castle; there to forget, in the midst of a large and knightly company, all the vexations and disgust caused by this strange disaster. Tebaldo, too, was already on his horse, riding slowly and sadly along; whilst Otto and the stranger set off in the opposite direction. Then the light-brown steed and the jennet began neighing, and striving to join each other; but their riders urged them on the way they had struck into, although they themselves could ill refrain from looking back in the deepest sorrow.

Otto had already ridden on for some distance at the

stranger's side, when they all at once heard a trotting behind them; and looking round, they saw that it was Tebaldo, who, however, stayed his horse as soon as Otto's eye met his, and with a most unwonted meekness—"Master," said he softly, in the German tongue, "I believe I was wrong, and I will fain go with thee again." Whereupon Otto stretched out his arms to him, and Tebaldo flew with joyful shout to his embrace; and whilst the two comrades kissed and clasped each other, the light-brown and the cream-coloured steeds neighed cheerily at the meeting.

Whilst now they all three rode on together, the noble huntsman evinced his joy at the reconciliation in the warmest and kindliest terms: it was well worth while for brave knight to bear anon with brave serving-man; for such a league would last out a dozen other leagues, for all they might be between king and king. And then he began to tell the prettiest things about his falcon, and about falcons altogether; and how they lived to be more than a hundred years old; and how, by the golden collars of the noble creatures, while still alive, people had found that they had belonged to mighty heroes long since dead; and how, after their master's fall, they had often winged about over distant lands and seas, and lived quite wild, till they found a new master worthy of the old one. Thereat Tebaldo grew quite a friend to these knightly birds, and discovered, without the least disguise, his remorse at having wounded the noble forager of such a lord.

But after a few moments of quiet, Otto had quickly remarked that the huntsman of the Frank country was the Baron Folko de Montfaucon; whilst, in the stately and richly-accoutred knight, the latter could not for a moment dream of beholding the pert stripling of the Danube's bank. Of a truth, the black silver mail glanced on him its solemn warning; but the youthful face, with its morning blush and flaxen tresses, suited those trappings too ill to allow any distinct remembrance to arise. All floated before the baron's senses like some dream-sent figure, which, when fully awake, we can no longer arrest—dark, vague, and soon utterly forgotten.

CHAPTER XIX.

In Sir Folko's castle, at the merry evening banquet-table, sat the noble knights of many a varied kinship, and other men too of buoyant life and spirit, among whom Tebaldo found fitting place. His sprightly Italian vein of merriment soon boiled up, to the amusement of the company, and was remarked with especial complacency by one of his countrymen, named Count Alessandro Vinciguerra; whilst Otto sat still and silent, unnoticed by any after their first astonishment at his handsome figure and bright knightly array was over. As the cups circled more quickly, filled with more fiery wine, they thought of enhancing their social pleasures by the recital of all kinds of pointed tales. Among knights of such renowned blazon and such distant travel, and so many noble masters in many a varied art, there could not possibly be any lack of adventurous matter; and they all begged the lord of the mansion, in common, that he should make a beginning.

"It will not avail us as an excuse for the host," said Folko, "that his garden boasts only sorry or ordinary flowers: it is enough if his noble guests crave them; accept, therefore, what I am able to bestow.

"It will be no unknown tidings to many of you, that my house had its rise in the mountain-ranges of Norway, and that we there may still number many a noble kinsman. Setting sail from those parts, my conquering forefathers landed on the Frankish coast, pushed forward victoriously into the domain which to this day is called Normandy, and, among many other curious legends, brought the following one with them:

"An old and far-famed warrior had a beauteous daughter, whose name was Fair Sigrid; they talked about her in every northern country, and many a suitor sought her hand. The splendour of her beauty was enhanced still more by her rare skill in every graceful and womanly art, and in divers lore too, the gladdening and the gay, as well as the secret and magical, which the ladies of those parts are specially fond of. Thus she knew, above all, how to prepare a certain draught, which, if prudently taken, would fire the combatant with unheard-of strength and glee, yea, even render him proof to every other but a charmed weapon. To this very hour there are said to be many dames in the northern lands who are skilled in mixing this wondrous beverage; nay, the secret of it is reported to be hereditary in one of the branches of our race. Now one day the old warrior said to his daughter, 'Fair Sigrid, be quick and go out into the wood, and gather red berries and green leaflets. To-morrow I need thy draught; for I march forth to a hot encounter.' 'With whom, then, father?' asked Fair Sigrid; and the old warrior replied, 'With Hakon Swendsohn, the young lordling who bids fair to outvie me one day in all the north country, if I bring not down the bold eaglet ere he is fully plumed. Moreover, thou knowest he is sprung of a race hostile to ours.' And Fair Sigrid went forth into the dark evening wood, all alone, as the charmed custom of the mysterious potion required.

"Up the rocks and down the rocks, over the banks of the wood-streams which the light bridge of the pine-trunk scarcely united, through many a dark valley, and along many a fearful precipice, Fair Sigrid pressed forward till she had found all the simples for the wonderful potion. And now she looked around her in the gathering darkness of night; and there she stood in an utterly strange part of the forest, all alone, and at a loss to find her way. Many a look had she given to the flowers and night-herbs, but not one to the stars; and brightly as they sparkled in the sky, Fair Sigrid could not at all set herself right by these puzzling, mute way-marks. As she was thus peering doubtfully into the gloom, she heard the branches rustling and snapping in the forest-trees near her; and just as she espied a black bear, rampant in grisly mimicry of man, coming rushing on her with a roar, a javelin passed whizzing over her, and the next moment the huge beast was rolling in his blood down the neighbouring precipice. With a winning smile a young warrior issued from the brushwood, and made offer to the beauteous maiden whom his spear-cast had saved to guide her homeward in safety. But Fair Sigrid wept bitterly; for all her witch-herbs and flowers had fallen out of her veil in the fright. To gather new ones, she would be forced, by wizard-law, to begin all over again; and the moon was now high in heaven, and the maiden felt the wood thereabouts quite strange and uncanny. 'Go on seeking and gathering as thou wilt,' said the young warrior; 'I too know well enough that it must be done quite alone and undisturbed; so I will course round thee at a distance, sweet maiden, to guard thee, that no one may hinder thee; and ere morning breaks, I will escort thee home again to the rocky castle of thy father.' So the young chieftain vanished amid the brushwood; while, merrily and trustingly, Fair Sigrid plied her search; and if she grew timid at times in the strange lone wood, she soon felt cheered and relieved again when the gold-mail which the young warrior wore sent its guardian rattle through the whispering leaves.

"At length she had done gathering her herbs, and was minded to brew them up at once in a golden flask that she had by her, and thus to take the wondrous draught easier and safer to her home. Her first and slightest signal brought her guardian to her side; and scarcely had he heard her wishes, before he piled up a heap of light twigs and boughs; and in a trice, at the maiden's bidding, the flame flashed up cheerily, through the dark green forest, to the lone vault of night. But this brewing of the weird potion lasted long; and when at last it was ended, Fair Sigrid began again to weep bitterly, for she felt that she was no longer able to begin her long way homeward without taking some repose.

"'Sleep in safety, beauteous maiden,' said the gallant warrior: 'I will take good care to watch over thee, and to wake thee at the fitting time.' So, with his mantle and a plentiful store of moss, he made a soft, warm couch; and as she stood bashfully by the side of it, he vanished at once into the dark shades of the grove.

"She awoke just as morning was breaking, at the sound of some war-horns in the distance, and the young warrior again stood at her side. 'Thou must haste and hie thee home,' said he, 'for those are Hakon Swendsohn's horns that are blowing, and they summon thy father to the fight. Take up thy draught quickly, and come.'

"And he led the maiden on through the strange by-ways of the forest, till they were close to her father's castle. On taking leave of him there, she besought him to tell her his name. 'I am Hakon Swendsohn,' said he; 'and I know full well that thou art Fair Sigrid, the old warrior's daughter; and that, to my ruin, thou hast sought and brewed the potion in the mountains. But too long have I been fired with the love of thee, Fair Sigrid; and the feud between our races is the death-blow to my hopes. Now right gladly will I die by the famous sword of thy father, and may he thrive on the potion!' Albeit Hakon, with these words, was darting off to his followers in the thicket, yet Fair Sigrid would not let him go till he had followed her into her father's castle. There she told all that had happened to her. The two foes embraced each other, and Hakon Swendsohn and Fair Sigrid became a happy pair."

The company were well pleased with the story. "Yes," said a noble master of the painter's art, "the sportive dalliance of light is ever and every where a welcome greeting; but where the rainbow throws its span athwart the threatening thunder-clouds, we thrill with the keenest joy. Thus welcome, too, are these looks of love and gentleness, darting forth from the roughest regions of the north. Glad astonishment and sweet surprise, mingled with delight in the bright picture, enter at once into delicious fellowship."

"You are right, noble master," said the Count Alessandro Vinciguerra, "if the sight of the rose seems more wonderful to you in northern lands than in our blossom-teeming Italian gardens. But we cannot be astonished at the fair flowers of knighthood and comely bearing that bloom among those noble Normans—we, I mean, who have seen Normandy, and know her high-born sons and beauteous daughters."

In the meanwhile, several of the company had turned to a Spaniard, Don Hernandez by name, of fine stature and sunburnt visage, and begged him to tell a tale of his fatherland. "Many a wonderful thing must take place," said they all, "in a land so rife in beauty and knightly prowess, where Christian swords have ever had to stand their ground against the armed hosts of the cunning and gorgeous Saracen." Hernandez craved a lute. He would rather sing his tale, he said, than tell it. His wish was granted; and waking the strings with the most lovely sway, he sang the following words:

"'Don Gayferos, Don Gayferos,
Knight so wondrous, knight of glory,
From the castle thou hast charmed me,
Lovely one, with thy beseeching.

Don Gayferos, leaguers with thee
Were the wood and evening's cressets:
Lo, I wait thee; tell me only
Whither wilt thou wander, dearest?'

'Donna Clara, Donna Clara,
Thou art mistress, I the vassal;
Thou my guide, and I the planet;
Spell of sweetness, speak thy bidding!'

'Sooth, then, let us down the mountain
To the crucifix beneath it;
Wending then along the meadows
By the sainted chapel homeward.'

'Ah! why need we by the chapel?
By the crucifix why need we?'
'Speak; for why wilt thou gainsay me,
Who methought wert my true vassal?'

'Nay, I wend me, nay, I wander,
Lady, as thy will commandeth:'
So they rambled on together,
Communing of love so sweetly.

'Don Gayferos, Don Gayferos,
By the crucifix behold us;
Why hast thou not bowed thee lowly
To the Lord, like other Christian?'

'Donna Clara, Donna Clara,
Could I gaze on aught around me
But those little tender fingers,
Whilst they sported with the flowerets?

'Don Gayferos, Don Gayferos,
Couldst thou find no fitting answer
To the holy friar's greeting,
As he murmured, Christ be with thee?'

'Donna Clara, Donna Clara,
Could I hear the lightest breathing,
Or a single earthly whisper,
But thy soft sweet tale, "I love thee"?'

'Don Gayferos, Don Gayferos,
See, before the chapel glistening,
Stands the little hallowed fountain;
Come and do like me, beloved!'

'Donna Clara, Donna Clara,
Very soon shall I be sightless;
For a single moment's gazing
On thy bright eyes hath undone me.

'Don Gayferos, Don Gayferos,
Do like me if thou wilt serve me;
In the wave thy right hand steeping,
Sign upon thy brow a crosslet.'

Don Gayferos mutely started;
Don Gayferos fled away thence;
Donna Clara turned her timid
Trembling footsteps to the castle."

Now striking a few pensive chords, Hernandez passed into another and a gloomier key, and continued his song as follows:

"Then at night the lute rang sweetly,
As it oftentimes had sounded;
Then at night the handsome stranger
Sang as he so oft had sung there.

And again the casement trembled—
Donna Clara gazed beneath it;
But her timid glances hurried
Coyly through the dewy darkness.

And in lieu of love's sweet whisper,
Soothing tale, and tender tiding,
She began conjuring harshly—
'Say, who art thou, darksome wooer?

Say, by thy love and by my love—
Say, if thy soul's peace thou prizest,
Art thou Christian? art thou Spaniard?
Art thou of the Church's liegemen?'

'Lady, sternly thou conjurest;
Lady, thou shalt hear the tidings.
Ah! no Spaniard am I, lady,
Nor the holy Church's liegeman;

But a Moorish king, whose bosom
Love of thee to flame hath kindled;
Great in power, rich in treasure,
Matched by none in knightly prowess.

Crimson blooms Granada's garden,
Golden gleam Alhambra's towers;
Warriors wait their queen to welcome—
Fly with me, then, through the darkness.'

'Forth! thou soul-destroying false one!
Forth! thou fiend!' she would have shouted;
But before the word was fashioned,
On her lips' sweet bourne it melted.

Helplessness its darksome coil
Wreathed around her form of beauty;
Straightway to his steed he bore her,
And fled onward through the night-gloom."

Again Hernandez changed the key; and in a stately, hymn-like march he closed his song.

"Up the early sky of morning,
Pure and smiling, soars the sun;
But there's blood upon the meadow,
And a steed with rider gone,
Round and round affrighted runneth;
And a vassal-band is there.
Moorish king! thou hast been smitten
By the valiant brother-pair,
Who beheld the hardy venture
Thou didst in the greenwood dare.
By the corse the lady kneeleth,
With her gold dishevell'd hair;
Little now to hide her fondness
For the fallen doth she care.
Brothers plead, and priests reprove her—
Vain alike reproof and prayer:
Suns may set, and night-stars follow,
Eaglets soar and sink in air,
Every thing on earth is changeful—
She alone unchanging there.
So at last the faithful brothers
Build her shrine and chapel fair;

And her life is spent in praying,
Day by day, and year by year,
Like a slow-exhaling offering
For the soul of him so dear."

The sounds of the guitar died away in slow vibrations, and the gaze of the listeners was overcast with gloom.

Hernandez was the first to break silence. With a tone of the most courteous sweetness, "I should both reproach and condemn myself, ye noble knights and masters," said he, "for darkening your merry banquet with so stern and sorrowful a tale, had ye not yourselves craved a story of my fatherland. But every thing there just now takes a very gloomy cast; for where Christians and Pagans fight for their lives with each other, sorrow, and even death, too often sits at the helm."

"It needeth not excuse," rejoined the Baron de Montfaucon. "Think ye, then, we do not gladly weave dark flowers, too, in our garlands? Thank God, we Franks are not degraded to such mountebank fellows, that we either mistake or avoid the noble gravity of Castile; and who, of all my gentle-born guests from divers European lands, hath not gladly drawn from the deep spring of life and poesy in the bright soil beyond the Pyrenees?"

"You speak graciously of us," said Hernandez, "and we hope that we are worthy of such favour. But, however that may be, the beautiful garland will pale before too many dark flowers. A flame-bright fire-lily might fitly be blended with it; and sorely am I mistaken if such gay little blossom is not just now upon the lips of the noble Count Vinciguerra."

"Spaniards and Italians form ready fellowship," said Count Alessandro; "and if such be your pleasure, I would fain tell my story too.

"In magnificent Naples, which, both for its situation and beauty, may be called a very city of the sun, lived some time ago a warrior of the name of Dimetri, high-born, wealthy, and of far-famed prowess, though well advanced in years. As he wished now to crown his toilsome life with a cheery and refreshing old age, he gathered around him all the fairest things those rich domains afforded, in tapestry, fruit, wines, blazonry, sculpture, and whatsoever could minister to delight; but the most beautiful gem of all was a young wife, Madonna Porzia, whom he had taken to his home from one of the noblest families of the land. Therewith, however, no little discomfort installed itself in his mansion; for however modest, gentle, and compliant Donna Porzia might be, still the consciousness of his own gray hair, and the decay of his personal charms, raised such jealous thoughts in the good old man's breast, as left him but small store of peace.

"If he, however, on his part, was a prey to uneasiness, still more so was Signor Donatello, a young nobleman, whose winning manners, knightly beauty, and graceful bearing, made him a favourite with every one; for since he had by chance seen Madonna Porzia at mass (and to any other place the anxious Dimetri never let her repair), he could think of nothing else but the enchantment of her beauty. Accordingly he resolved in one way or other to gain her love, or to lose his life in the endeavour. Yet he did not set about this like most foolish youths, who, by messages from the chattering lips of female envoys—by riding and galloping past in full array of splendour, and waving their greeting the while—only awaken the fears of jealous husbands; or, by thrusting presents upon their mistresses, and like acts of indiscretion, strike such terror into their tender hearts that they must blame themselves if there be no more room for love there. But so artful and circumspect was his demeanour, that albeit the fair Porzia took knowledge of his flame,—as one bright look is ever quick to strike fire from another,—yet she at the same time felt assured that Donatello held the safety and happiness of his mistress far dearer than the attainment of his wishes.

"So it happened, then, at last, that she herself devised safe means of sending him her thanks for his attentions, and the tenderness of his court to her; and after many sendings to and fro, Donatello was at last empowered to promise himself all he most ardently longed for, if he could but gain an entrance into his lovely mistress's house.

"The favours which by this time Donatello had showered on Dimetri had not fallen to the old warrior's lot in all the length and breadth of his eventful life; yet so cleverly were they tendered, that no obtrusiveness of design was for a moment discoverable. That, however, which might greatly advantage the youth with the beautiful Porzia, was his greatest drawback with old Dimetri: the handsomeness of form and feature, to wit, in which he shone above all others of his age. Had it not been for this, Dimetri would long before have bidden to his dwelling a comrade so congenial and winning; but now the venture appeared to him too fearful; and friendly as he invariably continued to Donatello, Donatello as invariably continued a fixture outside his door.

"The enamoured youth had soon spent a considerable part of his fortune in tokens of good-will to his veteran rival, and was still not a whit nearer his goal. At length a thought, which had hitherto been but a dream, ripened into a well-ordered plan; the wish, namely, that Dimetri's life might be perilled, and that he, by saving him, might gain his confidence and friendship for ever. To this end he hired certain assassins, who were to fall upon the old man unawares in some retired part of the city. But as soon as he was seemingly in the height of danger, Donatello was to hasten up, and the venal bullies, after a feigned resistance, were to take to flight. The trick was played off most cleverly; Dimetri believed himself saved by Donatello, thanked him with the greatest warmth and earnestness; but his threshold remained barred as before, and he himself seemed still more morose and uneasy. The facts of the case were these: The belief that Madonna Porzia could never love an old man like him—one, too, so utterly unskilled in the art of pleasing—he sought to stifle in his own breast, by calling to mind all his renowned and truly wonderful achievements, and at the same time conjuring up all that great poets had said about the love of fair dames for mighty warriors. Whereupon he failed not to tell the young dame in glowing terms of his combats and adventures, and to put books into her hands wherein many of them were chronicled. But it always seemed to him as though she heard and read that sort of thing with no other emotion than she did the histories of warriors that had long since mouldered into dust; and, beyond a doubt, he would fain have freshened up his fading laurels by some new campaign or other, despite his tottering health, had jealousy allowed of his straying so long from Donna Porzia's side. And when he now and then had young chargers led into the courtyard of his mansion, or cross-bows brought him, that he might show his lovely young consort the dexterities of his once-admired youth, he felt too keenly how little he then shone in those featly exercises; while a certain anxious trait of concern in Madonna Porzia's features told more of the fear of a daughter for her feeble father, than the anxiety of a wife for her hair-brained spouse. How much more keenly must the heart of the old soldier have been wounded by his inglorious fray with the bravoes, and his rescue by the hand and arm of so comely a stripling. He disengaged himself more and more from Donatello, whose every thought of entering the house had now to be relinquished. After hopes so often blasted, the young lover's patience could stand it no longer. To be sure, a faint glimmer of hope that his wish would one day be granted kept him still gentle and friendly towards Dimetri; but to the rest of the citizens he was a very torment, since he thought, if *his* best wishes were in vain, others should never see the fulfilment of theirs. So that he, who before was the favourite of Naples, and praised by her every tongue, came at last to be by all Naples execrated and hated; till some young men, whose path he had too often jeeringly and spitefully crossed, resolved to lie in wait for him without more ado, and if not to murder him, at least to wound him in such a manner as to make him thoroughly shy of his own bickering and banter. One evening he fell into the snare; for as he could not help sauntering, by night at least, in the neighbourhood of that well-loved roof, it was easy to fall in with him there; and bravely as he defended himself, yet the surprise and number of his foes left him open to two severe wounds. But, hark! the old swordsman heard from his palazzo the shouts and the clashing of the combatants; and eager to play the Orlando, both before himself and the beauteous Madonna Porzia, he girds himself to the fight, and runs out at once with his huge two-handed battle-blade. Whether he, equipped as he was for the fray, was really a dread warrior still, or alarm was most potent with Donatello's foes,—enough, they fled before the giant spectre, and Donatello was saved. Now, every shadow of scruple vanished from the eyes of the triumphant conqueror. He brought in his rescued friend to Madonna Porzia as a trophy: nothing would do but she must undertake the nursing of the wounded one herself; and as Donatello knew his own game too well to talk of aught to Donna Porzia, so long as Dimetri was present, but the heroism of her spouse, dwelling on his feints and wards, his menacing postures and unheard of daring, he continued, even after his recovery, his daily and privileged guest. Dimetri often found him alone with his wife; but every germ of distrust was crushed in a moment, as he always heard Donatello recounting the story of his valour, and Donna Porzia applauding it.

"My tale may teach us, I think, that one man's cunning is of little avail against the wits of another; but when the fool in our adversary's breast declares for us, the game is at once our own."

CHAPTER XX.

MANY tongues grew loud about the adventure of the old warrior and young Signor Donatello. Now the lover was praised for his refined secrecy and reserve; now Madonna Porzia for understanding and honouring so delicate a suit; and now again every personage in the story, even old Dimetri included, were termed happy, since each had met with the fulfilment of a long-cherished hope: in short, there was no end to their laughter and the motley tissue of their remarks Meanwhile, with the watchfulness of a worthy host, the bright eyes of Sir Folko de Montfaucon circled round the table; and as it seemed to him that Otto was sitting there in sad and sullen thought, he strove to raise his cheer, and make him better acquainted with his company. "My noble German guest," said he, "you hear how this and that is praised in Count Alessandro's story: what seemeth the most praiseworthy point in it to you? and do you find it in the knight or in the lady?"

With eyes darkly glowing, a deep voice, and an austere look, that matched but oddly with the witty mirthfulness of the company, "I know not," replied Otto, "whether in such a knight and such a lady there can be the least mite of any thing to praise. If you ask me in which of the two all that is most abominable, most infamous, and most devilish is to be found, I might find a readier answer, and even then it would be hard for me to choose. Out upon it! Far above all she deserved, the renowned warrior chose the smooth, sleek puppet, placed his honour in her hands, trusting to her to light up the peaceful evening of his valiant life with the goodly ray of love and tenderness and truth; and now, vile truant from the high path of her destiny, her eyes rove in search of wanton lemans! Out upon it! The pretty sauntering coxcomb succeeds in making the old hero fond of his company,—an honour, by the by, at which every right fellow's heart would leap with unmingled joy,—but only in order to set his toils the more artfully! He mates and mixes with bravoes! Why not with poisoners outright? And at last the old battle-prince saves him in earnest, unlike his own wicked toying; wields for him in truth and bravery, and perhaps for the very last time of all, the fame-crowned sword; and then, instead of the sniveller sinking to earth under the burden of his shame—But spare me, good sirs, the pain of dwelling on it more largely: I have already gazed on it longer than is good for healthy eyes."

All at the table were silent; many a cheek was glowing with a deep flush of shame, which Count Alessandro Vinciguerra felt kindling on his own. Yet, thinking to struggle out of it, "You take things too severely," said he, "noble Allemanian knight. From your point of view, you may be right; but, prithee, from your side of the Alps level not your shaft of reproof at my fiery countrymen. We are other than you are, and so things must go otherwise with us than with you."

"Are there points of view, or whatever you call them, in such matters?" said Otto. "I know sure enough that, on the other side of the Alps, folk are as little fond of going to hell as on ours: and hellward leads the road that your story would teach us; you may take my word for it."

With all this there was a sober earnestness, a freedom from every thing spiteful, and at the same time a quiet, childlike grace on Otto's features, such as we see on the angels' heads of old German or Italian masters. A light shudder, a presage of measureless eternity, thrilled through the assembled wassailers. The proud Vinciguerra riveted his eyes on the ground. Hernandez, on the other hand, had quietly risen and stationed himself behind Otto's chair. At a friendly tap on the shoulder, the young knight turned round, and a joyful, loving ray of light came streaming from the Castilian's eyes.

After a long interval of silence, the Baron de Montfaucon rose from his seat and addressed the young German: "Sir knight," said he, "you have put us one and all to shame; but you have led us one and all too into the right path; for you sound forth, like a clear church-bell, the behest of Christendom and of knighthood. My inmost, warmest thanks to thee. I acknowledge thee the noblest jewel in my castle." Thereupon he bowed solemnly before him, and all the knights and masters rose and did the same.

Otto's cheeks were brightly flushed with modest embarrassment. "Kind sirs," quoth he, "I ween ye bow to the good God, and not to me, and so it is all very right. Were it meant otherwise, I, poor stripling knight, dare not approve it."

"We crave your name, noble sir," said the baron, "and the story of your life."

"Whether any at all, or what kind of story my life will produce," replied Otto, "rests with your sword-grasp, my noble host. Remember you still the youth on Danube's bank, at the time when you worsted the stalwart Count Archimbald von Walbek? I *have* now the golden spurs, and the three flat sword-strokes too."

"Good, sir knight; and ye come for Gabriele's ring?" said Montfaucon. In courteous approval, Otto bowed his head. "At your service," said Folko, in friendly guise; then turning to the banqueters, "Sirs," he continued, "the young German knight has told you no tale; but he will let you see the germ of one if ye will honour us so far to-morrow as to bear us company to one of my Norman castles, whither I will bid the wondrously beautiful Gabriele de Portamour, and there to be witnesses of our encounter." He then told them how he had formerly met with Otto at the castle of Trautwangen, and what they now had before them; that, moreover, the lordly mansion where they were to fight before Gabriele was the principal seat of those baronies to which the contested ring gave a paramount right, so that the beautiful lady would not be slow to repair thither. All the guests present had already accepted the invitation, when Otto, with a graceful meekness, went round the circle, thanking so august an assembly for their readiness to behold how his almost deedless youth was honoured by a combat with the great Folko de Montfaucon. Every heart beat warmly for the friendly stripling; and Alessandro Vinciguerra kissed him fondly. "Truly," cried he, "if fate wished for a stern preacher to chide and put a damper on my arrogance, it could send me nothing more lovable and true-hearted in the whole wide world than this!"

CHAPTER XXI.

With the earliest beams of the following morning, the whole of the noble company set forth for Normandy. A fair sight it was to see how they rode along together, now over blooming plains, now through shady avenues or thickets, now across bright green meadows; warriors, and cunning masters, and liveried servants in glittering medley; and here and there sumpter-horses richly laden with baggage, over which lay sparkling coverlets with fringe of gold or silver. Among the proudest of the train was Count Alessandro Vinciguerra, whose gaily-emblazoned arms shone gorgeously on high from the silk-embroidered groundwork of his escutcheon. Costly braids of beadwork were enwound with the dappled chasings, forming in many a varied festoon some pretty motto or warlike device. The plates and splints which peeped forth from his rich raiment or saddle-cloths were of the purest steel, inlaid with gold; while feathers of countless hues fluttered in the wind from his barret-cap, or proudly waved adown his slender girth. Strange was the contrast formed by the Spaniard Hernandez. He had made things quite comfortable to himself, in true travelling trim; he wound his way on a wondrously fair and prettily caparisoned mule, with no other weapons than a falchion of elegant form, and a little glittering targe, both of which hung on the velvet trimming of his saddle. But not far from him, a squire led his snorting Andalusian charger by a golden chain-rein, and another his beauteously flashing arms on a sumpter-horse, in as fair array as one could well conceive,—the closed vizor fastened high upon the top of them, with its far-waving heron-plumes.

The brave baron and Otto mostly rode at each other's side, engaged in various converse, and growing mutually fonder every moment. And Folko's silver-gray, and Trautwangen's light-brown too, were of friendly accord, little as the latter was wont to order himself peaceably towards stranger steeds. Of the parley of the noble foes, be it granted me to note the following.

"I scarcely thought to find you again in Frankland," said Otto. "At the Holy Grave, thought I, we shall meet, or at least on our way thither. But doth not every great heart in Europe throb towards that blessed loadstone which, in the night-shroud of the grave, engirt by the godlessness of Paganism, spreads through all the world its still yet mighty sway, and summons us to burst the chains of its bondage? And your heart, my noble foeman, must assuredly beat time with the best of Christendom. Why, then, weareth not your shoulder the cross of red?"

"Because not only doth the Saviour need warriors at His grave," replied Montfaucon, "but my king too must have barons in his blooming realms. For the very reason that my noble liege himself is marching forth into the East, he maketh it his high wish and behest that my mates and I shall remain behind to keep guard for him over the earthly garden of France, whilst he conquereth Palestine, the garden of God. The Moors in Spain are not so very far off, nor is there an arm of the sea between us and them; and if the brave knights of Castile seek to make head against them, we must either help in strengthening our noble bulwark, or appear in our own eyes but craven idlers. I think of bending my march thither in the company of the valiant Hernandez, and, maybe, in yours too, if it so chance that I fall in the fray, and yet survive it; for, as conqueror, you too will become a vassal of France." Otto looked on him questioningly, and the baron continued: "I thought you already knew," said he, "that the fair Gabriele de Portamour has promised her own passing lovely self to him who wins for her the wondrous ring. Oh, how your eyes sparkle again, you hope-exulting champion!" And, sooth, Otto's soul flashed forth with a joy till then strange to him; and yet he could not but doubt more than ever of his victory, and even whether he should live till the day of strife, in such sudden and overwhelming glory did that fair fortune beam upon him. Folko smiled with keen delight at the stripling's enthusiasm, and yet his look was soon changed to one of pensive sorrow; haply he was reflecting that this very warrior-glow was urging the young knight on his fearful, and, to many a foe, deadly lance-point. So they both sought, by divers parley, to forget that they shortly would close for life or for death; and on Otto asking the baron what he really knew about the wondrous jewel, the latter gave him answer as follows:

"The ring is an heirloom of my stepfather's, a very doughty man of war, Messire Huguenin by name, who was of high account at the court of our king. Although he had come a stranger into the land from the East, or, as others said, the North, his valorous achievements had gained him the grant of many mighty feoffs in the realm; and this, too, with such unfettered ownership, that he might bequeath them to whom he would, whether lady or knight. Glittering at all the galas of the court, he was smitten by a beautiful damsel, of one of the noblest houses, betrothed himself to her, and promised her the wonderful ring of enchantment, which he was said to have brought with him from the wonder-lands of the North. The jewel was, moreover, to serve as a pledge to the fair possessor for the feudal feoffs obtained by him in Frankland. And the damsel is even said to have been seen pranking with the golden circlet on feast-days, yet it always returned again into Messire Huguenin's hands.

"About this time he travelled into Normandy to see his fine castles for the first time. They lay close to the ancestral seat of our family, where my mother lived a lonely life, busy only in bringing me up to be a brave knight, not unworthy of the name of Montfaucon; yet harassed in her forlorn state all the more, because her seemingly never-failing and luxuriant beauty still outshone the fairest and youngest lady-flowers of the land, and brought upon her a number of suitors, who were one and all a plague to her. I still remember quite well how the glorious Messire Huguenin came riding up the first time to our castle; how my whole heart enkindled at his princely array; with what knightly courtesy, yet well-bred ease, he spoke with my mother; for I was then more than ten years of age, and well able to see the difference between him and our other neighbours. If since then I have now and then been happy enough not to be displeasing to noble ladies, I have always been obliged to say to myself that Messire Huguenin was my best teacher, without ever being quite able to come up to this pattern of noble bearing. By my beautiful mother, too, he was more than commonly prized; and, on the other hand, her heavenly charms made every union but one with her unbearable to him. His first care, therefore, was to release himself from his earlier betrothal; and a dread of the favour in which Huguenin stood with the king, and of his own valiant arm, kept the lady's kinsmen so thoroughly within bounds, that all passed off in the utmost peace: the knight retained the ring; and it was not till long afterwards, when she was already Huguenin's spouse, that my mother heard a single word of the matter.

"Willingly had the fair Wittid intrusted her life and her happiness to the renowned Messire Huguenin, and, what she had much more at heart, the knightly rearing of her son. How the first two costly jewels were cherished by him, I know not; for the rosy spring-bloom of his love was as brief as it was beautiful. Scarcely more than two years, during which my stepsister Blancheflour was born, an embodiment of her mother's every charm, did the stately Sir Huguenin dwell in our castle: after that he set forth on the seas, and never came back again. For the sake of his honour and his soul, let us think that he met with a speedy and a glorious death. My mother never heard of him more; and the greater the happiness he had yielded her in the short term of their union, the more surely did he wind his own dark shroud round her beautiful life. For a few years sorrow preyed upon her health, and then, sorrowfully smiling, she sank into her peaceful grave.

"The other pledge—namely, myself and my knightly culture—he had honourably kept. Grave and tender, stately yet kindly, like some beckoning pillar of flame, he ever strode on before me. During the day he talked but little to me, but showed me rather what was noble and animating in feats of arms, and horsemanship, and the chase. At eventide the legends and stories of far-gone times fell on me from his proud lips in plentiful flow: little or none were the warnings he blended with them; but he told his tale in such wise that the soul and life-giving power of each achievement stood ever in fair embodiment before me, holding out its hand, as it were, to mine, and bidding me join fellowship with the shining league. And this I did with heart the more devoted to the cause, because I knew that it was a mighty hero who was recounting all this to me, and one who had compassed no less exploits than those of which he spoke to me. And in those two years I too —without boasting, be it said—had followed closely in his footsteps; wherefore, on the eve of his departure, he took me with him to his chamber, and locking it after us, 'Folko,' said he, 'I am going to other lands; for how long, God knows: perhaps for ever. Thine eyes already sue me to take thee with me to battle and to victory; but that must not be, as I have fashioned thee to a higher destiny. Thou must tarry here as warder to thy mother and the little Blancheflour; for though thou numberest but thirteen years, yet, in spirit and skill to wield thine arms, thou art half a dozen years older. And withal thou art fond of me, and of poor little Blancheflour too. Her, then, be it thine to ward, and the wondrous jewelled ring which I bequeath her, and which, I foresee, will be assailed on many sides. But let it not be taken from her, young lion of Montfaucon: and see, when both of you are older, that she one day bears the name of thy lineage; for mine, though great and mighty, is not so well known here in the realm, and sounds strange and awkward to Frankish ears. Wilt thou now promise me all this?' Proudly and joyfully I vowed to do his bidding, and Heaven knows I have kept my word honourably to this very day. Messire Huguenin's earlier betrothed was afterwards wedded to the knight of Portamour, and became the mother of Gabriele. Thereupon the fair Gabriele, who was early left an orphan, heard much from her guardians of her right to the ring, for which her poor mother is said to have raised her cry in the hour of death, as a dear and promised dowry. Hence, then, all this fighting took its rise. If your good fortune and the will of God will have it so, to-day or to-morrow may put an end to it. For see, the towers of the castle to which my fair foe is bidden are already peeping over the tree-tops."

CHAPTER XXII.

At the foot of the castle-hill, in a fresh green beech-wood, the train had halted beneath the broad and shady branches, to enjoy the balmy spring-breeze of evening as it curled through the wood; whilst a squire was despatched in haste to the mansion to announce the arrival of the knight and his noble guests. But scarcely had they alighted from their steeds and filled the wine-cups, when the messenger came hastening back with the news that Lady Gabriele de Portamour was already at the castle; and that, at her suit, Lady Blancheflour, as hostess, had ordered their evening meal and supper to be served in the forest beneath; and that the escort of the noble damsels was already in motion down the hill. And now the flash of polished arms, silver table-services, and rich attire, might be seen through the webwork of the branches. The Baron of Montfaucon turned to Don Hernandez and the Count Vinciguerra, and begged them in the meantime to give the ladies greeting at the head of the brotherhood of knights and minstrels; "For," said he, "it is fitting that we two foemen appear in comelier guise before the beautiful Gabriele than our journey and surprisal will just at this moment allow of." So saying, he strode with Otto down a little copse-covered dell. Tebaldo and a squire of the baron's attended them.

The young warriors armed and arrayed themselves with eager haste. Carefully were plate and vambrace rubbed up and furbished, the straps buckled closer, and their ends concealed, their ruffled helm-plumes smoothed again, and their sashes beaten, and more daintily wound round them. When they both placed their helmets on their heads, Folko looked on the young knight with amazement: "Now first, at the sight of the eagle-vizor, I get to the rights of what seemed so strange, and yet familiar to me, in your black and silver mail. Is not that the armour of Count Archimbald von Walbek?"

And on Otto's replying that it was, "I shall soon beg of you," continued he, "to tell me more at large how you, so young a flower of knighthood, come by this austere war-suit; and I will recount to you, on the other hand, what strange things I have dreamt about fighting with a silver-black eagle, that kept flying across the Rhine from German soil, and pecking with its sharp beak at a garland on my brow. Now, when I awoke with my own strugglings, I said to myself, Thou must surely think of hot encounters with Count Archimbald von Walbek; but his word binds him fast, and debars him from the tilting-ring. Here, however, the eagle is, and ready for war. Follow me, my young eaglet; the dames await us." And the two knightly comrades strode hand in hand up the slope of the dell.

Through the circle formed by fair ladies and noble knights on the lawn above, Gabriele's beauty shone with such wondrous lustre, that Otto, at the thought of the fray and the happy prize, cast his eyes meekly to the earth. Folko stepped up to the lovely lady of Portamour: "Never should I forgive myself," said he, "for coming, like tardy host, later than so beauteous a guest, if it were not still unsettled who is really to remain host and who guest here. If such be your pleasure, this brave young German holdeth himself ready to adjust the point of strife."

Gabriele cast a hurried glance at Otto. Now she seemed to doubt his youthful inexperience and the issue of the struggle; and now, in his youth and artlessness, he took the semblance of a ministering angel. "Wert thou not the stripling on the bank of the Danube?" said she, trying to recollect herself.

"The same," answered Otto softly; "and I am come to redeem my vow." Gabriele looked at him complacently; yet still, it seemed, in doubt. But the knight of Montfaucon stepping up to her, "Lady," said he, "prithee choose this noble cavalier to be thy champion. I stand not in the repute of craving powerless foemen: and this one I would gladly see confronting me in the lists." And straightway the lady Gabriele drew the pretty glove from her swan-white hand, and tying it fast to the knight of Trautwangen's sash, "My right and my hope," quoth she, "are wedded to thy brave sword." And then with faltering voice she added, "and Gabriele shall be the conqueror's guerdon." He was about to return an answer, when a cooing, as of the soft turtle-dove, sounded close at his ear; and looking up, he beheld a form of passing loveliness leaning on Sir Folko's shoulder—one which, by the description given him, he knew at once to be the lady Blancheflour; and now he heartily believed all that the baron had told him of the never-fading beauty of his mother. Was not that lovely flower still triumphing over the grave, and spending its sweet bloom on the world? But Blancheflour bent meekly to Gabriele: "Oh, one boon only, noble maiden!" whispered she. "One, one brother only have I, and must he fight all his life long for that little ring? Must I never gladden myself in the young warrior with safety? Oh, let the pending combat decide for ever! If my dear brother falls, lady, then the ring is thine, And again, if thy champion be defeated, then once for all let thy claim be waived. Oh, prithee hear me. Too noble-minded I know thou art to play so ill-matched a game for ever."

It was easy to see that Gabriele underwent a fierce struggle with herself. But at length she kindly raised her eyes. "Be it so," said she. "Sir knight," she continued, turning to the Trautwangen with a high-born though anxious air, "now rest my woe or weal with thy bold hand and heart."

"Oh! can I not fight this very hour, then?" cried Otto, in ecstasy.

"Not so," said Gabriele, in a solemn tone; "very well do I know the mail that thou wearest. Haply it may be destined to repair my earlier ill-fortune; or, maybe, to complete it. Yet if I then was rashly eager for the ill-starred tourney, to-day I will curb my zeal. To-morrow, therefore, at the hour of noon, hold ye ready for the fight in the castle-court. Till then away with all such solemn matters. But rather, if I may speak the boon I crave, let sport and festival be gaily sped, and care unthought of."

Folko bowed, and with skilful grace he had soon arranged the company beneath the greenwood bower. Wines and viands were handed round in delicious variety; and sweet lays were warbled the while by this banqueter or that. Then many a lip besought the lady Blancheflour to sing the lay of Abelard and Heloisa with one of the noble minstrels. She chose, therefore, one of the minstrels from her brother's retinue, named Master Aleard; and their alternate strain began as follows:

BLANCHEFLOUR.

O'er the vale and woodland lonely
  Evening's flowery buds are laid;
But her Heloisa only
  Is the flower to droop and fade.
    Cloister-garden,
    Cruel warden
Will not let the bright one through;
    She may not fly;
    But only sigh
  Unto life a last adieu.

ALEARD.

Heavens! the crimson gloaming sparkles;
  'Tis the night-bird's witching prime;
Soft and cool the evening darkles;
  Ah! this wont to be the time.
    Hush, sweet wooer!
    Sterner, truer,

Sounds the solemn cloister-bell;—
Song is over,
Flown the rover;
Over, all but dirge and knell.

BLANCHEFLOUR.

Heloisa, bent on flying,
Long'st thou for the blooming train?

ALEARD.

Over field and meadow hieing,
Com'st thou, Abelard, again?

BOTH.

Earth hath tried us;
We would hide us
Where its woes are all unknown:
In the ruing
Love's undoing,
'Tis not sad to be alone.

BLANCHEFLOUR.

Over distant seas it pealeth:
Comes it, Abelard, from thee?

ALEARD.

O'er the far woods echo stealeth:
Can it Heloisa be?

BOTH.

Warblers roaming
Through the gloaming,
Sing their last ere spring is flown:
Close, ye bowers;
Hearts like ours
Do not grieve to be alone.

The tears stood in many beautiful eyes; nay, in the eyelids of many a valiant warrior; so touchingly had Blancheflour and Aleard sung. Otto felt the strain echo from the very depths of his heart: it seemed to him as though the whole lay were made for him, little as it tallied with his present situation; and he could not keep from secretly murmuring to himself the few closing lines. In the meanwhile Sir Folko de Montfaucon looked gloomily before him; very differently to the light-hearted knight's usual wont. At length he cast a keen look towards the lady Blancheflour, who at that moment was speaking with great concern to Master Aleard; and she hastened to her brother, sat down beside him, and stirred not the whole evening from the spot. He, on his part, caressed her in the fondest and gayest guise; devising a thousand pretty things to divert her with. Yet ever and anon there was, as it were, a little pearly tear in Blanchefleur's gentle eye; and then Master Alcard withdrew to the deepest shade of the bower.

Evening now drew its cool veil over the landscape; damp vapours stole from the fallen beech-leaves: so rising to the strain of a merry march, they passed onward to the castle. And strangely through the gathering darkness glimmered the tapers and torches that lit the train up the winding mountain-path.

CHAPTER XXIII.

Early at dawn of morning on the following day there was a busy scene in the courtyard of the castle, on its fresh greensward, and beneath the shade of its lofty lime-trees. Stakes were set up, and spars let into them, as a grating to defend the tilting-ring from the pressing crowd, while rich tapestry was hung over the barriers. Into the lists themselves wagons poured their loads of fine white sand, and a number of serving-men spread it smoothly and carefully over them, that the war-horses might have a firm footing, and curvet and caracole at will, without slipping on the smooth turf; and that, if the knights should chance to grasp the keen falchion for the fight on foot, their armed heels might find a trusty stay. With all this, Don Hernandez and Count Vinciguerra strolled up and down, to whom, as umpires of the fight, the chief survey and arrangement had been deputed on the evening before. They measured the rounds, fixed and marked out the standing-posts of the combatants, giving each equal advantage of sun and wind, and all this with the maturest deliberation. For the ladies a high and beautiful platform was placed amid the leafy network of the old linden-trees, so that from the thick leaves that shaded and warded them they had a free, open view of the tilting-course, peeping forth like fruits touched with life from heaven, or rather like angels from the bowers of paradise. A throng of spectators had already gathered, waiting impatiently for the coming of the knights and ladies who were to grace this fair death-festival.

In the meanwhile, in separate chambers, the baron and the knight of Trautwangen were girding on their arms. About the latter his comrade Tebaldo was busied with the utmost care, and with a soft-heartedness at the same time which was but seldom seen in him. From the eagle-helmet down to the golden spurs, he looked at every thing ten times over; tightening a buckle here, giving more play there; and yet it was never quite the thing, to his mind, for his knightly master and friend. "Heigh, Diephold," said the latter, looking at him kindly, and using the German name by which he was fondest of calling him in their tenderest moments,—"Heigh, Diephold, thou makest such a sorrowful face about it, as though thou wert arming me for the last time of all!"

"That may well be, saving your noble prophetic lip!" said Tebaldo with a sigh; and he bent over the still-ungauntleted hand of his master.

Now the doors flew open; and with gleaming mail, flashing blue and golden, like the starry night-sky, surmounted as with a glory by an unclosed helm of the sunny metal itself, the Baron Folko de Montfaucon stepped in, followed by a squire with a huge sparkling sword. "Dear comrade of war," said he to the knight, "we have lived in good accord till to day, and have often looked each other trustingly in the face. But now it will full soon come to pass, or at least bids fair so to do, that after the closing of our vizors, the one shall never again see the eye of the other; at least not living, and with my unbroken. So hitherward am I come, heartily to mingle my kisses with thine; and we will pray together before the altar in the chapel." And wide he stretched his arms apart, while Otto rushed fondly to his embrace; and the two mail-clad men of war enclasped each other, as though the hard shell that encased them would melt at the brotherly warmth of their love. But a trumpet sounded without, and they tore themselves hastily apart.

"The first signal-call!" said Folko; "now gird me on my sword, my noble foe, and I will do the like service for thee." What the baron craved was done; and, whilst they were girding each other with the superbly-flashing weapons, they told each other—the one, how his stepfather, the other how his father, had for the first time placed the gold-chased falchion in his hand. Then they strode arm in arm down to the chapel, and kneeled in still prayer at either side of the altar; there, burning for the fight, yet with hearts overflowing with love, they awaited the second call of the clarion. On rising, they again looked kindly at each other; and then closing their vizors, they stepped forth together to the sun-bright court of the castle.

The fair dames were already on the balcony; and Folko said to his companion, "In the northern lands where my lineage sprung, they have a legend about the golden apples of immortality. Seest thou them up above there, comrade?" He only wished to say something pretty and sprightly; but hollow as the voice came from forth the close-locked helmet, softened by no smile of the lip or gay twinkle of the eye, with the cold metal vizor stark and motionless over the face, it sounded not like sportiveness, but like the stern watchword of death. The knights then shook hands, and each sought his charger. Whilst now the baron was approaching his silver-gray on the left, his noble falcon, almost healed of the wound given him by Tebaldo, flew down from a window of the castle to Folko's golden helm, and would not stir till his master took him down again. He stroked him kindly, and then turned him over to the hand of one of his serving-men, who drew the velvet hood over the faithful bird's eyes, and straightway went off with him. At this hap, a strange murmur arose round the lists: some holding it to be a greeting, foreshowing victory to the baron; others regarding it as the good creature's farewell, and the omen of its master's bitter death. But now the herald wound the third trumpet-blast; every voice was hushed; and the warriors, addressed to the fight, rode from opposite sides into the lists.

And at the foot of the balcony where the ladies sat rose Don Hernandez, in a magnificent suit of mail, calling aloud from beneath his open helmet, "Hereby be it made known to high-born dame and knight, and all true-hearted folk here present, that my fellow-umpire, Count Alessandro Vinciguerra, holds in his hands the casket which contains the contested ring. The fight with lances and the keen sword-blade, on horse and on foot, is open to both the noble combatants; and whichever can approach Count Vinciguerra with comely greeting, take the casket from his hand, bear it to his lady-fair on the balcony, and place the ring on her delicate finger, without his foe being able to hinder him, shall be held victor, and the strife be ended and quashed for ever. Are ye content to have it so, ye noble knights?"

Both foemen bowed their plumed heads of sturdy metal in sign of approval; and Hernandez, in stern dignity, took his seat beside Alessandro. Now a deep silence held the assembly in thrall, but only for a moment, for the trumpet-blasts rose on all sides with dreadly echoing joy; the spectators started, and crowded closer on each other in fear, and the two combatants spurred on their snorting and far-neighing steeds. In the middle of the fighting-course they met, and with such a terrific crash, that it sounded loud above the prolonged flourish of the trumpets; and the silver-gray and light-brown stood facing each other on their haunches, plunging with their fore-hoofs to keep their balance, after the stupendous shock that had shivered the lances of both the knights into a thousand pieces, and hurled them far away over the barriers. Firm sat the knights, both bending to the saddle-bow, both pricking for a forward spring; but after tottering and reeling awhile, and in vain seeking to recover their balance, both horses brought their masters with a backward crash on the sand.

A shrick of horror burst from the balcony and from the spectators that encircled the lists. But scarcely had it died away, the fallen chargers still struggling on the ground, when the nimble combatants had already freed themselves from ponderous steeds, and saddle, and bridle, and were hasting, with their swords drawn, to the spot where Count Alessandro Vinciguerra was posted with the eventful jewel. But soon seeing that neither would give the other law for the accomplishment of the stated conditions, they came to a stand-still opposite each other, firmly clutched their falchions, and then, each keeping his foeman in his eye, they strode leisurely back to the place where they had fallen, and where their shields were still lying. As if at a signal-call, they both had seized the bright orbs at the same moment. Each found his steed at his side; for the noble animals had helped themselves up again, and trotted faithfully and gladly hither and thither after their masters. And touching it was to see how the baron's silver-gray, with shoulder wounded by the shock, came limping on three legs behind its knight, and how it now stood still and stretched out the leg that had been lamed, neighing cheerily the while, and snorting from its dilated nostrils, true to its warlike sense of joy, though so sorely bereft of warlike power. Otto, seeking no advantage, and pitying his faithful charger, said, "Let us have the war-horses led from the ring, my noble baron." Folko gave him a courteous and thankful salute. "As you will," said he; "you prove yourself what I ever thought you to be." So the chargers were led from the course.

But scarcely had the foemen raised their shields and stridden to the fray with their flashing sword-blades,—scarcely had their first strokes fallen, rattling on the sounding plates of their helms and corslets,—when lo! fiercely dashing aside the squires who held him, Otto's light-brown flew over the lofty barriers, and, with many a wild caracole and gladsome battle-neigh, rushed to the aid of his master, and fell foul on his antagonist. But "Halt!" cried Otto, and catching at his charger's rein, he led him back to the outlet of the lists. There he delivered him to his squires, and with sternly menacing gesture, "Still, fellow!" said he; and anon he stood so motionless that they no longer needed the golden bridle to hold him.

A friendly salute from the baron's sword was waved to Otto as he returned; then the weapon was uplifted to deal a doughty blow, and the fearful fray began anew. Now the strokes of their falchions fell thick as hail; now their shields only clashed together as they pressed to and fro, letting their bright blades rest till either espied an opening that would tell, and then came the shrill whirr of the weapons as they flew asunder. But at length Folko's blade flew, swiftly as the scathing lightning, down Otto's left side, and the orb of the young knight's shield fell half-riven from his arm. "Halt!" cried the baron, and Otto stayed his falchion. "Are you wounded, my noble foe?" quoth he; "I myself am sound." "Your shield is not," rejoined Montfaucon; "and on mine the golden chevrons and ball glitter still untouched; wherefore I will rid me of it, for true battle calls for equal weapons." So saying, he beckoned to his squire-at-arms, and handed him his gold-blue targe. But Otto would not allow of this: then, "Young sir knight," said the baron gravely, "wilt thou this once take friendly counsel from me? I have been for twelve years or so longer in arms than thou, and know pretty well what beseemeth knighthood. If I erst thanked thee and honoured thy proffered grace when thou badest the chargers be led from the lists, thou, on thy part, I think, wilt not demean thyself too far by receiving a like favour at the hands of Folko de Montfaucon." "Thou art right, my noble guide in all that is knightly," quoth Otto, with a lowly obeisance; and the squire-at-arms bore the glittering shield away.

Now the combat was renewed with joyful ardour: but it was not long before a blow of Otto's, passing over Montfaucon's left vambrace, lighted between his gorget and cuirass, and with such mighty sway, that the fresh blood spirted out like a rosy fountain as he drew back his sword-blade. Folko himself soon began to totter, propping himself with difficulty on his sword; and before Otto could receive him in his arms, he sank to the earth. And Otto, too, at the same moment, was seen kneeling on the sand, fainting, as the spectators supposed, with an equally violent blow; but they soon saw that he was only endeavouring to loose the helmet, gorget, and cuirass of his fallen foeman. Blancheflour had hastened up to do him the same service, and was kneeling on the other side of the baron. She wept an anguished flood of tears; but Otto, looking kindly on her, "God be praised!" said he; "he lives, and the breast-wound reaches not to the heart." As Folko, too, just at that moment, opened his eyes, Blancheflour reached forth her hand to the conqueror, over her bleeding brother, with a smile that showed how thankful she was for those words of solace; while Otto imprinted upon it a reverential kiss, and then rising up, went to fetch the casket from the Count Vinciguerra, and carry it to the embowered platform. And as he now entered that leafy tent of green, and Blancheflour, with her sweet and heavenly smile, came forth to meet him, the trumpets without raising the glad flourish of victory, and knights, minstrels, and serving-men resounding his name, he sank upon his knee, as in the dizziness of some blessed dream; and whilst he drew the wondrous ring on Gabriele's swan-white hand, a soft kiss fell glowing on the brow of the too-happy conqueror.

CHAPTER XXIV.

Now Otto doffed his arms in his chamber, and arrayed himself for the bright betrothal banquet, after which Gabriele was solemnly to declare herself his bride. Squires and serving-men crowded on one another's heels; some sent by his virgin prize to wait upon him; others with necklaces, rings, baret-plumes, and other trappings, received at her beautiful hands. In the sweet delirium of his joy, and the reflection of it in all the brilliant colours around him, Tebaldo's absence first appeared strange to him, on his entering an apartment alone, whither Gabriele had bidden him, that he might lead her thence on his arm to the gorgeous banquet-hall. With his heart ready to burst with the good fortune that was being showered down so richly upon him, he would fain have disburdened it in confiding converse, and felt surprised and puzzled that Tebaldo still kept in the background. But just then he entered the hall at a side-door, in such unwonted gaiety and grotesqueness of bedizenment, that at the first moment the knight did not know him. Seeing this, "Yes, yes," said Tebaldo, "you are not altogether wrong, for I look very much changed: but then, every thing changes in the world. Just look here yourself now, and see whether the knight in the silver-black eagle mail has so much as a thought of him left." So saying, he turned the knight lightly round to a large pier-glass opposite; and before the brilliant image it presented, the noble stripling stood spell-bound with a blush of astonishment. Like a flower from its rich wreath of leaves, the blooming visage sparkled over the close and crisped lace ruff; curling and clustering under the green-velvet baret-cap were the fragrant tresses of his golden hair, well-nigh more golden than the splendid egret that confined the nodding plumes of his head-gear. The white-velvet jerkin, barred with green and gold, and girded round above the hips with the golden sword-belt, fitted nicely on the well-knit yet slender form; whilst over it, in carefully-arranged folds, fell the short green mantle, faced with ermine, and edged with pearls.

"Well!" said Tebaldo, at length, with an almost sarcastic smile, "that is not, I ween, the travelling-suit for Jerusalem?"

"As little so as thine can be named one," replied Otto, turning sullenly away.

"But pardon me, noble sir," said Tebaldo; "mine is a travelling suit, though; and if ye lay not too much stress on a little circuit that I have to make, it is one for Jerusalem too. I wear the colours of Count Vinciguerra,—in bright Italian fashion, you know; they are a little gaudy; and this very moment I am off with him to my blooming home; and then, taking ship to Naples, we shall pass on to share the holy war among the leaguers of the Lion-heart."

"What harm, then, have I done thee?" cried Otto sorrowfully. "Why wilt thou wound me when my happiness is at its height?"

"You have done me no harm," replied Tebaldo in a kindly tone; "but you know I seek the clash of arms, and not the peace of home: so that you were quite right this morning; for I really was girding you to the fight for the last time. The zest of war, and much beside it, hurries me away. I would fain kneel once more at the flowery mound where Lisberta slumbers. God knows why they let me play there so often in my childhood: but now it seems to me as though my life's best treasure were buried beneath it; and ever and anon I must away to the spot. But as for the wounding you, good knight, while your happiness is in full blow, prithee thank me kindly if I really do so. Know you not, then, that the trees are wounded when they grow too full of sap? And remember you not the story about Polycrates, who cast his ring into the sea to still the envy of fortune?—let me only be the ring, and God grant that no sea-monster may bring me back again into your hands."

"But why, then, in such haste?" asked Otto.

"That is Count Vinciguerra's fault," said Tebaldo; "for, indeed, I have pledged my word to him to travel with him as he shall choose."

"And he — ?" said Otto.

"Well, then," replied Tebaldo, laughing, "to tell the truth, he is a little sore with you and your youthful tongue for the rating you gave him about the story of young Signor Donatello. For in confidence he avowed to me that the signor was himself. And so he cannot readily bear to see you in full array of splendour as the chief personage of the feast. He was well-nigh swooning with vexation when he had to give you the casket with the ring. Let us part from each other with a laugh about it, good knight, and not a word about any thing sorrowful."

"You have forgotten, perhaps," said Otto, "how hard the

parting was to you, then, when we had quarrelled about the falcon?"

"Yes, and just because we *had* quarrelled," rejoined Tebaldo; "but now we are parting in peace and good-will, and I leave you in all weal and happiness at the side of a most beautiful bride. Good speed to you withal!" And so saying, he went with a friendly nod out of the chamber; and when Otto at last stepped slowly to the window, the two Italians, like glittering parrots, were jogging cheerily, in their rainbow-hued attire, down the castle-hill.

The young German was still watching them in amazement and sorrow, when a little hand was laid upon his shoulder, and, turning round, he gazed on the full brilliancy of Gabriele's beauty in the costliest array. If the aid-imploring maiden had been beyond measure charming at the tourney, far more brightly beamed the conqueror-bride than that beauteous image. The jewelled wreath that sparkled on her silken locks, the black gold-bespangled velvet that enwound her peerless form,—these were but a dull foil, as it were, to set off the wondrous beauty of her every feature and her every turn. And, bending to the young knight with noble courtesy, in all the lustre of her pride, "Why so grave and gloomy, noble sir?" said she. "Cannot Gabriele's hand compensate for the flight of two humorsome comrades? Come, our guests await us; so lead me to the hall." Of all those charming words, the "our," on the mention of the guests, shot the gladdest flame through the soul of the happy bridegroom. He kissed the lady's little tender hand; he kissed—as a soft glance said he might—her blooming lips, and led her to the host of noble guests that thronged the glittering hall.

All bent to them as they made way for them, and gave them gladsome welcome; softly-breathing music played an enlivening march; flowers were showered from the hands of noble damsels on the beauteous and blushing pair, as with comely grace they tendered their thanks; and, on reaching the upper end of the table, Gabriele showed her bridegroom the noble Folko de Montfaucon reposing upon a silken couch, and supported and waited upon by his sister Blancheflour. "I knew very well," said Gabriele to Otto, "that nothing would give you greater pleasure than the sight of your noble foe so far restored, and taking cheerful part in our festivity."

"And," said Otto, bending thankfully over her hand, "I might know that nothing outmatched thy power, beauteous fay."

"Not a word about my fairy-power!" said Gabriele, smiling; "its healing virtues lie mainly in the ring which you have achieved for me in fight."

In the meanwhile, with Blancheflour's help, Folko had raised himself on his couch. He was still pale; yet with the kindliest smile he held forth his unmaimed sword-hand to the victorious Trautwangen, who pressed it with emotion, and could scarce withhold himself from kissing it, like that of some fostering elder brother. They now sat down to the banquet; and every one was enraptured with Folko's grandeur and grace: there lay the hero-form beneath the gorgeous blue-velvet coverlets, set off with a rich gold fringe; while his still-wounded falcon was perched upon his pillow, and ever and anon stooping to fondle him, it would sip a tiny drop from its master's golden cup. "They treat me here like a sick child," said Folko to the company, smiling an entreaty that it might be excused. "They leave me my playthings at table." And some minstrels there were who, in secret whispers, were fain to compare him with the beautiful Adonis, the wounded favourite of the heathen goddess Cypris; and every one said that they were right.

Whilst they one and all now sat together at the table, that bloomed with its savoury viands, and sparkled with its fragrant wines, the shrill blast of a monstrous horn was heard at the castle gate; and shortly after a gigantic man, in loud-rattling full suit of mail, and a halbert of wondrous length in his hand, entered the hall. He gazed around him inquiringly for some moments on the amazed throng of banqueters, and then, with a courteous obeisance, he went up to Sir Folko de Montfaucon. "Noble sir," quoth he, "I am sent hither by the sea-king Arinbiorn, your kinsman and friend. He maketh halt before your stronghold, and hath strayed thus far landward simply and solely to give you greeting. He asketh, therefore, whether you have the will and leisure to give him entertainment, together with certain noble maidens and knights in his suite; though, as it chanceth, one of the damsels is somewhat strangely favoured."

"Did I still hold sway here," answered Folko, with his sparkling eyes wandering to the ground, "the wound which keeps me to my couch should not prevent me from tottering at least, if not walking, to welcome your noble master. But thus —"

"O valiant baron," said Gabriele, staying him with a kindly yet half-angry rebuke, "if thou demean not thyself here quite as the rightful host, thou wilt drive me and my champion away."

"Then things are otherwise," said Folko, turning to the stranger; "your lord and his train shall be most dearly welcome, and I will up to meet him."

He stirred upon his couch, but the giant-herald saw

Blancheflour's imploring look of pain. "No, sir knight," said he; "that I must forbid in the sea-king Arinbiorn's name. Even though the like effort may not be death to a vigorous man, yet the beautiful damsel there trembleth for the issue; and true-hearted warrior must spare sweet woman pain wherever he can. Therefore I beg of you, dear as you hold my master's wishes, break not now the repose of your couch. The sea-king will in a moment be with you." So saying, he shook his right hand with hearty cheer, and again bowing a farewell, he strode from the hall.

"The sea-king Arinbiorn," said Folko, as the guests turned their glances questioningly upon him, "is a brave Norman, my kinsman from times long gone by, when our race was divided, and the branch to which I belong rambled from those icy mountains to the softer plains of Frankland. Since then we have always kept faithful kinship with each other in many a doughty deed and league of arms; and these—since Arinbiorn is sea-king—have ever tended to my weal. This name is given to those warriors in the high-coast country, who own little or nothing on the mainland, but who sail round the earth in their barks, in the company of brave and most devoted followers; passing from the other side of the North Cape, nay, even from distant Iceland, down to bright Constantinople, and far along the coasts of blooming Asia, or the molten gold of burning Africa, where almost all other seamen are at fault, and where they, by dint of their resounding arms, may lord it at will with kingly power."

Folko would gladly have recounted further, and gladly would the banqueters have listened to him, but the mighty steps of the wondrous guests already sounded on the stairway, and every eye was turned towards the door.

CHAPTER XXV.

The doors of the hall flew open, and a man sheathed in mail of gold stepped in—a very prince to the gigantic herald, by reason of his mighty stature, no less than his rank, with two gold-embossed vulture-wings shooting from his flashing helm. Otto started and shrunk back involuntarily at sight of the metal wings; he could not help thinking of his fight with the skeleton in the chapel. Many a wondrous form came in the sea-king's train; but wholly riveted as they were on him, the eyes of the company saw little or nothing of the rest. With a reverential salute to the ladies as he passed, Arinbiorn strode straight to the Baron de Montfaucon, and, with a friendly grasp of the hand, "Heigh, Folko, what meaneth all this?" said he. "What! must I find thee, then, so smartly wounded at last, thou fondling of fortune? A famous champion it must have been that smote thee so doughtily; but he is dead and gone, I ween. For, as to what my henchman would fain have told me, that thou hadst had inglorious fight and lost the oft-contested ring,—in the whole world, there can be no likelihood, surely, of that."

"Alas! but so it is," said Folko, somewhat confused, and with glowing cheek. "I have, sooth, found my master; and the wondrously beautiful damsel there is now mistress of the ring and of the castle, and thy gracious hostess as well as mine, Arinbiorn."

The sea-king made gentle obeisance to Gabriele. Then he begged that they should show him the astounding foeman who had not only borne the mighty Folko's falchion, but mastered it too: his eye had singled out Don Hernandez. But when the youthful, ruddy Otto was presented, he gazed on him with the greatest tokens of amazement, till the stripling began to feel himself affronted, and was about to speak. But the brave Arinbiorn, bending graciously before him: "If, as I doubt not," said he, "there hath been naught but fair play here, by heaven and earth, young sir knight, to what fair fame wilt thou not mount at last, so great as early youth already findeth thee!" And again he bent with deep obeisance; and Gabriele, in proud transport at her young champion's prowess, laid her swan-white hand in Otto's palm, and sinking her blushing brow and floating tresses, "I am the noble knight of Trautwangen's betrothed bride!" she said. Then the minstrels and musicians woke their strain of triumph anew; the guests poured in their glad shout as they wished them joy; the beakers rang; and Otto, pressing his lip to Gabriele's, saw heaven in her softly-flashing eye.

"Mayst thou be happy, dear Otto!" said a voice like a soft flute-note behind him; and looking round, he recognised the sweet face of his little kinswoman Bertha,—so friendly it was, so serene and cheerful, though perhaps of a moonlike paly hue—just, indeed, what the Lady Minnetrost's halls had made it. A little behind was Heerdegen's scarred visage, scowling like a thunder-cloud.

"Then, haply, all has been but a dream!" said Otto; and he passed his hand to and fro across his brow, as though seeking to scare slumber from his eyelids. Heerdegen pushed forward, and seemed eager to speak. But now Bertha stepped up between Otto and Gabriele, enwreathed their hands in one, and poured forth on them such a flood of tender and gladsome wishes of happiness, that one might have fancied some sweet-tongued angel had winged its bright way thither from heaven to bless that beautiful bond. Even from Heerdegen's brow the cloud passed away at the sound of Bertha's honeyed words; and Arinbiorn said, "The young knight and maiden here were once my prisoners. I won them in the goodly holm-bout on the coast of East Friesland; and gladly would I have taken them with me to my hearth and home, as tokens of victory, and as my own dear brother and sister; for, Heerdegen and Bertha, have we not lived together as such hitherto? But now be ye for ever released from my wardship, as well in honour of this high festival as because ye must be dear to the young conqueror there!" And a new shout of joy arose in the resounding hall. Gabriele kissed Bertha, now recognising her again as the child of the Danube's bank, and kindly stroked her softly-tinted cheek; whilst Otto and Heerdegen pressed each other's hands in glad pledge of reconciliation.

They were now seated again at the banquet-table in friendly converse,—Bertha by Gabriele, Heerdegen by Folko, Arinbiorn beside Otto; when the latter remarked the tall form of a woman standing behind the sea-king's chair, with many tresses of gold, and a long sword at her girth of wondrous beauty, yet stern and motionless; and when Otto rose, and politely craving pardon, offered her his seat, she turned indignantly away, and strode out of the hall. "Oh, is that all?" said Arinbiorn, on hearing why Otto and the other guests had been astonished. "Ye ladies fair and noble knights, my parents once wished to betroth me to this warlike damsel. Her name is Gerda; and she is famed far and wide, in all northern lands, for her wizard-skill, and is, moreover, near of kin to our line. But I was held in thrall by a dreamlike form that I saw in some weird mirror—ah! so wondrous lovely, so soft and fair it was, and one that I even now behold again."

The sea-king faltered and paused in strange confusion. Pretty it was to see how a girl-like blush passed over the visage of the stalwart warrior! But he soon manned himself anew, and continued as follows:

"Thus, ye fair dames and warriors, our marriage came to naught. Gerda said, 'For that I cannot be thy wedded wife, I will be thy conquest-bringing Wallkura;' and ever since then, even though unbidden, she follows in my traces, often bringing me unexpected good fortune, and sometimes brewing for me the wonderful war-draught of our north country, which makes one a long time unconquerable, save by charmed arms; and as, in many a venture, I hold it unknightly to make use of it, she ever and anon palms it on me by covert art."

"The Baron de Montfaucon lately told us a tale about a like potion," said Don Hernandez.

"And the draught is all very well," continued Arinbiorn. "But since, when drunk incautiously, and with unchastened eagerness, it is said to work black and fearful woe, my warriors shun it, and Gerda too. And yet, of a surety, she means kindly by us; though I grant she is a little strange and odd withal. Sir Heerdegen, there, made her acquaintance in singular wise; it was on the coast of East Friesland, and not long before he fought the holm-bout with me."

And whilst now Heerdegen, at the desire of the banqueters, was giving the history of that evening, Gerda herself had again entered the hall unnoticed by the most of them; had again taken her stand behind Arinbiorn's chair, and, without the sea-king's giving any heed to what she did, had placed beside him a large gold beaker, brimming full of the pure beverage itself. Otto, who had seen her come, turned round to her and rose, but with a look of displeasure she signed to him to keep his place; and then, stepping shyly back, she went tottering up and down the hall like a dreamer. In this way he soon lost sight of her, and the more readily as, in the course of his tale, Heerdegen had let fall something about the Lady Minnetrost, after whom several of the guests at once made eager inquiry. Otto could not join with them; but his whole soul was by that bright and happy moonlight-form. Bertha's eyes were full of tears.

"Ah!" sighed the winning Gabriele, with teasing fretfulness, in her bridegroom's ear—"ah, how absent all at once, and on the betrothal-day, too!" And when Otto would have excused himself, "No, no," contined she, with a smile; "there must be some very great thing on thy mind. What! thou, German-born, and the cups so still before thee! Hast thou drunk a single one to the health of thy bride?"

"O my life, my all, my crown of conquest!" cried Otto; and in the sweet whirl of transport he emptied the drinking-cup next to him, never noticing that it was Arinbiorn's golden beaker, till Gerda touched him on the shoulder, and muttered menacingly in his ear, "There, there, a fine thing hast thou done! Take it, then, even as it is, since thou wouldest not have it better." In the meanwhile, the draught flowed down his throat like a scorching stream of fire; and he instantly saw Gerda standing opposite to him in a corner of the hall, busily muttering, and framing her wizard-passes over Arinbiorn's battle-axe, without once turning away her glance from him. At length she rested the battle-axe against the sea-king's chair, and, shaking her head, stalked out of the hall.

In the meanwhile, voices grew still gayer, and song circled still more gladly round the board: a hearty sense of good-will and good cheer seemed mingling as it were its double current, and the storied lays, thrown in anon by cunning masters, formed the crowning blossoms of the general mirth.

But in poor Otto's mind, the joyful tones around him fanned to wilder and wilder flame the dark, unblest struggle within him. Word and song broke piercingly on his ear, seemed levelled at him, or wafted over him; moulding all that environed him to strange deformity, shrinking the laughing vault of the banquet-hall to the narrow span of the funeral chapel, and contorting the features of Arinbiorn, Heerdegen, Folko, and Bertha, and even of Gabriele herself. He felt as though he were swimming on the endless roar of a deafening sea, where fishes, with the faces of men, were jeeringly snapping at him; one of which was passing horrible to view: it had a pair of huge vulture-wings upon its head, and carried a skull hacked with sword-strokes in its maw. "It comes from the castle-chapel," thought Otto to himself; and then he braced his nerves anew, remembering that it was none else than Arinbiorn, the brave and friendly sea-king, who was sitting by him at the splendid banquet. But soon he thought a sea-king might, after all, be a fearful fish of prey; and then he remembered what Heerdegen had aforetime told him about ladies of the mist and cave-sprites on the Finland boundary-line, and much other silly nonsense. He could scarcely bear up against a sense of dizziness, as well as of prodigious power, that glowed in his sinews, and went coursing through his veins.

Suddenly he started up, his eyes sparkled hideously, and his voice sounded through the hall like a dread peal of thunder: to the right and left of him, like affrighted hinds, they all sprang involuntarily to their feet, while with astounding nimbleness of limb he bounded to a corner, and seizing his falchion, he whirled and brandished the flashing weapon over his head. "Holloa! holloa!" cried he; "where is he, the wicked fiend? Holloa! huzza! I challenge him to the fight! I'll meet him like a giant!"

"Well-a-day, ah! well-a-day, he is possessed; he is the arch-fiend's own!" Such light whisper was it that passed shyly from lip to lip along the walls, to which knight and lady had thronged, in dread of the menacing and terrific raver.

"I will venture it with him again for life or for death!" quoth the bold Baron de Montfaucon, seeking to soothe his fair partners. But as he tried to rise from his couch, the wound opened anew with the sudden strain; he swooned and fell, and attended by the trembling Blancheflour, was borne out of the hall. Straightway Hernandez and three noble Frankish knights ran up to hold the raving stripling; but the moment after, smartly wounded by his fist, they were reeling towards the walls. He laughed, and took his stand in such wise that no one could now gain the outlet of the hall without encountering his menace. "Spears, ho! throw spears at him!" was the cry of fear and anger on all sides: and Bertha's soft entreaty, "Oh, spare him! throw not at him!" was overborne by the clamour. Knife and javelin flew; they struck the uncorsleted one, and recoiled without effect. The raver laughed. "Come, more of your spurting, ye fishes!" cried he, with a yell. And again a whisper passed through the terrified throng: "The devil is with him, and gives him charmed life; the devil is his master."

"Nay, say not so!" said Bertha, a very heaven of love and trusting tenderness beaming from her soft blue eyes: "Otto, dear Otto, in the name of Heaven, give me thy hand, and follow me in peace to thy chamber." She drew near to him so bravely and lovingly, that they all looked forward to her victory, as to that of the Virgin, who, in holy blazon, is seen standing on the moon, over the dragon; but the storm in Otto's distracted brain rose still more wildly.

"What would the witch, the pale witch?" he screamed; and Bertha staggered back with a sword-wound on her kindly-extended hand. Heerdegen caught his sister in his arms; his glances fell burning on the phrensied foe, as he sped his mad gambols about the hall; but he could not leave his snow-white burden, and rush to the attack.

The sea-king Arinbiorn now stepped forward with his battle-axe. "This devil's leaguer, though, shall rue the blood of the beauteous maiden," cried he, "or I will shed every drop of mine upon the red pavement with hers!" And with uplifted arm he strode to the fray.

"Hoo, vulture-pinion! hoo, death's head!" shrieked the madman. "Cravest thou another blow from me? Wait, then, Satan, wait!"

"Satan thyself," shouted Arinbiorn, in his very teeth; and over the whirling sword-blade and all its brandishing, down upon the baret-cap fell the mighty battle-axe. Mute and motionless, Otto fell to the earth.

CHAPTER XXVI.

It might be about noon on the following day when Otto, shaking off his long stupor, again came to himself; but he could neither open his eyes, nor move a single limb. At first he felt as though he were already lying there a corpse, save that the soul could not yet struggle out of the stiff-set body;

and as he by degrees called to mind many of yesterday's events, he fancied that the sea-king Arinbiorn had slain him with the ponderous blow of his halbert. Yet he soon became aware that he must still be living, and that he was reposing on yielding cushions, beneath carefully-arranged coverlets; that the wound, moreover, on his head pained him but little, and was possibly but a slight one; the more so, since a gentle hand ever and anon enwound it with cooling cloths; taking off the old bandages so softly, that he did not feel the most trifling smart. But the same inability to stir still lay rigidly and unalterably upon him.

Now he heard a voice, which he recognised to be Gabriele's, saying, "Then he is really out of danger now?" And he was gladdening himself with the promise of his tender bride's nursing, when a male voice—that of one of the cunning masters at yesterday's banquet—replied: "I pledge thee my body and soul on it, my noble mistress; ye and all of us may speed our journey now, without the smallest concern; for ye have all done your duty by the hapless youth. What still keeps him powerless is not that slight wound of his; for the blow was broken by the edge of his falchion and his baret-cap; but wholly and solely the weariness that hath crept over the limbs of this poor possessed and fiend-ridden wight since his demon-dance of blood." With every word in this address a fresh dagger struck deep into Otto's heart. The ghastly horrors of yesterday all rose before his mind's eye, and found freer play, as he lay there half stupefied and motionless. A low sobbing, which he heard at the head of his couch, mingled with the words of pity, "Ah, poor Otto! good, lost Otto!" fell like balmy dew on his wounded heart; but it sounded as from the lips of his sainted mother, a far echo of his peaceful childhood; and, alas! in this living world, no one knew or loved him. Then he again heard Gabriele's voice. "Moreover," said she, "I have already restored the Baron de Montfaucon his sister's ring, pending another combat; for, by the bewitched and charmed champion here, I choose not, and dare not, to win any thing. I can only thank God that the mask fell from that devil's face of his before I was wedded to the wicked sorcerer by the Church's holy bonds."

"Ay," said the voices of several men, "we soon saw there must be witchcraft at the bottom of it; or how else could a boy like him overpower the stalwart Baron de Montfaucon?"

"And yet it is such a pity for so fair a thing!" said Gabriele with a sigh. "When he raised that truthful blue eye of his, one felt as though one would gladly trust oneself and all the world to him."

"Take heed only lest he catch *thee* too in his wiles at last!"

said the warning voices of some women; and at that moment the door flew open, and serving-men brought word that all was ready for the journey. With a deep-drawn sigh, Gabriele turned away and left the chamber: the others followed in her train. Otto heard his bright day of love and his goodly fame departing; and still he had no power to move hand, or eye, or tongue.

But he was not quite alone: this he could feel by the cooling cloths that were still being wound round his hair, and by the low sobbing at the head of his couch. And ever and anon it seemed as though a gentle hand were coursing timidly over his cold cheek.

Now all at once Heerdegen's voice sounded like a trumpet-blast in his ear: "Sister," cried he, "wherefore shouldst thou tarry longer by this vassal of Satan? Is he to wake up and wound thee again? Come, haste thee! Our horses are waiting. The rest of them are already off, even Montfaucon and the lady Blancheflour; and the old gray castle is quite lone and deserted." And when Bertha sighed and murmured words of soft entreaty, "Drive me not mad," cried he warmly. "Many a noble knight would rejoice to confront death, if thy heart and hand were the guerdon. And is this fellow here to wound thee both hand and heart? I beg of thee, irritate me not; or I might do unknightly deed, and lay rash hands on the powerless one." And then Otto felt the cooling bandage wound around his temples, for the last time of all; and Bertha, led by her brother, flew sobbing from the room. Soon after this, he could hear their steeds, as they trotted down the paved horse-road from the castle.

Now he was quite alone. But fainting nature took pity on him, and once more shaded him with her darkling pinions.

It was late in the afternoon when he awoke a second time. That rigid powerlessness had passed away. He raised himself with a groan: the veil was taken from his eyes, and the beam of evening played aslant through the casement on the scattered pieces of his mail. Painfully he turned away from these witnesses of his yesterday's resplendent glory, and tottered to the window. He looked straight down over the castle-walls into the vale below; and, on throwing open the lattice to breathe the peaceful evening air, he heard warriors riding through the forest, and singing the following words:

"What though we tarried, still before us
We kept the path, and loved it well;
But none unfurled his banner o'er us,
And lone and blind, our spirit fell."

He recognised the lay to be the same which Blondel had

sung for Tebaldo and him on that beautiful evening in the forest. "Ah!" cried he, "if those were but the people of King Richard of the Lion-heart, and I might journey with them to the Holy Land!" And again he caught the sound of their song:

"Now every breast hath ceased its sighing,
And every tongue is loosed to sing;
We see the fearless banner flying—
'Tis Richard Lion-heart the king."

And at that very moment the mail-clad singers issued from the wood; they rode steeds of stately beauty, and wore the like equipments with those who had formed the escort of the noble minstrel Blondel. Otto was just on the point of calling to them to wait, and he would ride with them, when they halted of themselves, and fell into parley with a number of squires and serving-men, whom Otto had not till then perceived sitting by the stone wall of the castle. The pilgrim-warriors told how that they belonged to the train of the King of the Lion-heart, and formed his rear; that he himself had gone on long before them. Then they asked why all was so silent and so still in that stately stronghold.

"Yester-morning you would scarce have asked us that, I trow," replied an old serving-man; "but just now there is not a soul up above there, but a bewitched knight, who has given himself to the devil's keeping. Would to God he were but gone!" And then in fearful words he told the whole story of the day before; and they who sat around him confirmed what he said, with many a shudder at the frightful parts, and many a voucher for the truth of them. But when he came to Bertha's wound, the English heroes crossed themselves. "God forbid," quoth they, "that we should catch a sight of the monster!"—and so saying, they trotted shuddering away.

"My doom is fixed," said Otto, in an undertone. "I must only be quick, and withdraw my degraded self from every human eye. There must surely be some mountain cave where I may bury my arms, and shroud myself in endless night."

He then began to gather up the scattered pieces of his war-suit; and among them he found his good sword, cloven in two by the battle-axe of the sea-king Arinbiorn. "Little thought old Sir Hugh," quoth he, "that thou wouldst come to such an end!" Yet he carefully raised the shining fragments, and bound them up in a bundle, with the rest of his fighting-gear. Laden in this sort, as he made his way out through the antechamber, he came upon the very same mirror that had reflected his image on the morning before. "This looks quite another thing," said he, with a shake of the head, as the pale and burdened form peered on him from the glass, mocking him with its blood-stained bandages, and the flaunting disarray of its festal attire. His light brown neighed cheerily as he approached the stable. He shook his head once more. "Peace!" said he, "it is no time now for gladsome greeting!" Then binding the fighting-gear fast on the noble charger's saddle, he led him by the rein out of the gate. The people of the castle shrunk back on all sides; and he was presently lost in the deep umbrage of the wood.

Ah! let man take heed to himself when the things he wishes for are rained down upon him, and his heart knoweth no bounds to its joy!

END OF BOOK I.

BOOK II.

CHAPTER I.

After a long bleak winter, spring was beginning to peep over the mountains of Ardennes: but still cheerless it looked, with its gray mantle of rain-clouds, its damp, hazy breath, and its escort of rushing torrents. Now, one day towards eventide, a magnificent knight in golden harness, and mounted upon a tall charger, came riding over the wooded heights into the narrow vale below. A lone dell it was, as though the whole world had deserted and forgotten it. A mighty battle-axe hung by golden chains from the horseman's saddle-bow; two lofty vulture-pinions decked his helm. It was the sea-king Arinbiorn.

He had not trotted far into the desert vale, when a wild brown horse came galloping towards him; and commencing a grim combat with his charger, he tore it to the earth before he could dismount; so that they both lay together in a heap, whilst the infuriated animal stamped his hoof upon them unsparingly.

Arinbiorn's steed was already bleeding, and his mail was shivered in several places, when "Still, fellow!" cried a powerful voice from the cliff overhead, and the frantic creature, bending lowly to the earth, stood motionless as a statue, while Arinbiorn sprang to his feet, and helped up his wounded steed. Some one was instantly on the spot to proffer his aid; and on looking full at him, it proved to be a rough-looking man clad in shaggy hides, with hair and beard straggling wild over his face; yet so soft a voice issued from those matted locks, and the stranger's whole bearing was so kindly favoured, that Arinbiorn felt no scruple in yielding to his entreaty, and following to his dwelling.

They entered a rocky cavern, to which large trunks of trees and clods of turf formed a sheltering porch. Far within blazed a cheering fire, on approaching which Arinbiorn descried the full war-suit of a knight in upright array, and sufficiently lit up by the flickering flame to show the quaint moulding of the black and silver mail. On the top of it stood a helmet, with a silver beak projecting from the vizor: a bright sword snapt in two hung over it: in truth, all was such as we often see piled up in churches at the tombs of goodly knights. Arinbiorn at first thought that some such grotesque warrior was leaning against the wall there, and was on the point of giving him greeting. Then, again, seeing the hollowness of the harness, a suspicion of treachery darted through his brain: and might not his own gold trappings ere long, thought he, be glistening as fairly on the rocky wall? He clapped his hand on his battle-axe, which he had unhasped from the saddle, and brought it in with him.

"Be not alarmed, good sir," said the shaggy-coated man; "that is my harness, or rather *was* so, for I care not to wear it again, since people have given a death-blow to the best of me. But trust me; I level death-blows at nobody, and am loth to do any one harm."

"And sooth it was a foolish fancy of mine," said the sea-king. "If you had been bent on working me mischief, why save me from your savage horse? Why take such care of my poor roan either, lay healing salves upon his wounds, and bring him to a safe enclosure full of soft moss? For he who takes such thought for the horse must of a surety mean well by the rider. Pardon me my folly, my faithful host."

"Say no more," said the latter; "I pardon thee with all my heart, though little store of pardon hath the world vouchsafed to me." And therewith his voice grew very faint, and he turned away, though more perchance to hide the gathering tears than for the sake of the food which he seemed busied in producing.

"By heavens!" cried Arinbiorn, "you are the very man I was seeking. Ay! they told me of a silver-black war-suit, and of an eagle-helm, just like that one in the corner there. To be sure, I never saw you in your harness, but in merry festal trim, with the green-velvet baret-cap, and the pearl-braided mantle."

"Oh! I knew you from the very first," said the shaggy-coated man. "Could I forget the vulture-pinions? or the battle-axe, forsooth? Just look ye at the scar here that it left behind it." And so saying, he threw back his tangled hair, and bared the wounded skull. "I held it not needful," he resumed, "to discover myself to you; but he who seeks me shall ever find me. What will ye with me, sir sea-king? I am boon to render answer."

"You look me boldly and warrior-like in the face, my

young hero," said Arinbiorn; "but your care is vain. Gerda has already confessed to me all the evil she brought upon you by her cursed witch-brew. And I have therefore banished her for ever, both from myself and my followers."

"Ye should have put an end to her outright," cried the furious stripling, "that the like fearful ill fall on no other child of Christendom; could she not at least have given me clear warning, so soon as the dread liquid was coursing through my veins?"

"No, Otto! that she could not," said the sea-king. "The moment she perceived the disaster, in anxious fear for my safety, she had to ply my battle-axe with many a wizard-spell and word of power, that, with the charmed weapon, I might be able to withstand you: and he who mutters so many unblest witcheries in a single day is well-nigh forfeit to the world of spirits: it hurries him away with it, and tells him not whither. Thus, then, the tempest bore her along with it into the sear and yellow woods, and deafened her with the howling of wolves and the hooting of owls. And it was only on the second day after that, when I was far away from those parts, and almost down upon the sea-coast, that she came to me and told me all about the terrible disaster and mistake."

"Yes, she told you all about it," said Otto sullenly, throwing himself back on his mossy seat; "but what does that avail me? My hopes of fair fame and love are shivered, and her story-telling will never build them up again."

"Whom do ye take me for?" cried the sea-king, in noble indignation. "Your own sense might have told you that I at once scattered my train along every road that any of that company might be journeying, and pledged them one and all my sword and my honour that you were a true-hearted knight, and free from every taint of witchcraft. And I, of course, galloped back to the castle myself to comfort you, hoping still to find the flower of that noble company there. But you were gone, no one knew whither; and likewise Gabriele, together with Blancheflour and Folko, Heerdegen and Bertha. So I only left the rights of the story with the people in the castle, and then trotted off after those five travellers, who, for the present, were said all to have taken the same road. On the way I kept sounding my large hunting-horn, feeling sure that Heerdegen would be quick in hearing such a blast, for in Frankland the like are seldom wound. And it turned out as I thought. Heerdegen said in a moment, 'That's the sea-king's call; he is either warning us of danger, or something must have happened to himself.' So they stopped, and I came up with them, and told them the whole truth."

"And do they believe it?" asked Otto, in the bitter tone of doubt.

"How could they do otherwise?" cried Arinbiorn. "*I* told them it. Besides, Folko and Blancheflour have never thought but well of you; and if the baron had not been spent with his wound, and the beautiful rose Blancheflour with terror, neither of them would ever have left either you or the castle. How matters stand with Bertha you know yourself, I trow. But Gabriele and Heerdegen felt very much ashamed; and Heerdegen being really a noble-hearted knight, left his sister in Gabriele's care, and uttered aloud a solemn vow, that he would never rest till he had comforted you, and reinstated you in all your lost good fortune. Folko was not a little minded to join with him in the vow, for he is unspeakably fond of you; but as soon as Hernandez and he are healed of their wounds, they must be off to Spain to fight with the Moors. They had promised and bound themselves to that somewhat earlier. I too ought to make a vow, they said; and the fair damsels pressed me most earnestly to do so. But as from the very first I had quite made up my mind to go in search of you with might and main, I told them that nothing of the sort was needed. And so now, all through the winter, I have been coursing up and down the land; and at length, with the help of God, I have found you: and I doubt not you will shave off that beard to-morrow, and order the hair of your head, and then ride away to your bride, who, with the two other angel-maidens, is dwelling in a fair mansion in Gascony, in one of the most sweetly blooming vales of Frankland. But I am off to my old home the sea, for which I have this many a day been sickening. And so ends the whole business."

"What, then, is become of the ring?" asked Otto; "for Gabriele gave it back to Folko, because she would not receive it at my hands."

"Ha, with other clouds this testy scrupulousness has vanished too," replied Arinbiorn. "Gabriele has it again, I believe; at all events, they have come to a pleasant understanding about it, for they are the best of friends. I have already told you that, during the baron's campaign against the Moors, Blancheflour is to sojourn with you in Gabriele's lovely castle in the south of Frankland, where she, moreover, may gain speedy tidings of her valiant brother's battles and victories. Gabriele will ere long tell you all this herself."

"No!" said Otto, slowly and thoughtfully; "Gabriele will not tell me all that so very soon. You must know, sea-king, that nothing is more unbearable to me than to be pitied, and they would be sure to pity me for all I have suffered, if I were to go to them now. So I am resolved that they shall not see me again till I come riding on with such bright wreaths of victory round my helm, that they will not only be forced to do me justice, but will gaze on me with amazement to boot."

"A proud thought!" quoth Arinbiorn; "but I should belie myself were I to say that it displeased me. Now, hear what I have to propose, sir knight of Trautwangen. The folk within the Finland boundary-line, and many of the northern Swedes too, are still blind, stiff-necked heathens. I have promised to aid in their reduction, and there we may find store of adventure, with all manner of dangers and wreaths of victory. Heerdegen too, in case he did not find you this winter, meant to join me there towards the summer season. And there we will achieve many a bold emprise to the honour of God and the glory of our swords. Join the march with me, then."

Otto sat for a long while in silence: at last he noticed that Arinbiorn looked on him with astonishment, and with glowing cheek he cried aloud: "You perhaps fancy, sir sea-king, I am not in earnest about my fighting, and that I am one of those light-sped youngsters who dearly love to talk of grand exploits, and of their zest for the same, and yet swoon away when the things they long for are brought within their reach! Think ye so of me?"

"Sir Otto von Trautwangen," replied Arinbiorn, "I have been travelling after you the live-long winter. Little should I care to do the like for such a fellow as your tongue hath fashioned; believe me that were a sour errand, and not much better than if a sea-lion were to be many months without his native flood. But that you refuse to take part in so glorious and blest an enterprise doth somewhat amaze me. I cannot deny that, and fain would I know the reason."

"And I will tell you too," said Otto, "even at the risk of seeming childish to you. The golden vulture-wings on your helmet are the cause of it: and just now, while they lower at me so giantlike across the blazing hearth, my former dread of them breaks upon me with increased violence, and reminds me of bygone times, when my father used to tell me many a tale about a terrible man, gigantic as yourself, and with just such a wondrous headpiece. Now, my father is a doughty hero, and there are very few things that can change or ruffle his stern-set features; but when he told of the man with the vulture-pinions, his large black eyes were always lit up with horror, and he would rivet his gaze on some corner of the hall, as though the terrible foeman were rising before him."

"What did he tell you about him?" asked the sea-king, with a gloomy smile.

"Much, very much!" replied Otto; "and among other

things, how he was always drawn in the strangest way towards scenes of misfortune. For long, long miles, over sea and mountain, through vale and hollow, he was obliged to hie him wherever any fearful thing was going on. And at such times he would lend a helping hand on the inroad of distress; but as he was always its forerunner, every one quaked and trembled with fear so soon as the giant hero with the vulture-pinions appeared. And if any one had a weight of guilt on his heart, his every drop of blood would curdle at the sight of that mighty form. For vengeance was ever the dread charge of the warrior of the winged helmet, and once only did he fail in his errand; but my father would never tell me that story. It was far too ghastly and bloody a tale, he said, for so young an ear."

"Your father told you no fabled tale," said the sea-king, with a sigh. "There really was once so dread and splendid a warrior in our tribe; but now he is long since dead."

"I think I once fought with his skull in our castle-chapel," said Otto, with a slight shudder, though Arinbiorn failed to understand him. Then, in a louder voice, he continued, "That is the secret fear, sir sea-king, that now holds me aloof from you. Who knows what frightful spectres may be lurking in the olden darkness of your race and mine?"

"They lurk unseen in every time-olden darkness," rejoined Arinbiorn in cheerful guise; and so it ought to be, if a healthy day-beam is to issue from the gloom. No trembling, no rejoicing!"

"Ah!" cried Otto, with enthusiasm, "there you are right, and old Master Walther too, when he sings:

> 'Night flies away before the sun,
> And fear doth into transport run,
> And grim death into life.'"

"Well, look ye now!" said Arinbiorn. "If in our houses fear and death have plied their work before us, maybe it remains for us to rear life and delight from the darkling seed. Freshly to work, my brave comrade, and pledge me thy hand for a happy trip to-morrow by East Friesland and the sea to Norway, and thence to the Finland boundary-line!"

"Be it so, in God's name!" said Otto.

The two brave young warriors shook each other heartily by the hand, and soon afterwards, in high glee at their valorous and unblenching resolve, they breathed a refreshing and fragrant slumber on the mossy couch of the cavern.

CHAPTER II.

The early blush of morning on the mountains eastward was just shedding its first light on the cave, when Arinbiorn awoke with a start from the chequered tissue of his dreams. But when in the faintly-crimsoned gleam he beheld a youth of angel-beauty sitting beside him, like some friendly warder, with a countenance bright and soft as the spring, he thought it could only be another dream, and closed his eyes anew. But ere long, he felt the soft touch of the stripling's hand, and from his blooming lips came the gentle words, "Were we not to set out on our pilgrimage with the earliest dawn, my noble comrade?" And then Arinbiorn woke up thoroughly, and recognised the young knight of Trautwangen. The hair of his head and beard were neatly shorn and trimmed, and a remnant of the attire that he wore at that strange betrothal-banquet, though somewhat worn and faded, adjusted itself with undiminished elegance to the stripling's slender form.

"Good heavens! how fairly and gloriously art thou fashioned!" said the sea-king with a kindly smile, as he clapped his hands for joy. "The Lord's greatness showeth in His creature; and thou hast done right well to throw away those rough hides that so grossly disfigured His image, and, curtailing the rank growth of that hair of thine, that erst fell about thee like the straggling branches of some wild forest, to fashion and order it, as thou hast done, to the semblance of a sunbright garden."

"Why, when one chooseth to mix with his fellow-men again," quoth Otto, "one must take care to look like a man. Art thou ready now to let me gird on thine armour? And then, perhaps, thou wilt render me the like service."

It was done as Otto said; and now the two young heroes stood fronting each other sheathed in the panoply of war, the one in flashing gold, the other sparkling with mail of black and silver. Then the horses were saddled and bridled. Arinbiorn's steed, by dint of Otto's good care and healing herbs, was well-nigh fully recovered; but when the light-brown came trotting up at his master's call, it started in fright at sight of its savage foe. Sir Otto, however, spoke sternly and threateningly to his mettlesome charger, and again it stood still as a statue, and patiently allowed itself to be saddled and bridled, though it was easy to see that it had been many months unused to that sort of treatment, and now felt vastly astonished at it.

"Ha! how superb that creature must look," cried the sea

king, "when rightly tended and groomed! Even now, with its long shaggy hair and bristly mane, it makes such a fine display. And when in its native pride, it might safely herd with a breed that is reared in our country, and that has never yet been matched. Yes, yes! of a surety this must be one of them; for they are light-brown too, and mettlesome, just as this is; nor will they bear any but right doughty heroes for their masters."

"That he is such a thorough light-brown," said Otto, "makes him a special favourite of mine. Light-brown is to me a dear angel-colour. My sainted mother had large light-brown eyes, and as heaven beamed from them, the whole colour seems to me like a bright greeting from above."

When all was ready, Otto girded on his mounted scabbard, dropped one half of the broken blade into it, and then thrust in the other, which was still fast to the golden hilt.

"No!" said Arinbiorn, "so weaponless as that you must not ride with me. Here, take my battle-axe, and sling it securely at your saddle-bow."

"Weaponless!" replied Otto; "that I am not. My broken sword, I trow, will hew more fairly yet than many a faultless blade."

"Yet, prithee, take the battle-axe," said the sea-king; "if thou cleave any more notches in thy falchion, or get it jagged just at the broken end, it will afterwards be far harder for a man whom I will show thee in Norway to weld it together: for his wizard-charms and master-craft shall set it right for thee."

"That is quite another thing," said Otto; "and in this wise I will take the loan of thy battle-axe till the cunning smith shall have helped me to mine own weapon."

And therewith the two young warriors mounted their horses, and rode down together in a north-easterly course towards the blooming plains of Ardennes.

CHAPTER III.

Wouldst thou not, courteous reader, fain cast one backward look on old forsaken Sir Hugh? There the old man sits all cheerless in his castle-hall: the rich hue of his life is paled, and all is as a corpse to look back upon: for he gains no tidings of his only son, nor of Bertha and Heerdegen; and were it not that the old minstrel Walther visits him anon, the once lusty warrior would be grown quite a solitary, and his gray ancestral halls a knightly hermitage. Sometimes when he is sitting all alone in his large banquet-room, he chances to forget himself, and calls "Otto! Bertha!" and "Otto! Bertha!" echoes back upon him from the long lone corridors; and old Sir Hugh shakes his head, and smiles painfully at himself.

One evening he was sitting with Walther at the round table, with the silver beakers full of noble Rhine-wine between them: out of doors a spring-shower fell streaming and pattering as though it never would cease. "Patter on, patter on!" said old Sir Hugh, darting a cheerful glance at the casement, "for thou wilt keep good Master Walther by me in the castle here; so a merry greeting to thee, thrice-welcome God-send!" Walther rang his cup against his host's, and felt cheered by the beam of mirth that had broken from the noble and sorrowing soul; even as we feel when crossing a misty meadow-land, where we think we have lost our way, if the sun suddenly darts a bright ray through the clouds, and shows us the well-known path at our feet. "Sooth, good Walther," continued old Sir Hugh, "thou art right needful to me. We both of us, indeed, have hoary locks, but in very different guise. To me they are a burden, like a ripe tuft of moss that looms on high in the winter air on some weather-beaten old statue. But on you they sit like a trim silver cap, that the fair white hands of sweet ladies have graced you with, as the meed of lengthened minstrelsy. Oh! come to me oftener, then, thou smiling envoy from heaven, with thy gift of song, and tame my wilful mood!"

The two old men shook each other by the hand with emotion, and were just about opening their lips—the singer to begin a store of friendly and long-withheld questions, and old Sir Hugh to tell the kindred tale—when a serving-man entered the hall, and brought tidings that there was a pilgrim in the antechamber, who, in that heavy fall of rain, could not speed his way farther that night, and who begged for food and shelter. "A most unwelcome time for his coming," murmured Sir Hugh; and then aloud to the serving-man, "Well, show him in," said he; "that is but a thing of course, and chiefly so in such fearful weather. Draw another soft chair to the board, and send in more wine, and a silver cup for the stranger, and some food that he may break his fast withal."

The man had just reached the door of the hall, when the old knight called after him, "Has the pilgrim chanced to say what countryman he is?"

"A Franklander," replied the serving-man, and disappeared.

"Well, look ye now," said Walther soothingly; "if we are to be disturbed, it is as well that it is to be by a Frank. He, perhaps, can tell us some good news of young Sir Otto von Trautwangen."

"News," said old Sir Hugh, with a mien of great earnestness, "is not wont to be worth much in this world. I have a thorough horror of it, and the more so when a man cannot contain himself, but greedily hunts it out with his questions. So let us at least eschew that fool's-play, and pledge me your word that you will wait and see what the stranger may please, or may not please, to tell us."

"With all my heart," said Walther, "if that be doing you any favour; and you may not be very wrong, after all, with this dislike of yours. At least for friends, who come to visit friends, scarce any greeting, I ween, is more annoying than when the host says, directly after the first shake of the hand, 'Well, what news, good sir?' And is not the guest always *a friend*—above all, when he comes through the darkness and the rain?"

At this moment the pilgrim entered at the oaken door. He was neither old nor young, neither gloomy nor merry; but like a true Frank, he spoke largely and freely; and in a quick, though by no means a scant flow of words, he gave them to understand that he was a wealthy nobleman, that a vow made by his father before him compelled him to his pilgrimage, and that he now hoped to be best able to accomplish it under guard of the King of the Lion-heart's army; otherwise, he thought he should not, of his own free will, have taken to the pilgrim's staff. Old Sir Hugh's reveries were soon diverted from this shallow stream. He sat quite still, gazing vacantly before him; and as was his wont when alone, he quaffed remembrances of bygone days from the wine-cup with a sparkling eye; and Walther had taken his zittar on his lap, and roused a few broken, listless, and almost dreamy accords; whilst the stranger went on talking, eating and drinking, and courteously praising his host's hospitable cheer.

But at last the pilgrim happened to mention a name that darted like a lightning-shock through the hearts of the two old men. He began talking of the great Baron de Montfaucon, and both Sir Hugh and the minstrel knew very well how closely this bore upon Sir Otto von Trautwangen. The mighty Folko, said the stranger, had in the previous autumn engaged in single combat with a young German hero about a famous ring, and had been worsted in an unheard-of manner. The fame of this rencounter was speeding like wild-fire through the whole of Frankland: every lip was talking of the youthful German, whose first name was Otto, but for whose knightly title he could not find fitting utterance, the like being hard to Frankish tongues. Then he recounted at full length the whole manner of the fight between Otto and Montfaucon; and Walther, with a glad and powerful hand, woke the strings of the zittar to the tune of a warlike march. Old Sir Hugh, on the contrary, wore a very thoughtful look, and it seemed as though he were anxiously on the alert for the cheerless after-tone of that happy tale, which, of a surety now, could not be far behind. At last the stranger said: "To be sure, they wished to pretend that the young German had achieved all this by witchcraft." And Walther's zittar was hushed; Sir Hugh's brow was knit more darkly, and he nodded across to his friend, as if to say, "Ah! it is just as I thought."

"But not a soul believes any thing of the sort now," continued the pilgrim, quite heedless of his hearers' emotion. "The greatest and grandest knights of Frankland, on the word of Folko and another hero, throw the gauntlet down before any one who dares to say aught ungracious of the young German victor."

With these gladdening words the stranger closed the rich measure of his tale, wished the two old men a peaceful night, craved store of pardon for so early having been overpowered by fatigue, and then, a serving-man lighting the way, he followed from the hall.

Scarcely was he gone, when Walther again aroused the strings of his zittar to sounds of joy, and sang thereto:

"Young Otto, matched by no man
That graces knightly board,
Stood not on dying foeman,
Yet won the foeman's sword.

So let the spiteful growler
His cry of witchcraft raise,
The lie will show the fouler
'Mid noble foeman's praise!"

Old Sir Hugh beckoned with his hand. "Sing me not songs of victory, faithful Walther," said he; "no one knows better than I do, that Otto is far more than a match for Montfaucon; for in the early youth of two boys it is easy to settle that sort of thing, and I know them well, both of them; but a long dark shadow is lowering over Otto's life, and my ill-starred warrior-training casts him forth on the darkened ground. The issue of the poor boy's earliest rencounter was that mournful triumph over Heerdegen. Ah! good God in heaven, I am very sad. Ask me not, Walther, how that is; but let us in silence to our rest."

CHAPTER IV.

Unconscious of the forebodings which threw their dark pall over Sir Hugh's mind at this time, Otto rode on at the side of his noble comrade with all the gladsome hope of youth at the approach of spring. Scarcely were his feelings what they had been when he rode abroad for the first time at this season, picturing to himself behind every hill on the blooming banks of the Maine a palace full of wondrous adventures and the sweet guerdons of love, and thinking to find in every mounted warrior a signal friend or glorious foe. Sometimes a year can add to the age of a man much more than three hundred and sixty-five days; and so it had been with Sir Otto. Yet he still retained youth enough to presage the budding of wondrously beautiful flowers beneath the fallen verdure of his withered hopes, not only for the crimson morning, as every true and reasonable spirit does, but also for the sultry noon-day, to which, with a foolish exclusiveness, we are wont to give the name of life.

The two young heroes were already within the East Friesland boundary-line; and as they rode up the soft slope of a grassy hill, the sea suddenly lay before them in all the brightness of its beauty, spangled with a thousand sunny sparks, and waving and changing like some endless flower-garden. Otto had never beheld it before. He threw his arms wide apart in silent amazement, as though he could have embraced both sea and earth with godlike passion; he uttered a loud cry of joy over that glorious world, and then slowly and solemnly dismounting from his steed, he kneeled in silent prayer on the grass. He who has seen the sea, and can form a conjecture what must have been the feelings of such a youthful knight, will not be so very much astonished at all this.

Arinbiorn too set up a cry of exultation, whilst his roan charger neighed again as he snuffed the well-known sea-breeze. This was no sign of wonderment on his part, but rather the hearty greeting of a shepherd who returns from foreign lands to the often-grazed pastures of his home. He at once sprang from his horse, gathered brushwood and dry twigs from a neighbouring thicket, and kindled a merry fire on the summit of a hill; and scarcely had the glowing smoke spired up into the clouds, when a stately ship came sweeping round from the covert of a bushy island. "See," said the sea-king; "my comrades are already on the appointed spot, and keep good watch." And then turning to Otto, who had now risen from his prayers, "That is the bushy island there, dear fellow-traveller," continued he, "where I fought the holm-bout with Heerdegen; and on one of those hills here the Lady Minnetrost's wondrous castle must be to be seen, about which Heerdegen and Bertha had so many a sweet tale of fear to tell."

With yearning emotion, Otto looked around him for the castle which the tales told during that fearful banquet of victory and betrothal had made so dear to him. Every word that had then rung on his ear was stored up in his heart, and often chequered his dreams with the image of the mysterious mansion, with its lily battlements and the pious Druda. He now thought of modestly knocking at the magic portal, in the hope that the blest minstrelsy of the halls would waft its fair greeting on his ear, and that when the wise lady of the castle should peep over the flowery walls, she would perhaps tender him a kindly salute, and foreshow him his career of usefulness and honour; for surely she must see how hallowed and dear a place her image ever held in his heart. And he soon caught sight of a line of wall near him; but it looked very different to what he had imagined the Lady Minnetrost's castle to be. Moss-covered and ruinous ramparts of stone nodded over the castle-moat; instead of the lilies, nettles and other straggling weeds waved upon the battlements, and ugly birds with shapeless beaks peered saucily through them, or flew screaming on high, when some large fox came hardily stalking or stealthily sneaking along the ramparts, as though he were the warder, and were going his rounds through the deserted pile.

"Good heavens! what a disgustingly horrid sight!" said Otto, with a sigh; "that cannot surely—"

The words died upon his lips, and the sea-king answered the unuttered query. "I sooth cannot bring myself to think that she ever lived there," said he; "and yet it must be so, from the site of the ruins."

Whilst the two knights were thus standing and looking on in amazement, a peasant had joined them unperceived. He saluted them courteously. "Yes, yes, noble sirs," said he; "ye are two travellers from far parts, I ween, and have stood on this spot in better times. I can very well believe as much. The Lady Minnetrost's castle it still is; but the Lady Minnetrost herself is gone far from here, and no one knows whither. The flowers are turned to weeds, the clear lake to a noisome swamp; wild animals dwell in the halls, and even wicked spirits at night-time, so people will have it. That all comes of our turning our backs on our own handiwork, and leaving it to shift for itself. Then there is nothing but pulling down and tearing to pieces; for what we short-lived worms fashion is short-lived too, and if we do not keep a firm hand and a watchful eye over it, it will fall to pieces of its own inward frailness, even though it be as beautiful a pile as that of our dear Lady Minnetrost. And the peace of the land too is giving way behind her; for the whole year that she has been gone, the blades of the chiefs and vassals have been wet with each other's blood. Nay, people go so far as to say that the mad sea-king Arinbiorn is showing himself again on our shores."

"There you are in some sort right," said the sea-king, with a smile; "but this time he means you no harm."

"Ha! then of a surety we may thank the Lady Minnetrost," cried the peasant, as he pressed his cap in his folded hands. "For you must know, that she has not yet so utterly forsaken us. Twice or thrice, at the beginning, the sailors saw her standing on the shore in her white flowing robes and veil of green, as was her wonted garb. And her bright eyes beamed forth just like the moon, but she wept very sore and wrung her hands. They think she was looking for the maiden that was with her in the castle aforetime. For she beckoned with her veil across the wide sea; and when no one came, she drew her veil over her face and went her way; yet they could see quite plainly that she avoided the castle. Ah, heavens! there they are at it again in the valley; I must be quick and drive my sheep on one side, or the poor things will be trampled to powder."

With a few hasty bounds he sprang down the hill, and the two knights vaulted into their saddles. At that moment the clash of arms and the shouting of the combatants was heard from below; and soon afterwards skirmishing bands came dashing past them, some on horse and some on foot.

"It seemed to me just now," said Arinbiorn, "that you felt inclined to visit the Lady Minnetrost's castle. Be not disconcerted by these fellows here. In half an hour we will give them such a quieting, that they will thank God if they keep the breath in their bodies: for look! my second ship is making towards us already, and I'll be bound the rest of them are not far off."

"No! enough of that, Arinbiorn," answered Otto. "What should I be doing in those halls, where perhaps a she-wolf and her whelps would come howling at me, and make believe that she was the hostess? Or wherefore drive the filthy fowl from the chambers? Think only that the Lady Minnetrost's and Bertha's eyes have beamed there, and their sweet words been echoed there. It would be a hateful sight, and our brains might turn, till we saluted the hideous beasts, as though we had the beautiful dames before us. We had better think no more of it, but away to our ships."

"You are very right too in the end," said the sea-king; and therewith they trotted down the hill towards the strand.

Drawn up for the fight, and clad in their curious war-suits, Arinbiorn's giant sea-mates were standing below. The flower of the band, who had formerly accompanied their leader to Normandy, recognised the knight of Trautwangen in a moment. A whisper ran through the ranks, which rapidly increased to a shout of rejoicing, and at length burst forth in the following song:

"Featly warrior,
Folko's conqueror,
Ringing their shields armed Northmen salute thee;
Thou that didst once wrest
The ring from a Norman,
Conquer with us, and then lighter the task will grow.

Look, how foamy
The North Sea swelleth!
Cannot its bright plane lure thee along it?
Hie thee, my warrior;
Dash o'er the main;
Down from thy steed; the winged sea-horse awaits thee!"

And therewith they clashed their javelins against their huge brazen-rimmed shields; and Arinbiorn said to his companion, with a gladsome smile, "That is Northland vogue. No sooner does any thing happen, of a new and beautiful cast, than they at once give it forth in song; and this is often handed down to their children's children, and even farther still, together with the story of its origin, however silly it may sound to finer ears."

With a glowing cheek, Otto sprang from his horse, walked through the ranks, and shook the brawny hands of his future mates in war. And when they saw him in such pleasant mood, and so full of knightly kindliness, many fell passionately on his neck, and clasped him to their breasts, till his cuirass was well nigh forced into his shoulder.

Then preparations were made with all speed for the embarkation of the horses of the sea-king and the youthful knight. Willingly did the roan charger confront his familiar element; but Otto's light-brown reared and plunged with monstrous fury, and had not his master walked along at his side, continually crying, "Still, good fellow! still!" some of the Normans might have been quit of it with their lives before they had brought the furious animal on board.

CHAPTER V.

Far on the high North Sea, Arinbiorn's ships were sailing along in company before the gentle breath of a favouring wind. Nothing was to be seen but the sky and the main, while the evening sun shot his parting rays, like arrows of fire, over the lightly undulating plane. Otto was sitting on the deck; and whilst the sea-king stood by him, leaning in deep thought against a mast, he sang the following lay to his zittar:

"I glide along the glassy seas,
O'er mirror green and gay,
On pinion soft the southern breeze
Still wafts me on my way.
The snowy sail, unreefed and free,
Swells to its breath most beauteously,
As o'er the wave we roam;
Its airy hall seems proud to be
The shining warriors' home.

And she I love, in shadowy vale,
By some fresh fountain laid,
Plucks roses, pinks, and lilies pale,
To twine her flowery braid.
O dear one, whom, then, wilt thou bind?
O dear one, whom wilt thou enwind?
Thy fetters reach not me;
Yet every chain on earth would find
Me ever bound to thee.

Oh, would that to thy gentle breast
The flood of memory came,
When with thy visioned beauty blest,
My heart is all on flame.
In Fancy's prescient witchery,
Could'st thou hear stealing to the sea
The cool waves' quiet flow,
Then to and fro, 'twixt me and thee,
The sigh of love would go."

Whilst he still continued singing, Arinbiorn had taken his seat beside Otto, and his head had fallen listlessly on his hand. At length, as though embathed in the liquid and childlike softness of the lay, he sank lower and lower on the boards; and when the last sounds died away, he lay stretched at full length on the deck, with his eyes raised to heaven, and moist with tears. "Come, I will tell thee a tale now, good Otto," said he, "which thy singing has brought to my remembrance. But let me go through it just as I am now lying, with my eyes roaming through the veil of the blue tent above us; for such a view soothes and solaces a man, and makes him more trusting."

"I have often felt so in former times," replied Otto.

"The better hap, then," said Arinbiorn; "and as we glide over the waves, it is passing sweet. Here we have heaven above us and heaven beneath us, as though we were floating in the centre of one illimitable ball of crystal. Listen, then, right earnestly to what I say, and open thy heart, that my words may find an echo there.

"It was on my first campaign that I was chasing a mountain Finlander, who had several times snapped his cross-bow at me in vain, and who, seeing me in such hot pursuit of him, might perhaps think that there was little chance of finding mercy at my hands. He was wrong, however; I was not in the least exasperated, and was only bent on taking a prisoner home with me. It ended in his plunging desperately down a deep and rugged precipice. I know not whether he broke his neck or not, for I could neither find him alive nor dead. I searched about in the dell beneath till the night gathered, and I no longer knew by which path I should return to my comrades. The snow was already on the mountains, so that I had to look about me for shelter. And this I found in the shape of an old, half-ruined watch-tower, amidst the very wildest of the cliffs. I called at the gate, but no one answered. I was ready to fall with fatigue; so I groped my way up a winding stairway in the dark, opened a door against which I chanced to stumble, and, after testing the strength of the flooring with my sword, and finding it safe and firm, I lay down quietly to sleep. Towards midnight I woke again. The moon had broken through the clouds, and was shining brightly in at the lattice, lighting up something opposite to me, which I took for another window. Behind it I descried a handsomely-decorated room, and as I rose on my couch, a maiden of angelic beauty was seen glittering within it. I will not dwell longer, Otto, on the lovely smoothness of that light-brown hair, those fond, bright eyes, that sweetly-smiling mouth, or the endless grace that spoke in every motion of that slender form; for thou wilt soon discover that thou hast seen her with thine own eyes, and, indeed, such loveliness defies description. When I now rose in haste and saluted her, and sought to make a tender of my excuses, she was quite unaware of my presence; but, taking up a lute, she began to play upon it, and yet, near as I was (within the distance of six paces), I did not hear a single note, but only beheld those taper marble fingers gliding up and down the golden strings. Astounded by this, I drew nearer and nearer, and at last perceived that she was sitting in no room, but in a blooming and embowering garden, which caused the slim and tender stem of a white rose to shoot up so woudrously beside her, that it seemed to me as though it were trying, in its own flowery guise, to emblem forth her image. And at the same moment a youth stepped forth from the hedgerow with a music-leaf in his hand; and as he knelt down, he held it before her, and she sang from it, as I could easily see from the sweet motion of her lips, casting such a look on him—Ah, Otto, if I ever gain such a glance from her, I shall be the happiest man on earth; if I do not, I shall pine to death. I now drew nearer still, for jealousy and passion took place of every other feeling; and on reaching the spot, I ran against a mirror, on the surface of which I found those forms had seemed to live. A wild, tumultuous uproar arose in the glass, till, in the fever of my blood, I began to reel; and thus goaded on by a strange access of terror, I tottered down the stairway, rushed out into the darkness, over mountain and rock, and only recovered my senses on the following morning on finding myself near my own band again. A hundred times since then have I explored the mountains, both alone and with my comrades; but never has it been my lot to discover a single trace of the tower."

"Thou must have been dreaming, Arinbiorn," said Otto.

"Thou mightest have hit on a cleverer thought than that, my fighting-mate," replied the sea-king, with some show of vexation. "Am I, then, such a fellow as not to be able to distinguish between dreaming and waking? And what will you say when you hear how it has fared with me from that hour to this? The maiden's image never faded from my heart. I broke every tie that bound me to Gerda: I scarcely looked at the form of woman, save in the hope of finding my sweet mistress among the fairest of them. I found her not, and the others were, one and all, as nothing to me. But since we are fond of giving a name to what we love above every thing, and I did not know the right name of the beautiful one, I called her Rosalind, after the white rose that had sprung up beside her; and Rosalind was my war-cry in many a glorious fray. Neither had the flowery cipher told me false, but had imprinted the sweet name, as it were, on the edge of its chalice; for on entering the hall at your betrothal-banquet, I saw Folko's sister for the first time, and beheld in her my hallowed image of the mirror. And is not a white rose Blancheflour, and is it not called Rosalind too?"

"Well, I ween you are a happy bridegroom?" said Otto.

"No," said the sea-king, with a sigh; "for the youth whom I saw in the mirror sat with them at the banquet, and they called him Master Aleard. He sang some pretty songs too; and sometimes I could not help thinking that Blancheflour darted that sweet and well-known glance at him, though only hurriedly and quite abashed. Then, in timid doubt, I still was silent. O heavens! if song were all, and Blancheflour would rather be won by that than by fighting, I would gladly travel to the world's end in search of beautiful lays, and would turn minstrel on the gentle zittar, full of tender melancholy—

"What shouts are those from the third ship?" cried he, and his war-suit rattled again as he started to his feet. A captain approached them. "I have to report, sir knight," said he, "that there is a sail in view, with armed men on board. We hailed her, and bade her bring-to and say whether she were friend or foe. But her crew seem to take no notice of our signals; they are making all the sail they can, and plying their oars right lustily. They are already a good way ahead."

"Have you any of the Greek fire on board that we brought from Constantinople?" asked Arinbiorn; and on his captain's answering that they had, "Then wrap some of our arrows in flax and tow, add plenty of that fire, and send them at the saucy hull. They who will not hear must feel!"

Then straightway through the dusk of evening those arrowy messengers went flying at the outlaw vessel, like little birds of flame. Some might plainly be seen fastening on the deck, some on the sails, and soon they began to flare and eddy round, like growing stars. Then here or there a pair of these little orbs would merge into one; and at length, in many a blazing coil, there would be flashing up and down from the deck to the masts, and from the masts to the deck. Suddenly the flamy streaks and starlets fell hissing together, and the whole vessel was one glowing mass.

"Now out with the boats to the rescue," said Arinbiorn, "and fish the lads out of the sea, that none of them may come to any harm. By your souls I charge you."

Not long after, they brought the prisoners on board. Happily they all were saved, and there was greater joy on this account, inasmuch as by their attire and stature, and such few arms as the sea had not engulfed, it was soon seen that they were Normans likewise. A young and very handsome man was led before Arinbiorn as their captain.

"Ha!" cried the sea-king, in a tone of compassion; "Cousin Kolbein, was it you? That is really a pity!"

"Yes, indeed, it is a pity, for the sake of my beautiful craft," replied the stripling hardily; "and I never should have thought that you, Arinbiorn, would have been the man to burn it."

In a solemn voice the sea-king answered: "And who bade thee put out to sea before thou wert acquainted with our usages? When greater vessels hail a smaller one, the latter slackens sail, and gives fitting answer, or else makes foes of its friends. So to-day thou hast been taught how little such daring is in the right."

"It was not those fiery bolts of yours that should have convinced me," said Kolbein; "yet when so brave and renowned a seafarer maintains it, I am convinced enough, and humbly crave your pardon for having demeaned myself unbecomingly."

"Trouble not thyself," replied Arinbiorn. "Thus much of the art of war thou hast now thoroughly by heart." They then pressed hand in hand, and one and all made a right merry meal.

CHAPTER VI.

EARLY one balmy night of spring Otto had fallen asleep on deck, and it was nearly morning ere the cool sea-breezes, playing over his face, awoke him. He rose to his feet amid a flood of the brightest moonlight, and a chain of high, steep cliffs, not far from the ship, were looming aloft beneath the deep blue of heaven. Vast beech-woods rustled on the summits of the crags; the pinnacles of watch-towers, or mountain battlements, jutted out here and there from amid the trees and savage rocks. Eagles, that had their eyries in the cliffs, came swooping down or flying over the ship. The young knight felt strange feelings of awe, and yet he was so happy the while, and sang the following words:

"As some low unbidden lay
O'er a weird lip finds its way,
Fear awakes in me;
Here time-olden woods are glistening—
To the moonlit ocean listening;
Oh! this must Norway be."

While Arinbiorn's voice was heard behind him thus:

"Here is Norway; here dwells Norman;
Here the love of arms is wakeful;
Here the Scald his lay is weaving;
With a healthy flow it telleth
Of the faithfulness of beauty,
Of the valiant warrior's prowess.
Sweet the cup, by fagot blazing;
Hail, then! hail, then! well-loved Norway!"

The sea-hero stood at the helm, himself guiding the flagship to the well-loved strand; and they were already near to a small landing-place at the foot of the cliffs, when the anchors were dropped; and, full of glad impatience, Arinbiorn leaped overboard, sheathed in armour, and swam ashore; and when the rest came after him in the boats, he was blowing loud blasts on his bugle-horn, as a greeting and announcement of his arrival to his friends on the mountains. In the thick beech-forest above there was a light, as of single sparkling stars, and soon many windows of a large and beautiful castle might be seen lit up with bright tapers, that now revealed the once half-shown pile in its full magnificence. At the same time the glad sound of horns returned answer above; horses were heard descending the rocky path, and the arms of the riders rattled as they came. Arinbiorn pointed cheerily aloft. "That is the time-worn dwelling-place of me and my fathers," said he to Otto. "Thou shalt see many a gallant sight there, dear comrade-in-arms."

In the meanwhile the war-steeds had been brought ashore, and, horsemanlike, they were leading them up and down the strand, to give new strength and suppleness to their limbs after the unwonted constraint of the voyage. Otto's light-brown reeled like a creature intoxicated, and could scarce regain his fearless restiveness; whilst Arinbiorn's roan, from long acquaintance with the sea, in a few moments had completely recovered, and was capering and neighing round the once dread light-brown in the merriest spirit of defiance, as though he sought to make the best of his enemy's present powerlessness.

The castellans of the sea-king had now descended from the heights, tendering a reverential salutation to their lord and his guest, as also to the young Kolbein, and greeting their own companions-in-arms with familiar cheerfulness. They had brought chargers for the knights. So all dashed joyfully up the pathway to the castle, and in a quarter of an hour they were trotting through the arched and resounding gateway of the stronghold into the torch-lit court.

And now from forth a dark doorway, through which bright coals might be seen glimmering, stepped a tall form, black and sooty, though of knightly bearing, and offered the sea-king his hand. Arinbiorn grasped it warmly. "Good morrow, Asmundur, thou mighty armourer," said he; "hast thou finished many a beautiful piece of work in my absence?"

"I ween I have forged death for many a foe," replied Asmundur, with a confident nod.

"I bring thee a friend who needs thy skill," said Arinbiorn, pointing to Otto. "The costly sword that hangs at his side I have shivered with my battle-axe, and I wot thou canst weld it together again for him, and make it better than it was before."

"Yes, forsooth, if it be worth doing," said Asmundur; "for I could make a new one as easily. Just let me see the blade."

Otto drew one half of it from the scabbard, and shook the other out after it. The craftsman took up both of them, and examined them narrowly; then, "If the man be like the sword," cried he, "the two will scarcely find their equal; though he whom the sea-king Arinbiorn brings with him, and trusts with the battle-axe that I forged myself, speaking a good word for him to boot, must sooth be a gallant knight. But since at best I ply the hammer for very few, and wholly and solely for the deftest hands, I should rather see this or that feat of arms from him first."

"With all my heart, Asmundur," replied the sea-king. "He will give thee full satisfaction. But thou knowest he must rest him a little after his first voyage on the high seas."

The brave smith gave a willing nod, and was about to withdraw to his sooty hall, when Otto cried out, "Wherefore, then, should I rest? A sorry champion he would be who should lose so much of his strength by a little unwonted travelling. Let us to it, then! Morning already sparkles so brightly as to make the torches useless. Will any one name some fair exercise in arms? for I fain would meet his challenge."

"We mean to say," said Arinbiorn, "that you, as a stranger, cannot be skilled in our way of war."

"Why not?" cried Otto. "Think ye, then, that my father travelled for naught through so many foreign lands? He well understood your way of fight, and carefully instructed me in it. What, then, is there among you that I should not know? Can it be the casting of your long spears, of which a whole mass is lying yonder?" And he flew like a ball from his steed, grasped a javelin, and hurled it whistling through the air with such mighty sway, that it flew across the whole breadth of the courtyard, and fixed itself in an old elm-tree at the further end. Heedless of the astonishment of the Normans, "Ye must not be too hard upon me with this first cast," said Otto; "I am a little out of practice, and this is only to show you that the use of your weapons is not quite strange to me."

Then they all gazed on the young stranger as on a chosen hero, and each tried to outvie the other in measuring his strength with him in this or that feat of arms. Thus the high noon came, and still Otto was not tired of wrestling, throwing the spear, or fighting with the blunted and two-handed sword, nor was Asmundur weary of watching the young victor's exploits. Nay, at last he even stepped up to him himself.

"I know very well," said he, "that you will worst me; but it must be a keen pleasure to feel such doughty blows as *you* deal; and besides, I would fain show you that I am armourer to be sure, but still no despicable swordsman either." And it turned out as Asmundur had said. He received many a sword-blow at Otto's mighty hands; and, after a brave resistance, the sooty smith's weapon at last flew nine ells or more across the court; and gallantly and skilfully as he afterwards planted himself in the wrestling-bout, yet he was throwu on the sand, whilst Otto, lying on him, pinued him, arm and leg, motionless to the earth.

"Loose me!" said Asmundur, with a groan; and as Otto raised him, "This very night," said he, "I will forge thee thy hero-sword, young hero, and at the noontide banquet we will sit together over the cup; for well I ween thou wilt be as hard to vanquish by mead and wine as by any warrior in the world."

CHAPTER VII.

THE cups were emptied, night had fallen, and Otto, receiving from all the banqueters the parting words of love, slept upon his couch, after the exercises of the day and his unwonted travel by sea. But as early as midnight, a hollow knocking and ringing broke upon his slumbers, at first enweaving itself with his dreams, and at length fully awaking him. Looking carefully rouud, half in dismay, and half pleasurably moved by the unusual sound, he at last remarked that his lodging was over Asmundur's smithy, and that the stern craftsman below was working at his shattered sword, singing a song the while about the great Siegmund Wolsung's sword: how it broke in battle beneath Odin's spear, and how the wizard craftsman again soldered it together for Sigurd the snake-slayer, Siegmund's son. From his early childhood, his father had told him many an inspiring tale about this hero-legend, and he could not now repress his curiosity to hear the same from the lips of a Norman, especially as the old story about a doughty warrior, named Hugur, was alternately blended with the song, and Otto knew nothing of this as yet, though his heart was all on fire to hear it. He rose softly from his couch, grasped his cloak and battle-axe, cautiously glided down the stairway, and following the sound of the song and the forge, he suddenly entered Asmundur's hall. The craftsman rose angrily from his work, and brandishing his glowing hammer, he advanced to the intruder. But no sooner did he recognise Otto, than he turned away in peaceful mood, only laying his finger with solemn portent on his lip. He then set himself to work again, and in obedience to his significant look, Otto silently took his place opposite him on a half-sunk anvil. Then, as he plied his work afresh, the armourer renewed the solemn chant, till the black vault resounded with the exploits of Sigurd no less than with the strokes of the hammer. But at every close he changed the key, and sang the following words:

> "But as untowardly Hugur the mighty
> Wielded aforetime the smoking sword-blade—
> Ah! how sweet woman sobbed in the death-struggle!—
> So let none wield thee, sword of the lightning-flash.
> Well-a-day, Hugur, ill was thy deed then;
> Oh! let no warrior-son do so after thee!"

Now the strain changed again to the exploits of Sigurd, and then plaintively told of the mighty Hugur. And still the restless hammer swung, and still the glowing iron sparkled, lighting up in fearful splendour the form of the giant smith. At length the sword was finished: Asmundur drew it from the coals with his tongs, and, while it looked like a weapon of flame, he laid it down to cool. Then he opened his lips, and spoke to Otto. "If thou hast aught to say to me," quoth he, "begin at once. Thou mayest now do so, without in the least endangering either thyself or thy sword."

"I came not to speak," replied Otto, "but to listen only; for old legends are very life-blood in my veins. With the achievements of Sigurd thou seemest to have done; and I know most of them myself. But if thou wouldest only tell me what that was about the mighty Hugur, thou wouldest tender me a special grace."

"That is easy service," said the smith; "but I will first go and fetch me a horn of mead, and thee a golden beaker of wine." And having placed both of these on the half-sunk anvil, he brought forth two cuirasses, on which the two warriors took their seats fronting each other at the iron table, and Asmundur began to relate as follows:

"Nearly forty years ago lived a knight in this country, of the name of Hugur. Hugur was the fairest and strongest of men, and as he had come from strange parts, many people fancied that he had been sent hither in magic wise by the time-olden Odin, from the beautiful land of Gottheim, which so many mortals have sought for in vain. How this might be, I know not. I have been signed with the sign of the cross, and am become a good Christian; yet when mortal tongue speaks of Odin and Gottheim, my whole heart leaps at the thought of them. Mere lying fables, my young hero, the olden legends about the gods can never have been. Well,

Hugur soon proved himself to be the most victorious warrior in the whole of Norway, a single one excepted. Yet the more dearly the folks hereabouts were minded towards Hugur, the less favour did that other champion find in their eyes, because his presence always betokened some untoward misfortune. Manful as he was in giving them aid, and unequalled as he was as an avenger of their wrongs, yet he never could make up for the panic which his appearance caused among them, and the injury it did to their health, their happiness, and even their lives."

"Was that not the Avenger with the vulture-wings on his helm?" asked Otto, with a shudder.

"Ah! you are at home among us already," rejoined Asmundur. "Well, Arinbiorn, I ween, has told you about it; for he is of the same race of heroes."

Otto turned his glassy gaze on a corner of the vault, as though the intruder with the vulture-pinions would be seen rising from the earth, and Asmundur continued as follows:

"Now at that time of day there was an earl in Norway who had almost as much power and golden store as a king, and two daughters of wondrous beauty, and very like in face. The eldest was named Astrid, the youngest Hilldiridur. Astrid was like a thousand other maidens, modest, kind-hearted, and cheerful among her playmates. But Hilldiridur, though equally good, and not less comely in her behaviour, had received from her stars a yearning and a bias towards that mystic and wizard knowledge which is in vogue in northern lands; and therefore, in her early childhood, she had been adopted by a kinswoman of hers, who was powerful in that grave lore, and had been carried over with her to a flaming yet snow-clad island.

"Now almost all the great warriors of Norway made suit unto the beautiful Astrid, and the Avenger with the vulture-pinions among them. But as the maiden shrunk with fear at the thought of the stern behest which Heaven had imposed on the latter, the mighty Hugur more easily bore away the prize, and the day was fixed for the bridal. The Avenger left them, but not in anger, for he was ever of a kindly turn, revenging other men's wrongs, but never his own. Yet at the espousal-banquet, true to the secret power that swayed him, his golden vulture-wings peered in at the hall, lured thither by the approach of misfortune. He excused himself for coming; he could not do otherwise, he said. The bride turned pale, and, with sorrowful courtesy, the bridegroom received him as a noble guest. At night-time the castle was struck by a thunderbolt, and enwrapt in flames. The hero with the vulture-pinions saved the bridal pair by the most venturesome daring;

for, stifled in their first sleep by the sudden rising of the smoke, they were lying almost lifeless on their couch. But the mighty Hugur conceived a rancorous hatred to the Avenger, and bid him stay away from him for ever.

"'With all my heart,' said the vulture-winged hero, 'if thy misfortune force me not upon thee!' And as he said, so it happened: Hugur was exposed to many a disaster; and whether he himself, his beautiful mate, the child that she had borne him in the first year of their wedlock, his noble charger, or his harvest, were threatened, yet the vulture-helm might always be seen beforehand beneath the porch of the castle. Despite the succour, however, which he afforded them, Astrid and Hugur grew suspicious of the Avenger. As a slighted suitor, they said, he purposely brought those evils upon them which he afterwards strove to stem. And it at last ended in Hugur's swearing to their vulture-helmed visitant, face to face, that he would cut him down without further warning, if he ever again let himself be seen within the boundaries of his domain. The Avenger shrugged his shoulders, and sorrowfully went his way.

"Not long after this it happened that fair Astrid, as was her wont, went all alone into the neighbouring copse. She had a light javelin in her hand, not so much for the sake of wounding any thing (for she was no huntress), as that she might carry with her some pretty glittering toy. And there, on a spot where the bushes were very thickly intertwined, she found the Avenger lying asleep, with his vulture-pinioned helmet near him on the grass. She started in the greatest alarm, and yet she could not help standing where she was, and looking closer. Thus we often feel at the sight of fearful objects. At last the thought came across her, whether there might not be some weird spell in the helmet, which might be broken if that guardian thing of fear were removed from its owner's head. No sooner said than done; for she gave the Avenger credit for no good intentions, and so she wished to render him as powerless as possible. Then wandering back through the dark tissue of the branches, the helm in her hand appeared so fearful to her, that in order to hold it out more at length, she poised it on her javelin, and thus bore it before her.

"But at this moment the mighty Hugur came riding through the forest. The golden vulture-pinions darted up all at once close to him from the brushwood, and as he could only suppose that the Avenger was lurking in ambush there, he swore a fearful oath, and dealt a blow at his fancied foe with all the strength he was master of. The blade glinted off the helm and lighted on the bosom of his darling wife; and that was fair Astrid's death. But before she died, she wept very sore, for she was dearly fond of life. And Hugur, when he saw his hapless mistake, was ready to die of grief and remorse. They say that in the strong flow of song which our language supplies, and in which Hugur himself was very skilled, they both sang thus ere she died. Hugur sang:

'Oh! have I slain her, my sweet little roe?
Oh! have I stricken her fair limbs with death?
Well-a-day! well-a-day! what is all to me now?'

Astrid sang:

'Then alway remember thy little roe;
And make her a grave on the soft green sod;
And sing a lorn lay, for thy little roe loved thee.'

Hugur sang:

'I have requited her many sweet gifts
With the hateful guerdon of grisly death!
Here begins woe for me; where shall it end?'

Astrid sang:

'Many a giddy draught grows on the earth for thee,
And as it trickles, thy heart will grow glad!
But me cold slumber enfoldeth—good night!'

Therewith fair Astrid closed her bright and roelike eyes for ever, and just then the Avenger came through the wood in search of his helmet. Hugur fell on him with tremendous fury, and it seemed as though his avenging office were now at an end. His unconquerable strength forsook him, and after a short conflict, he lay, with a severed skull, at Hugur's feet. The mighty Hugur bore him on his back, took fair Astrid's corpse in his arms, and thus he entered the castled hall of his father-in-law. There he upbraided himself with the disaster, and sought to tender his own life as an atonement for that of his spouse; but the earl, hearing how it all had happened, made Hugur quit and free of blame. He only demanded of him that, mighty champion as he was, he should always march forth to his aid when he needed him. The mighty Hugur bent low before the earl, and dipped a spear-iron in fair Astrid's blood; then he held it out to the earl. 'Send me that,' said he, 'and though I be at the world's end, I will hasten to Norway to help thee.' And that was the atonement for fair Astrid's death.

"But Hugur's son was present when his father dipped the spear-iron in his mother's blood; and this filled him with such dread horror, that Hugur could never lure him to him again. So he was obliged to leave him behind with his grandfather.

"Afterwards (and the mighty Hugur was in Italy at the time), the earl sent him the spear-iron, requesting him to come to Frankland forthwith, to the aid of certain Normans of his race. And Hugur honourably redeemed his pledge. And thence again the earl called him away to a cruise on the sea; and after the mighty Hugur had completed this with renown, he met a ship as he sailed homewards, manned with Icelanders, and bearing the beautiful Hilldiridur to Norway. They met in a cove. He saw that form of grace, whence Astrid's loveliness broke on his dazzled gaze in twofold bloom; and hearing who she was, he took her by main force, for he was well aware that he never would be able to gain her father's consent. Fair Hilldiridur knew nothing of his fearful deed, nor the Icelanders either; so, partly terrified by his angry violence, and partly won by his knightly splendour, she surrendered herself to him, after a Christian priest had first spoken over them the blessing of wedlock. At the same time Hugur made her vow that she would never again use her wizard arts so long as she should be united to him. He either felt a natural abhorrence for them, or he feared that by their means she might discover the blood that clave to his hands. The Icelanders, whom he had dismissed with presents, told all this in Norway. But they found the old earl already dead, and since then no one has been able to discover what has become of the mighty Hugur and fair Hilldiridur."

CHAPTER VIII.

Otto sat silent awhile, gazing, in deep emotion, on vacancy. The death-song of fair Astrid and Hugur had pierced his very soul; and when he again aroused himself from that tearful sadness, and was on the point of asking, among other matters, how Arinbiorn was of the Avenger's kindred, he heard the tramp of horses in the courtyard, and people calling on him by name from this side and that.

"They could not find you in your chamber," said the smith, "and are now in search of you. Come, take your sword, and let us go forth anon."

Bright was the flash of the spotless weapon in Sir Otto of Trautwangen's hand, and still more fairly shone the young knight himself, as with the sooty smith he issued into the courtyard, now gleaming and glistening in the fresh light of morning. Arinbiorn stepped cheerily forward to meet him, and wished him joy of a sword forged by Asmundur's hand. With store of thanks, Otto returned him the battle-axe; and straightway the sea-king ordered the eagle-mail to be brought, and whilst he was busied in girding on the young German's trappings, "See you the merry band of horsemen there?" said he. He pointed to a numerous squadron in the court, whose steeds, mostly of the light-brown hue, were impatiently pawing the ground. "Those," continued he, "if my bidding be done, you shall lead into Swedeland, to make war on the Finlandish heathens; whilst I will put to sea with my ships, and, sailing round the coast, will fall on our enemies' flank and rear, and give them battle on their native soil. Do you agree to this?"

"Why not?" returned Otto. "Let us set forth this very morning."

"In a moment," said the sea-king. "It only depends on this one thing. Your horsemen would gladly see a trial of their captain's strength, just to know whether both man and horse can stand the brunt of it with the best of them. Will you ride a round with the trooper there on the light-brown charger?"

"Nothing were more to my mind," cried Otto; and his accoutrements being complete, he sprang, in his rattling mail, to the adjoining stable, saddled and bridled his steed, now recovered from the constraint of the voyage, and rode out of the courtyard through the high arch of the gateway. Cheerily did his courser neigh, snorting on his strange mates from his smoking nostrils. The mounted troop filled the air with huzzas at the sight of their stately leader. With a reverential obeisance his rival rode up, and asked if it were the knight's pleasure that they should begin their race. "Lead me to the course," said Otto; and riding a little way on their flank, the horseman replied, "It lies straight before us, noble sir." He checked his steed on the brow of a steep descent, interspersed here and there with single pieces of the crag, which now were seen peering ruggedly on high, and now winding in formidable smoothness aslant over the turf. "There lies our course," said the Norman gaily; "it matters less, in our mountain-ranges, whether a horse can scour fleetly over the plain, than whether he can bound swiftly and securely down such break-neck places as these."

"Enough," said Otto, with a smile, though his eye swam the while, as he gazed on the fearful depth. However, he nerved his courage all the more, as his light-brown foamed at the precipitous path no less cheerily than the steed of his rival, and champed the bit with like impatience for the struggle.

"Let the signal be given with the clarions, Arinbiorn," said Otto, turning to the half-circle formed round them by the troopers, with the sea-king and the smith at their head; "I am ready."

The trumpet-blast sounded, the riders gave the horses their heads, urged them with the spur to more adventurous bounds, and warily threw their weight over the crupper, to preserve the equilibrium of their flying steeds, as they sped onward with the swiftness of the storm. Otto's eye grew dizzy, his ears rang again, the plumes on his helm went whistling through the air; anon he felt as though the flight were becoming a fall, and he must check his wild course with the rein; but remembering that thereby his rival might possibly shoot before him, he plied the spurs rather than the bridle, and wilder flew his light-brown over the bristling crags or smoothly winding layers of stone. In the vale below, man and horse made halt, and the victorious animal neighed cheerily on the morning breeze, whilst the antagonist horseman came rattling down the neighbouring cliff; but no sooner was he in the vale than his horse fell furiously on Otto's charger, despite all he could do to restrain him, and the two light-brown steeds stood biting and plunging at each other on the plain; ere long, however, the strange steed and his rider, both wounded alike, lay floundering on the earth. Otto dragged his angry charger away. His antagonist rose, and, as he was wounded on the foot, "Mount my steed, good friend," said Otto, "and ride up to the castle."

"Sir knight," said the Norman, drawing back, "what task would you set me? Now I know of a surety that your steed is of the noblest and most formidable breed of the light-brown chargers that we rear in our country. Why, he would tear me in pieces were I to come near him; for his own master cannot sway such a war-horse after the fray."

"That depends on who his master is," said Otto. "Take my word for the event.—Still, my fellow!" cried he, as he alighted; and with his wonted obedience, the creature stood still. Otto helped the wounded rider to mount, and gently and warily as a sumpter-horse the light-brown clambered up the steep after his master. When they reached the summit, all the horsemen lowered their spears before the knight and his steed.

"That is a captain," said the oldest among them, "such as all our lives long we have never had!"

And then, still seated in their saddles, they drank the early stirrup-cup all round; and soon afterward Otto's troop was trotting through the valleys, and Arinbiorn's swelling sails were flashing over the blue mirror of the sea.

CHAPTER IX.

OVER many a desert heath, and through many a wood and mountain-pass, Otto had marched onward with his troop. They were already on the Swedish lands, when they learned that the army which had taken the field against the Finlandish idolaters and their leaguers had advanced to the frontier line of hills, and were every day looking forward to a decisive battle. Otto's squadron, in their impatient march, were often warned to be on their guard against hostile parties, who were ever and anon hovering in the enemy's rear. But the knight and his Normans only laughed at this. "It is for them to be on their guard against us," said they; "if they are wise, they will keep out of our way."

One day some mounted scouts, who had been sent out to see that the road was clear, brought word that a party of horse, much stronger than their own, was marching to meet them. To judge by their stature and accoutrements, they could not be Finlanders, but noble Swedes: "perhaps," added they, "they have been worsted in battle, and this may be a part of the army on the retreat." The troopers knit their brows. But to the same stripling who had ridden the race with him at Arinbiorn's stronghold Otto intrusted the command of the squadron, and pricking forward on his light-brown, he gave them orders to halt, and only gallop to the rescue when they heard the call of the golden war-horn, which, as the sea-king's gift, he always carried at his side. Some called after him, and would fain ask, wherefore he, their leader, should rush thus venturously to the very first onset? "Sigurd," quoth he, "the great warrior, of whom ye so often sing, always rode out alone to reconnoitre. Let me follow in his steps." And so saying, he trotted merrily on through a little bushy glen, and then ascended a hill, whence there was a good view all round.

Halting on its summit, he beheld not only one, but three strong companies of horse, moving forward from three different directions, yet united one with the other by means of single troopers, who each kept their eyes on the man that was nearest them. By the whole manner of their march, he could easily see that they were gallant warriors; while the knightly splendour of their array, their heavy accoutrements, and the close order of their line, showed that they could not be Finlanders, but true-born Swedes. As he was eyeing them thus, a mighty chestnut charger came tearing up the steep through the brushwood before him, bearing a tall sinewy rider in heavy mail, from whose helmet a long black horse-tail flew wildly in the wind.

"Who goes there?" cried the rider, from whose open vizor beamed the countenance of a light-haired and beautiful youth.

"A Norman!" replied Otto.—"Swedish brother's friend."

"That is as it may be," said the stripling. "Ridest thou forth for Odin or for Christ, with that troop of thine in the vale below?"

"Fie on the sinful challenge!" cried Otto. "Is not the Norman land turned to the true faith, and thinkest thou that we are recreants from the cross?"

Here the Swedish knight brandished his javelin. "Ward thee, then," cried he. "My kindred and I keep true to Odin and the customs of our fathers, and neither thou nor a single man in all thy squadron shall reach the Christian host."

"Ay, now it is my turn to say, that is as it may be," retorted Otto. "Brace thee to the fight, thou heathen foeman."

Then both the young heroes dropped their clashing vizors, and brandishing their spears, they caracoled round each other on their fiery steeds. Ere the lapse of many moments, Otto beheld his foeman's hand quivering for the cast, and then the heavy lance sped with such a thundering crash against his head that, stunned as he was with the blow, he rolled in the saddle, and painfully strove with his plunging and impetuous light-brown. But the eagle-helm turned aside the deadly point, and the wild bounds of the charger kept back the Swede as he sought to fall with his drawn sword on the rider, till, with a firm seat and nervous arm, Otto again poised his lance, and hurled it with shattering force through the vizor of the foe. The next moment his hand was upon his sword; but the Swedish knight had already measured his length on the grass, and the chestnut steed flew in dismay through branch and brushwood into the vale below. Slowly rode the conqueror up to the corse, and pensively he beheld the youthful countenance looming from the shattered vizor, with the lance in its brow.

But suddenly there was a rustling in the thicket all around him. Four or five of the fallen Swede's comrades dashed up on their foaming steeds, and fell with infuriate cries on the knight of Trautwangen. Fair time had he then to try Asmundur's blade; and it did gallant service. Right and left they reeled from their saddles on the grass, and as soon as Otto gained time to wind a blast on his golden horn, his Normans came rushing up to his aid from the valley. Now a furious fray ensued with the enemy, who seemed to swarm thicker and thicker on the brow of the hill: but as the noblest among them had fallen at the very first onset, and but one hollow path led up the steep on their side, they fought shyly and awkwardly; and when the first group above took to flight, it bore down those along with it who were hastening up to its aid. Many a Swedish corpse lay strewn on the field; and, on the very same evening, with store of captured steeds and accoutrements, Otto and his Normans reached the Christian camp.

The huzzas with which they greeted him, when the mail of the Swedish knight was seen, showed the victor more fully what a decisive cast he had made. The fallen foe had been the terror of all Christian warriors; and when his bloody mail and his shattered helmet flashed through the avenues of the camp, the lust of fight and trusty cheer fired every heart for the coming battle. The general of the forces, a prince of the blood-royal, well advanced in years, and with the stern, staid look that told of many a field, stepped forth to meet him, thanked him with kindly dignity, and led him by the hand into his tent. There he asked him concerning his march, and what he knew about Arinbiorn. When Otto had given a full report of every thing, and had detailed the manner in which the sea-king was sailing round the Finlandish coast, the princely leader cast on him a keen look of pleasure. "Here our good God sends me a truly gallant hand," said he. "The death of the mighty pagan has proved your strength and valour, and your clear speech shows at once that you have the soul and the glance of a warrior. Young hero, I will not conceal from you my intention of giving battle to-morrow to the enemy's hordes. Your mounted men shall march on the left wing of the army; but you shall bide with me in the centre, till I shall clearly have pointed out the spot to you, where you may gallop off, fetch a compass round the right wing of the enemy, and thus fall upon him flank and rear. Sorely have I been wishing to have one such as you for this service. God be with you, and sound sleep attend you, that you may bring me a keen eye and a stalwart hand for to-morrow."

Whilst in the still glow of enthusiasm Otto passed onward in the darkness to his troop, he heard an old Swedish horseman say, "To-morrow we shall have battle."

"Why so?" quoth his comrade.

"Ah!" said the veteran, "seest thou not the kites and the ravens, how they are trooping down before us to the plain? Such folk know the errand they are bound upon. And there are eagles too among them: they scent a royal meal that shall dye the green turf red for them."

Otto paced onward in solemn thought on that fearful festival, and fain would he have been a watcher that night. But the prince's caution about a clear eye and a stalwart hand made him wrap himself in his cloak; and despite the images of woe that hovered round him, he at last yielded to a refreshing slumber.

In a few hours the beam of morning shed its sparkles over the grass, and at the same moment a trumpet-call sounded in the warriors' ears, summoning the horsemen to saddle their steeds, the footmen to the arrangement of their bows and quivers. Otto leaped upon his light-brown, drew up his troop, and then trotted on to the appointed post on the left wing of the army. There, once more making the stripling of yesterday's race their leader: "Ye brave Normans," said he, "hold ye still till I come to you again, and lead you a way of your own to deeds of death and victory. Till then, move forward on the flank of the army! Your word on it now that I shall find you here?" "Scrip, faith, and honour be our pledge!" cried the Norman horse-troopers; and Otto galloped on towards the centre of the line, where the princely chief was already standing with his staff around him, and many of the mounted warriors who were skilled in blowing the horn.

"Stay by my side, young soldier," said the prince to Otto, with a friendly greeting. "I shall soon send thee on thy way. Seest thou the groups opposite to us, which are pouring over the plain like wood-streams from the rocky passes? Hearest thou their wild howling? He who seeks to stem their path hath a thankless task, and oftentimes achieves but little; for like dust they scatter themselves, and thread their way through us one by one, in mockery of our close array. He who breaks their flank and their rear-line breaks their strength at once. To this task have I chosen thee. When we get farther up, I will show thee more clearly what I mean. Now, in the name of our God, to the charge!" He cast his spear on high, and caught it with a dexterous hand. Then the clarions sounded around them like the roll of thunder; from every troop the sound was echoed, and with measured and even march both horse and foot moved sternly across the plain. With a dismal howl the Finlandish forces pressed forward to the attack, while their light skirmishers, on horse or on foot, dotted the plain before them like so many gnats or flies, as they came darting their shafts on the advancing Swedes. But from among the forces of the latter, also, a merry body dashed forward with their crossbows and spears; and boldly answering those volleys in glad mimicry of the fight, they thus diverted the hostile missiles from the Christian troops.

Nearer and nearer the two armies advanced: with a more lengthened huzza, with more eagerness for the charge, and yet solemnly at the same time, as though sounding a farewell, rose the melody of the Swedish march. Otto's heart beat high with enthusiasm that he had never known before. What was all the inspiriting parade of single-handed fight to this mighty gathering—this march to victory in the defence of a noble cause—this holy death-league, that, with tongues of flame as it were, spoke forth in those rich clear tones, and shouted from flank to flank, "Onwards, onwards! Together we live and we die. Wife and child, and bride, adieu! Peace be with ye; we die and conquer here!" The single combatants now disappeared more and more from between the armies; many a band of horse or foot had already dashed to the encounter with indecisive effect. The Finlanders began to extend their line, dissolving like a cloud that is passing into mist, and winnowing their way here and there through the Christian squadrons, just as the old prince had foretold. Suddenly casting his flaming glance on Otto, "Dost thou see the broad trench there on our left?" said he. "They have planted their right wing behind it, for they think that neither man nor horse can pass over; but thou and thy Normans, I ween, can clear it."

"We have tried many a bolder thing among the mountains," replied Otto, with a smile.

"Mark me," said the prince, and he raised his finger in grave token of warning; "think not too lightly of the leap; remember, ye must take it twice: first on our left here, to fetch a compass round the foe; and then on the right again, to fall upon his flank."

"All the better," said Otto: "so we shall soon get a little practice, and the horses will lose some of their untameable spirit. A good foaming gallop, and then they are just what they should be."

"Well, so far all is right," said the prince; "thou hast good soldier-like faith. Only ride on behind the hill there; in that way the Finlander will not catch sight of thee when thou leapest the trench. And when thou hast to clear it again, and fall upon him flank and rear—ay, young hero, then thou must have thine eyes about thee. Thus much only I warn thee of: not too soon, or thou wilt only take a few of the nearest groups by surprise; and not too late, or thou wilt be forced to ride far in chase of them before thou comest to blows, and they will bring up their squadrons rearwards against thee."

"Have you aught else to command?" asked Otto, with the confidence of victory on his brow. Bending in his saddle, the prince pressed his hand in friendly token of dismissal, and, with the fleetness of the wind, the young mettlesome warrior flew over the heath to his squadron.

The Normans greeted him with a loud huzza: "Now," thought they, "we shall go straight on to the foe!" But when the knight turned off to the left with them, and pursued his course behind the hill, many a face in the troop was overcast. Some young soldiers were even on the point of speaking, and asking their leader whither they were riding, when two or three veterans gave them a warm rebuke. "Have ye neither manners nor discipline?" said they; "pretty shambling warriors, truly! Our captain has given us the word, and we must follow him. Can *ye* tell us better what to do? Come, turn captains yourselves; but away from our troop first."

And therewith all were silent, and reanimated with the most cheerful obedience. Away they flew over the trench. Not a horse stumbled—not a single one fell; and reaching the other side, they trotted on against the enemy's flank, under the continual cover of a low range of hills that ran between them and the trench. Otto rode near enough to be able to see over them, without himself being seen. Denser grew the dust of the battle-field, and wilder the cry of the contending hosts, while the Finlandish troops were seen pressing to the advance. Now it seemed the right time to leap the trench again, and rush to the onslaught. Otto's heart throbbed with impatience and yet with doubt, whilst thus on the brink of hazarding his first essay as a captain. "Not too soon, and not too late!" said he within himself, as he repeated the words of his commander, and took a keen survey of the enemy's line. "Would it be too soon now?" he murmured. But the next instant, in a loud voice, "Ay, by heavens, methinks this is the lucky moment; and one may best lay to whilst one can!" So saying, he swung his flashing blade over his head. With the quick turn of lightning his troop flew onward to the right, cleared the trench amid tumultuous huzzas, and fell rear and flank on the foe. Old Sir Hugh's pupil had cleverly watched his time. The pagan horse and foot set up a frightful howl, and dashed in disorder from the trench; whilst the Norman troopers, without troubling themselves about fugitive stragglers, sped fleetly onwards wherever denser groups might be seen. "Down with them! At them again! Sons of the Norman! Down with them! At them!" cried Otto; and every lip caught up the cry, and each rose with an exulting shout in his stirrups. Now they flew apart with the speed of the storm, to hinder the gathering of the broken ranks; and now they closed again with the force of flame, when some concentrated assault was to be made, or, like avenging gods, they scoured in their rattling mail over the field. The Swedes pressed onward with a loud shout of victory, and the pagans were stricken with still wilder disorder; many of them were slain, and many of them gnashed their teeth in chains.

But the old general came riding over the crimson heath,

and kissing the young knight of Trautwangen, he cried aloud to his troops, "Dear Swedish Christians, behold here a young saplin, beneath whose shade the whole land may one day rest and be glad."

CHAPTER X.

MEANWHILE it happened that three young dames were riding with an escort of waiting-women and squires through a blooming wood in the beautiful country of Gascony. By the whole array of the merry band, it was easy to see that they were not bound on this or that journey, but merely on a pleasant jaunt in the embowering forest, where the sunshine flashed so fairly through the network of the branches, and the breeze played on them so coolly from the neighbouring sea. Hither and thither floated many a pretty lay from the lips of the ladies and their squires up to the blue summer sky; while the birds opened their little throats to vie with them in song. "Oh, how different is it now," said the middle lady of the three to her right-hand companion, "and how much better too, my Blancheflour, than when the ring was always entangling us in unhappy variance!"

"Yet I ever beheld it as I do now, Gabriele," returned the other, "sparkling on thy white bosom, without any envy, as it hung from its little gold chain. If it had rested with me, thou hadst long ere this have called it thine own, and my brother's silver-gray charger, that now is bearing thee, would never have been ridden lame in the lists."

"Dost thou pity the silver-gray?" said Gabriele, with a smile. "Methinks thou hast no cause to do so. As he now ambles on with us on our light jaunts over mead and wood, till perhaps the wounded limb pains him, and, warned by the noble animal's uneasy toil, I alight and nurse him with double tenderness,—is not this better for him than being spurred on by thy brother among the Moorish knights in Spain, and falling to the care of some sturdy horseman, in case of receiving a hurt?"

"Thou art right, I think," replied Blancheflour, as she stroked down the mane of the silver-gray. "I wish thee joy of thy wound, good, pretty creature!" said she.

"That depends," said the lady on the left, in a graver tone, "whether or no the silver-gray is contented with thy benison. He looks to me like a true knightly animal, and, in that case, no tender nursing will make amends to him for the career of renown of which he is debarred."

"What harsh things thou canst say, Bertha!" rejoined

Gabriele. "Wert thou not oftentimes so wondrously gentle, with that maidenly soft mien of thine, I might anon be tempted to take thee for some masked knight, and be on my guard with thee."

"Do not so, my noble hostess," said Bertha, in a soft and kindly tone. "In the whole world thou findest none more devoted to thee than me, whom thou receivest and protectest so hospitably. Besides, art thou not my kinsman Otto's betrothed bride? aud whom, then, could I cherish in greater faithfulness and honour?" Gabriele drew a painful sigh, aud in the depth of her musings pressed Bertha's hand in hers.

At this moment a dainty squire dashed forth from the thicket. Brightly flashed the gold embroidery on his blue-velvet jerkin; little bells of gold ran sweetly on the saddle and head-gear of his palfrey. At sight of the ladies he made halt, leaped from his seat, and bending the knee before Gabriele: "Lady," quoth he, "my lord and master, the Baron de Montfaucon, craves permission to present himself before thee, together with a noble guest, who bears him company." A lovely flush of red mantled on the cheek of the beautiful damsel; she waved her tender hand in token of greeting.

"Good squire," said she, "give welcome in my name to the noble baron and his guest. Thanks to the bright summer day that hath lured me forth thus early to meet him!" Then the squire bounded lightly on his steed, and, with a deep obeisance, galloped back into the green shade of the wood.

"Who can the guest be that thy brother brings with him?" said Gabriele, as she turned to Blancheflour.

"If it were but a minstrel!" replied the latter; "but it is surely not such a one." And here she paused, and her blushing face drooped in strange embarrassment to the little forget-me-nots on the fresh green lawn.

Forthwith Sir Folko's mail of blue and gold was seen brightening through the bushes. The chestnut steed with its coal-black mane, which he had ridden since the wounding of the silver-gray, sprang gleaming from the shade. The knight lowered his lance to the earth; then bounding lightly from the saddle, he threw the weapon to one of his squires, and with courtly grace, and his beautiful falcon-gentil on his hand, he approached the ladies. But his companion, who leaped at the same moment from his trim Arabian charger, and drew near to the fair damsels with as comely a greeting, was indeed no minstrel, but one of the noblest of youthful warriors. Round his slender, well-knit frame floated the rich attire of a Moor, of unequalled beauty both in texture and embroidery; a white turban of the finest lawn enwound his brow, confined by a rich egret of diamonds, and surmounted by a heron-plume of royal splendour.

"Lady," said Folko, with low obeisance to Gabriele, "allow me to present to thee Prince Mutza, the bravest of all Moorish knights, who fought with us on Granada's plains."

Mutza bowed his head before Gabriele and the other dames with the most refined air of courtesy; then, in a tone of gloom, he added, "Were I so distinguished a knight as the baron is pleased to make me, he would not feel thus sorely ashamed of his victory. He forgets, sooth, in the presence of the loveliest ladies whom I ever yet beheld, to announce that I am his prisoner, which, by the by, it can scarcely be worth his while to do. Know, then, ye fair stars of earth, that, albeit Prince Mutza now boweth his head only to the radiance of beauty, he ranks but among the lowliest of the knights of his fatherland, at least since he has been a captive; in which guise he craves of thee, loveliest image of woman, that thou wilt take from him the weapon which his noble-minded conqueror hath left too long in his hands." So saying, he had unhasped the golden diamond-studded sabre from the silver chain at his girth, and in reverential posture he now held it towards Gabriele.

The beautiful damsel accepted it, moving at the same moment, as if to dismount from her silver-gray, when Mutza, starting quickly to his feet, assisted her as she lightly sprang to the earth.

"You made your own self my servant, princely sir," said she; "but it beseemeth noble ladies to have armed servants:" and therewith she hung the sabre at his side, again allowed him to assist her on her steed; and in company of himself and Folko, who in the meanwhile had greeted his sister and Bertha, they rode back to the castle.

On a high veranda, which caught the last glow of evening as it streamed from the far mirror of the sea, and where the fragrant flower-beds of the garden enwreathed them in perfume, sat the three ladies and the knights, diverting themselves with the lute and the song, and the recital of graceful adventure. In this soft circle, Folko and Mutza sought to outvie each other in noble grace and finished manner, as they had formerly done on the battle-field in knighthood's prowess; and if victory there stood long in abeyance, no less indecisively did it sport with them here.

Distressed by Mutza's look of flame, Gabriele succeeded in evading those lightning-shafts by a thousand turns of her eye, or bright sallies of wit, and inclining with an enchanting air to the Baron de Montfaucon, without seeming to cast a slight on the Moorish prince. That little head that was so prone to droop, Blancheflour gladsomely raised, while her revered and beloved brother was near her; and her sweet face beamed so beauteously, that the emblem of the white rose seemed scarcely enough to betoken such a rich flood of radiance. Bertha alone sat immersed in silent, and one might almost say moody reverie; and no honeyed speeches from Folko or Mutza, nor gay banter from Gabriele, nor Blancheflour's pretty signs and entreaties, could that evening win from her either story or song. Thus, at last, in that cheerful group, she was almost forgotten, or at most only gazed on, without being addressed, not unlike a beautiful statue about which four living forms were moving, without either understanding her or being understood by her.

In the midst of that cheerful parley, the Arabian took up a guitar, and sang the following words:

"Gloomily o'er gloomy mountains
Passed the captive knight Alarbe,
Darker 'mid the blooming landscape
Was his fallen visage shrouded:
For like venom to the angry
Is the merry laugh of mortals.
But in pleasance-ground enchanted,
Here are beams of heaven's beauty;
Like the lustrous stars of ether,
Gentle eyes, ye glisten round him!
Sooth, for you his bosom gloweth
Like a bed of flaming blossom;
Sooth, both soul and sense are melted
To a stream of sweet complaining.
But when farther he shall wander
O'er his lonesome path to-morrow,
Ah! how wildly in his bosom
Will those flaming blossoms kindle;
And when they in ashes smoulder,
Sorrow's stream will bear him onward."

Now Folko took a guitar from Blancheflour's lap, and sang responsively to the prince:

"Oh, would the merry morning light
Could find a morrow never, never!
Oh, would the stars that bloom so bright
Could bloom as brightly on for ever;
And o'er a changeless field of wit
Content to flit,
With knightly bards three ladies fair,
In airy sport, would ever wander there!
Ah! those sweet times are flown,
And Merlin's mighty spell no longer known!
Then dare my Carthagenian princely game
Be trusted unto lovely dame,

Until,—when I,
Returning from my jaunt, shall hither fly,—
Again the castle-gate
Shall ope to me in hospitable state,
And welcome me, nor then be wanting
Sweet greeting glance and word enchanting?
Ah, no! too soon shall we be driven away
By that same look that lures us so to stay;
And—if 'twere not vainglory
To cite the bravest names of olden story—
The sad Darius hand in hand will wander
Upon his way with sorrowing Alexander."

"Right gladly would I keep Darius here till Alexander should come again," said Gabriele, with a smile, "if the conqueror, on his part, could consent to rest him, for a week at least, in the company of his sweet sister in the castle; and, more than all, if his words were not merely the pretty sport of song, but the genuine language of his heart."

"What a week have you lavished on me," said Folko, with a graceful reverence to Gabriele; "and what a month on the prince! for so long, at least, it will last till I come back from Normandy, whither I am summoned by my duties as banneret and baron of the realm. Mutza, thou art this lady's prisoner; and from this spot must thou contrive thine exchange for the noble Castilian in the manner thou hadst before resolved upon."

Mutza took his seat at Gabriele's feet. "This is a prisoner's place," said he; "but one thing I tell thee, Montfaucon,—thou hast put me in fairy bonds, and that is against our compact. Knowest thou, moreover, that in this wise thou givest me back my word of honour, and that I am now free to escape as best I can?"

"The fairy bonds may see to that," replied Folko; "but, captive, if that be thy place, henceforth let any one rather be called a free-man than me." And so saying, he let his sword, sash, and baldric fall to the ground, and sank down beside Mutza at Gabriele's feet.

Now Blancheflour sang to the guitar, which Folko had resigned to her:

"I speak a riddle; who shall render
The answer fair?
A queen in more than queenly splendour
Sits throned in air;
Her name, her loveliness unfoldeth
An angel's dower;
And with an easy sway she holdeth
Her fairy power:

For at her little feet reposing
Two forms recline,
In war's dread rage and bloody closing
More wont to shine.
A lion one, a tawny rover
On Tigris' strand,
The while his eagle-mate flew over
The northern land.
And now they eye the queenly fairy,
And wait their doom;
And she will choose—ye listeners wary,
O tell me—whom?"

Blancheflour had only sung in sportive jest; but the three hearts into which she had unwittingly hurled the flaming brand were quick to blaze. Both eagle and lion, with that changeless eye and eager glance in which their whole souls were seated, looked inquiringly up to the queen for their doom; while she, with a downcast glance and crimsoned cheek, seemed, as she sat between them, to drop a green twig which she chanced to have in her hand towards the head of the baron. Scarcely perceptible as was the motion, yet it appeared an almost magnetic sway. In the meanwhile, Bertha had seized the guitar, and with a few more chords of thrilling plaintiveness, she had aroused the rest from their reverie. Every eye was turned upon her, as though a picture were becoming musical, whilst she sang the following words:

"Where is the coal-black harness,
With glistening silver sheen?
And where the light-brown war-horse,
So noble and so keen?

The silver mail is vanish'd,
The noble steed hath strayed;
They saw it gallop fleetly
Around a broken blade.

And lost, too, is its master,
With mail and falchion fair:
Ah! if he ever cometh,
The bride will braid her hair.

Till then, all mournly, sadly,
Sing ye, whose hearts do bleed:
Alas! for hero-harness!
Alas! for noble steed!"

Folko sprang to his feet till his armour rang again, and hastily girding on his sword and sash, he bade Gabriele farewell. When he came again, he added, he would summon Mutza with the sound of the clarion to the neighbouring mead, near the wood. Gabriele dared not venture on remonstrance, though, haply, beneath the dark veil of evening, the warm dew would trickle down her cheeks and Folko's. Pensively did the baron kiss his sister; while in brushing past Bertha, "Thanks," said he softly, "thanks to thee, severe and noble maiden!" He heard not the astonished Arab demanding the reason of his hasty departure, and repeating with a laugh, forsooth, yet not without a solemn meaning, that he no longer held himself bound by his word of honour. Rapidly hurried the noble Montfaucon down the steps of the veranda into the castle; and soon the fair dames above saw him trot out of the gateway with his train, bend low his flashing gold helm in the glimmering light of the stars as a last salute, and then, giving his charger the rein, fly off to the darkling woodland.

CHAPTER XI.

Some weeks afterwards the three damsels were taking their pleasure on the seashore, enjoying the breeze that blew so cool over the waters, and diverting each other with that lively chit-chat, of which the most unconstrained confidence and the sweetest retirement could beguile their blooming lips.

"Thy brother," said Bertha to Blancheflour, "has not done right withal in leaving us all alone in the castle with the Moorish prince; and, above all, since this strange visitant is anon assuring us that his word of honour shall henceforth be unbinding. I know he means it in jest, but I am terribly afraid of him."

"There you are playing the grave German girl again," said Gabriele, smiling. "So prudish and shy! Yet there are few men, you must confess, who surpass the noble Mutza in refined demeanour, princely grace, and courtly sprightliness of tongue. Moreover, I have seldom seen one so handsome; and one bright image more in our halls is no despicable ornament to our castle."

"Ah!" replied Bertha, slowly and musingly; "do ye both think so? When I turn the matter over, I cannot altogether say that you are wrong; but it would scarcely have occurred to me of itself. I grant you he is tall and slim, has beautiful eyes, an arched forehead, and a kingly gait; when he dances the toca, with loose and fluttering turban, a pretty sight it is to look upon, and almost like some visibly-revealed fairy-tale.

But when he opens that mouth of his, full of those long, sharp, white teeth, I feel as though I had a tame tiger beside me, which may every moment return to his former wildness, and scatter ruin around him. The tiger, too, people say, is a beautiful creature; but I, once for all, should never have a taste for him."

"And what says my pretty Blancheflour to this?" asked Gabriele. That gentle form started up from her dreamy musings: "In good truth," said she, "I know not who he is; but just now, again, I hear those sweet sounds wafted from the sea-cliff." The two other damsels smiled at Blancheflour's absence of mind; but they were hindered in their parley by soft, enchanting notes that came stealing over the waters from the very place she had spoken of, and breaking upon their ears in nearly the following words:

"O! give me wings, that they may waft me to her
Through twilight air;
And in a net of dreamy gold I'll woo her,
Enwoven there.
Ah! fleeting phantom, cease the fond endeavour,
And hope no more,
Or live in love's soft plaintive song for ever
On this lone shore."

The song died away. "Thus I often hear him sing," said Blancheflour, as the tear glistened in her eye: "and even when the moonlight is streaming down from heaven, he sends those sweet tones through the flowery trellis-work of my window. Think ye, then, sisters, that it is Master Aleard?"

They had no time to reply; for, advancing from a clump of trees that fronted them, divers forms appeared in motley array. They were men with monstrous beards, and of strange attire; and suddenly making halt, they talked with vehement gestures, glancing and pointing towards the beautiful damsels. The latter were about to retreat in terror, when a like number of frightful forms appeared behind them on the brow of the hill; whilst some of them, in swift career, came darting down the slope, and uniting with those under the trees, drew a circle round the ladies. Then, crossing their hands on their breasts, they all bowed reverentially before them, till their heads almost touched the earth, adding thereby to the fearful hideousness of the scene. From the midst of them stepped forth Mutza before the astonished ladies, more gorgeously apparelled than ever, and glittering in gold and jewels, and divers colours, followed by two youths of equal splendour, in Arabian costume.

"Upbraid me not," said he, with a graceful bow to Gabriele, "if I tell you that I am about to depart; and tremble not, when ye hear that ye must bear me company. I lead you to a bright and joyous existence, and have sent for these two young knights, of a race princely as mine, to aid me, promising them that they will here find fairer flowerets than in Mahomet's paradise.—And have I kept my word?" said he, turning to his comrades; while one kneeled before the beautiful Blancheflour as she dropped lifeless on Gabriele's arm; and the other threw himself at Bertha's feet, who scornfully turned her back upon him, and strode towards a little mouldering wall, on which was a time-worn cross of stone. She clasped the stem of the cross with her left arm, signed the young Arabian away with her right, and gazed, as if in deep thought, on the blue vault above her.

In the mean while, Gabriele had recovered her consciousness, and breathed more freely, as she boldly reviled Mutza for violating the rights of hospitality and his own word of honour.

"Twice," cried he, "I declared myself, in the presence of Montfaucon, utterly released from my word; and when thy heavenly beauty lights up my every sense like the dazzling sun, enkindling all in the bright hues of the rainbow, who can seek for rhyme or reason in what I, poor dazzled wight, may do?" And so saying, he wound his arms round Gabriele, and with many a caress and soothing word he bore her shrieking for aid to a light shallop, that in the meantime had been rowed to the shore. The young Arabian caught Blancheflour in his arms, and bore her away after his guide; but when the other Moorish knight was advancing with a bolder step towards Bertha, "I call God and man, and heaven and earth, to witness," cried she, with inspired voice, "what heinous outrage is being committed here. Whether a miracle will happen to avenge and arrest it, I know not; but beware, ye wicked men; that may indeed happen. And this I tell ye,—and I feel sure of it as of life itself,—that he who drags me with him to the ship, brings death and ruin upon his own head."

The Moorish knight recoiled in terror from the angry maiden as she stood there, in all the glory of evening, showering down her reproaches upon him from the trunk of the cross. His warrior-band withdrew timorously to the shore; and when Bertha again raised her threatening hand and signed her lingering foe away, he shrieked aloud, "There is a demon in her," and, staggering away to the boat, he at once put to sea.

The maiden had not yet stirred from her post, when a pale youth in a minstrel's cloak came winging his steps along the strand.

"In the name of heaven, cried he, "have the Moors borne away Blancheflour?" And scarcely had the "Yes" passed from Bertha's lips, than he answered swiftly as the wind: "Forthwith send a messenger to her brother. I must make my way after them." And again he began to fly, rather than to run, along the shore; nor, till he had vanished from her sight, did Bertha become aware that Master Aleard had spoken to her.

CHAPTER XII.

At this season the storms of autumn were howling over the northern mountains; and on the very same evening on which his betrothed bride was carried off, Otto stood on a hot and shadowy point of the battle-field. He had alighted from his light-brown, and clambered up a steep and narrow ravine, in order there to bar the way of the advancing pagans; for they outflanked the Christian army on all sides, and the latter was already giving ground. The princely general called after the young hero, and asked what he could now be about, since he was almost alone. Otto gave answer: "But then the pass is narrow; they can only come one by one against me, and one by one they shall find their man." And there he really stood, like a guardian cherub, at that mountain-portal, opposing his fair face and comely form to the black swarm of little hideous pagans that came buzzing forth against him. In many a flashing circle flew his tireless whirring blade, and every time it descended, it rose again crimsoned with gore, and spirted little drops of blood all around him. Already there lay, as it were, a bulwark before him of shapeless and bloody corpses; and it seemed as though this stubborn mole gradually made the broken billows recoil. Then a bright lightning-gleam flashed upon the throng, and the horse-tail on a warrior's helm was seen fluttering on high. A Swedish and pagan hero, tall and handsome, and arrayed in a shining war-suit, rushed in his rattling mail against Otto. His spear flew whistling past the young knight's head, and forthwith his sword-strokes fell thick as hail on the eagle helmet.

"Thou slewest my brother," cried the infuriate foe; "full well do I know thee in thy silver-black mail. Dost thou remember how thou smotest him on the wooded hill? Thy javelin dashed him from the chestnut steed. Now, blood for blood! Now vengeance lights on thee! Heigh! heigh! Thou wardest thee in vain. Odin here! Odin and Swerker's sword!"

But Otto's blade was keener still. With one of its ponderous blows, dealt directly over the crest of the helm, the pagan knight began to reel. The conqueror seized the falling youth by the horse-tail plume, dragged him to him across the rampart of corpses, and hurled him to the small knot of followers in his rear.

"See him safe," he cried, "and tender him well! I shall require him at your hands!"

At sight of this the Finlanders fell back amain, and began talking in a murmur. It was not possible to understand what their evil plot was about; only chance discordant sounds fell on Otto's ear. But he grasped the spear which the pagan knight had cast at him, and hurled it into the midst of the group. Two of the foe fell to the earth, bathed in blood; while the rest flew with a wild howl asunder, and crouching singly behind the cliffs and bushes, they sent a rattling shower of bolts on Otto's war-suit. Trusting to his well-wrought mail, the young knight stood motionless at his post, save that he turned his polished targe to the left of him, in order the more securely to bar the narrow way, and to cover the more lightly-armed warriors behind him. The shooting continued, but did harm to no one.

"Sorry fighting," said Otto to himself; "it is of no use to them, and makes time hang heavy with us." So, by way of pastime, he began counting the shafts that recoiled from his silver-black harness.

All at once there was a rustling close behind him. He looked round, and the visage of a pagan grinned on him from a narrow covert hollow among the tangled bushes. Then indeed his Asmundur blade stood him in good stead, for it cleft the grinning head in twain; but a host of Finlandish warriors came thronging after their fallen leader with a hideous howl; it was almost as though the goblins of the hills had entered into league with the heathens, and were now coming forward to their aid, or, at any rate, had revealed to them the time-olden nooks and passes in the mountains.

Otto and the few Swedes with him—for the Normans were fighting on horseback in the plain—made a firm stand both before the hollow and the footpath. But their numbers were lessened by the absence of those who had borne off the pagan knight by their master's order; and it became very plain, both from the increasing multitude and vigour of the enemy, as likewise from their own weariness of arm, that the moment of defeat was nigh. At this very crisis another protruded a hideous banner from forth the hollow, on which some dragon-like idol was blazoned, crying, "Now, too, your god is here: forwards, bold Finlanders, forwards!" The foe pressed on with a merry huzza; but Otto, slinging his shield behind him, grasped his sword with both hands, and, in desperate fury, cleft a path to the loathsome banner. Wherever he struck, the wound was death. And soon he clutched the fearful standard, tore it with gigantic strength from the grasp of the bearer, and hurled it mightily over the cliff.

"Your god is in the abyss!" cried he; "try what ye can do without him, ye host of madmen!"

For a moment the pagan hosts fell back in terrified surprise; but soon their angry howl grew wilder, their advance more furious. Then Otto, fighting with the last remnant of his strength, began a strain of the solemn cast which in those northern lands he had learned to frame and sing. It ran thus:

"Come, pile me stones, heroic stones—
A token in this vale of death!
Here manfully the Swedemen fought;
Here gallantly the Swedemen fell!"

And his followers sang after him:

"Here manfully the Swedemen fought;
Here gallantly the Swedemen fell!"

And thereupon, in accordance with their song, they began cleaving right and left, with all their might and main; and though the greater part of them were already red with blood, exhaustion made them deadly pale.

But of a sudden there was a rumbling as of brazen thunder in the rear of the Finlandish warriors on the hills. The song sounded from above:

"But cheerily from his bark he sprang,
The tall and stalwart Arinbiorn;
Sharply he fastened upon the foe
With his pointed fangs. Ye foemen, fly!"

At the same moment Otto looked up, and beheld the golden vulture-wings peering over the mountain-heights, and Arinbiorn's shield too, large and bright as the moon, with his whole mailed band of heroes; and now, like a shower of hail, the lances of the Normans rattled down upon the Finlandish throng. "They fly! they fly!" came the shout from the plain; "at them, Swedes!" And "At them, Swedes!" cried Otto, with his gathered band. All forgot their weariness and their wounds; and up the rocks, down the rocks, they dashed on with the flashing sword of vengeance after the routed foe.

CHAPTER XIII.

EVENING already spread her mantle over the valleys. The storm raged more wildly, and the clouds drew a darker pall over the sky. Otto stood alone in a tangled thicket, whither he had been lured by the lust of fight; but neither friend nor foe was near him now, and, spent with conquest, he sank upon the earth among the leaves of autumn. After a brief and refreshing repose, he gazed around him, without being able to descry any familiar object that might set his course aright. He clambered up a leafy height before him, in the hope of gaining a more extensive view. But the copse grew thicker as he ascended, and instead of espying the darkling night-sky between the branches, he could see nothing but a bristling forest of firs towering over the oaks and beeches, and stretching out its needle-like arms through the green trellis before him. Like one long wall of green, the fir-trees wove their boughs behind the beeches. "Scarce a bird can thread this maze," said Otto; and at the same moment he remembered that he must have heard the like words before. He was endeavouring to recollect himself, when the howling of a wolf caught his ear. The sound was plaintive rather than savage; and on drawing nearer, he descried a grave-mound just on the boundary-line between the firs and beeches. A white she-wolf was lying upon it, and uttering that mournful cry; but on Otto's nearer approach, she rose ready for the fight, and two sharp rows of teeth shone in fearful array from her blood-red maw. Otto hurled his spear at her; when an old man, in a long habit, came slowly up the hill from the other side, holding a large crucifix in lieu of a staff, and the wolf fled affrighted into the fir-wood. But the story of the hermits and the wolf, which Heerdegen had formerly related to Tebaldo and him on the banks of the Maine, flashed suddenly on Otto's recollection. "Can it really be?" said he to himself, in a musing tone—"ah, yes; we are on the Finlandish border-mark. Can this really be the grave of the knightly recluse?"

"Yes," replied the old hermit, "it is indeed my poor son's grave; and as I am just going to pray there, I would fain bid you leave me in peace, noble knight. But plunge not into the Finlandish forest; it is a weird hour now."

Otto turned away, pondering in strange alternation of thought on a tale which he had received with a cast of doubt, yet to the truth of which he now was himself a witness; and he strode with a quickened step down the leafy slope, led on by a sound as of horns and trumpets from below, which seemed to betoken the neighbourhood of commingling friends and foes.

But, in the valley beneath, all was still as he had left it. The shroud of night grew darker and darker ; and he could not help thinking that his own senses must have played him false, when he seemed to hear the noise of battle in the grave-like silence of that lonely region. Then again, wafted on the northern breeze, came the clang of warlike instruments. Still more anxiously pondering on the cause of this, and gazing still more eagerly round him, Otto at length found that he must incline his head backwards to catch a glimpse of the harmonious choir that was sailing far on high, through the blue ocean of the night-sky, in white and close array, like a flock of winged lambs, and cleaving with heavy wing their invisible path. The legend of the wild army, which he had brought with him from Germany, now flashed upon his remembrance. He wondered whether this might not be something of like sort, and yet it was so different again ; solemn and thrilling, to be sure, but the minstrelsy was lovely, and not at all wild.

Suddenly a heavy-armed warrior came rattling forth from among the cliffs. Uncertain whether he had friend or foe before him, Otto planted himself in the posture of war, whilst the stranger, without taking notice of him, swept hastily by. But a single glance at that warrior-visage bereft Otto of strength, froze up his marrow, and made his blood run cold with horror. It was his own face, the very face of the young knight of Trautwangen himself, that shone upon him from beneath the strange helmet in the light of the rising moon.

"It is not true, it cannot be !" said Otto aloud, as he broke the long silence of awe-struck astonishment. "Here I stand, firm and hale, with my trust reposing in God ; how, then, could I be gliding along the rugged cliffs at the same time, in hideous mockery of myself ? Am I crazed ? Or is it a Finlandish goblin that thus shamelessly dares to affright me ? I should have looked boldly in the face of the witless juggler, and thrown up my beaver. My darkening vizor alone it was that gave him spirit. With eye to eye, I wot, he would never have had effrontery enough thus to sport with my image."

Then came the sound as of the gentle voice of woman from the heights above him. "Otto, Otto," it cried, "wild Otto, glide not so rashly down the precipice."

Horror thrilled Otto to the very heart. He stood for a moment as if paralysed in all his limbs. But soon he roused himself with a violent effort ; and looking upward, he shouted in the direction of a moss-grown watch-tower, whence that call had sounded : "Otto is here," cried he, "standing firm on his feet, and not scrambling or bounding in mad sport over the crags. God only knows who that is that does so. But if the fellow says he is Otto von Trautwangen, he lies. I only am he."

From the moon-bespangled casements of the watch-tower a white form seemed to shrink back at these words; but the upper half of his strange counterpart rose behind the ledge of a rock, turning its frightfully confirmed semblance to the moon. "Who goes below there?" it shouted across the dell. "Let him take care that I do not fall foul of him; I am in no very prime mood. He may call himself Otto as long as he likes, for all I care: my name is Ottur, and the brain-struck woman of the tower is calling after me. It were better for one to have his ears about him, before he has any thing to say. Ottur was called, and not Otto. Only let that dotard below there open his mouth again before he is spoken to, and I'll cleave his head in a thousand pieces."

"Come down, if you have heart enough!" cried Otto, raising his beaver. But in a moment his counterpart turned deadly pale with terror, and dropped with a rattling fall behind the rocky wall.

Now Arinbiorn's voice came sounding along the valley; the vulture-pinions peered on high, and the golden shield flashed through the branches. Otto rang him answer with the hilt of his sword on his mail, and with a loud huzza the sea-king flew into his truant comrade's arms. "The princely leader is asking for thee," said he, "as for his only son. About a hundred of the noblest warriors are on the mountains in search of thee, and God knows with what hearty eagerness I have sought thee; and so for me, too, was reserved the joy of finding thee. Oh, a thousand times welcome, then, young sapling, that bearest victory as another does its blossoms in the spring-tide. We have been chasing them, comrade, like the hart and the roe. We have made the Swedish woods too hot for them for many a long year; and as soon as autumn and winter are past, we will hunt them up in their own lairs. Hast thou heard the news? The pagan banner, that thine own arm won and dashed down into the abyss, was brought up again by one of thy comrades in war. The Finlandish captives howled when they saw it, and cried out that their god had forsaken them. And hast thou been told that the young Swede whom thou tookest prisoner was the brave Swerker, the hope of the whole pagan army? Oh, my tongue leads me astray in the sweet sense of victory, and the joy of having thee once more. But say, why standest thou dreaming thus, as if fettered to the earth? What has befallen thee, young conqueror? Art thou wounded?"

"No," replied Otto; "but I have received a shock from all sorts of frightful things in the valley."

"Ay, indeed," said Arinbiorn; "these northlands of ours enclose many a wondrous sight. They are like strange and monstrous riddles, cast upon the ocean-tide beneath the gleam of our northern sky; so that it is no wonder if even a hero's heart should beat quicker at the sight of them, when he comes from distant parts."

"Hark, now! there, for example," said Otto, as he pointed to the dark heavens overhead, whence that mighty minstrelsy was descending again in martial flow, and the dense white train sweeping onward on resounding wing.

"Is it nothing but that?" replied the sea-king. "Those are no evil wizard forms, but only tuneful swans, winging their autumnal flight from our country to the south. Thou mayest well gladden thine ear with them, and bid fear be gone. Hark, now, how merrily they sing! And look, with what a bright span of white they glisten!" But whilst he was thus following their flight with his eye through the blue realms of air, the old watch-tower met his glance, and he started back like a wounded man. "Yes, Otto!" cried he, with a shudder; "now I can very well believe that horrible things have befallen thee in this valley. There stands the tower of which I formerly told thee. Up there it was that I saw Blancheflour's image on the glass."

"Shall we make towards it?" said Otto. "Shall we at once tear aside the veil from mysteries that both allure and affright us? Of a truth, I think the veil itself is more fearful than all that can be lurking behind it."

Arinbiorn remained a moment in thought. "Night, my gallant comrade," replied he at last, "is a mighty leaguer with such foes. Let us not enter the unblest pile just now. Though, sooth, if thy mind be really made up—" They both were silent. All manner of ghastly visions rose before Otto's fancy, and one more than all the rest. His fell counterpart, he thought, would perhaps be sitting at a table when they went in, and reading in a book full of devilish characters. The sea-king haply noticed the inward horror of his friend. "Besides, we have a long step to the camp," said he. Whereupon both the knights strode hastily down the mountain-side, and Arinbiorn wound many a merry blast on his horn. He said it was to give the other searchers a sign of his good luck; but it might as likely be to scare from the heart of himself and companion the dismal imaginings of the night.

The morning-star was already sparkling in heaven when they descried the camp-fires on a wide plain at the foot of the frontier hills. Arinbiorn's horn, with its well-known salute, awakened the Norman knights, who were slumbering on the outer line of the bivouac. They leaped upon their steeds. and, with a loud huzza, they galloped off to meet their dear leader Otto; whilst the light-brown, defying all control, bounded forward in advance of them, and then standing still by his lord, he laid his head coaxingly on his shoulder, and drowned, with many a gladsome neigh, both the acclaims of the horsemen and the clash of their ringing shields.

CHAPTER XIV.

A BRIGHT and fragrant morning in autumn beheld the whole army in fair array and glistening armour on the plain. The captains rode up and down the lines, rendering their thanks for the achievements of yesterday's fight, whilst the horns blew many a merry note of cheer.

But there was one among that warrior-throng whose heart could not quite yield itself up to the mirthfulness of the hour, and he was Sir Otto von Trautwangen. The apparition of his counterpart peered forth like a darker shade from the gloom of the bygone night, and dimmed all the gladsome images of the morning. And even though horror became mute and pale before the brightness of day and the greeting of his friends, yet he could not help frequently summoning it up again, just as we are very often unable to keep from straining our eyes in pursuit of some object that troubles and perplexes us. Even with thy mind's eye hath it often happened to thee thus, dear reader; and in such cases be of good cheer, and do as Otto did. He, forsooth, could not hinder the troublesome guest from breaking stormily on his soul, but like manful hero he stood his ground; and at last, looking as though the strange disquieter were no longer there, he remained what he had ever been—a gallant and merry-hearted knight!

The princely leader came riding along the line. His greeting was most friendly; and halting on a little mound that fronted his centre, he brandished his flashing spear in the crimson gleam of morning, and rang it three times against his shield, till the loud alarum echoed again from the mountains. The clarions threw in their merry strain; all the troops, both horse and foot, wheeled cheerily round to the rising ground, and formed a half-circle round their leader. The captains put spurs to their horses, and dashed up the ascent. Whilst they were closing their ranks, young Kolhein came brushing past Otto, and with a low obeisance, "Mighty warrior," said he,

"I too lent a hand yesterday with Arinbiorn's squadron. Prithee give me a kindly glance now."

Otto grasped his hand with hearty pressure, but was prevented replying by the voice of the old prince. Clearly and sonorously, like the sound of the bugle, it rose from his sturdy breast. Every warrior could hear the hoary hero rendering his thanks to them all, in the name of his fatherland and of his holy faith. Then he looked around him on the circle of chieftains, and his eye rested first on Arinbiorn. "Sea-king," said he, "you decided the day. Your coasting manœuvre, your quick landing at the right point, and your well-timed onset—such are the deeds of great generals only. But the eagle, who maintained the pass on our left with the victorious stroke of his pinion, till, with your vulture-speed, you could come to the rescue—that eagle we do not forget. Thanks to thee, my dear son;" and he reached forth his war-hand to the knight of Trautwangen. "From the very first moment of our acquaintance, I took thee for what thou art." And then, turning round, he took from the hand of a trooper the heathen banner which Otto had won, and delivering it over to him, "Thine own arm," said he, "hath already made this standard thine. But, as a momento of the love which all Swedes bear to thee, we have had a scroll inscribed upon it, with which we bid thee store it up in the hall of thy fathers for thyself and thy children's children."

Twined round the staff, Otto read the following words, emblazoned in glistening Runic characters:

"On Finland's border-line he fought,
And tore this banner from pagan hands;
Then he showered his blows for Sweden's sake—
Anon doth the Swede the conqueror prize.
Sir Otto is his name;
Von Trautwangen his knightly race."

"Thanks to thee, heroic prince—thanks!" said Otto, as he bowed his head; and smiling kindly on him, the old champion continued as follows: "Good knights and warriors all, a matter of the greatest weight lies before us. The foe is driven back within his borders: our peasants have their seed in the earth, and await the crops of the coming year in cheerful confidence. That the hopes they rest on a kindly heaven may not deceive them, and that the winter may be passed in peace and quiet, God hath charged us to see to. To this end, it is fitting that one or two of our companies stay the cold months of winter in the passes before us, doing the best for themselves that they can, and steadily maintaining their position. Truly, as folks report, elfs and goblins dwell there; and the season there, too, is very trying. But still, methinks, a true-born son of the north will, for once, be right glad to ply his sport with the like of them. Who of you may feel inclined that way?"

The chieftains stood in silent thought around him. It was easy to read, in the coutenances of many of them, that they would gladly address themselves to the task; but still they were fain to hold counsel with themselves beforehand on this matter and that. In the meanwhile, the eyes of Otto and Arinbiorn had met; and, as though he had signed them to him, they both rode up abreast to the general. "We would fain try our fortune in the mountains," said they; "but if the event be otherwise than you hope for, be well assured that our good will is not in fault."

Thereupon the old prince closed in rapture with their proposal, and bade all the chieftains to a parting banquet. It was, moreover, resolved, that the two comrades-in-arms should move off that very afternoon to the mountains—a boon which they themselves were fain to crave; for they were skilful soldiers, and knew very well how much the maintenance of such posts depends on the occupation of this or that superior height.

Whilst the exulting troops were again on their march towards the camp, Otto said to Arinbiorn, "I thank God that He again sends me into those parts where those fearful mysteries of mine inhabit: else they would always have lurked in the hidden depths of my heart. But now, with one manful, though maybe terrific, peep at them, all will be set right again."

"I feel just the same," replied the sea-king. "And now I will find out the way of the mirror, and get to the rights of it, or shiver my own mirror of life in the attempt, and thereby learn the mystery of those wondrously-fashioned glasses which we are wont to call our senses."

At the door of his tent Otto found the brave Swerker, his prisoner of yesterday's fight. The stripling riveted his gaze, in the deepest gloom, upon the earth; but when he heard Otto's light-brown trotting towards him, he raised his eyes and surveyed his conqueror, as it seemed, not without satisfaction and confidence.

"Hark ye, Swerker," said Otto; "we will make a covenant together."

"It depends," replied Swerker, "what that covenant may be."

"In the first place," said Otto, "thou must receive Christian doctrine."

"Shower thy doctrine on me as thou wilt," retorted Swerker; "if the doctrine be good for any thing, I will fain take it unto me; but if not, all thy teachings will be empty smoke."

"Of course," said Otto. "Thinkest thou I fight for a mere vain puff of wind?"

"Thy blows speak not the like of that," said Swerker.

"Well and good," quoth Otto. "Then I will send thee, on thy word of honour, to Germany. And there, in Suabia, on the banks of the Danube, thou must go in search of a knightly castle. It is called Trautwangen: my noble father lives in it; and he is called old Sir Hugh. Bear him greeting from his son; take him my banner; and give him tidings of all that hath happened here. Then come back hither again to me; tell me the whole story of thine errand; and listen to Christian doctrine. That it shall bear fruit in thee, Christ Himself is my warrant. Wilt thou now abide by all the conditions I have stated?"

"So Odin help me," answered Swerker.

"Thou shalt learn, I ween, a better oath than that," said Otto. "But now take the banner, and set off on thy way. Thou mayest choose thee one of the baggage-horses from those of my troop; and take a few pounds of silver from my travelling-pouch." And herewith they shook each other by the hand and parted.

The cups at the old prince's banquet were still unfathomed, and many a fine song of the northern lands had still to be sung, when Arinbiorn and Otto rose to take leave of him; and gladly as he saw them at his side, he dismissed them without demur, for he well knew the irrevocable value of time, and, above all, in war. With a voice that quivered with emotion, with sparkling eyes and outstretched hands, he spoke his blessing over the two youthful warriors, who now headed their companies of horse and foot, and marched forward to the mountains, filling the air, as they went, with sounds of glee and songs of victory.

The best positions, in hill or dale, were soon warily yet courageously chosen; sentinels were set for the protection of the whole mass and the connecting of single groups; and whilst the footmen began to erect a shelter for themselves, and the cavalry for their horses—which were the first objects of their care, being well aware that they would have to winter in those desert parts—Otto looked at the sea-king, and said, "I think our duty, for the present, is done, and the sun will not be setting just yet: we might at once go forth on our adventures, as they will rather lead us forwards than backwards."

"So I should say too," returned Arinbiorn. "On our front, a little to the left, the mysterious old tower must lie. Man is never properly at his ease, after all, till he has thrown some light upon that which was the cause of so much tumult within him; and so," continued he, in a louder tone, as he turned towards Kolbein, "kinsman, take the chief command upon thee for a time, and exert it gallantly. Otto and I have an errand in the mountains." Kolbein bent low in token of obedience, with the true grace of knighthood; and the two friends trotted rapidly forward through the shadowy vales.

Ere long they reached a mountain-path. Between the scattered shrubs that crouched beneath the overspreading branches of the loftier trees, the battlements of the old watch-tower were soon seen towering on high. Silently and slowly they rode towards it; and as the old gray pile became gradually more visible through the leaves, they beheld its glass lattices glistening brightly, bespangled by the crimson gleam of evening. "It is very strange," said Otto to his friend, "but now that the setting sun plays upon the glassy panes, the whole tower no longer appears so ugly and dismal to me. I feel as though I were riding to the halls of my home; nay, I never felt my heart so inly touched with hope and expectation as I do at this moment."

"What! is it so with thee too?" said Arinbiorn. "I have no home, so to say; for what is my motherless, fatherless, and joyless stronghold to me! But now a something comes over me, as though Blancheflour could be living here, and I be coming back to her from the pagan fray as her wedded lord. Ah, heavens, what an evening of bliss that would be! And thou, Otto, thou too mightest find thee at home here. Thou mightest perhaps prove to be Blancheflour's brother. Wouldest thou give me thy sister, if it were so?"

"Of course I would," said Otto, with a hearty grasp of Arinbiorn's involuntarily proffered hand. "If I had a sister, and she were pleasing in thine eyes, by this hand she were thy betrothed bride. But just now I can give little thought to bride and bridal, scarcely even to my own; so keenly do I feel as though I were coming back to scenes of home again, like some merry child after a distant pleasure-trip, and as though the smoke of the paternal hearth were wafted on the breeze to meet me. I could knock at the gate, and ask for my father, if I gave my spirits vent."

At this moment, they perceived a knight in harness standing before the tower, and seeming to speak with some one in the chambers above. That they might discover what the meaning of this was, they checked their steeds and tarried awhile in silence, without being noticed by the stranger, as his face was the other way.

The sweet voice of a woman issued from a window in the tower. "Thou wild youth, art thou angry with me?" it said. "Is my motherly care too much for thee? What else is a mother's care than a beam from God, that taketh up its abode wheresoever it can find the pure heart of woman, and filleth it with such a heavenly kindliness, that to form of earthly mould it often seemeth to be a pain?"

"But I am not your son," replied the froward knight. "What need ye to sorrow for me? Why must you be ever sending after me your doves, and swans, and dreams, with their endless warnings? Leave me alone, or aid me in the love I bear to the weird and beautiful maiden beyond the vale."

"No, wild man of war," retorted the voice. "God hath not in store for thee that thou shouldest win the weird and beautiful maiden. That were as though the flame should woo the flood; both are mighty, impetuous, and dread, but they are for ever incapable of union."

"What is this that thou sayest?" cried the stripling in anger. "I must surely know best myself what I will have. And ah! I will have naught else in the world, but the lovely and wondrous maiden only. If I win her not, then forsooth will I become a flame that shall waste all your Christian land for you. Thus I swear by Odin and the gods of the north! Help me, then. Though little, sooth, will such aid avail thee. For when she is mine, the more cheerily shall we sally forth in angry fellowship against your vassal fondlings. And mine she will be; my renown in fight, my true service and watchful tarrying at the rocky portal of her dwelling, stand pledged to me for that."

"Her heart itself is a rocky portal to thee," returned the same sweet voice, "which thou wilt never subdue. Yield thee, poor stripling, yield thee; and cease thy foolish threats. The Saviour from His throne in heaven guides His people to their weal and to victory. Didst thou not witness this so late as yesterday, poor wayward recreant?"

The knight set up a scornful laugh, and turned round as it seemed to descend the crags on the other side, when Otto rode forward from among the bushes.

"Yield thee, sir knight," cried he; "we are too much for thee. We will prove to thee now, by force of arms, that the voice in the tower was right."

The knight turned round upon Otto, and furiously hurled his spear. Then both of them, looking each other in the face, shouted as with one voice, "Ha! art thou here again, thou terrible one?" and turned away with the paleness of death. But Arinbiorn dashed impetuously forward: "What! shall the miscreant escape us?" he cried. But when he gained the edge of the rock, and the clambering knight glanced back upon him, he too turned pale with affright, and swaying round his roan with a violent effort, his ash-pale lips trembling the while, "Art thou, then, doubled?" said he to Otto. "And art thou, or that fugitive yonder, my rightful comrade?"

"Arinbiorn," said Otto, "yonder fugitive hath done outrage to God and the Redeemer; how canst thou ask whether I am thy comrade or not?"

The sea-king pressed his hand: "Thou hast spoken true words of comfort," said he. "Thus, then, I have thee, I embrace thee, and no hellish jugglery shall palm another upon me, thou dearly-loved, true-hearted friend."

And the soft sweet voice came sounding from the tower, as on the evening before: "Ah, Ottur, wild Ottur; dash not so rashly down the cliffs!"

CHAPTER XV.

"Where that voice is heard, I cannot stay away," said Otto. He alighted therefore, unbridled his light-brown, and with a stern tone bade him be quiet and orderly. He then went forward towards the gate of the tower. Arinbiorn seemed to shudder at the sight of the building; yet he could not think of remaining behind, while his dear comrade-in-arms led the way. So he followed in the knight of Trautwangen's steps, and ever and anon said to him as they went, "Dost thou know this voice, then, that lures thee to it with such magic power?"

"No, I know it not, nor whose it is," replied Otto; "but my whole heart becomes trusting and sorrowful at the sound of it."

At the entrance of the watch-tower appeared the tall and noble form of a lady, in snow-white attire, with a green veil thrown over her head and face; yet two gentle light-brown eyes, soft as those of the roe, gleamed through the light tissue of the veil, as the sun does through the closely-woven leaves. She stood still in astonishment before the knights. "Ha!" said she, "how quickly art thou come back, my Ottur; and how is it that thou hast donned the strange silver-black mail? And thou lookest so much more gentle and friendly too. Thou hast bethought thyself, I ween, of the wrong thou hast done me, and art now become more peaceful and lowly,—is it not so?"

"Lady," returned the knight, with a noble reverence, "my name is not Ottur, but Otto, with the title of Trautwangen; but better and more seemingly will I comport myself than he whom you call Ottur, if you deem me worthy to be a sharer in that maternal favour which you lavish on that savage man."

The lady stood awhile mute and motionless; then, in a soft,

low voice, she said at length, "So, then, it was no dream, when I thought I heard your voice yesterday in the rocky valley." Then she hung her head, and added, in a kindly tone, "Enter in at my door, Sir Otto von Trautwangen, and bring your comrade in with you, if you desire it. This mansion henceforth shall often give you the welcome of peace, and every friend of yours whom you shall choose to bring with you." Joyfully did Otto yield to her invitation, and with a hesitating step the sea-king followed him.

They went up a number of strangely wound staircases, through long resounding galleries, and chambers filled with all manner of wondrous furniture. In one of these, Arinbiorn pulled Sir Otto's arm, and signing towards a curtained frame: "That must be the mirror," whispered he, "or I am utterly mistaken."

"Noble lady," said Otto to his beautiful guide, "your goodness makes me bold to crave one boon. Will you grant me to look behind the curtain that hangeth from that golden frame?"

"If you desire it, Sir Otto," answered she, "you may do so. But thus much I tell you: there is a mirror behind it, on whose glassy lake the whole happiness of my life I once saw founder, and afterwards my every hope of ever regaining it. Since then I have always kept it shaded, and only at certain seasons do I leave it open, when its magic nature is impatient of being veiled, and when I myself am generally away; but if you wish it, it is at your service." She stepped forward to the purple curtain, and grasping its golden cord, she stood waiting for Otto's decision.

"God forbid," said the knight, "that I should covet aught that your will opposed!" And looking round upon Arinbiorn, he continued: "Or it were a matter on which the whole weal of thy life depended, my good comrade-in-arms; and, in all truth and honesty, I do not believe this mirror will yield it thee." In sorrowful token of dissent, the sea-king shook his head, and reverently bowed to the lady of the mansion, as though he besought her to step aside from the curtain. She did so, and led her two guests the way into another chamber. Here it seemed as though Arinbiorn, contrary to his usual wont, were altogether subdued, and shy, and estranged; whilst Otto, with childlike frankness, gave free utterance to his thoughts before his solemn hostess. She, on her part, testified her delight at this, by gentle words and a cheerful playfulness of tongue, that threw its gleam across the grave tenor of her speech, like the little glow-worm shining on the solemn moonlight.

"How well I feel, how truly well!" cried Otto, whilst they

all three took their places at a round table in a little dimly-lighted room. "One thing lies like a weight upon my heart, and preys like a canker-worm on my sense of joy. Is he, then, whom ye call Ottur really a man? Or can it be a hideous reflection of my own self—a wizard goblin, that has sufficient power over me to filch away my likeness, and to tear me in pieces in the snare of perplexing jugglery?"

"Calm yourself, gentle youth," said his solemn hostess. "Poor Ottur is really a man, a fond and warm-hearted creature. He puts his whole life at stake to win the favour of a pagan girl, who lives on the Finlandish mountains over against me in a time-olden chasm of the rock, whence she would send over your Christian land all the evil spirits over whom she holds sway, if my tower did not happily interpose to avert the storm. She and I keep up a silent, unseen, and yet mighty struggle together. Far over there, in the light of the rising moon, ye may behold her fortress cliff."

The knights stepped to the casement and gazed upon the savage scene, looking so dreary in the sad hues of autumn. A strange pile was seen towering from the rocks over the gray, dank mists, with an arched entrance in the form of a gateway. They could see far within it, through the varied arcades of ponderous and moss-grown stonework; and in the remote background rose the flare of a dim blue flame. "That is the glow of a horrid caldron," said their hostess. "It is there that the wizard maiden conjures forms as hideous as she herself is graceful and lovely."

"But who is the warrior in the heavy mail," said Otto, "who is pacing up and down before the entrance so gravely and slowly in the pale moonlight, like a soldier upon guard? How doth his horse-tail helm-plume flutter in the wind of autumn! How doth his long and ponderous halberd loom on high!"

"That is poor Ottur," said the lady. "In this way he thinks to soften her stubborn heart; but his every hope of that is for ever vain. What has he not suffered? what foes hath he not combated and defeated for the sake of that terrible maiden? but he will not listen to me—he runs headlong to ruin." Here she cast her eyes pensively on the ground; then looking with a smile on Otto: "But Otto is not Ottur," said she; "the gentle German is no wild Norman. No, thou goodly youth, thou wilt obey the rein, wilt thou not? thou wilt not rush so headlong into ruin?"

"God, I trust, will keep me from it," returned Otto, with a friendly voice and folded hands; "and, next to God, I feel as though your kindly guidance would often be a safeguard to me in my wanderings." The lady too now folded her hands on her bosom, and looked forth with a glad gaze on the darkling night-sky. They could see that her heart poured forth its praises unto God.

In a few moments she turned her face towards the room again. "Now come," said she to the knights, "ye brave young warriors, and refresh yourselves with a repast." The round table in the centre of the chamber that a moment before was empty was now furnished with several flasks of noble wine and delicious viands. "Be not astonished," said their hostess, "and still less be afraid." Then, making the sign of the cross over liquor and viand, "You see," she continued, "they stand the test."

"Who could doubt of that," said Otto, "when you tender them, most beautiful Lady Minnetrost?"

"Lady Minnetrost! Lady Minnetrost!" repeated their hostess again and again, as she gently waved her head to and fro; "and how comest thou, young sir, by this forgotten name?"

"You could, in all truth, be no other," cried Otto, with a cheek that glowed with joy. "God be praised that I have found you! About your life on the coast of East Friesland, Heerdegen and my kinswoman Bertha have told me."

"Otto," said the fair dame, and she held up her finger long and threateningly, "thou shouldest look graver and humbler when thou speakest of thy kinswoman Bertha." Otto cast his eyes abashed to the earth; but, with returning gentleness, and her wonted sweet smile, his hostess added: "I am truly the Lady Minnetrost of whom thou speakest. Thou art a dear and welcome guest in my halls, and thy comrade too. I know very well that he is the sea-king Arinbiorn, and that he has been here once before, albeit somewhat sooner than he was bidden." And then, too, a severe look fell on Arinbiorn, so that he dared not raise his eyes; but the Lady Minnetrost, with an air of angel gentleness, now bid the youths begin the repast; and they soon felt more easy and cheerful than in the whole gladsome tenor of their lives they had ever felt before. On their taking leave, "Twice a week ye may come to see me," said the lady; "and it shall be my care that no disaster befall your forces while ye are away from them."

CHAPTER XVI.

Now the mountain breezes of that northern autumn were wafting the last leaves from the branches; winter was spreading its ice-bright coverlet over vale and hill; the Finlaudish fir-woods alone towered boldly up from the deserted hollows in their sad and dismal vesture of green: but still in their lonely winter-camp our friends were happy. Whether they were trotting through the hoar wood in pursuit of the beasts of the forest; or were making their earnest sally against the bands of pagan marauders, that, by bold attack or stealthy manœuvre, every now and then sought to win their way through the well-guarded passes; or, tired with victorious effort, were sitting at the low hearth of their warm log-hut, pledging each other in the brimming horn of mead, and holding parley on the future, or cheering their spirits with the past—their minds were still unclouded and cheerful. They felt well aware that they were true bulwarks to noble Swedeland, and to Arinbiorn's dear Norway likewise. And between those stern days, when blood often besprinkled the snow, and those evenings spent in brotherly and peaceful converse, the hours passed in the Lady Minnetrost's dwelling spread their brighter gleam, like flowers that, amid storm and snow, bloom smiling on in fadeless beauty. Even Arinbiorn too had cast doubt aside, and now felt more at home in the wondrous watch-tower. Songs, riddles, and marvellous tales played ever and anon on the lip of the pious Druda; or if she at times became silent and thoughtful, it was no sultry noon-day heat that lay oppressively on their minds, but the cradling repose and gentleness of dewy evening. One only thing there was that the youthful warriors wished for,—to see the face of their kind hostess and helpmate unshaded by the veil. For, sweetly as came the bright smile of the large brown eyes, reflecting the slightest impulse of that motherly and gentle spirit, yet her other features remained shrouded in impenetrable gloom. Otto once spoke to the kindly Druda about it, but she merely answered, in the softest guise, "Oh, no; not a word about that yet!" and her favourite did not dare to question her further.

Late one evening the two young heroes were sitting in sober and friendly converse at the round table in the Lady Minnetrost's hall, when of a sudden her voice was hushed. Laying her finger upon her lips, she bade the knights be silent, and, listening as it were to some mysterious sound, with a fixed and sparkling eye she gazed aloft. Then, stepping to a casement, she looked eagerly forth on the star-bespangled night-sky. "To horse, young soldiers! to horse!" she cried. "To your troops, with the speed of the storm! The arms of the pagan are bare! Pagan witchery is rampant! Bear ye bravely. To-night is the decisive struggle!" The ready warriors had already donned their helmets, girded on their swords, grasped their javelins, and tightened the buckles of their mail. Then lowly bowing, they took a cheerful leave of the Druda, who signed over them the holy sign of the cross, and again cried, "To horse! To your yeomen, with the speed of the storm!" They sprang into the saddle, and their horses flew with them down the steep path of the mountain.

A hollow and confused din resounded, as they sped forward, from the neighbouring dells. Fire-signals flared hither and thither from the snowy mountain-tops over the Finlandish fir-woods. Aroused by these unusual alarums, they found their yeomen already under arms beside their horses; and when the two champions appeared, all were filled with confidence again and eagerness for the fight. "Mount!" cried Otto. "The light foot forwards!" cried Arinbiorn. And in comely array they were soon seen trotting and scouring over the narrow vales before them, under cover of the guards that had been posted on the other side; while the latter, under the command of young Kolbein, with a dense volley of arrows and javelins, stood the howling onslaught of the Finlanders.

Now fiery starlets flitted ever and anon over the heads of the advancing Normans. "The foe shoots flaming shafts!" said some. "It is witch-work!" shouted others; "charmed serpents of air are let loose upon us!"

"Let it be as it may," cried Arinbiorn and Otto to their squadrons. "We are on a goodly road. Christ and our country are with us!"

The inspiring call, the only one which could lead Christian warriors on to victory in confidence and glee, sounded like redoubled thunder from a thousand lips, and at once they sallied forth from the hollow passes against the hideous foe.

A small gloomy plain was the scene of the fight. The troops met in closer war; and friend or foe were scarcely distinguishable in the darkness of night. But again that winged flame flew at intervals over the contending squadrons, discovering to the Christians by its doubtful glare that grisly forms were fighting among the foremost ranks of the pagans, which less endangered the body by the swords or lances that they swayed, than they filled the soul with dismay by their horrid ugliness. And forms still more hideous were seen in the valleys, towering on high over the pagan bands: it was hard to tell whether they were wizard-banners or gigantic demons. Nevertheless the Christians pressed forward with joyful prowess, raising their cry to the great God above them, whirling their swords and driving back the wild rabble, whether they were witches, goblins, or hideous beasts, into the vales below. Arinbiorn and Otto sought to order their line again before they continued the pursuit, stationing knots of horse and foot on the little plain as a corps of reserve, and executing such other manœuvres as clever generalship might suggest; but in this wild tumult and disorder not a word more could be said about it. Soon as the Finlanders were routed, black night spread her rayless mantle over the mountains; the meteors of air gleamed on them no more; Otto's eagle-helm, Arinbiorn's mail of gold,—all were lost in the furious press; nay, even their mighty war-shout and resounding bugle-note were drowned by the howl of the flying foe, by the bellowing of the growing tempest, and the unbridled huzzas of the Norman warriors. If the two chieftains wished to escape being trampled under foot by their own squadrons, they could only give their steeds the rein, and dash blindly forward through the trackless gloom.

It was not long before their stormy career brought them to a wide and deep mountain-basin, as they could judge from the long recoil of the echoes, and from the bands of pursuers streaming in on every side, with their resounding war-cry and neighing chargers. Here they thought a far more advantageous fray would begin for them; but the airy shafts of flame again hurtled through the gloom, and shapes of horror were discovered in their gleam, squatting and grinning at every cranny in the rocks. It seemed as though the whole region around them had become one monstrous temple of idolatry, held in ban by ugly spells, where, without further hope of fighting, the devoted strangers could only shed their blood. The restive chargers, boldly as they were wont to confront a nobler field of peril, snorted wildly at the horrid sounds and forms that met them here; heedless of the spur or rein, Otto's light-brown not excepted, they swerved violently round, and bore away their angry riders in ungovernable and disordered flight. Then the Finlandish warriors howled in mockery as they fled; then their shafts hurtled after them with the swiftness of the lightning, and unhorsing many a noble rider, they laid him low in his gloomy death-shroud; while many a Norman, bravely fighting on foot, and now forsaken by his mounted comrades, fell a sacrifice to the fury of the conquering pagans. It was only in a narrow dell that the two chieftains at last succeeded in taming their own infuriate steeds, and gathering a knot of their faithful followers around them.

But lo! from a snowy height before them came the flash of a circling wheel of fire, and in the midst of it appeared the enchanted maiden in all the terror of her beauty. Her long gold tresses fluttered on the breeze; threateningly in her uplifted right hand gleamed a flaming sword, while with her left she waved a green branch on high, as if in mockery of the icy season.

"Do ye know me now?" cried she to the knights. "Gerda stands before you,—the slighted, rejected Gerda. Now your lives are in my hand. If ye be slow to make peace with me,

I will let my fiery serpents loose upon you, and in this narrow dell shall ye and your horses destroy each other in all the madness of dismay. Then the morrow's sun will rise upon you as upon a smouldering pile of gory bones, and mirror itself in the frozen filth that hath trickled from your hearts. Or choose ye to fly from me? Look! left-ward lies the way."

They involuntarily turned their eyes in the direction she pointed, and beheld an immense sheet of ice stretching far away over a lake, whence the blazing fire-wheel shot up its long smooth flash. Gerda laughed. "Will ye gallop over it?" said she in a mocking tone. "If ye and your horses are mad, it will be pretty to see you tumbling about upon it, and shivering your limbs one against the other on the cold, unyielding plane."

As if by concerted agreement, Arinbiorn and Otto put their bugles to their lips, and prepared to sound the signal for the charge, resolved to stand the honourable brunt of war as long as sense, hand, and horse were obedient to their will. Then said Gerda: "Halt awhile; I leave you one choice more. Victory and joy and honour be with you, but make a league with me. Start not; ye shall not be obliged to renounce your champion Christ: a goodly peace shall be concluded with the land for which ye fight, and then, as light-hearted adventurers, we will wander through the world together. Are ye agreed?"

She cast a lovely look on the vale beneath her. In a moment young Kolbein was off his horse, and clambering up the snowy mountain slope. "Oh, thy threats dismay me not," cried he, "but thy promises wind me fast in their toils, thou beauteous being. I will be thine adventurous mate; thy leagued adventurer will I be the whole world through."

The sea-king and Otto called upbraidingly after him, and stretched out their arms to him in brotherly entreaty: but Gerda extended her lovely left hand towards him with the enchanted spray of green; and as if drawn up by magnetic power, the stripling was soon seen standing beside the maiden in the sparkling circlet of flame, smiling with delight, and beckoning his comrades to follow him.

Arinbiorn and Otto looked at each other gravely and almost pensively in the face. "There will be an end of us sooner than I thought for," began the sea-king at last.

"Yes, indeed," returned Otto, "and I am free to confess to thee I would fain have fought and conquered a little longer in the world."

"And I too, from the bottom of my heart," rejoined the sea-king.

"But as things are come to this pass," said the knight of

Trautwangen, "and the witch is likely to harry our senses soon, let us take a brotherly farewell of each other, and forgive every thing beforehand in which one may thoughtlessly have done the other a wrong."

And therewith they kissed each other tenderly, and, calling out to their troops, "Children, die bravely, and cleave to Christ in your hearts!" they shouted to Gerda, "Now begin, if ye will. We are bound to blow the noble war-horn."

And with the first bugle-notes a soft gleam stole on every thing from behind them. They looked round in astonishment. It was only the full moon that just then came wandering forth on her bright and kindly path over the mountains. But, in the fulness of her gleams, on a neighbouring height, the Lady Minnetrost's lofty form stood in thankful prayer. "With the help of God ye have withstood the temptation," cried she. "In His holy name, to the charge!"

Gerda's giddy fire-wheel had vanished. In the light of the moon, that now lay in all its solemn brightness on the snowy mountain-turrets, the Norman warriors dashed victoriously on the enemy. And in unbridled disorder the black Finlandish hordes went flying over those glistening regions of snow.

CHAPTER XVII.

At the dawn of morning the knight of Trautwangen left his charger with his troop, and clambered up a snowy rock, that he might better see how to direct the pursuit, and whether they should dive still deeper among the valleys, or at once face about for the return to the camp. The cliff above was parted by a broad and very deep cleft. Otto took his stand close to its margin, and rejoiced to find that they had run far over the boundary-mark: that they, moreover, were in a condition to place strong outposts on the Finlandish territory, and thereby insure greater safety to the land of the Christians. Whilst he was still engaged in these considerations, a tall knightly figure came towards him through the morning mist from the other side of the cleft, and planting himself with his beaver up on the opposite margin, began taking a like survey of the country. But suddenly the two heroes quivered with fear; for again did Otto and Ottur behold the striking semblance of each other's faces.

"I neither can nor will bear it any longer," said Ottur fiercely. "Thou wilt drive me mad at last with that face of thine. One only such countenance ought to live. Besides, last night thou puttedst our hosts to flight; and when thou art clear of this world, the army of Odin may have better hopes of revenge. Brandish thy spear, therefore. The rocky cleft forbids us reaching one another with the sword, but our lances are ready for flight. Anon to it. Ere the sun is fully risen, it must be decided who may wear this countenance, thou or I." And he brandished his javelin with mighty power over his head.

"Wait awhile," said Otto. "I ween we shall find but little peace in that way. How should he afterwards live, who had slain his counterpart? Why, that would be as though he had put an end to himself."

"Sooth it would," returned Ottur. "But we will close our beavers: in that guise it will not be seen how our own features grow stark in death, and swim in blood." And so saying he let his vizor fall, and again brandished his spear.

"But we might be brethren-in-arms and friends," said Otto pleasantly, "and in a closer bond of union too than any two heroes in the world."

"Wilt thou follow Gerda? Shall I leave her?" cried Ottur, in a hollow voice, from his well-closed helmet. "So quick to the bloody work. If thou throw not hither, I will make my cast at thee. And a fugitive from the field my counterpart can never be."

"God forbid!" returned the knight of Trautwangen; and like Ottur, he closed his beaver and addressed himself to the fight.

Whilst now the two warriors, aiming from beneath the covert of their ponderous shields, stood expectantly confronting each other, something came panting through the thicket of firs behind Ottur. A monstrous bull, haply aroused and irritated by the din of battle, with ready horn and sparkling eye made straight for the heathen knight, who, in the eagerness of the pending struggle, was unaware of his approach. In a moment Otto levelled his javelin, and hurling it high over his adversary's head, he planted it with unerring aim in the neck of the infuriated beast, and threw him on the snow.

"What art thou about, Otto?" said the pagan, as he lowered his spear. "Thy want of skill forced thee not to so sorry a cast. Thinkest thou, then, to sport with me?"

"Prithee look round now," returned the young German. And casting a glance behind him, Ottur beheld the stricken bull convulsively pouring out the last drops of life.

Then, turning to Otto, he threw up his beaver, and Otto did the same. The morning sun, just then rising, shot a beam of glory on the countenances of the two youthful heroes. They gazed on each other with kindly animation of look.

"Shall we exchange swords?" said Ottur at length.

"I dare not part with mine," said Otto. "It is a sacred keepsake of my father's, otherwise I would gladly do so. But I will tell thee what we will do. Henceforward name thy sword Otto, if thou hast conceived a liking for me, and I will call mine Ottur."

"With all my heart," replied Ottur. "I feel altogether as if thou knewest how to manage every thing better and more cleverly than I, for all thou mayest be several years younger."

"Yea, thou lookest to me a little older than myself," replied the knight of Trautwangen: "otherwise we are wondrously like."

"So, then, his name is Otto now," cried Ottur; and his sword rattled again as he struck it.

"And this is Ottur," returned Otto, while he too let his gauntleted hand fall rattling on the hilt of gold.

Therewith the reconciled champions nodded to each other their smiling farewell, and each strode down the hill to his squadron.

From that day forth the winter passed in sober peacefulness among the hills. The routed pagans ventured forward no more to harass the Norman warriors, whose two chieftains again whiled away many a serene and solemn hour in the Lady Minnetrost's lovely watch-tower. The pious Druda at such times wore a smile of stilly pleasure, like the sweet harvest-moon. Once only, when Otto at the round stone table sang the parting lay of Fair Astrid and the mighty Hugur, she began quite piteously to weep, and besought the youth not to sing it to her again. He observed her request as though it had been an imperial ordinance; and their life passed on in such a sweet and unbroken flow, that the two knights could not help being astonished at the shortness of the long northern winter. For before they thought of any change of quarters, the breeze of spring was already whispering through the vales, the rivulets, released from ice, were purling over their beds, and little blades of grass and budding wild-flowers came peeping from the earth.

CHAPTER XVIII.

Whilst now Otto was leading so renowned and joyous a life in the far lands of the north, winter had passed in gentleness and quiet, nay, even in cheerful serenity, over the head of old Sir Hugh. The hoary minstrel, Master Walther, sojourned for many days together in the castle of Trautwangen; and if he occasionally went away, it was only for a short time, when he would soon come back again to the knightly recluse, and gladden him with converse and with song. But what might be deemed a special blessing to the aged Sir Hugh, were the beautiful dreams which, during those lonely months, were wont to hover round him; whether it chanced that he lay at night on his antiquated and closely-curtained couch, or was dozing at noon or eventide in his great arm-chair in the hall, where he had dubbed young Sir Otto a knight. Hence it was that he felt no little store of joy when weariness drew its sweet shadow over his eyelids; and he now yielded more willingly to it, and more frequently than before.

At such times the garden of his chequered youth would mostly open on his view, save that in lieu of the nettles that ever and anon had sprung up there, nothing but blooming roses were now to be seen; in the place of poisonous roots were healing herbs; and the whole scene was like one large sunflower, turning continually to the full glory of the bright orb of day. And in the midst of the blooming parterre appeared the form of the young Sir Otto, childlike and smiling, and gathering with luxuriant choice the most beautiful fruits and flowers.

Thus, one afternoon, old Sir Hugh had fallen asleep, pleasing himself, as he sank into slumber, with the thought of the fair world of promise which to his mind's eye might soon be unfolded; but it turned out quite otherwise than he had hoped for. It seemed to him as though the heavy tramp of a mailed warrior came sounding up the stairway, till the casements rattled again, and anon a gauntleted hand struck three ponderous blows on the oaken door of the hall. The "come in" seemed fast pent up in the breast of the dreamer. At length he thought he had found breath for it, when the oaken valves swung apart with an ill-boding creak, and suddenly, with ghastly face, all bloody and distorted, and upraised fist denouncing death, in all the terrible pomp of a shrouded corpse, the Avenger with the vulture-wings stood before him. Sir Hugh awoke with a shudder, and started to his feet; but scarcely had he reminded himself that he had been dreaming only, when, in the broad daylight of his senses, he really heard that heavy martial tramp upon the stairway till the windows rattled again, and the thrice-repeated ponderous knocking of the gauntleted hand on the door. Rescuing him from the madness that might follow so terrible a blow, a deep swoon enveloped him in its misty shroud.

The serving-men and menials whom Sir Hugh still retained about him in his peaceful stronghold were not one of them at home: some were plying the chase, some had gone in quest of the old minstrel Walther, while others had been despatched to the neighbouring town, to fetch all sorts of things for the entertainment of the wished-for guest. When, on receiving such errands, they now and then ventured to make a demur about leaving their lord thus alone in the old and spacious pile, the latter was wont to answer: "Old Sir Hugh is at his right post in the bannered hall, among plenty of swords and suits of mail; and, in case of need, he would be quick to lay his hand on some olden sword-blade that his fathers have wielded."

But now, the first of the menials who entered the hall saw that quite a different foe must have broken in there to what Sir Hugh had reckoned upon; and as the old man sat so motionless and deadly pale in his chair, it seemed as though death himself had been his foe: so that the servant set up a loud cry of woe, and drew all such of his comrades around him as had returned to the castle.

Just at this moment Master Walther came riding over the drawbridge, and hearing their shrill cry, he said to himself, with a sigh: "Ah! and couldest thou not live, then, till thy son was returned from his renowned wanderings, thou aged hero?" But when he reached the hall, and surveyed the pale giant-form in the arm-chair, it seemed to him quite plain that old Sir Hugh could not be dead.

Nature is fond of the children of song; and if they know not how to climb the toilsome height of learning by the common ladder, their kindly foster-mother often throws to them undeservedly and unasked some tiny spark or posy, with which they achieve most wondrous things, to the astonishment of songless souls. And in this way it was that Master Walther was in the possession of a deliciously-scented salve. He held it to the lifeless sire's nostril, and in a trice old Sir Hugh rose to his full height, and opened his eyes. "I had a horrible dream," cried he. "Where, then, is he that sought to mimic it when I awoke? Where is he whose iron tramp sounded slowly up the stairway, and who knocked thrice at my door with his gauntleted hand?"

Not one of the menials knew aught of the matter.

"But some one must have been here," said the old man, at length, "and bodily too; for look ye at that odd thing that standeth at my side!"

Looking the way he pointed, they beheld a strangely-fashioned banner in a corner. The image of a hideous dragon glared on them from the staff, but round it was a shining scroll of golden letters, which the cunning Master Walther quickly recognised, and read as follows:

"On Finland's border-line he fought,
And tore this banner from pagan hands;

Then he showered his blows for Sweden's sake—
Anon the Swede doth the conqueror prize.
Sir Otto is his name;
Von Trautwangen his knightly race."

Then all the serving-men and menials broke forth in a loud huzza, and wished their lord joy of his treasure-trove. But old Sir Hugh took his little green-velvet cap from his head, and folded his hands in silent prayer. Then, at last, he cried, "If the goblins bring us such trophies as these, we may well put up with the frightful dreams they send us."

CHAPTER XIX.

In the midst of one of the enchanting gardens which slope from the Spanish city of Cartagena to the sea, at the foot of an oleander-tree, sat Gabriele, with her beautiful eyes fixed on the blue of heaven; while Blancheflour, reclining at her side, wove a wreath of flowers from the clustering beauties of that teeming soil. At a short distance, a black female slave touched the strings of her zittar; and, astonished at the seeming indifference of her mistresses to her music, she at last said, "Shall I sing to you, perhaps, ye fair, sorrowful doncellas?"

And when they both, without knowing what they did, gave a nod of assent, the slave, in the sweetest strain, began the following song:

"'Montjoye! holy Dionysius!'
Cries the mighty Christian warrior
Knightly Folko de Montfaucon;
And the Moorish brides are weeping.
Now Guadalquivir comes flowing
One long gleam of bloody purple:
Tell it at Cordova's towers—
Tell it further in Sevilla—
Tell it on the shores of ocean—
How the baron bold hath warred.
Fifteen sallied forth to meet him,
Fifteen of the stoutest horsemen,
And they swore to take him captive;
By a deep oath were they bounden:
Fifteen sallied forth to meet him,
But not one of them returned—
Nothing but their blood flowed homeward,
Envoy mute of bitter sorrow.
'Montjoye! holy Dionysius!'
Cries the mighty Christian warrior
Knightly Folko de Montfaucon;
And the Moorish brides are weeping."

"And many other brides weep besides the Moorish brides," said Gabriele; and she buried her glowing cheeks in her fine Indian handkerchief.

"Allah knows," said the frightened slave, "I thought to make you quite merry with my lay, as I sang the achievements of your valiant countryman. Wherefore, then, do ye weep?"

Without giving further heed to what she said, Gabriele continued her converse with Blancheflour. "Oh, what a glorious brother you have!" said she. "Shall we ever see him in this world again?" Then Blancheflour burst into the tenderest flood of tears; and the two beautiful damsels embraced each other as they wept, and clasped each other fondly to their bosoms.

Then, with a noble grace, in all the splendour of a Moorish knight, Prince Mutza entered the garden; but when he saw the ladies weeping, he stepped back with the greatest token of respect, and beckoned the slave to follow him. "Is that the service," said he, in an undertone, "that I expected from thy skill? I heard the sound of thy lute; but thou hast melted the beauteous damsels into tears. What silly lay thou choosest, I know not; but this I know, thou shalt for the future be quit of the sweet charge of waiting on Gabriele."

But the lovely lady of Portamour noticed Mutza's displeasure. "Rebuke not the maid," said she. "She is not in fault about our weeping; or, if her singing hath brought the tears to my eyes, they are sweeter to me than all the beautiful things that you can offer me in your luxurious castle."

Then the prince placed a sparkling diamond in the hand of his swarthy slave, and led her back to her mistress. "Allah be praised," cried he, "that ye deign for once to lay upon me either restriction or command! Oh, that ye would only command me freely!"

"I command you," returned Gabriele, "to lead me back with my friend to the shores of Gascony."

"Ah! that one thing," said Mutza, with a sigh, "that one thing, dear lady, ask not." And Gabriele turned indignantly away from him.

Along the terraces of the garden, close by the golden trellis that surrounded it, a cavalier rode past them in the gorgeous costume of the Moors. His figure was tall and slim, his countenance stern and thoughtful, yet not wanting in engaging sweetness, though embrowned and touched with the fire of well-matured manhood; his jet-black beard fell in rich flow from his chin and upper lip; and his whole bearing and gesture was that of a king. One of the noblest Arabian steeds of coal-black hue neighed under him; and men, whose costume and demeanour betokened lofty rank, rode like servants in his train. Gabriele and Blancheflour rose from their seats, without exactly knowing why, and saluted the brilliant stranger with a marked tone of reverence. The prince returned his thanks to them with dignified courtesy; then halting, he beckoned Mutza towards the railing, and the proud youth hastened up in humble obedience to the signal. Whereupon the stranger threw his further leg over the neck of his docile steed, that he might sit more conveniently on the side where Mutza stood, and forthwith began a parley, which Gabriele and Blancheflour, who had by this time learned the language of the Arabs, for the most part understood. Its purport was as follows:

"Are those the beautiful women there," began the brilliant horseman, "whom thou broughtest with thee from the land of the Franks?" And on Mutza's reply to that effect: "Sun-bright pearls they are of the fairest mould," continued he. "But mark me, young prince, it nevertheless appears to me thou hast left the most beautiful and most inestimable jewel behind thee. Or is it perhaps untrue, what they tell me about the frowning maiden, who scared thy kinsman from her when she towered so fearfully on high beside the crucifix of stone, in the solemn light of the crimson evening?"

"That is all as they have reported it to you, most noble sir," replied Mutza; "and that woudrous maiden in Frankland is called Lady Bertha von Lichtenried."

"Then this I vow," cried the kingly horseman, "that to him who should bring her to me to Cartagena, unharmed and unsullied in all her virgin purity, would I relinquish a third part of my treasures,—for him and his whole house for ever!"

Then a dusky but richly-apparelled little man rode forward from the train. "Are you in real earnest, most noble sir?" he asked. "The Lady Bertha von Lichtenried, then, must still be to be found and taken captive within the bounds of Christendom."

"Thou dost not look as though thou couldst do as much!" replied the haughty Arabian, with a faint smile of scorn.

"I only ask whether you are in earnest about the third part, most noble sir?" continued the ill-favoured Moor.

"Thou knowest well enough, Alhafiz," was the answer, "that I do not jest with my promises."

"Then we will set our brains to work," replied the knight, "to see how the wondrous Bertha may be yours, and the third part of your treasures be awarded to me. But since time gained is every thing gained, I beg to take my leave of you at once, without a moment's delay." So saying, he bowed low to the earth, and rode away. The gorgeous stranger followed him with his eye, shaking his head and smiling, and shrugging his shoulders repeatedly in token of pity; then, with a friendly nod to Mutza, and a low reverence to the ladies, he again threw himself into the position of a rider, and trotted lightly forward with his train into the bright country of the south.

"Who is that wondrous and magnificent stranger?" said Gabriele to Prince Mutza, when he again stepped to the ladies on the terrace.

"It is the great Emir Nureddin," was the reply; "the most potent and heroic Arab that the world hath ever beheld. After scattering in the flaming East his starry host of valiant deeds and gentle conquests, he hath passed over to us here in the West, in order to enwreathe his brow not only with the palms of Asia, but with the laurels also of Spain and Italy. Our wise men deem him the wisest in their schools, and our generals account him the great lord of the battle-field; and that, in your presence, O maiden so wondrous fair, beams of his favour and friendliness have fallen upon me, makes me not less proud and happy than if I had victoriously sustained a conflict with those heaven-bright eyes."

"We understood your parley with him," replied Gabriele de Portamour, turning proudly away, "and we hope that the only true God will defend the lady of Lichtenried from falling into the hands of this brilliant tiger. Well ye do to look up to him as your master, since he can turn his thoughts so quickly to the commission of rapine among women." And a cold, imperious look drove the dejected and embarrassed Mutza from the garden; a second glance sent the astonished slave after him.

Again couched on the flowery grass at the foot of the oleander-tree, Blancheflour eyed her friend, as she still stood before her, with such a sweet look of hope and secret joy, that the latter was struck with amazement, and could not refrain from asking what bright sun could have mantled her sweet cheek with the fair flush of morning. "God be praised that we are for once all alone," said Blancheflour, with her happy smile, "and that I can open my heart to thee without reserve! But take thy seat by me on the grass; for though no listener be near us, yet I would far sooner whisper of such matters than speak aloud." And when Gabriele had done as she desired, the blushing maiden hung her little ringleted head, and said quite softly, "He is here; Master Aleard is here. These few last days I have often seen him lurking round the palace and the garden."

Gabriele was about to give vent to her delight at these hopeful tidings, when, all of a sudden, and they knew not whence he came, a stranger stood before the ladies in the garb of a slave, with a youthful mien, a bright black eye, and the most winning smile. He bowed low before them, not in the manner of Arabia, but of Europe.

"Who art thou? Has magic brought thee hither? Dost thou know, too, that to be discovered is to be lost?" Such were the words with which Blancheflour and Gabriele greeted him.

He replied with a calm and kindly air. "Allow me, ye high-born and beauteous beings," said he, "to answer your questions in reversed succession; protesting to you, that I am neither so ignorant as not to know my danger, nor so hairbrained or awkward as to run recklessly into it, if I did not feel pretty certain of my safety. Then ye ask me, whether enchantment hath brought me hither? and I answer, No; but simply a few golden rails, which, for these three or four nights, have been cunningly filed through by me, and seemingly restored to their fixings. But to the question as to who I am, although you place the rest of your queries before it, I have but paltry news to tender, namely, that my name is Tebaldo; that I am an Italian trader, who, in the retinue of Sir Otto von Trautwangen, attended that fair evening festival in the autumnal beech-grove when the lady Blancheflour and Master Aleard sang the beautiful ditty of Abelard and Heloisa; that I the next day set off with Count Alessandro Vinciguerra on a journey through Italy to join the troops of the king of the Lion-heart at the Holy Grave; that not far from Naples we were taken prisoners by two Arabian galliots, and doomed to serve as slaves here in Cartagena; but above all, that I deem myself much more fitted to serve you, beautiful ladies, than my gray-bearded master; and that for this very purpose I have stolen into the garden."

The two damsels looked on him with astonishment, gradually calling to memory the features of the once unheeded youth; whilst Tebaldo, with kindly caution, made clear to them that he had formed a league with Master Aleard to rescue two such heavenly beings from the grasp of plunder, and at the same time to secure the freedom of himself and the Count Vinciguerra; but at the close of his discourse he uttered the following singular words: "I have told you, noble maidens, that I am a merchant; and such a man is far better pleased with a thousandfold than a hundredfold. Now, the lady Gabriele has a wondrous ring by her, to which I deem myself to have a right, since a late visit that I have paid to a certain grave-mound in Italy. I do not see the thing quite clearly, but she who should give me the ring would really make me her unchangeable ally; and I can most confidently assure you that I am a very efficient and trustworthy one; nay, perhaps, a most necessary one, so severed as we are from other Christian folk, and with such a perilous enterprise before us."

All this time his countenance was marked by so strange a mixture of gravity, menace, and hearty friendliness, that Blancheflour whispered in concern to Gabriele, "Give him, oh, give him the unhappy ring! Hath it ever brought either of us peace or joy?"

Gabriele remained a long, long time in thought; then at last she drew the little golden chain from her snowy bosom, with that jewel that was still so strange and mysterious in her own eyes, and unhasping it, she said, as she handed it to the Italian merchant, "There you have the guerdon you crave of me; but beware how you play with it—it is a dangerous toy."

Tebaldo's eye sparkled as it fell on the glistening stone. The one seemed to kindle brighter and brighter at the flame of the other. "Welcome to my hand at last," he cried, "thou hallowed, but still deeply-veiled treasure! Yet we soon shall understand each other; and do I not already feel a light flashing on my soul?" Then, turning to the ladies, "You are saved," he said, "most beauteous maidens! and thou, lady Gabriele, hast lost but little, though thou hast lavished such endless wealth upon me. These lips shall praise thy bounty, so long as the fair breath of life streams through them." Then, with a graceful salute, he strode back into the bushes.

"What an extraordinary man that was!" said Blancheflour, after a pause of silence; "and at the end of our parley, did he not appear quite otherwise than at the beginning? Somewhat grown, methought!"

"Yes, indeed," replied Gabriele; "there was more meaning, solemnity, and prowess in his look. Despite his slavish garb, one might have taken him for a baron; yet not for so glorious a warrior as thy brave brother Folko, for whose sake the Moorish brides are weeping."

But hark!—light pinions were heard fluttering around the damsels, who at once looked up with amazement in the air. A falcon-gentil, of wondrous beauty, adorned with a golden necklace, circled close over their heads, and at last, flapping its wings for joy, sank in the lady Blancheflour's lap. "Good heavens!" cried she, pale with terror, "what can this mean? It is the falcon of my lord and brother; and they say such noble creatures only quit their noble master when he is buried, and that they then fly far away to seek them an equally noble and worthy lord!"

"Talk not of such horrible things," said Gabriele, with more self-composure, though her cheeks too were blanched with woful pallor. "What if he came to thee a a messenger?

For a sorrowing fugitive, he looks far too bright-eyed and cheerful." Whereupon they examined the golden necklace of the kingly bird, and found a rosy slip of parchment inside it, upon which a pencil had traced the following rhymes in delicate characters:

"I falcon will the envoy be
Of hearts that love each other;
'Tis Folko sends his bird to thee
With greeting from a brother.
My falcon only stays his wing
For hands as true and tender;
And so, on far and trackless fling,
I send him forth to wander.
The fight was slow, and I am fain
To come, a masked stranger,
As merchant with a brilliant trai ,
To bear thee off from danger.
And if two maidens would declare
When I should come to greet them,
I'd hie me from my castle fair
With morning's light to meet them.
Then write to me, sweet sister, write,
My falcon saileth gaily;
And wilt thou do me service bright,
Oh, greet me Gabriéle!"

Now the two damsels kissed each other, and wept for joy as fondly as they but just before had embraced each other in sorrow. "They all are here!" said the smiling and delighted Blancheflour, "my brother, Master Aleard, and the falcon. I feel as though we were at home again already."

Then, as soon as she had taken counsel with her friend, she traced the following words with a golden needle on the rosy slip of parchment:

"Gabriele greeteth thee;
Come to-morrow carefully,
When the sun is on the lea,
And the dew-drop gleameth;
Day-star thou of mailed men!
Pass in shadow through the glen;
Then on steel flash forth again:—
Ah! how maiden dreameth!"

Then the little leaf was again placed in the falcon's necklace. Joyfully he soared through the sunny blue of ether, and joyfully did the maidens stroll across the beaming lawn to the palace.

CHAPTER XX.

SCARCELY had the blush of morning mantled on the eastern hills, when, through the flowery trellis-work of their lattices, Gabriele and Blancheflour were looking for the arrival of the Frankish warrior. They were the more anxious to gain a glimpse of him, since the airy phantasies of the dream-god had the whole night long been weaving them such a wondrous tissue of truth, presage, and fable, that neither of the maidens scarcely dared to believe that the ministering falcon-gentil had really come to them the day before, on an errand so bold and rapturous.

But, ere long, the sweet clear sound of the horn, the cymbal, and the flute, came wafted along the white and level way that swept across some blooming meadows at some distance from the palace. A squadron of Moorish horsemen covered its van, followed by a line of camels and other beasts of burden, laden with high piles of merchandise, over which were spread azure coverlets of velvet with fringes of gold. Blancheflour and Gabriele descried with joy the noble emblazoury of the Montfaucon escutcheon, and smiled on each other with an increased glow of confidence. Then came the musicians, playing on varied store of instruments, the metallic parts of which were of the purest gold or silver; while jewels sparkled on the necks and bridges of the same, or wherever they might be disposed to advantage. At length appeared the master of the train himself. His noble mule was so richly caparisoned in blue and gold-embroidered velvet, that its slight limbs alone were seen pacing in dainty grandeur beneath it, whilst his large rolling eyes looked forth, as from windows of gold, over the bright margin of the embroidered head-cloth. The noble baron himself, arrayed so curiously in silken robes of blue and gold, that one could scarcely tell whether he wore the costume of the Christians or the Moors, sat on a cushioned saddle after the fashion of a woman. In his hand he held a guitar, upon which he was rather seen than heard to play; for those tender tones which he seemed to cherish as something delicious for himself alone were lost to other ears amid the merry riot of the march; but still it might be seen, by his flashing eye, that the strain had changed all at once to the sweetest song: it was at the moment when he seemed to descry Gabriele behind the flower-wreathed lattice.

The ladies knew him at once; though a false black beard hung far over his lips, and another floated downward from his chin, while a sort of Turkish tire of azure hue concealed his clustering locks, yet Gabriele and Blancheflour would have been quick to discover him even in a much more deceptive mask. The falcon, moreover, kept sporting and hovering on triumphant pinion over its master's head, as if to point him out with greater certainty to the only two who were as yet permitted to recognise him. Mutza, indeed, had no suspicion of the presence of his noble and bitterly-deluded conqueror. On the contrary, he rode in easy guise from his palace to meet the cavalcade, asked for costly wares, bargained for many of them, and at last bade the strange merchant to a banquet in his castle. But Folko declined his invitation. He avoided putting the self-possession of the ladies to any dangerous trial; and, besides, without any other need of approach, had he not the speediest and most trusty messenger in his falcon? This faithful winged envoy flew forth many times in the next few weeks, bearing the rosy parchment with divers words of greeting to and fro, by which means the Baron de Montfaucon and Master Aleard kept up a communication with Tebaldo and the Count Vinciguerra. Don Hernandez, with some galleys, which, as had been agreed upon with the baron, he was to bring up before the port of Cartagena, alone was awaited, to put the bold and cleverly-conceived plan of deliverance in execution.

One evening, as the eventful hour drew near, the two ladies were again in lonely repose beneath the oleander-tree. The falcon had brought another message, and sat meekly on Blancheflour's white little hand, taking good heed not to rase the tender snow with his talons. But, in doubtful mood, Gabriele still held the rose-coloured parchment in one hand, while the other toyed with the golden needle with which she was accustomed to write, quite unable to grave a single word on the yielding tablet. Blancheflour entreated her to be quick. "We may be surprised," she said; and then, lowering her voice, "If thou canst," she added, "oh, write the poor brother of thy playmate something gentle and comforting." Gabriele shook her beautiful head in sadness, and a sigh escaped her heaving bosom: then she once more ran over the words which Folko had written on the parchment, and which were nearly as follows:

"To Gabriele.

The hour of freedom soundeth. Freedom's hour
Shall smooth full many a knight his gory bed;
If o'er mine eyes the hallowed death-cloud lower,
And spent for thee be life's last stream of red,
Let not with me thy tenderness, thy power,
And my sweet misery, die all unsaid.
Oh, bless thy Folko ere his spirit flee,
Who loved thee, Gabriele, only thee!
A sister's right, my stern vow to defend her,
Had made us foes on life's tempestuous main;

Then, when at peace, my trembling lip grew tender
With sweeter utterance, friendship cried—'Refrain!'
But now, since haply this fond heart shall render
The blood for thee that warms its inmost vein,
These erring blissful words my way prepare,
And pray soft answer, fairest of the fair!"

Gabriele began to weep bitterly, and Blancheflour too was bathed in tears. "And wilt thou give no answer?" she said; "not a single word to the poor dear champion? Shall he, then, go so uncomforted to meet his death for thee?"

There was a rattling at the gate of the garden, and Mutza's voice was heard without. The falcon flapped his wings, and darted a timorous glance of impatience around him. "Oh, quickly, quickly!" whispered the trembling Blancheflour. "Thou wilt be the death of him, if thou send back his envoy without an answer."

Then, in all the haste of twofold fear, Gabriele wrote the following lines on the rosy leaflet:

"Oh, live, my hero, live
For me, who give thee all that love can give!"

Then, covering her friend with her kisses, in the ecstasy of gratitude, Blancheflour hid the little leaf in the knightly bird's necklace, and, swiftly as a sunbeam, he darted with his costly booty through the air.

CHAPTER XXI.

Tebaldo arrived at the hostelry of the Baron de Montfaucon just as the latter had finished loading a mule with a store of beautiful weapons, that he might present himself, as requested, before the great Emir Nureddin in his assumed character of merchant; but as Tebaldo, about an hour before, had descried the galleys which Don Hernandez was expected to bring up to the mouth of the harbour, and, by the concerted signal, had already given the noble Castilian the hint, Folko made the emir wait, and agreed with the adroit Italian that the deliverance of the captives, and their flight by sea, should take place that very night.

But, in the midst of this most important parley, the baron's glance seemed suddenly to rivet itself on a golden chain which peeped out from Tebaldo's slave-frock, and which, as the merchant stood speaking with all the lively vehemence of the south, at last shook completely out, and displayed Gabriele's pendent ring.

"Whence hast thou that?" asked the baron sharply, with the flush of rising anger on his face.

"For such trifles," replied Tebaldo, with an air of cool effrontery, which he invariably put on when harshly or imperiously addressed,—"for such trifles I should think there would be time enough when we are on board; but as it is a matter of such vast consequence to you to know, I may as well tell you. I had the jewel from the lady herself; and, in fact, she gave it me on my desiring it in lieu of earnest-money towards securing my alliance."

"The bargain is null and void!" said Montfaucon, with ill-repressed wrath. "More noble has been the flow of blood on this ring's account than should allow of your taking it into your keeping, because a timid maiden, in trembling helplessness, was unable to deny it to your pert demands. Come, up with it—up with it, I say, without further parley!"

"Ye might as well ask my life-blood of me," replied Tebaldo: "and I warrant you, you will neither get the one nor the other out of me by a few despotic baronial words. But moderate your wrath now. I renounce every claim that the ring may give to lands or castles. Wholly and solely on its own account do I desire it; and I can assure you that I am not altogether without a right to it."

"To think of my bargaining and haggling with this merchant-fellow for a peerless gem like this!" cried the baron. "I will show you what there is in baronial words, as you term them!" And so saying, he made so stout and sudden a grasp at the chain, ring, and collar of the Italian, that the latter, despite his adroitness, stood spell-bound to the spot, and would have lost his gem in a moment, had not Count Alessandro Vinciguerra stepped up, and said, with an air of distinguished grandeur that brightened through the garb of a slave, "What are ye at with my serving-man, sir baron?"

"Messire," said Folko, loosing his hold of Tebaldo, "make him deliver up that ring; that I demand of him again in the name of the lady Gabriele de Portamour, and I have no other business with him of any sort."

"I perhaps should have commanded him to do so," returned Vinciguerra, "had it pleased you to couch your petition in other words."

"You would perhaps have commanded me," retorted Tebaldo, whilst he looked down on the knight with a smile of unusual grandeur; "but just as little would have come of it for that matter."

Vinciguerra cast a look of displeasure on his saucy mate; but Montfaucon, heeding only the answer of the count, took up the words he had last let fall. "*Petition*, should I?" said he. "I petition nobody but my king. From other people I *demand* my rights. Is it your pleasure now to grant me them, or not?"

"You would be a good deal more civil and gentle towards me," replied Vinciguerra, in scornful anger, "if I stood not here as a weaponless captive before you."

This fell like venom on the pure and noble spirit of the Baron de Montfaucon. His brave soul rose in a ferment, and seemed labouring, as it were, to eject again the dark, unsavoury poison, regardless of the time, or place, or the common danger that threatened both himself and his adversary. With lightning speed he tore from the pack-saddle of his mule two Persian swords, with blades bent inwards in the form of a scythe, and holding them out crossways to Vinciguerra: "Choose, sir count," said he. "They are both of the same length, and both as sharp as a razor. The arms of European knighthood I unfortunately have not at hand."

Whilst now Vinciguerra, with a firm resolve, though somewhat taken aback, was making choice between the two curiously-fashioned blades, Tebaldo endeavoured to remind the knights how little a divided kingdom could hope for victory, and what a dangerous foe looked them one and all in the face. A contemptuous glance from the baron was the only reply, save that it was followed up by the summary caution: "My honour is at stake. Keep to your ell, sir merchant."

With a shrug of the shoulders and a proud insensibility to chagrin, Tebaldo turned away. "Ye will want me, after all," said he. Then he walked down for a stroll on the strand, whilst the two knights fell on each other with infuriate violence. In vain did the falcon hover over his master's head with Gabriele's heavenly missive, watching for the moment to alight. Inflamed just then with far other thoughts than those of love's sweet tidings, the knight left the falcon unheeded.

Scarcely could either combatant have ever had so odd a weapon in his hand for the purpose of serious medley, but the pupil of the far-travelled Messire Huguenin was unskilled in no kind of warfare. Soon might the scythe-like sword be seen whistling as lightly in his hand, and with as manful an effect, as his knightly blade itself; and whilst his perplexed adversary often showered his blows with the blunt and outer edge of the scimitar, Folko clave coolly down with the inner one, till Alessandro Vinciguerra, with three deep wounds on his breast and arm, reeled lifeless to the earth.

"There, you have made a pretty business of it!" said Tebaldo, who at this moment again took his stand by them. "Only just be off with you now. It is ill tarrying here. Trust me for getting the wounded man out of the way." So saying, with a gentle yet powerful effort, he hove the lifeless count on his shoulders, and vanished with him among some adjacent summer-houses.

Still the baron stood advising with himself what to do, and gasping out the last breath of fury, quite at a loss to gather the meaning of Tebaldo's parting words, when all at once it was but too clearly revealed to him.

"Dare I believe my eyes? Was such saucy hardihood ever heard of?" cried a well-known voice close beside him in the street. It was the Prince Mutza, who, surrounded by a rich train of followers, stayed his pure Arabian charger, and, with an astonished gaze, looked the baron full in the face. The latter was instantly for returning to his merchant character, but he now perceived what had escaped his notice in the heat of the combat, namely, that one of the blows which Vinciguerra had dealt with the blunt edge of the Persian sabre had torn the riband from his head, and the false beard had fallen with it to the earth. With his rich brown locks flowing round him, and the trim knightly beard on lip and chin, the Baron de Montfaucon stood fully revealed before him in all the splendour of the Frankish warrior, with the bloody scimitar still glistening in his valiant hand. He, however, shook off his confusion much sooner than Mutza, tore a steel gauntlet from the store of arms that formed the burden of the mule, and dashing it in the prince's face, "I challenge thee to single combat, sir prince," cried he, "with such weapons as thou shalt choose thyself, though far too great is the honour that I show thee thereby; for not only art thou a perjured varlet escaped from knightly keeping, but more than this, like a common robber thou hast carried off two noble damsels, one of whom was thy hostess."

A deadly paleness mantled over Mutza's visage. Was it that of anger, or were viler feelings at work within him? It were hard to decide, since every step from the plain path of honour puts even the best of us under the control of hateful powers, whose very existence, till then, we did not so much as guess of. However it may even have been, Mutza soon showed himself sunk low enough in villany to call out to his retinue, "Lay hands on him! Does this assassin of a merchant fancy that I shall fight with him?"

Then the warriors and attendants in the prince's train leaped at once from their steeds, and rushed on the baron in fell superiority of numbers. But Sir Folko, after wielding his Persian scimitar so manfully as soon to make two or three of the foremost of them rue their venturesome advance, tore down a number of daggers, arrows, javelins, and battle-axes from the lading of the mule, and hurled them on the knot of wavering opponents. Then a howling and moaning arose on every side, while in the fierce outburst of fury he cried anon, "Try the merchant! Try him! These are his fiery wares!" Mutza's faithful followers were already giving way; not one of them had any inclination to renew the fight.

Meanwhile the prince was boiling with fury and shame. "Then I must try my strength with him myself," cried he, "if ye are one and all such pitiful cravens!"

He was about to alight from his horse, upon which he had hitherto remained a quiet spectator; but Folko cried out to him, "Thou thyself art the most pitiful of all the cravens that surround me; thou art no longer worthy of the single-handed fight!" And at the same moment he hurled a battle-axe at his adversary with so sure and powerful an aim, that its sharp edge sank deep in Mutza's lofty brow, and the reckless young robber reeled lifeless on the grass. Whether it happened in the convulsive agony of death or during the last efforts of his rage, the dying man cast his Damascus sabre against the Frankish hero's breast; and the blade made so deep a wound, that Folko at the same moment with his adversary lay senseless on the earth. Furiously did the attendant band rush forward on the fallen knight to revenge the ignominy that had been cast both on themselves and their master; and with three wounds on his breast, and several others on head, shoulder, and arm, his noble life gushed forth in a rich purple flood. On anxious wing the faithful falcon hovered over the grisly throng.

But lo! like twin beams of snowy light, two beautiful ladies came brightening towards the spot, and the frantic crowd reverentially made way for them. They were Blancheflour and Gabriele, who, amid the universal tumult that filled the palace on the occasion of the Prince Mutza's death, had threaded their way through its enclosures. Over the Baron de Montfaucon's stiff and bloody form they sank in tears; now kissing the pale hero, and now each other, and praying God with the voice of wailing that they might die.

For a time the people and the slaves stood round them in astonishment, as if holy greeting had been sent down upon them from higher worlds. But by degrees their evil hearts flamed forth again with wonted savageness; first in random murmurs, then in distincter utterance, and at length in a wild resounding cry, their grisly lust of revenge broke loose, demanding the sacrifice of the enchanting Christian maidens as those whose fascinating loveliness had lured the lustrous Mutza to his death. Behind the silver veil of their tears, the two fair damsels knew nothing of all these unholy doings; and shrouded as they were, they would suddenly and unexpectedly have come by a violent death, had not one stepped up amid the confusion who resembled a demigod more than a man in the power and beauty of his form, and whose heroic valour held sway over the multitude no less than the outward splendour of his array. It was the Emir Nureddin.

"The ladies are under my protection," said he. And no sooner had these simple words passed his lips, without the least exertion of strength, without menace or anger, than the crowd fell back in reverential awe, and not a recreant whisper did they venture upon: so that with comely gentleness, and all the kind consideration of a father, the emir succeeded in withdrawing the maidens from the baron; and then, helping them with the fairest show of deference into a brilliant litter, he ordered them to be conveyed to the chosen apartments of his palace. He then returned to the bodies of the fallen. The Prince Mutza's eye was glazed, and death sat brooding over his distorted features: in woe and wailing his kinsman bore him away. But the Baron de Montfaucon likewise, though the wisest leeches were summoned,—men familiar with all the balsams and leech-craft of Arabia,—was declared to have died of the many deep wounds that covered his body: upon which the emir commanded it to be deposited for the present in a neighbouring hall, where none but the remains of princes were wont to be seen.

The bidding of the mighty Prince Nureddin was done. On slow and heavy wing the falcon followed the woful train. When they closed the jarring gates of the sepulchre, he kept hacking at them with his beak, and scratching with his claws. Then suddenly rising, in mad despair, he winged his swift flight far away over the sea.

CHAPTER XXII.

"On Northland mountains, high and grand,
The twilight gleam is waning!
And now a stripling sitteth there,
And pondereth on a maiden fair;
What would he know, if she were nigh,
What would he reck beneath the sky
Of peril or of paining?

And list! at love's enraptured call,
The German minstrel singing;
The blooming meads have caught the ay,
The flowery summer looks more gay;
And shadowy vale and hill along
A thousand feathery mates of song
Their gladsome flight are winging.

Ah! well they know the woodland ways,
And fortress grim and hoary,
And beacon-rock, and Runic stone;
As pure, his every heartfelt tone,
As when the Scald, in days of yore,
A sainted light was wont to pour
Round legendary story.

And now a hallowed light on you,
Ye guardian towers, gleameth;
For oh! an angel form doth sit
Upon my lip, entrancing it;
The hoary peak and mountain line
Have changed them to a temple shrine,
Where fairest beauty beameth.

My soul shall give her best of song,
My lute shall answer gaily:
Ye guardian mountains, join with me
To wake the chorus note of glee;
From stream and flower, vale and hill,
Oh, let the sweetest echo still
Be—Gabriele."

It was a beautiful evening in summer, when Sir Otto von Trautwangen sang this lay to his zittar on one of the Swedish heights on the frontier of Finland. He was not far from the Lady Minnetrost's watch-tower, for the inroads of the Christians on the pagan lands had been gradually delayed till the fine season was far advanced, by reason of the negotiation set on foot by the pagan hordes concerning their submission and conversion. Otto and Arinbiorn, therefore, were still on the wonted spot with their band. Just at this moment the young knight was about to quit his station on the heights in order to return to the dwelling-place of the pious Druda, when there came a fluttering as of some timid fowl around his curly tresses. Thinking it must be the bats, or such other ugly denizens of air as night sets free, Otto clapped his hands to scare them away, and then raised the cheery cry of a huntsman. But this seemed to be just the right note of invitation for the winged fluttering thing, and all at once a wondrously beautiful falcon-gentil nestled itself in fond familiarity on his breast. The practised sportsman was quick to recognise Montfaucon's faithful forest companion, and the more easily so, as the well-known necklace of gold, with the baronial hue and token, was wound round the glistening feathers.

"Good heavens!" said Otto, with a sigh. "Is the valorous Folko, then, fallen so soon?" For he knew very well, from what Montfaucon had formerly told him, that the like noble creature would only leave his lord when he was dead, and then he would circle far and wide over land and sea to choose another master that was equally worthy of him.

"Would to God," said Otto, looking on the bird's sprightly eye, "that thou couldst answer me a word or two. A host of questions are rife in my breast." And as a thing is often granted us that we foolishly petition for, often bringing us more woe than weal, so it happened now. A rose-coloured leaflet of parchment peeped from out the falcon's necklace, and when Otto drew it out, he read the glowing love-suit of the lustrous baron; read, too, Gabriele's acceptance of the same, that had never reached him whose eyes were to glisten with the blissful vision, but had sprung forth on poor Otto like a sharp and bitter death-shaft.

You who have loved some one being in the world above every thing,—who have been drawn to her by scenes of enchanting promise that outshone your fairest hopes, and now, because she has suddenly turned away from you, stand like a wanderer in the desert, whose moon has unexpectedly gone down,—oh! you will understand poor Otto's bitter pain. Should this book fall into the hands of one who is more wont to give wounds like these than to hide them in her own bosom while they rankle there, she may perhaps curl her lip with a disdainful smile. But God will keep ye, beloved and well-meant lines, from such readers as these; and much have I cause to hope that he who scans you will pity the sorrow-stricken Otto, and yet look with pleasure on the youth, seeing that he has strength enough still to keep those bitter pangs for himself alone, and with his zittar on his arm, and the falcon-gentil on his wrist, to stroll up manfully and calmly to the Lady Minnetrost's watch-tower.

CHAPTER XXIII.

As he was clambering up the bushy stone-way that led to the tower, the iron tramp of a war-horse sounded in the valley below. Involuntarily looking down, he perceived a horseman on a gray charger, and both steed and rider seemed familiar to him. Whilst he was still endeavouring to recollect himself, the horseman raised his eyes, and catching sight of Otto's face, as he peered through the trellis-work of green, he suddenly checked his steed, and with a lowly reverence, "Welcome, my noble conqueror and lord," cried he. "I have to announce to thee my return from the pilgrimage enjoined me, and that I have duly conveyed thy banner to the fortress of Trautwangen on Danube's bank."

Then Otto at once recognised Swerker, the brave young Swede, his prisoner and messenger; and with a heart that yearned still more fondly towards his father and his fatherland since the happiness of love was lost to him, he sank down on the rocky ledge of the path, and "Tell me at once, Swerker," said he, "just as we are, from beginning to end, how thou foundest every thing."

With a pale and troubled countenance Swerker gazed on Otto. "Sir knight," quoth he, at length, "Odin knows ye have dealt with me like unto one of the glorious princes of Asgard; and now, as a meed of thanks, I must be the bearer to ye of right unwelcome tidings, far other, I ween, than those you wish for. But to command is yours; and I will frankly and honestly give you what my message-bag contains, good and bad the same.

"Castle Trautwangen, on the bank of the Danube, still standeth firm and strong. Long ere I reached it, I beheld its stately gable towering over the fruitful plain. The people made me comely reverence when I asked after old Sir Hugh, and confirmed what you had already told me, that he lived in the castle there a stern and lonely life. The man at whose hostelry, about a quarter of a day's journey from the mansion, I gave the last provender to my horse, had formerly been a servant there; and he told me a lengthy tale of the hoary warrior's venerable mien, and how he always sat so straight and stern in the high chair in the bannered hall, with the little green-velvet cap on his head, and the round table before him; on which stood the silver cup moulded out of costly medals, and filled with the rich old wine.

"A mingled thrill of love and awe came over me as I passed the fenced bulwarks of the fortress. In the peaceful security that the name and dignity of their venerable lord commanded, the portal-valves stood wide apart, and the drawbridges lay peacefully across the moat. Neither serving-man nor squire came forth to take my rein. I dismounted, therefore, without more ado, tied my horse to the whipping-post in the middle of the court, and strode alone up the great stair-way, which I thought must lead me to the bannered hall. But I went slowly up, and purposely made my spurs and armour rattle, to see if any one would come, either to greet me or to marshal my way. Not a soul appeared. Not a word nor footstep sounded in the spacious pile. So at last I stood before the large oak-doors, and guessing that here must be the entrance to the bannered hall, I struck upon them three several times, loudly and slowly, with my gauntleted hand. No sound from within! I made the lock clink and rattle; yet all remained still! So at last thought I, 'I have now done all that a guest should do to announce his arrival, and he who is so deaf or sleeps so very soundly as all this, cannot take it ill if I enter without a marshal. Besides, I am a messenger, and have important tidings to deliver!' In this mood I gently opened the door and stepped in with the banner. There I was, forsooth, in the high hall itself; but, with all its array of arms and harness, it looked like the empty mail-suit of some buried hero. For although in the far background old Sir Hugh sat, so tall, and stern, and straight at the table, with the little green cap on his head, and the silver goblet of wine before him, yet the eyes of the hoary knight were closed, his countenance deadly pale, his forehead icy cold, and his strong hands clenched convulsively. Then I soon saw that the venerable hero must just then have died. I placed your banner before him, and was minded to keep watch beside the noble corpse till some one should come. But Odin knows how it fared with me! In that strange and tenantless chamber a fearful panic seized me; I felt as though the dead man would suddenly move, open his eyes anew, and start in the same ghastly horror at the sight of me that I should feel before him. Then his fearful howl would thrill me to the very soul, and I should run forth on the wide world an incurable madman.

"Sir knight, I trust ye have already proved that I am no coward; but on the spot where I then stood my blood ran cold. 'Besides,' thought I to myself, 'hast thou not fulfilled thine errand? Thou hast brought the old hero the banner, and they can lay it with him in his grave. And, moreover, thou mayest report to his son, that his father sits and quaffs in Odin's halls, or whatsoever Christian folk may rather please to call them.' Thereupon, hastening down the stair-way, I galloped off on my charger, and ere I had got far from the gates, I heard the wail of the squires around the body of their lord. And now behold me here, with such tidings as I have brought you."

"Hast brought me!" said Otto, heart-broken and sighing, whilst the thick gathering of night concealed his troubled countenance from Swerker. He ordered the latter, in a kindly tone, to ride to the camp, and there await his coming: then, on his own part, he turned his upward steps to the Lady Minnetrost's castle, without being able to prevent some scorching drops from trickling down his cheek beneath the dark shroud of night.

At the round table of that soft-bright chamber they would have been quick to recognise the pale and sorrowful look, the dishevelled hair, and rolling eye of the youthful knight, as signs of the deepest inward suffering, had not, besides the Lady Minnetrost and the sea-king, a third guest been present, to whom they were listening with the most eager attention, and who, on Otto's entering, sprang joyfully from his seat, and flew into his arms.

"Hei, heavens! Heerdegen, is it you?" said Otto, with incredulous amazement, though the broad deep scar which his own sword had left on the knight of Lichtenried's face might at once have set every doubt at rest. The two friends, who had so often been at variance, and were now reconciled anew, embraced each other in the warmest glow of affection. Each had something to forgive the other; and perhaps no feeling acts more acutely than this in knitting the souls of two good men together. To have made a formal explanation would have been not only unnecessary, but even ill-timed and out of place, and every temptation of that kind was at once removed; for the eyes of the Lady Minnetrost and Arinbiorn were so intently riveted on Heerdegen's lips, that one might clearly see what important matter had just escaped them, and was still hovering on their threshold.

"A wild time this in which we live," said the knight of Lichtenried, as, in accordance with their eagerness to hear more, they had reseated themselves at the round table, listening attentively to his tale. "What I have already told both of you, and what Otto does not know, I will once more briefly repeat, forsooth, that King Richard of the Lion-heart, at the siege of Ptolemais, happened to quarrel with the Duke of Austria; and thereupon, when the king, in the hardy spirit of knighthood, was returning homeward as a pilgrim through the Austrian demesnes, the duke set liers-in-wait for him, and took him prisoner."

"Lord of my life!" cried Otto, "then KNIGHTHOOD itself is taken captive, if King Richard the Lion-hearted be in durance."

"For that very reason, all belted knights must take lance in hand," cried Heerdegen. "It only remains for us to find out in what fortress, in hill, or vale, or lake, the great King Richard is concealed. The duke denies the fact. To-day he says, Richard has not been taken prisoner at all—to morrow, that he has been delivered over to the emperor—the next day, that he has escaped. What now shall an honourable knight be at in such a medley of purposes? One's head grows giddy—one's heart stands well-nigh still; and, with the greatest exertion of the power within us, not one single deed is done that dare even half reveal itself to view."

"We have a poor life of it altogether in this world," said Otto. "To angels or devils, at a distance, it may look better, perhaps, or more ludicrous, forsooth; but he who is in it has but sorry store of joy."

The bitter spirit of defiance with which these words found

their way over a lip whence soft and gentle speech was ever wont to flow, drew every eye to the face of the speaker; and, just as when we behold in ruins a scene that erst was the abode of gladness, without being able to guess in the remotest degree from what the sad ravage has resulted, so now did they all stand with their glances mutely fixed on Otto, till the Lady Minnetrost, with difficulty, found words to address him. "In the name of Heaven!" said she, "what has befallen thee, young hero?"

"Ah! it mattereth little," answered Otto, in the same fearful tone. "Only my bride is faithless, and my father is dead; so that henceforth I stand alone—all alone in the world. It is nothing else but this."

And as Arinbiorn and Heerdegen flew towards him, and clasped him fondly in their arms, he suddenly added, in a softer voice and kindlier feeling, "Grieve not about it, comrades; things cannot be altered now. Ye have stood truly and honestly by me, Heaven knows, as the very best among frail mortals could do; but still, for all that, I stand alone; for a band must be enwoven with the inmost holiest impulses of our being, knitting us to father, mother, brothers and sisters, to a dear wife or blooming child. All other living and loving is nothing—a mere shade it is that skims over the meadow. Good night."

And so saying, with a gentle yet powerful effort, he disengaged himself from the embrace of his friends-in-arms, and strode towards the door with sorrow preying on his heart-strings. But now the Lady Minnetrost stepped forward from the round table. The green veil floated back from her face, as if chidden by its moonlike gleam. Suddenly, though without any hasty effort, she stood at Otto's side; then, embracing him amid a warm flood of tears, "No!" said she, "thou art no shadow that glides over the meadow! No, thou standest not all alone! for I am Hilldiridur, thy mother, the mighty Hugur's faithful wife."

CHAPTER XXIV.

What would be your feelings, ask yourselves, ye who reckon a beloved mother among the dead, if she whom ye so long believed lost, and at a time too when your spirit most needed her support, should suddenly stand before you, and, gladdening your souls once more with her sweet words of solace, should smile on you in all the peaceful enchantment and gay innocence of your childhood? But you who still enjoy the unspeakable privilege of holding on your course beneath a mother's eyes, I will not counsel you to the frightful fancy of contemplating for a moment as lost what is the gentlest joy and the purest charm of your life. Without that, ye will be able to imagine the healing heavenly flood of transport that shed itself in a moment over Otto's bleeding breast. Beneath Hilldiridur's moonlight glance his heart became a smiling parterre of childlike trust and hope. Reft of the veil, his mother's face now shone on him in all its well-known soothing gentleness, though not so sorrow-stricken as formerly in the wood, nor so pale and rigid as on the chapel-wall during the night-watch beside his arms.

It lasted long ere they could come to any explanation. Otto was still kneeling before Hilldiridur. "O dearest, dearest mother!" said he, "have I found thee again? O heavens! why hast thou been away so long? Thy poor child has sorely wept for thee." And Hilldiridur's sweet tears flowed freely over his face, and her soft fingers sought ever and anon to dry them. With folded hands, Arinbiorn and Heerdegen stood motionless on either side, like forms that we are wont to see standing in old German pictures beside holy men or women.

At length Hilldiridur dismissed the three young heroes, bidding her son come alone the next evening to hear the history of his parents from his mother's lips. Half rejoicing, and half in tears, Otto rode back through the clear bright moonlight, his comrades, in kindred mood, bearing him company.

On reaching the camp, Swerker came running up to them, and offered to hold the knight of Trautwangen's stirrup.

"Not so," said the latter, waving him aside; "thou art no squire of mine, but a dear brother-in-arms of equal birth with myself."

"In no wise so, sir knight," replied Swerker; "I am not a Christian yet, and who knows if I ever shall be?"

"That you certainly will," said Otto. "If we had but a regular priest in our troop here, he should expound to you our doctrine in all its power and godliness; and of a surety thou wouldst receive it without scruple."

"List to me, sir knight," said Swerker. "Methinks you might address you to the work yourself. Knight speaketh best with knight; and so, in all true faith and hearty sincerity, we should certainly agree. If it turns out that you are right, then I will follow you to Christ; but if truth be on my side, you will then come over with me to the olden worship of Odin."

"Agreed," said Otto; "and to-morrow, by sunrise, we will begin. Wondrously hath it pleased God to gladden this heart that He so lately wounded; and I doubt not I shall triumph."

It was done as they said. The whole of the following day the two young heroes wrestled with each other in fiery argument. Otto felt the spirit with which his own words inspired him, and the victory they promised him; and when evening gathered, he rode joyfully to his dear mother in the Druda tower.

She came to the gate to meet him, and led him up the stair-way, amid a shower of caresses, into the chamber where the round table stood, and which that evening was more bright and cheerful than ever. On the round table itself lay many brilliant thiogs: a splendid helm-plume, confined by a costly egret of jewels; a large golden cross, with a rich chain attached; a green-velvet sash, whose golden embroidery sparkled with dazzling brightness; and other noble gifts befitting knighthood. "These shall be thine, my dear son," said Hilldiridur, as she placed her newly-recovered fondling before the glittering store; and whilst his astonished gaze fell first on the rich array of presents, and then on his mother, she contiuued, with true bright tears in her light-brown, moonlike eyes, "For so many a long year I have given thee nothing at Christmastide or birthday festival, poor forsaken boy! Now, then, I will do so all at once." And so saying, she began to deck her beloved child in all the splendour of that sparkling store, till the young hero soon stood before her like a fairy-king, so bright and so beautiful; and when, in the rapture of her soul, she had gazed on him once more with all the foud satisfaction of a mother, she bade him sit down opposite her at the table, and, without ever turning away her eyes from him, she began to speak as follows:

"Thy father, my beauteous, gentle boy, was beauteous as thou art, but not so gentle. A dreadful frowning warrior he was, who made every one tremble while they loved him, as they would before a fair summer's day with murky thuuder-clouds hovering on its horizon. Thus, then, it was that I, whom, partly by promises, partly by threats, he had made his wedded wife, when our barks met in the North Sea on my voyage home from Iceland, feared and shrunk from him amid all my truth and devotion. Still my blood runs cold when I think of the terror that oue day seized me. We had just returned from a merry banquet given in honour of him in a sea-port town of Hollaud where we had been living several months, when he found a Runic wand in my room; and, with a countenance that suddenly changed from the fondest expression of love to the most furious anger, 'I have already heard,' cried he, 'that thou art a mighty sorceress; but beware of letting me see any more of this craft of thine: such moment were thy last.' In thoughtless dismay, and heedless of the power of the wand, I threw it into the fire on the hearth, which instantly blazing up at the touch of the unblest visitant, flew wildly up the chimney, rove the brickwork in twain, and fastened so rapidly on all around, that Hugur scarcely had time to snatch my fainting form from the flames. Would that they had devoured all my wizard-gear at once, and, above all, the fearful mirror which is let into the wall there, and which I at that time used to have carefully packed, carrying it about with me every where! But its secret virtues had driven back the flames; and, much as I stood in fear of Hugur's anger, I could not disengage myself from all the furniture and mysteries of my magic art. Ah! my son, whithersoever an inborn longing drives a man, thither he must go, though he lose all his earthly happiness in his struggles on the way. Yet I made a compact with myself that I would keep all those mighty implements by me, and refrain from using them, especially as Hugur's rage would be likely to wax fiercer in remembrance of the fire.

"He compensated to the owner of the house according to the dictates of his kingly munificence, and then removed with me to the favoured town of Coblenz, situated on the confluence of the Rhine and the Moselle, whose blooming landscape might fairly vie with any spot in the world, even though Asia's beautiful fields lay brightening before us.

"There, in a knightly castle, not far from the town, among blooming fruit-trees, and on the gentle slope of a hill, whence, wrapt in the embrace of those two beautiful rivers, might be seen many a golden glebe and flowery meadow—there, my beauteous child, wast thou born! Rocked in thy cradle on the balcony of the castle, with what sweet unconsciousness wert thou wont to smile on the greeting of the bright world beyond thee; and, little as thou then couldst understand either thyself or it, yet I can well believe that the fragrance and light of those dreamy hours break sometimes even now on thy sleeping and waking."

"Mother, I feel so too," said Otto. "Thy words summon pictures before me that have lain like some sweet riddle in my thoughts which I could not unravel. And did we not travel on farther, when I began to understand things better? Did not our way lead us over lofty hills, pendent with beautiful vines? and did we not once stand on the very outermost ledge of a foaming, thundering water-flood? or was it some angry storm beneath us, with its clouds of paly blue?"

"That was the glorious Rhine-fall, dear Otto," answered Hilldiridur. "I remember quite well how you clapped your little hands again, and shouted for joy, while the glad sound was drowned amid the thunder of the falling flood; and your little cheeks glowed, and your eye sparkled so brightly, while the very planks trembled upon which we stood. Then the mighty Hugur kissed us fondly and fervently, and his lionlike cry rose above the din of the waters, 'Here is my true-born, valiant boy! Thanks to thee for the test, mighty Rhine, thou prover of heroes!'"

Otto's eye sparkled with joy as he gazed on his mother. "And since then," she added, with a smile, "you have not changed more than was necessary to pass from a boy to a full-grown knight. I knew you in a moment."

"And concealed yourself from me so long?" said Otto pensively; "and debarred us both so long of the hours of transport we now enjoy?"

"My son," said Hilldiridur, with a deep-drawn sigh, "it is a heavy penance to look too often into the wonders of nature and the world of spirits. I once talked of this to Bertha. While *ye* wend your way, hoping and wishing still, in childlike unconcern, a thousand mystic signs and warnings hold *us* in their grasp; and these we must follow, if we seek to be free from sin against the solemn gift which the counsels of Heaven have awarded us. The fitting hour had not yet come."

"Before that," said Otto, "did you never take my strange counterpart Ottur for your son, whose name my sword now bears?"

"I did so for a brief space," replied Hilldiridur; "but I soon saw who he was. You will learn that too, for my story draws toward the fatal crisis; it was fully revealed to me how inly and fearfully his wondrous destiny was wrapped up with yours and mine." And, after a solemn pause of silence, she continued as follows:

"For nearly three long years we had roamed through the blooming plains of the German land, when a longing for his home awoke in the breast of your father. In these parts he was no more called the mighty Hugur, as we in northern speech had named him, but Sir Hugh von Trautwangen. I, too, soon accustomed myself to call him so; and while I amused my fancy with the sweetest pictures of the fortress of Trautwangen, they pleased me the more, because they were ever blended with the only dear name I loved on earth. With what thrilling joy and lively hope did I think of the castle, and yet I never beheld it till long afterwards in the fearful mirror; and that fearful mirror it was that really deprived me of the sight of it.

"For, as we drew nearer and nearer to the fortress, my dreams rose every night before me in stranger array, urging me in the most indescribable manner to peer into the magic mirror, and read therein the events in Sir Hugh's life that were but just gone by. On awaking, although I could not clearly remember of what forms I had been dreaming, I felt a powerful longing within me to fulfil the behest of the vision; yet my love for Sir Hugh, and the dread in which I stood of him, always gave me strength enough to withstand the mysterious temptation; until one night, which we passed in our tents in the depth of the wood, my dream became most terribly distinct, and remained clear to me even after I awoke.

"It continually appeared to me as though Fair Astrid, my sister, of whose death I as yet knew nothing, was rambling about under the trees in search of flowers, when ever and anon a moonbeam would glance athwart her face, and I would keep saying to myself, 'How strange it is, though—night makes every thing look so pale! It is so like the face of a corpse!' And then I always felt awe stricken and sad. In the mean while Fair Astrid would go on with her search, winding and weaving a brilliant wreath, till only one flower was wanting; but scarcely was this last one braided on, when the beautiful gems of the garland would fly asunder, and spitefully burst in her face like a cloud of gray ashes, till her eyes swam with tears, and she herself, in that mask of dust, would look a very corpse. Then she would wring her hands in doleful wise, and begin her search anew, and then all would come to the same sad end again.

"I tried to rise and help her, but the dream lay like a leaden weight upon me. I could not move; and when Fair Astrid saw my struggles were all in vain, 'Trouble not thyself,' she said; 'they are earthly flowers, and none can give me those. Foolish it is of me to weary myself for the sake of them, for I have long since been dead!' So saying, she took her seat at my head, and spoke as follows: 'Thou *must* look into the mirror, and ask after the mighty Hugur. What hast thou the glass at all for? Never will I leave thee in peace till thou hast looked into it: after that, fain will I let thee go to Castle Trautwangen, if thou wilt; but till then, no rest—I say to thee, no rest till then for thee!' All this she uttered in so vehement a tone, that my head throbbed with pain, and I started screaming from my sleep. This time I knew my dream very well. The owls were hooting in the wild forest outside—my waiting-women were fast asleep—and the watch was snoring at the door of the tent. Shuddering with horror, I again sought to plunge into the sheltering depths of sleep; but so surely as I closed my eyes, Astrid's pale, gravelike visage appeared bending over mine, and her quick, shrill murmur rang painfully in my ear. Thus frightened from sleep into watchfulness, and from watchfulness into sleep, I at last sprang up, and ran in wild terror to the baggage, among which I knew the mirror lay. All slept around me—the fires were out—the moon had set—and the night was dark and still.

"At the touch of my hands, their familiar mistresses, each lock and seal beneath which the fearful hoard lay hid flew quickly open. With a strange weird light it flashed upon the pitchy darkness, and lightened still more awfully and dazzlingly from forth its frame, when I poised it against the trunk of an ancient oak, and questioned it, as the vision bade me, concerning the past life of Sir Hugh.

"What it revealed to me, it needs not my tongue to tell. You already know it from the grave recital of the armourer Asmundur, as also from the death-song of the mighty Hugur and Fair Astrid."

Here Hilldiridur and Otto melted into tears, and in this guise they remained for some time, sitting opposite each other in silence. Then his mother again began to speak as follows:

"In the mirror, too, I saw the beauteous boy who afterwards grew up to be poor Ottur; for he was Fair Astrid and the mighty Hugur's son. That your half-brother is so like you, is in truth no wonder. Your mothers could scarcely be told one from the other. Astrid and Hilldiridur, like two gentle roes of the same growth and colour, were sung of in all the lands of the north.

"I was still weeping to see Ottur turn away from his father in timid wrath, when the latter dipped a spear-iron in my sister's blood, as a token of peace between her father and him,—when Sir Hugh von Trautwangen stood in menacing guise behind me. The blood-red glow of the rising morn lit up his furious features. 'Thou hast been at thy witchery again,' said he, 'and thou must die.' And at the same time he whirled and brandished his broad sword like a fire-wheel in his hand. This was the very same blade, my son, that now hangs glittering at your girth, and which, as you said a few moments ago, is called Ottur."

Otto cast a shy look of fear and disgust at the weapon that but just now was so dear to him; and it seemed as though he were moving away from it. But, "The good sword did me no hurt, after all," said Hilldiridur, in a soothing tone, "although my life was forfeited to it by my disobedience. For whilst I fell on my knees, and threw back my neckerchief in meek resignation like a convicted criminal, and awaited the avenging stroke, 'No,' cried Sir Hugh suddenly, in relenting tenderness, 'God forbid that I should ever wound thee; but separate myself from thee I must, for now my whole trespass against Fair Astrid is known to thee, and I am far from being softhearted enough, or brave enough, whichever thou mayst choose to call it, to pray to be forgiven. Besides, I am afraid of such a busy sorceress. So haste, then, and leave me. I must keep our boy, and I will tell him thou art dead.'

"But I never ceased entreating till he let me say farewell to thee, my beauteous child. They told thee, that death was just drawing its curtain over mine eyes; and well I ween I may have looked like a dying creature, for sorrow at our separation, and remorse for my trespass, cast me speechless upon the flowery grass."

Mother and son again kissed each other with the fondest fervour, and their joy at thus being united once more was endlessly greater than their sorrow at having lost each other so long.

CHAPTER XXV.

From that day forth the three knights came almost every evening to Hilldiridur's watch-tower. The pagan hordes were at rest. Otto could gain no tidings of his half-brother Ottur, though his heart yearned more fondly towards him every day; nor could Arinbiorn gather news of his cousin Kolbein. They were often on the point of wishing that Gerda's witchcraft would rouse itself anew to some decisive struggle, if it were only for the sake of looking once more on the dear and truant warriors. But it seemed as though the flames both of hatred and of love were alike extinguished on the Finlandish boundary. On the other hand, the light of Christian doctrine kindled brightly in Swerker's breast. He hung with fond and watchful fervour on his knightly master's lips; and after the stern struggle of the first few days, he made solemn confession of the faith, which beamed on his loving soul as the only true path, either in this world or the next, to life and happiness. Therewith the two knights consoled each other for the loss of Ottur and Kolbein, rejoicing that they had gained over one soul—and a truly heroic one it was—to the doctrine of the Cross.

But while the outer world around him was at rest, Otto felt every day more keenly the pangs of blighted love. In the depth of a sorrow, which he strove to conceal from his brother-warriors, and even from his mother herself, a sullen sense of chagrin awoke within him when he thought of the ill-starred destiny of his parents, of his own long deprivation of a mother's love, which threw its shadowy veil over the day-star of his earlier life; and of all the pain he had since then suffered, and from which he was not altogether wrong in imagining that he might have been preserved under the fond guidance of a mother. He would now often ride far into the wild depths of the forest, till he had passed the Finlandish boundary-line; partly for the sake of finding his half-brother at every hazard, and partly that he might shake off the moody sorrow that harassed him: so that he sometimes would come at a late hour to Hilldiridur's moonlit chamber, and long after Arinbiorn and Heerdegen had taken their places at the round stone table.

One evening this was the case again. The smouldering sparks of discontent in Otto's breast had been chafed to wilder flame by the speed at which he had ridden; and as he strode all alone up the winding stair-way, threaded the lonely vaulted corridors, and at last reached the room where the mirror with the blood-red curtain was let into the wall, he seemed urged by necessity to deal one manful blow that very evening, and to shiver the enchanted glass that had been the cause of so much scathe and misery. "Out, comrade!" said he to his sword. "Thou hast still to atone for thy fault in the forest, when thou wert doomed to threaten my dear mother with woe. Purify thee now, then, by taking vengeance on this baneful witch-work." And at the same moment the good sword called Ottur flashed on high in the stripling's hand; then it fell with a jarring clash on the purple curtain; and after a few ponderous blows the floor all around him was strewn with the glittering fragments of the magic glass.

A loud clap of thunder rolled over the watch-tower: its basements trembled, a sullen howl rose from the subterraneous cells, and a cry of wailing sounded from the vaulted roof. Hilldiridur, Arinbiorn, and Heerdegen, with countenances pale and troubled, now entered the chamber.

There Otto stood, as if petrified, in the middle of the room. His hair rose on end, and, with a strange smile, he looked on the glassy fragments around him. "That I have shattered the mirror," said he to his mother, as he pointed to the place where the tattered curtain was now waving in the wind on the bare white wall, "that is of small account, forsooth. It deserved nothing better. But that Bertha's image was probably playing at the time on the shrouded plane, and that now, multiplied a hundredfold, it smiles sorrowfully on me from every single fragment—that is an unhappy business. Oh, heavens, mother! surely I cannot have done as the mighty Hugur did? Surely I have not slain my faithful love? Ah! with this same sword, too, Fair Astrid was slain. O mother, mother, was it not so?"

The voices now howled more wildly; invisible pinions came flitting through the room; and Hilldiridur buried her face in the green folds of her veil. "Hurry your friend away from these ruined halls!" cried she to Heerdegen and the sea-king. "If ye lay not hands on him quickly, madness itself will seize him."

The knights did as was commanded them. Leading, dragging, and carrying him, they hurried the bewildered Otto through hall and gallery, down the winding stair-way, and to the foot of the rocky height, Hilldiridur bearing them company. The thundering and howling on the tower grew still more terrible, and the three warrior-steeds sprang rearing and snorting at the side of the fugitives. A little grassy vale, engirt with dark alders and hazel-trees, and slumbering in the gleam of the dewy moonlight, received them in its still caress. They made halt, and began to collect their scattered senses, while the horses grazed peacefully on the high grass and fragrant clover; yet, from the distance, the din of the watch-tower came wafted on the breath of the dark night-air. In the full beauty of the unclouded moon, Hilldiridur threw back the green folds of her veil: then turning to the knights with a saintly smile, "We have escaped a great danger," said she; "let us praise the Lord in silent prayer." Whereupon they all knelt down on the green carpet of the vale—not excepting Otto, who had become quite calm and rational—and prayed in fervid devotion. When they again rose to their feet, Hilldiridur turned to her son. "Shall I thank thee, or shall I upbraid thee," said she, in a solemn yet kindly tone, "for scattering my spell-work on the air, and making an everlasting breach between me and the fearful powers that hitherto have attended on my steps? Dire helpmates indeed they were, and oftentimes hard to hold in check.—I thank thee, dear Otto," continued she, after a pause of silence, whilst she folded her fondling to her breast; "I thank thee, for good was thy deed, and if now thou hast a less mighty mother, she will only be more entirely thy mother on that account. The time of enchantment is over for me, or with endless toil I should have to wind my way up a steep, where but half an hour ago I held peaceful sway: and for this I have neither strength nor inclination now."

Otto kissed his mother on her hand and brow still more trustingly and fondly than ever; Heerdegen called her his dear good kinswoman, and drew close to her with a look all peace and cheerfulness; but Arinbiorn stood apart immersed in thought. "Who shall wield enchanted arms now," said he at length, "against Gerda and her crew? For the swords of her friends we are an easy match; but how shall we withstand the bewildering juggles of her demons?"

"Fear not," replied Hilldiridur, as she rose from the embrace of her son; "I have brought knowledge enough with me from the enchanted tower to be able to tell you that Finland hath made a peaceful surrender of itself, and that Gerda, Ottur, and Kolbein have taken to the sea in savage anger, resolved to roam through Christendom as the Christians' foes. Ye will find the envoy of peace awaiting you in the camp; and then it will be for you to choose whether ye will travel with my son and me to Castle Trautwangen, for which I feel an unspeakable longing, or whether ye will set forth on other knightly wanderings through the world. But for the present, let us make haste and get farther from the tower. Its angry spirits are already stretching out their fiery tongues from every loophole in the wall."

Otto took his mother behind him on his steed, and the light-brown neighed cheerily beneath the beauteous burden, trotting more gently and daintily through the valleys than was his usual wont. They had ridden nearly a league from the spot, when a fearful clap of thunder and a sulphurous pillar of smoke announced the entire demolition of the enchanted pile.

On nearing the camp, Swerker came forth to meet them with the tidings of peace; and after a brief repose, the whole triumphant troop, singing songs of love and heroism, passed down into the plains in the first light of the morning sun. Carefully leading a beautiful palfrey which he had chosen for his mother, Otto rode on in advance, with Montfaucon's falcon-gentil on his wrist, and Arinbiorn and Heerdegen on either side.

"For the present we shall remain a long time together," said the sea-king, as a parley arose as to the future plans of the knightly brotherhood.

"Ay, surely," quoth Heerdegen; "I at least think of taking my course through Germany into France, for the purpose of fetching home my sister."

A bright flush of red mantled on Otto's countenance. "I would fain ask you," said he softly, "to carry her a word of greeting from me, but I am unworthy of so fair a favour."

Then, silently yet kindly, Heerdegen gave him his hand, and Hilldiridur stroked his glowing cheek. Freshly and fragrantly the beam of morning broke over them, and every heart felt a new spring of hope in this early foretaste of a joyful future.

END OF BOOK II.

BOOK III.

CHAPTER I.

Bertha von Lichtenried sat reading a large book one evening at Gabriele's castle in Gascony. It contained the histories of pious saints and martyrs; and she was the better able to brood over its pages, as in that stately pile, saving the few menials of the mansion, she was all alone; and thus she had many days been vainly awaiting Folko's return and that of the two hapless maidens. The last greeting of the parting summer was rolling without. A fierce thunderstorm it was, and the red lightning flickered over the dark trees around her, revealing the surface of the sea as one dread mirror of flame. A gentle shower pattered on the terrace of the garden, and the silvery note of the bell in the little tower of the chapel might be heard, by which the warder sought to avert evil from the castle. In the neighbouring villages of that fruitful land, chime followed on chime, till it almost seemed that the mighty car of the thunder was borne along on the pinions of that goodly harmony. Bertha felt a threefold blessedness in the hour, from the awful words of the Deity, that sounded on high above the clouds, from the harmoniously soaring orisons of men, and from the pious histories, which, as she pondered over her book, floated in vision before her.

Suddenly an old Moorish waiting-woman entered the chamber. Her visage was black, for she was born in the depth of scorching Africa; but so completely had she conformed herself to the fashion of Europe, since her conversion to the Christian faith, that she might have been taken for an ordinary housewife, as far as her dress and manner went, save when her dark face was seen peeping forth so strangely from between the white ample plaits of her coif.

"What tidings, Zulma?" said the maiden.

And the old woman replied: "A pressing boon, which is specially craved of *you*. A Moor is lying on the plain there, mortally wounded. I know not whether he has been attacked by robbers, or slain in single fight. He wishes to receive Christian benison ere he breathes his last; but from no other than you, who have been renowned in all the Moorish country ever since the day that you leaned against the cross of stone, and with wondrous power put Mutza's bold comrade to flight. Not far from that stone cross the wounded Moor is lying. I found him on my way back from the farm."

"Call the chaplain, that he may go with me," said Bertha, as she looked round for her mantle and veil; "and have some of the grooms ready, both for our own safety and the aid of the wounded man."

"The chaplain," replied Zulma, "is already in bed, and the grooms are snoring in the stables. Long before we can rouse them, and themselves get ready, the wounded man will have breathed his last. And where he is to go to, if he dies without Christian solace and benison, you yourself must know much better than I."

"Ah, Zulma," cried the lady of Lichtenried, "how fitly and fairly dost thou rebuke my laggard mood! Truly, so long as he is in God's ways, no mortal child need tarry long for comrades and protectors; let us go at once to the wounded man. Good Heavens! what great works the holy men of whom I have just been reading used to do; and shall I be slow to such a trifling errand! How anxiously, perhaps, the poor dying man is looking for me."

Screening herself in her mantle, she strode with Zulma down the stair-way to a secret wicket of the castle; and taking the little solitary lantern that burned there to light them on their way, the two women went forth into the storm and rain. Zulma knew the way to the stone cross much better than Bertha would have given her convert credit for. She passed with a hasty step through the darkness, so that the lady Bertha had a hard matter to keep up with her, though she could not help feeling a kindlier regard for her, when she saw her zeal for the salvation of the wounded man.

Over wild and thickly-wooded hills, through intricate valleys, the nightly wanderers pursued their path; and when Bertha doubtingly asked, why they strayed so far out of the way, Zulma would reply, "It is the most direct road, lady; trust an African woman for skill in such matters. On our desert wastes of sand, where the storm at once covers up every footstep, we soon learn the art of setting ourselves right."

And in real truth, so often as the flashing lightning revealed the hills, towers, trees, or other objects, it turned out that the Moorish woman was going on quite the nearest way to the cross of stone. But Bertha soon remarked that

Zulma was led by mysterious signals; for very often she would send a harsh, shrill whistle through the night air, and the like shrill sound would give answer, determining the direction they had to pursue. She started involuntarily several times; and when Zulma noticed this, she said to her, "It sounds not sweetly, my lady, but it helps us through the darkness to the wounded man. Happy it is that he is skilled in this Moorish signal-craft, although he is not one of us black Africans, but a white Arabian follower of our crowd."

While she was speaking thus, a flash of lightning discovered the stone cross, now quite near to them, and a man, too, in the Moorish garb, half reclining, half sitting on the brickwork of the basement. "God be praised that you still live," cried Bertha, hastening up to him, and leaning over him. "I am Bertha von Lichtenried, she whom you asked for; and I bring you the consolations of God and the holy Church."

But what were her feelings, when he whom she supposed suffering from a deadly wound suddenly started to his feet, clasped her wildly in his arms, whilst that harsh, shrill whistle sounded close to her ear, the hills and edges all around seemed to spring to life, and a dense circle of Moorish men came pressing onwards towards the cross? Zulma broke into a loud and shameless laugh, shouting and screaming, "We have caught thee, then, have we, rare, shy little bird?—we have caught thee!"

In the mean while, Bertha struggled free from her adversary's grasp with a strength and adroitness that surprised and dismayed him in so tender a form; and then, flying, as she had aforetime done, up the little wall at the foot of the crucifix, she wound her arms in trusting fervour round the holy symbol. Touching it was to see the beauteous virgin clinging fast to the divine tree of life, while the lantern in her hand shed its bright rays over her, or cast a stray beam here and there on the throng of hideous menacers below. Zulma had already wreathed her veil round her black head in the manner of a turban, and then, with an impudent grin, "Now I am a Moor again, just as I always was," she said. "Did you really think your sober way of living could ever suit me? You must come to Cartagena now, and there you will learn something better than in your whole silly life you ever dreamed of."

Bertha turned contemptuously away from her, and implored the leader of the troop to bethink himself of knightly truth and honour, and not league himself any longer with an abandoned woman, for the violent capture of a noble damsel. But the shameless fellow burst on his part also into a scornful laugh. "This time," cried he, "that cross of yours and your prudish, dignified beauty will avail you naught. Ye have no sighing lover before you now, but the arch Alhafiz, the envoy of the mighty Emir Nureddin, who will bear you without fail to the arms of his lord in Cartagena."

"Let none lay a finger on me whose life is dear to him," retorted Bertha. "I know not who has implanted the thought in my bosom, but I know for certain that it is true—he who tears me hence with violence shall pay the penalty of a bitter death: heed ye, therefore!"

Alhafiz laughed, and strode towards the cross. A mighty thunderbolt rent the clouds, the robber and his vile gang fell dazzled and stupefied on their knees, and the recreant Zulma with them.

"God hath spoken," said Bertha, "and that is the last token of grace He will show you, if ye persist in your evil purpose. Be wise, and return in peace to your ships."

It seemed as though the circle were about to dissolve, in obedience to the behest of the glorified Bertha; even Alhafiz was speechless, and he now turned away from the beams of the lantern in the virgin's hand. But all of a sudden rose the cry of the hateful Zulma: "Think, Alhafiz, of the third part of Nureddin's treasures! Thou shalt not lose that, nor I the eighth part, as thou hast promised me." And with the nimbleness of a cat, she sprang up the wall, tore the lantern rudely from Bertha's hand,—"Now," cried she, "the witch can dazzle thee no more; off with her, then, at once!" And at the same moment Alhafiz wound his arms round the maiden, and bore her away to his bark, while his train followed him in triumph, as though rejoicing over a victory.

The lightning flashed no more. In cloudy darkness they reached the strand, and in darkness as deep they took their way across the waste of waters.

CHAPTER II.

STRANGE things had happened in Cartagena before the occurrence of the event just related. In the night on which, by the commands of the Emir Nureddin, the body of Sir Folko had been deposited in the old tomb of the princes, and the gates thereof been shut, a man, closely veiled, had come to the grating of the vault, and, taking his stand before it, so that the Moorish watch might both see and hear him, he had rung upon the brazen bars with a metal substance that he held concealed in his hand. As the sound died away, an irresistible lassitude weighed down the eyelids of the Moorish soldiers;

so that, just as they were on the point of springing forward, and asking the mask what he was about, they fell, reeling and staggering one over the other, and, as if seized with a swoon, lay motionless in sleep.

In the mean while, with a strange and thrilling sound, the metal kept chinking against the bars, till, within the vault, a heaving and stirring was heard as of a strong living form awaking. It was Sir Folko de Montfaucon, who rose up from among the bloody cloths with which they had covered him; and, in a hoarse and dreamy voice, "Good heavens!" said he, "how cold and dark is my bed!"—and, after a moment's silent recollection, he began anew:—"or, if I have died of my feverish wounds, why do they burn so madly now? and why do I not soar up, a disembodied spirit, into the happy blue of the skies?"

"Sir knight, you really live!" said the mask from without; "only the cure is not quite brought about yet. Chase slumber from your eyes, lest you begin to dream. I will be with you in a moment, and then I will heal you thoroughly."

And the more the wondrous stranger continued the chinking against the grating of the portal, the more strange were the fantasies that passed before Montfaucon's eyes, or sported round his brow. It was almost what we feel when we lie in half-conscious slumber; and the baron, who had just been awoke from a deathlike trance, would have relapsed again, under the influence of the same tones, into the sweet embrace of sleep, had not the stranger coutinually kept crying, "Drive away your dreams! keep your dreams away from you!"

At length the ponderous gates of metal creaked on their hinges, swayed solemnly and slowly apart, and the masked stranger entered the hall of the dead. "My wounds are grown cold," said the baron, his voice quivering with fever the while; "they pain me grievously."

"We will soon put a stop to that," replied the stranger; and, drawing a lantern from beneath his apparel, he began dropping a gentle balsam into those red breaches of war, and made a light pass over them with a glittering ring; and, while pain ceased, and new strength and animation sped through every limb, Montfaucon, in doubtful amaze, recognised the ring to be Gabriele's long-contested property, and the powerful leech to be the Italian merchant Tebaldo. "Now you see," said the latter, in a kindly tone, "how much better it was that the ring remained with me. You looked upon it as a part of your knightly equipments. Gabriele played with it as with a pretty toy; but a merchant was the person needed to elicit the true virtues of the gem, and to wield it in the aid of fair dames and noble knights. If you feel yourself fresh and strong enough, come with me into the Emir Nureddin's palace. He has undertaken the guardianship of the two beautiful ladies, aud we will release him from the burdensome charge by carrying them off. Hernandez is waiting with the ships at the mouth of the harbour, and one of his boats, ready manned, is lying close in."

The baron sprang to his feet, and, shaking off the last remains of weariness, he grasped his scythe-like Persian blade. Noticing the spots of blood that stained it, "Vinciguerra, I ween, still lives?" said he, with a sigh.

"Yes," replied Tebaldo; "I healed him before you; but he is in such an ill humour about his ill luck throughout the whole affair, that he has gone moodily down to the strand, and will be very loth, if he can help it, to show himself either to you or to the ladies." And therewith the merchant laughed most heartily, and, in merry Italian fashion, made many a pert grimace in mimicry of the sullen count, holding up the lantern to his face the while, that Folko might the better see him.

"Bethink yourself, you wondrous mortal," said the latter, in a solemn tone, "that we are in the vault of death! But Mutza, the perjured robber, you surely have not awoke him?"

"Heaven keep my hand from such godless folly!" cried Tebaldo: "besides, even if I had wished to do so, the virtues of the ring would not have compassed that. Your battle axe dealt too fair and deep a wound. It is now his turn to be carried off, and by a very black set of fellows too, I trow."

"Judge not," said Montfaucon, as he solemnly stalked forth from the vault, "but lead me quickly to the rescue of the ladies." With a strange motion of the head, that looked almost like contempt, aud yet either dared not or could not venture forth in words, Tebaldo walked along beside the baron.

On a lonely height, not far from the city, lay the palace of the mighty Emir Nureddin. The fearful howling of a beast, such as Montfaucon had never heard before, issued from the main wall that skirted the foot of the hill. "That is a tiger of monstrous size, brought from the land of Asia," said Tebaldo: "the emir takes him about with him every where, and has the animal chained up at night-time on his threshold, that he may guard his dwelling." The baron flourished his Persian sabre once or twice, by way of practice, making it whistle again in the air, and then he tried its edge and point with his fingers.

"Ye will not need to use it against the savage beast," said Tebaldo; "pray, keep it in abeyance. There is no telling but what unforeseen things may happen, though I do not exactly think they will." Then, drawing an arrow from his girdle, he began chinking with the ring on its silver-bright point, when music ensued, exquisitely soft and beautiful, and yet with such wizard virtue in its tone, that they fancied they could hear it quivering forth across the plain in sweet vibrations, and then dying away in the farthest regions of air. No sooner had Tebaldo repeated this weird minstrelsy for several times together, than the roar of the tiger became fainter and less frequent; and at last it ceased altogether.

"The monster sleeps!" cried Tebaldo; "but I must make more music with the ring, that he may not wake again, and that other eyes in the palace may be closed. If a fit of drowsiness should come over you, sir knight, only make the sign of the holy cross on your brow, and the charm will be reft of its power." Folko did as Tebaldo had advised, and they both strode onward to the lofty pile.

Overcome by sleep, the gigantic tiger had stretched himself at his full length on the threshold, so that, when the gates opened at the touch of the ring, the adventurous pair had to stride over the savage guard. At this moment the wandering gleam of Tebaldo's lantern fell on the wild and subtle visage of the beast. It almost looked as though a *man*, thus frightfully misshapen, were lying at their feet; and they hastened shuddering away from the hideous spectacle.

They mounted the hill by a beautifully-paved footway that wound along between hedges of roses all bloom and fragrance, though they were also obliged to pass through two or three gates with gratings of gold or bronze, at which a numerous watch was stationed. The guards sank into slumber at the soft music of the ring, and bar and bolt yielded noiselessly to its touch. In this manner they arrived unperceived in the body of the palace: yet, many as were the gold and silver lamps that burned in the corridors and on the stair-ways, Tebaldo stood still and shook his head in doubt, as if uncertain how to find the right way, through this magnificent labyrinth, to the chambers of the two captive ladies. But Folko's martial glance and eagle eye wandered keenly and unerringly around; and, soon setting himself right as to which side of the building they were on, when the merchant had pointed out the chambers of the ladies from the outside, "Straight up this jasper-stair, Tebaldo," said he; "it must lead us, without fail, to our load-stars."

They did as Montfaucon advised and commanded; and so in the galleries above he found out his way in like manner, till they at length stood still before a door adorned with glistening garniture of green and gold. "Here," said he, "must lie the apartments of the captives."

He then made a light clinking at the silver latch; and as

nothing was heard to stir within, he at last whispered through the keyhole, "Blancheflour, Blancheflour, open to us! thy brother Folko stands without, and he is come to save thee and Gabriele."

"Speak a little louder," said Tebaldo; "the music of the ring has doubtlessly weighed down their eyelids."

Folko repeated the same words in a louder voice; and scarcely had he finished speaking, when two female voices uttered a shriek of terror in the apartment; and the moment after all was still as death.

"What foolish work we have been making!" said Tebaldo, in a tone of chagrin; "we forgot that they thought you dead; and so, what you have just said, they must take for the words of a ghost. What are we to do? If we open the door by the virtue of the ring, they will then really take us to be spirit-forms, and, in the frenzy of fear, they will set all our magic at defiance, and scream till the emir and all his palace awake; and if they swoon away—which, perhaps, would be the greatest help towards our carrying them off—how shall we bring them down to the strand, as we must always be prepared against the possible chance of an attack?"

They were still standing in doubt, and considering what they should do, when the lock rattled, the door swung softly on its hinges, and the figures of Blancheflour and Gabriele, wrapped in their white night-robes, and with tapers in their hands, stood at once before the two astonished comrades like beauteous sister-spirits.

"We know very well, brother," said Blancheflour, "that thou didst die yesterday of those burning wounds of thine. Thou wouldst of a surety not have come merely to tell us that. Nay, thou speakest of rescue: and oh, if shame or dishonour threaten us, we are ready to follow thee even to thy grave!"

In maiden fear, her tender limbs quivered as she spoke—her voice trembled; but a firm, unbleuching resolution shone through those few coy words. In the height of his astonishment and emotion, before Folko had time to reply, "August shade!" said Gabriele, "on the other side of the tomb the eye seeth all things clearly; and thou knowest well how fondly I love thee—how truly I am thine; and thus it was even when thou heldst thy wanderings over the earth, though my lip never told the tale. Command thy maid, O noble hero!—she is ready to follow thee to death."

Then, with the bright flush of joy on his cheek, the knight of Montfaucon knelt reverentially before her. "Still do I live, heavenly Gabriele!" cried he; "still is my immortal soul a prisoner in this mortal body; but thine angel-words have granted me, while yet on earth, a foretaste of the bliss of heaven."

Blushing deeply, Gabriele drew back, abashed at her own confession of love, and also at the presence of Tebaldo, whom, till then, she had not perceived to be an unbidden witness of her love, and yet unspeakably enraptured at the restoration of her knightly favourite. Weeping tears of joy, Blancheflour lay in her noble brother's arms.

"Time wears apace!" said Tebaldo, stepping in like some droning watchman between the transports and greetings of love. Folko sprang to his feet, offering his right arm to Gabriele and his left to his sister; and the maidens followed their stately guide without further scruple or question. Tebaldo strode on hastily before them. He dared no more make music with the ring, lest the tender damsels should again fall asleep at the sound. He therefore used all possible despatch to leave the palace and reach the boat, fearing that, by some untoward chance, the sentinels might be aroused from their slumbers, or the savage tiger start up and assail them at the entrance. But he still slept soundly. The ladies, however, drew timorously back, and could not resolve to pass over the hideous monster.

"Riddle his neck through with your sword," said Tebaldo to the knight, "and then these charming tremblers will the sooner step forth to freedom."

Montfaucon stood hesitating what to do. "I cannot make up my mind," said he at length, "to fall on the beast while it sleeps."

"No, indeed!" replied Tebaldo, with a moody laugh; "I almost fancy you extend your knightly conscientiousness to a tiger."

"Jeer as thou wilt, and welcome," said Montfaucon; "but something always bars my way when I seek to draw my sword on the snoring monster; and this will do as well." Whereupon he raised Gabriele gently in his arms, and bore her forth over the savage guard; then he did the same with Blancheflour, whilst, with a shrug of the shoulders, and a sinister shake of the head, Tebaldo emerged from the portal.

But scarcely had the noble baron placed his sister on her feet, when the tiger started up with a roar, and buried his fangs in Folko's flowing vesture. "Hei!" cried he, clutching promptly at his Persian blade, "if thou wilt not have it otherwise, it is all one to me. To the strand with the ladies, Tebaldo! I shall soon have settled matters here." And truly the merchant had gone but a few paces with the trembling maidens when Folko overtook him, released him from his charge, and dropped his reeking sabre into its sheath. Without further hindrance they reached the shore, and, at once taking ship, they sailed out of the harbour, Vinciguerra bearing them company, yet turning his face sullenly away from them all.

"I am heartily sorry, Alessandro," said Folko to him, "that you are still so sore about a bygone encounter; but if you cannot help yourself, why, no one can." With all the heartier joy he turned to the stout Hernandez, who, as commodore of the galleys, received the ladies with distinguished courtesy.

When the Emir Nureddin, on the following morning, heard of the flight of the damsels, and the other wonders of the night, "Since the tiger is felled," said he, "I doubt not that the valiant baron has risen from his trance, and has taken the beautiful spoil along with him. In hero-hands the maidens are worthily tended. Let no one take upon himself to follow them; though, if that little jewel Bertha had been with them, I might, indeed, be prone to feel otherwise."

CHAPTER III.

Both now and before this, the mighty emir displayed a mysterious and incessant activity, in which his whole soul seemed absorbed. Ships were fitted out, soldiers were levied, stores of arms and provisions were amassed, and nobody was able to give the remotest guess as to where Nureddin's spirit was bent on expanding its gloomy pinions. The very character of the princely hero was a guarantee for some great and critical end being in view: for never was he yet known to sally forth either with a trifling armament or on a paltry quest.

Late one evening, after a busy day, Nureddin was reclining on purple cushions in his hall. He held a lute in his hand, on which he played in an unwonted strain—now luring forth tones of wrath and defiance—now others of a sweeter sound; or rather tearing them by main force from the instrument, which seemed to groan again under the stormy hand of its master. His slaves imagined he was resting from his work; but he who could understand the flashing roll of his eye, the wrangling tones of the lute, and those quivering lips, might soon be aware that the real struggle was just beginning, and, forsooth, with the mightiest foe that the emir had hitherto encountered, with—himself. This was the sole and only one before whom he was at times wont to tremble.

A captain of his forces, Abdallah by name, now entered the room with tidings for him. He was a tall, austere warrior;

with a hoary beard and flashing eye. Whilst he delivered his report, the emir looked him steadfastly in the face, and yet still continued tearing at the strings of the zittar. At last they snapped asunder with a note of wail, and the emir shivered the instrument against a pillar. "That all comes, lute," cried he, "of thy not understanding me. It is thine own fault." Then he signed to the attendant slaves to retire; and, begging the captain sit down beside him, he began to speak as follows:

"Abdallah, my heart throbs within me, as though it would rive my breast asunder, since I cannot breathe freely out, in my own way, what is pent up within it, into some ear that is skilled in listening, and in laying *to* the heart that which came *from* the heart. I know well enough that the like feelings are best shown forth by deeds, but the latter take up so much time before they come to light; and if one could but exchange a word or two about them in the mean while, one might fashion forth things of far greater glory, and such perhaps as one otherwise would never think of for a moment."

"Words are the mightiest of all shafts," said Abdallah. "Trees they are, that not only spread their fruit in upper air, but even send it back again into the lap of their mother—into the breast that bore them."

"Right, Abdallah!" cried Nureddin: "I think we understand each other. Long did I ply my search among the votaries of youth, thinking that in their flaming pleasure-groves the hero-tree must grow that should give me the fruit I longed for; but my quest was in vain. One and all, they blazed and crackled the moment that I let the least spark fall upon them; but mark me, the sterling core—the genuine being that makes a man what he is—that was either not to be found in them, or it was at most unripe and crude, and, in its dim conceptions, was as far from the goal I aspired after as heaven is from earth. They were mostly glad to have business with the great Emir Nureddin, and to be able to say to people, 'To-day I was chatting with him for an hour or more:—Did you see how he walked with me?' and a thousand other sorry conceits of that sort; but they troubled their heads little enough about any thing further."

"Pardon me, mighty lord!" rejoined Abdallah; "but when thou hadst once taken them up with thee to thy wonted elevation, it was thy duty to teach them to fly. The veteran eagle stands pledged for that."

"It was not that—not at all that!" cried the emir, with some show of impatience: "they ought to feel with me in things that cannot be taught—they ought to learn to know themselves, and thereby legitimise themselves as holy death-brands in the hand of the Lord of hosts. Is it not so, Abdallah?"

The latter looked on him awhile, and shook his head in silence. With increased fire and vehemence, Nureddin continued as follows:

"Abdallah, thou hast lived twenty years or so longer in the world than I. What has been made plain to me in my mature manhood, while age still keeps aloof, must long ago have been revealed to a hoary sire like thee. Seest thou not, by the increase of war, and the clashing swords of the Musselmen, Christians, and heathens, that the anger of God and of the Prophet hath kindled the vault of heaven to one mighty furnace, in which the nations are to be melted? They, most of them, have life and strength in them; but, that the noblest particles of them may not pass away in smoke, *we* too must further the fusion, or in a few centuries the One great Alchymist will have nothing remaining but a lifeless and spiritless mass. The best of us are placed here as lights,—that is to say, as torches; so round with the brand, and whisk the fire about. Like furnace-rakes, too, we must harry the sooty blackamoors out of Africa. Only quick to work, and set the masses in fusion; for as yet we are getting on at a desperately slow rate."

"My lord," said Abdallah, in utter amazement, "as it seems to me, you aim at the subversion of peace and the rights of nations; and what will remain to us then?"

"The rights of men, of knights, of women!" cried the impassioned emir. "The individual shall be had in honour by the individual, and the masses shall be stirred up together, till the fusion is complete, and they of themselves relapse, as they cool, into more beautiful forms."

"But, my lord," returned Abdallah, growing more and more astonished, "who has told you all this? and who has deputed you to the charge?"

"Is there not a fire here," cried the emir, as he smote his breast, "that maketh a very torch of me?" But suddenly pausing, he cast a long and penetrating look on his captain. "Thou of a truth," said he at length, "art no firebrand; so begone, and make the best of it."

Abdallah rose from the sofa, and bowed his head in no little alarm. Then Nureddin, in kindlier mood, extended his hand. "Well, if thou art no firebrand," said he, "yet thou art a gallant soldier. I will not deal with thee as with the broken lute there; nor would *it* have fared so at my hands if it could have been of any other use—as a shield, for instance, or something of that sort; but a mere lute must understand one, or be content to be shattered. As far as the rest goes, old soldier, forget what I have said. Think I must have been tasting opium, or that I have even transgressed the command of the Prophet, and been drinking wine. Good night to thee." So saying, he signed him in friendly guise to the door, and, when left alone, he threw himself back on the cushions, sighing and gnashing his teeth.

He had not long been lying thus, when the shrilly sound of the cymbal, the sackbut, and other festal instruments came pealing through the palace. The emir started to his feet in fury, and clapped his hands for his slaves. They entered, still hurraing and rejoicing; but, heedless of this, the angry prince called out to them in a threatening tone, "Who dares raise this shouting and jingling without my command? It shall go hard with ye for ruffling my troubled mood with your refractory and senseless glee."

Then the slaves fell on their faces. "Let not the anger of our lord lighten upon us," said they, "if we have trespassed against him. Nobody but Alhafiz is in fault. He just now came into port with his galley; and he brought a veiled maiden to the palace, saying it was the long-wished-for pearl of our lord, and bidding us shout and dance for joy in honour of her. He would answer with his head, he said, for the consequences. Let, then, no one suffer, just ruler, but he who is the author of the evil."

"In gold and purple will I array Alhafiz," cried Nureddin. "Moreover, he shall have the third part of my treasures that he hath won. He shall sit on my left hand at the banquet, and ride at my side in the battle, if his words be true. But if he lie to me, and bring not the pearl, then there shall be no lack of savage coursers to tear the sorry boaster limb from limb, on the four winds of heaven, in return for the wound that he hath given to my peace."

The emir had not yet finished speaking, when the green-velvet curtains, with fringe of gold, rolled back from the cedar-panelled door; and as the latter swung open on its silver hinges, it discovered the tall figure of a female, in simple vesture, and closely veiled. At her left hand was an ugly black woman, and on her right the repulsively smiling Alhafiz. "I bring thee, my lord," he began, "what I promised thee, and the black dame here was my helper. I commend her to thine especial favour; and hope thou wilt also do by me as thou didst promise."

The emir signed to him to be silent. "Thou hast an unlovely voice, Alhafiz," said he; "and thine unseemly caution has just given me a new proof of thy clownish spirit. Break not in thus harshly on this solemn hour of my life. I am free to confess that thou hast achieved infinitely more than I ever believed of thee, or than I at present can comprehend; and of a surety thou shalt not be the first to whom the Emir Nureddin remained a debtor."

Alhafiz and the black woman winked on each other with sinister glee, whilst the princely Arab rose from his cushioned couch, and, reverently approaching the maiden, "Lady," said he, "by the pulse of my life thou art she for whom my heart hath yearned so fondly. Now I make entreaty of thy favour; let me no longer be debarred the sight of the purest and loveliest countenauee that of a surety earth can show."

"Your blandishmonts,' was the damsel's stern reply, "should never win the veil from my face; but since God has permitted me to fall into your power, and since it is not unseemly in a noble Christian maiden to unveil herself in the presence of stranger men, I obey the behest of my most unlawful lord."

Her veil floated back. In the still majesty of features, whose sterner cast was suffused with unspeakable loveliness, Bertha gazed on the astonished emir from beneath the dark shade of the lashes that curtained her clear blue eye. Her light-brown hair was smoothly parted over her angel-brow, though some few little stray locks played around it. There stood that beauteous form in calm purity and lofty resignation, less dazzling at first sight than refreshing to the continued gaze, and ever entwining round the soul the rapt, chaste bond of love.

For a long timo both were silent,—the maiden in the consciousness of the strength given her from above—the emir in the sense of hero might that had been subdued and humbled; till at length he began to speak in the following words: "O noble lady! what saidst thou just now of a lord, and of commands, and of power? I will not suppose for a moment that any one hath had the insolence to fetter thine own free will,—at least not in my name. He who stands at the door once heard me promise the third part of my treasures to the skilful hand that should bring thee to me, without doing the smallest outrage to thy dignity; for, by heavens! that lies near as my own honour to my heart; and I take it for granted that he can only have lured thee across the sea by pretty entreaties, or the fairy enchantment of music and song."

"I know not what you call pretty entreaty, or fairy enchantment," returned Bertha, while a smile mantled over her features as sweet as it was severe. "Your envoy there and his band tore me violently away from a stone monument of our holy cross, which I clung to for protection. The black woman at his side was my servant, and she betrayed me to him."

"Can it be possible!" cried tho emir, while his frame quivered with rage; and he strode towards the wall of the divan, that was richly hung with all sorts of weapons.

"Prince," shrieked the terrified Alhafiz, "I have brought thee the maiden, and without outrage or injury too."

"Dost thou call that without outrage?" said the emir in a voice of thunder; "and couldst thou gaze on this angel form, and think of violence? Silence, ye dogs, where her voice is heard, and be silent for ever."

At the same time he took down two sharp-pointed knives from the wall, and swaying either hand with a motion almost imperceptible to Bertha, he hurled them with such fearful truthfulness of aim at Alhafiz and the Moorish woman, that the glittering blades of death quivered in their sinful hearts, and the culprits sank almost voiceless to the earth.

"Out with them!" said the emir, signing his slaves to approach. "A cunning lawyer shall come and divide the whole of my treasure into three equal parts: when that is done, call the next heir of Alhafiz, that he may choose such third part as suits him best. I seek not to belie my promise further."

The slaves covered up the bodies, and bore them away. Bertha shook her head and sighed as she saw them carried forth. "I knew very well, ye poor creatures," said she, "that ye would pay dearly for your trespass; and I told you so too. Why did ye not cease from the wicked deed? God have pity on your wretched souls!"—Then, turning to Nureddin, "What I am to make of you, stern avenger, I know not," she said. "Were you really, then, chosen to be their judge?"

"Yes, I would fain believe so, noble lady," answered Nureddin. "For the present, I beseech thee to be pleased to repose after the toil of travel. I would encourage thee to lay aside alarm; but silly fear, I ween, thou knowest not. With thee, it is but as the hovering of holy pinions over thee,—a hallowed meteor that weaves a guardian light around thee, repelling all the unworthy thoughts that are too prone to rise in the breast of man. But think no evil of me on my wicked envoy's account. I longed for thee, not as a paramour, but as a young and beautiful sister, who at the same time might be my loftier and more heavenly friend."

"God's will be done!" returned Bertha. "If He have destined me, a simple maiden, to guide a dread lion on his way to Him, it will doubtlessly prove so at last."

In the mean while, at a sign from the emir, honourable matrons had entered. To them he intrusted his beauteous guest, to be cherished with the tenderest and most respectful care; and then, crossing his hands on his breast, with a deep obeisance he bade her farewell.

CHAPTER IV.

On the following day a Moorish knight presented himself in the antechamber of the lady of Lichtenried's apartment, asking if the emir might be allowed to appear before his lovely guest. Bertha accorded the permission he craved. Nay, she even felt a sort of joy at Nureddin's coming, partly from a wish of knowing more certainly into whose hands her strange fortunes had led her, and partly because she was not unfavourably inclined towards the Arab, by the whole tone of his behaviour, and by a certain faint resemblance in his features to a pleasant face which she had somewhere seen, without clearly being able to remember how or when.

The emir entered with a lowly reverence; and when, according to Eastern custom, he had taken his seat on the yielding cushions opposite the lady, "Yesterday, noble sir," said Bertha, "you gave sterling judgment, not only as the avenger of innocence, but also as the maintainer of your princely word, by devolving to the next heir of Alhafiz what the rapine of the culprit had won. How is it, then, that you lose sight of strict justice with regard to me? If Alhafiz was a robber, and worthy of death, then I am quit and free as a bird of the air of any and every claim that you can urge to me."

"That you are, lady," replied the emir; "and it only rests with you to say what part of the world you will brighten with the splendour of your beauty, or ravish with the sweetness of your voice: only, I cannot be your escort now—I dare not be so; for a matter with which God and the Prophet have filled my soul holds magnetic sway over my goings. Wait a few days only; bear me company on a short trip by sea, and then you shall travel under Nureddin's protection wheresoever your heart desires. But haply, by that time, your heart may change, and desire no more than to tarry for ever under Nureddin's care."

"I cannot think so," replied Bertha gravely; "and to prove what I say, I request you to prepare a proper escort at once, and bid them convey me to the Gascon shore."

"If you insist upon it," said the emir, after an interval of silence—"yes, so it shall be." But again he paused, and gazed long and ardently on Bertha, till at last his feelings burst from him thus: "Thee shall I leave? Thee—thou beauteous image—thou heavenly phantom, and let thee wander with a strange escort to a distant land? If they honour thee not as they ought—if they offend thee by word or deed, or even by the harsh sound of their voices—shall I not foam with rage at the very thought of it? Oh, trust thyself to me, and to me alone. In a father's arms thou hast never known safer slumber." And truly there was something fatherly and pure in the warmth of the emir's love, so that Bertha could not feel afraid; and, saving her brother, she could think of no one under whose protection she could have felt herself so calm and secure. She therefore insisted no further on her hasty departure; but simply demanded a promise of the emir that he would escort her whither she chose as soon as he possibly could. He gave it with the utmost true-heartedness and a well-bred sense of delight at the confidence reposed in him by the maiden, who now, during the few days previous to embarkation, sought to make herself acquainted with the palace, and the manifold wonders it contained in the way of costly furniture, curious books, and beautiful works of art.

Rich are the lands of Asia, and blessed are they above all other regions of the earth, as though Nature were still fond of the sainted soil of tradition, on which man, her most glorious gem, first sprang from the lap of paradise, and where, in later times, both on him and her, blessings infinitely greater were lavished.

All that was most noble and brilliant in its produce, whether it chanced to be the intellectual offspring of its denizens, or the gleanings of wood and water, field and plain—all these, so far as the tender nature of the fair blossoms would permit, the emir had deposited and drawn up in pleasing array in his palace. He himself walked like a mighty enchanter through this pretty enigmatic maze, deftly solving its every riddle, and engrafting it upon the heart of every worthy listener; and to whom rather than to Bertha could he wish to speak of his bosom's best and noblest stores? Wherefore they often met each other with mutual pleasure in the wondrous and boldly intertwined arcades of the palace, in the shady bowers, on the bright green lawns, beside the clear mirror of the lakes, and the silvery fountains of the garden. With a keen sense of delight, Bertha listened to the olden tales and legends which Nureddin sought to amuse her with, partly reading them from cunningly inscribed palm-leaves, partly letting them flow from his lips, as they had been solemnly transmitted to him, in a tone betwixt discourse and song. She became so fond of them at last, that she requested to be taught the Arabic words and characters, in which these graceful treasures were embodied; and when she tried to imitate the foreign sounds, they received quite a new charm—so the emir thought—from her pretty utterance; for, in the aptness of her voice, she perhaps surpassed all other ladies in the world.

One day she was walking up and down with Nureddin, beneath the leafy umbrage of some lofty laurels, when he told her the following tale:

CHAPTER V.

'Far in the sea hight Archipelagos
There lies an island, large, far-famed, beauteous,
Fresh, bright with fruit and wine of golden sheen.
Now, in the heathen-time it must have been
That there was born the sorcerer so bold,
Whom folks afterwards for a god did hold.
The island is Creta hight, and Zeus its charmed son:
And there, with many a spell such power he won,
That soon the happy land where he drew life
With golden, laughing, frolicsome things was rife;
And not very long ago was planted there
A little rosebud, bright and passing fair:
Of all the beautiful buds on flowery stem
In that blooming land, it was the queen of them.
Now from Damascus town this rosebud came,
And kindly was tended by a little dame,
Whom from Damascus city, so grand and gay,
Some plundering band to the island had brought away.
She was just planting the pretty rose-twig, when
Her flowery sport was spoiled by robber-men;
Yet in her robe she brought the little flower
Over the sea so far to her Cretan bower;
And there it throve wondrously on the island-strand,
Tended by maiden eye and maiden hand;—
The rose of Damascus, the fairest far and wide—
The maid of Damascus, more fair than all beside.
Then oft to the rose, in secret, she would say,
'We both are strangers here, poor little spray;
Let us make a true league, then, on this island-strand,
And closer and closer draw the pleasant band;
Neither of us shall hie to her native home
Till the other, too, to the same glad port may come,
And the one shall fade when the other is snapt or dead.'
Then the rose always seemed to nod its little head.
Not long after this, the lovely maid looked out
Upon the main, where the billows danced about,
And a little boat came rowing along the sea:
In it was a wondrous man, so frank and free;
Right and left with the oars he smote the stormy wave,
As though 'twere a slave of his, a rebel slave,
Whom he did chasten and bow beneath his yoke,
Till the pride of the naughty slave at last was broke.
The seaman with eagle eye descried from afar,
At the lofty casement, that glistening morning star;

Anon he rowed up, moored his boat to the rail of gold.
'Who art thou, lady bright?' was his question bold.
'The child of a king,' quoth she, 'by robber-hand
Hitherward carried away from Damascus land.'
Then he: 'Such life, I ween, must be lone for thee?'
'No! the sweet little rosebud there is my all,' quoth she;
'See how it blooms and brightens the livelong day.
I *would* bring it with me when I came away.'
'Ha!' cried the seaman, 'I won a falchion fair;
In all Damascus never was blade so rare.
Maid, rose, and sword from Damascus, they are three;
And lightly the sword will make rose and maiden free.
Trust to me. I will save thee, if thou darest.'—
'Who art thou, sailor, that such bold emprise declarest?'
'No sailor, sooth, am I, but a belted knight,
Roaming the fields and the main, and the mountain height,
Seeking for sport and for spoil, with heart on flame;
And in this country Hygies is my name.'
'Art Hygies thou, the mighty man,' quoth she,
'Of whom they tell and sing so wondrously,
Who already hath won so much with his own stout hand,
At sea and on shore, in the Grecian and Persian land?
Ah! noble sir, then soon shall I be free.'
'Yea, maiden, this very night I will come for thee.'
'And hast thou swift ships to bear us from the shore?'
'Next year they will come, fair maid, but not before.'
'But, heavens! till then, say whither shall we wend?'
'Trust Hygies' wit to compass Hygies' end.'
Then she nodded gently; he rowed him along the sea;
Came again with the ladder by night, and she was free.
Deep in the mountains, overgrown with green,
A secret cavern lies, roomy, lone, unseen;
Whence fear keeps little coward man away;
And there was born in olden time, they say,
The Thunderer Zeus, the mighty wizard child.
Thither, then, into the very deepest nook,
Hygies his little smiling fondling took;
And often would come and talk the whole night through,
And bring her food and wine, and carpets too.
But the maiden would sigh, as from an inward smart.
'Thou wilt rescue me, and my good man thou art;
Then heed thee faithfully,' she would often say,
'That my poor rose-flower may not fade away;
Has Damascus given thee maid and falchion fair,
Oh, tend the Damascus rose with kindly care.'
And he cherished the maiden, and tended the little flower.
Then far and wide in the land, from hour to hour,
They wondered and wandered a whole year round and round,
And knew not where the fair maid might be found:
But Hygies knew it, and great was his delight;
And since the deep cavern did not please him quite,

Wherein his dear little Damascene love to hoard,
Blow followed on blow from his Damascus sword,
And wondrously hither and thither the falchion flew,
Until to a roomy dwelling the hard rock grew:
They say no princess ever had house so brave
As this beautiful home of hers in the Thunderer's cave.
Love bringeth sorrow, and stolen caresses bring sighs;
From warrior wooings after warriors rise;
And thus, ere the first year of love its course had run,
The beautiful princess bore a little son,
A lustrous child, as the cavern might well produce
That had been the cradle of the Thunderer Zeus.
So Hygies pressed to his heart the noble boy;
And the mother's woe soon changed to a mother's joy.
And soon after this, there came a flashing throng
Of white sails over the sea, borne swiftly along;
A part of Hygies' wealthy barks were they;
In the evening still and proud they anchored lay,
And messengers came to tell their knightly chief;
To his heart such glad news was a sweet relief.
He went to fetch his Damascus love by night
From the cave in the rock, while moon and stars were bright;
And as they wandered forth in stilly joy,
And the fond mother pressed to her heart the sleeping boy,
Then the beautiful lady sighed and hung her head;
'Ah, heavens! how all my joy is changed!' she said;
'Oh! must I leave on the strange shore, all alone,
This little plant that I so long have known?
We have alway loved each other so tenderly;
And promised each other, that if the one were free,
The other should ever bear it company.
There stands the little flower, oh, give it me!'
But the knight will not; he hurries her quickly by,
And she passes the dear spot with a deeper sigh;
Then the rose-bush, as with a thorny hand, took hold,
And tangled itself in her garment's sweeping fold,
Dragged the weeping fugitive back to it anon,
Till she sank and shrieked; and thought and sense were gone.
Scarcely had Hygies time to seize the child,
Ere she lay still and stark Then, in medley wild,
From every wicket and gate, a busy rout,
Woke by the shrilly shriek, came streaming out,
With arms and torches bright, all Cretan men,
And soon they knew the beautiful maid again.
There as she lay by the rose, they made ado
As if to seize her and seize on Hygies too;
But Hygies gave the sport another cast,—
Onward they came, and he clave them down as fast,
Till the blade of Damascus trickled again with blood,
And cowed and daunted the wilful robbers stood.

Now arrow and lance they showered, fierce and fell,
But Hygies warded himself and his dear ones well,
Till under his golden shield an ill shaft flew,
And pierced the heart of the lovely lady through.
She sank and swooned in the gentle arms of death,
And gave to the red rose-leaves her parting breath.
Then, wild with grief and rage, the knight bore away
The boy to his wealthy barks that at anchor lay;
Doomed to leave rose and lady on the strand,
With naught but the sword of Damascus on arm or hand,
And the boy too—who soon became a brand of war
That was more than a hundred thousand bright swords are."

CHAPTER VI.

BERTHA had listened to this recital with great emotion, and on several other days Nureddin had to repeat it. He did so with manifest satisfaction, and with a faltering voice that he ill strove to conceal. Then she sometimes asked him who Sir Hygies really was, and whether he knew no more of him than might be learned from the story?

"Not much more," the emir would reply. "He came from foreign lands to the Grecian soil as a stripling who was every where admired and feared; and I have never been able to make out whether his real name was Hygies, or whether he received this latter as a surname; for Hygies, in the Hellenic tongue, means a hale and jocund fellow." With such words as these he would suddenly stop short, while a moody cloud gathered over his hero-brow.

One evening Bertha and the emir were sitting in an airy verandah. Over the blooming orange-trees of the garden might be seen the boundless mirror of the sea, and their souls seemed to fill with tender yearning for the distance. The east wind played coolly over the waters, whisking up the leaves from the tops of the orange-trees, and wafting them towards the maiden, as though it would garland her brow. "Does it blow from Creta?" said she to her companion, with a smile; "and does it mean to tell us what is become of Sir Hygies and his boy?"

"You never yet have asked after the poor boy," said the emir.

"I know not how it is," returned Bertha; "at heart I have always felt a great desire to hear more of him; but when I am going to speak about him, a seal seems set on my lips, and I am mute."

"That is strange enough," said the emir; "I have always

felt tempted to speak to you of Sir Hygies' son; but then I have been kept back, from a fear that you would fly from the son of the adventurous knight—the offspring of the enchanted Cretan cave—for I myself am the very man."

Bertha looked on him with signs of astonishment. At length she said, "Why, then, should I be afraid of you, because you are the offspring of Hygies and the beautiful maid of Damascus? You must be all the dearer to me on that account. From such a bond of heroism and roselike loveliness a very star of honour and gallantry must have risen on the world."

"A comet, you meant to say," cried Nureddin. "A comet has risen on the world in me, vengeful, destructive, yet fraught with weal for future generations."

"They must be very bad," said Bertha gravely, "if they expect deliverance from a single champion, and not from themselves."

"It is just in order that they may not grow so bad," rejoined Nureddin, "that I am sent before them. I am to heap on fire, purifying, ordeal fire, till many a roof and many a land shall fall to ruins, to rise in all the greater glory hereafter. Believe me, noble maiden, the race of man has one and the same nature with the phœnix. It must from time to time perish in the flames, and rise anew from its own ashes, if it wish for immortality and endless vigour."

"I think you are fearfully in error," replied Bertha, slowly waving her lovely head to and fro; "but God will soon help you out of it, and most surely He knows how to shelter true and pious souls from the fire of your frenzy."

"We shall soon see whether He will do so," said the emir. "To-morrow we sail with my galleys for Ostia: this is the long-intended trip, in which you are to bear me company, till I am able to convey you whither you desire. At Ostia we shall run into port. Rome is but feebly manned; and when I bury the triple-crowned priest beneath the ruins of his churches, the whole rotten pile of Christianity, as they term it, keystone and all, will soon be a heap of grisly rubbish; more especially so, since the light of knighthood, the great Richard of the Lion-heart, is held in durance by the brethren of his creed."

Then a gentle smile passed over Bertha's face, betokening such childlike glee and unconcern, that it might almost have been called a laugh. The emir rose in amazement from his seat.

"Ah, well-a-day, thou beautiful being," cried he, "how canst thou make a jest of such solemn matters? I seemed in the spring-bloom of my life again at thy side, and fancied thou understoodest every thought of my soul; and that, although thou wouldst shudder anon at its revealings, in womanly wise, thou wert nevertheless thoroughly sensible of their greatness, and wert ready to rise on the wings of rapture when thy trembling was sorest! But, now that I give utterance before thee to purposes which hitherto my fondest and most secret prayers have betrayed to God and the Prophet only, thou hast nothing but a childish laugh for all my hero-scheming: thou tremblest not even at the thought of the ruin and death that threaten the creed which thou espousest."

"Would it, then, be a creed," said Bertha, with the same unconstrained smile, "if I could think of its death or ruin? The true faith can never die. God will preserve His Rome; and I thank thee from the bottom of my heart for intending to take me with thee to Ostia, where I shall be able to look on with admiration, and see by what bright envoy the Lord will baffle the wrathful man of war, whether by an angry cherub or a peaceful seraph's smile. O heavens! for thy sake, I would fain wish it may be the latter."

The emir bowed low before his lovely companion. "Pardon me," said he, "for misunderstanding you. Am I in fault, then, if you bestow upon me so much more favour than even an heroic soul can expect?"

Bertha kindly gave him her hand. "Good night," said she, "wondrous son of Hygies! To-morrow we must be up early for our voyage."

"Yes, indeed," answered Nureddin; "but, I beseech you, call me not the son of Hygies. I honour my valiant father; yet, that he neither sent me to Damascus to my royal parents, nor took me with him to his unknown home, but intrusted me to the random nurture of roving Arabs—lady, the remembrance of this gnaws fiercely at my heart; and I am tempted to think he may perhaps have been worthy of his Damascene sword, but not of the tender roselike maid of Damascus." So saying, he made a lowly reverence, and left the verandah.

The next morning the sun glistened brightly on the golden garniture and brazen beaks of Nureddin's ships, the spring-breeze wantoned in the silken streamers, and impatiently swelled the snow-white sail. Through a bushy avenue of the terraced garden, Bertha strolled down towards the seashore at the side of her strange protector. As they drew near to the glittering trellis-work of the portal, the low song of a minstrel outside broke on Bertha's ear, and she listened with that yearning fondness with which we meet some well-known token of long-past happy days. The words of the lay were nearly as follows:

"Ocean strand,
With thy bushes green and darkling,
With thy sparkling
Leafy verge of garden-land;
Tide of splendour,
Borne in morning's gleam along!
Thine should be my minstrel song,
If the tender
Yearnings that my bosom throng
Could but leave me for an hour,
Who so haplessly have sighed
For the little snow-white flower,
That was once the garden's pride.
Cruel star!
She who tarried here so often,
And could soften
All my woe, is now afar.
Here, *I* wander,
Winged trembler flown away!
Sighs come mingling with my lay,
All the fonder
Sobs my bosom—'Well-a-day!
Life the lingerer, passes fleetly,
And what promised bliss for ever!
Hope and love deceive us sweetly,
Doubt and trembling—never!'"

It seemed as though the minstrel, whose song issued from a thicket that lay close by the outer gate, would fain have pursued his love-plaint further, if a gentle flow of tears had not checked his voice. The zittar only with which he had accompanied himself still rang with a few pensive accords.

In her eagerness to catch the sound, Bertha involuntarily stood still; and the emir, attentive to her every wish, stood motionless likewise, signing to the slaves and handmaids to do the same, as they followed their beautiful mistress with parasols, cushions, and other conveniences for the voyage. When the song ceased, and Bertha's eyes wandered in quest of the minstrel, Nureddin passed hastily out at the garden-gate; then, glancing through the thicket with his bright warrior-eye, he soon discovered the weeping youth with the zittar, and, beckoning him to him, he led him before the lady. Without any token of fear, with a grave yet gentle mien, the minstrel approached her, and with glad surprise Bertha at once discovered him to be Master Aleard. She asked him, in a tone of kind sympathy, what had brought him to those parts, and whether she could in any way improve his seemingly untoward fate. "Speak freely," added she, as the hesitating youth cast a sidelong glance of doubt at Nureddin. "What you have to say, my noble minstrel, this hero without doubt may hear."

Then Aleard related, without any reserve, how he had come thither to rescue Blaucheflour; that, after the wound received by her heroic brother, he had felt so disgusted with Tebaldo and Vinciguerra, that he had resolved to consort with them no more; and how he passed tho whole night in thinking what plan he could devise in order to liberate the lady, and convey her to her home: then, on the next morning, he had heard from every lip of the baron's wondrous recovery and the ladies' rescue. "Now I live here lone and forsaken," added he, "wandering among sounds and faces that are equally strange to the cravings of my soul: my friendly zittar alone remains to me. It takes care during the day, in the houses of rich Moorish knights, that I need have recourse to no menial or wearisome work to gain a livelihood in a foreign land; and morning and evening it sweetly soothes me with the strains of bygone days. I had already made a firm resolve to live here forgotten and unknown; but, while my life is brightened by that beauteous form of thine, ere now so often seen at Blancheflour's side, the sweet longing for my dear home thrills my breast again with tender pain. I see ye are ready for travel. Could ye take me with you to a Christian land, ye would shed the fresh light of morning on my existence; if not, it will at least be an evening ray, and the stilly night will draw its gentle veil the sooner over my yearning sight."

"No; I will be your morning dawn of happy omen, if it be God's will," replied Bertha. "My noble comrade here will of a surety make no demur."

Kindly did the emir grasp the right hand of the minstrel. "What the lady Bertha wishes," said he, "is already done, so far as Nureddin's power can compass it; and your noble craft itself is dear to me. We Arabs are a people fond of the tale and the song; nay, sometimes even, when lute and lay chime fairly together, I myself cherish the proud thought that I belong to the poet throng."

And now engaging in lively discourse on the minstrel art, the noble triad strode down the strand in the crimson light of morning, and entered the ship.

CHAPTER VII.

The joyous halloo which had followed the galleys of the great emir, as they sailed from the Carthagenian shore, had now died away, and the Spanish coast was lost to the eyes of the seafarers. Over the deep blue sea, and beneath the azure heaven, the vessels were wafted on their smooth, swift way before a favouring wind.

Nureddin and Bertha sat on the deck of the flag-ship under a baldachin of olive-green silk, holding lively converse with each other, now in the Arabic, and now in one of the European languages; while the awe inspired by the emir's solemn mien kept every listener far aloof. Even Master Aleard, the noble troubadour, was not summoned to take part in their earnest conference. It is true that it began with the jest and the song, and Bertha's zittar still lay in her lap; but it soon became of another and a loftier cast, as is commonly the case with the discourse of two eloquent souls that are filled with aspirations after the great and the beautiful. People say that the eagle naturally soars to the sun, and mostly strikes into this path, though he begin his chase with the roe and other denizens of the forest.

What the two lofty forms, who sat opposite each other, discoursed of, the story-teller of knighthood, named by our forefathers Dame Adventure, and by our kinsmen of Roman lineage Damozel Aventure, cannot undertake word for word to report. Her sport, though in truth a grave one, is oftentimes chequered with many a shadowy figment; and, by very reason of her goodly meaning, she ventures not to place the grand truths of our holy religion on one and the same footing with her gaudy fantasies; and of these grand truths was the converse of Bertha and Nureddin. The emir clothed his argument in all the flowery lore of Arabia, Persia, and India: the maiden's words were few and childlike, condensed in little, simple phrases; while the tones of Master Aleard's zittar sounded pensively and faintly from a vessel in their wake.

In the mean while, evening rose over the sea—night followed with her solemn vault of starry gems; and the emir, committing the lady to the care of her handmaids, withdrew in thoughtful guise to his cabin. Bertha sported more gaily than ever with her attendants; and as she sank to sleep, a sainted smile mantled over her angel face.

The next day beheld the renewal of the calm yet mighty struggle of these two noble spirits. The emir brought with him into the olive-green tent several written scrolls of the palm-leaf; and in the intervals of his argument he would read aloud some cunning adage, or, sometimes, pleasant rhymes from hero-lays, or songs of love and wisdom's higher lore. Bertha had no book to aid her. She possessed, indeed, a copy of the book of books, bound in black velvet, with silver clasps and mountings, and graced with gentle, goodly blazonry; but this she had left behind her in Castle Trautwangen; and the beautiful histories of sainted men were in Gabriele's fortress in Gascony: yet had the good child conued those hallowed pages with such pious care, that she never lacked their succour. She would sometimes pause to recollect herself for minutes together, till one might have thought she was becoming embarrassed and dismayed by the glittering fruits and flowers that rose from Nureddin's rapt and royal soul in all the shadowy glory of the Alkoran; but soon she spake the simple words that breathed of love, and faith, and hope; and soon she foiled, like an artless dove, the garish serpent-craft of Mahomet's creed.

Things went on thus for many days. Their life during the voyage was quite different to what it had been expected to be. A solemn silence took the place of the warlike songs and splendid carousals on which all parties had reckoned, and seemed to throw its shroud even over the firmament and the sea. The wind swelled the sails no more than was necessary to bear the fleet towards Ostia without severe toil on the part of the crew. The shining expanse of the waters was smooth as a mirror, ruffled only by the light play of the waves, and furrowed by the cloven wake of the galleys.

CHAPTER VIII.

Early one morning on Ostia's strand there was a wild scene of dismay and confusion. Old men, women, and children were flying with their baggage along the high road to Rome, hastening up the Tiber in boats, or anxiously laying hands on their movables: whilst others shot, screaming, past them. "Away, away!" they cried, "their pennons are peering above the horizon!" Men and boys assembled in armed groups; but there were many pale faces among them, and a murmur passed through their ranks—"It is Nureddin; it is the fearful Alarbe himself!"

Some captains soon joined them with succours from Rome; but their number was small, and their countenances told of no blither cheer than those to whose support they had been despatched. He whose spirit was highest would anon call out, that it was not the great emir at all; it was nothing but a loose swarm of African pirates. Then from ten to twenty others would raise their voices against that single one, who partly had seen with their own eyes from the top of beacon-towers, partly had heard from the crews of barks that had been sent out to reconnoitre, that the fleet of the dreaded warrior himself was approaching, and his flag-ship among the rest. All this they knew by the decorations and streamers, the rigging and build of the galleys. The words died away on the lips of the captains as they sought to impose silence on the messengers of evil; and with an ill-omened shudder, each would whisper his neighbour, "It is all too true: it is he himself, and our fairest meed must be a noble death."

The sails flashed brightly on the crimson gleam of morning, between sea and sky, borne along by a favouring wind in numerous and well-ordered array. The captains of the forces dared not dispute the strand with so vast a multitude. They therefore retreated inland, that they might thence take advantage of any oversight that the Arabs might be guilty of on landing, or surprise them whilst engaged in plundering the deserted town of Ostia: or, in case the forces of the enemy should disembark with caution, and move against them in order of march, they would the more surely and speedily be enabled to make good the retreat towards Rome. In a moment the companies who were the first to muster gave ear to the word of command for retreat; every soldier turned his back on the sea, and each strode hastily along the Roman causeway. But not so promptly were the leaders obeyed when they bade the troops halt on a new position, and again turn their faces towards the foe. To that simple burgher-throng, strangers as they were to war, and intimidated by all manner of staggering reports, the way to populous Rome was too inviting and rich in promise. The more the leaders cried "halt!" the more hasty grew the march of the soldiery; and when their captains railed at them, and threatened them, laying hands on some of them, and turning them round by main force, the march became a run, and the run a wild, disordered flight. Some few well-tried warriors only stood stanchly by their forlorn commanders.

In sorrowful pride that little band looked around them. They were fain to feel that they were the true wheat among a heap of chaff; but sad it was, for all that, to find so little genuine grain; while even their very fame must bring them inevitable death. For Nureddin's ships were already coming to anchor, and the dense cloud of shining warriors was fast forming on the strand, and spreading almost as many bright banners on the air as there were opponents assembled to withstand them. Yet no one thought for a moment of taking part in the shame of the fugitives. He who up to a certain point maintains a firm resolve has nothing further to do with doubt or trembling.

While these heroes stood thus mute and still, and ready to die, leaning on their swords, lances, morning-stars, and halberds, so brilliant an apparition passed along before them, that they at first thought some heavenly envoy was come to fortify and cheer them in the last and bitterest hours of life. And on the like errand this messenger was come. The holy father the Pope, in all the glory of his office, passed up and down the ranks. Every knee was bowed before the most venerable ruler of the Christian world; all hands were stretched imploringly forth to him.

"Children," said he, "if the Saracens be conquerors here, those runaways will neither save Rome nor its sanctuaries. Therefore am I come forth to you, to live and to die with you, for God forbid that a Pope should think of his own safety, when the holiest domes in which the Lord is adored on European ground are to perish. To judge as man judges, to this pass it must come; and it behoveth us to shed our blood on this green plain for the honour of His name, and for our own happiness hereafter: but as God appointeth, it may, indeed, happen otherwise. Let us be prepared for every thing, whether He send us joy or sorrow, and with meek yet manful hearts receive ye His blessing."

The holy father extended his arms and blessed the noble troop; which forthwith rose at his bidding, and waited the event with happier cheer. The Pope stood like a field-marshal at their centre, armed with the holy symbols of his office.

With a merry war-strain, and the sound of tambourine and drum, Nureddin's troops moved in dazzling array towards the hill. Suddenly they halted; in a trice the martial clang was hushed; two lofty forms, a man and a woman, came forward together, and boldly drew near to the Christian forces, without first sending forth any herald or envoy of peace. On a nearer view of these sudden apparitions, the soldiers were struck with amazement at their beauty; at the gorgeous dignity of the man, and the commanding meekness of the wondrously-beautiful woman. No one could think of raising his arms for a moment against such peerless forms; but still, to prevent every possible outburst of despair or fury, the Pope signed to the captains and soldiers to remain where they were; and then, with a solemn salutation, he advanced a few steps towards their wonderful visitants.

The latter at once bent the knee, and the lady began to speak as follows: "Descrying thee from afar, holy father, both by the solemn magnificence of thy vestments and by the venerable grace of thy honoured old age, I deemed it unneedful to think on further preliminary ere we should do what we do at present. Here we kneel, holy father; and I, who am a Christian lady of German lineage, named Bertha von Lichtenried, bring thee the noble Emir Nureddin, who meekly craves the grace of receiving at thy hand the sacrament of holy baptism."

A solemn silence followed this astonishing address; the Pope turned his wondering and thankful gaze, as if in ecstasy, to heaven.

After a short interval, Bertha continued: "The warriors who are making halt on the plain are minded to follow the example of their mighty leader. The few who turn recreants to him, and cleave unto Mahound, are just now taking ship again, and they will not venture wilfully to bruise even a blade of grass on these shores, which, from this day forth, will be under the wardship, next to God, of the mighty Nureddin."

"So the true God help me, and His holy Son!" added the emir, protestingly; "both of Them, and Him who proceedeth from Them, this virgin seraph hath taught me to know."

Then the holy father kneeled down, and with him the Christian warriors, and all prayed in silent emotion to the God who had so wonderfully protected them. Then rising from his knees, the Pope bade the emir and the lady do the same, and follow him to Rome to the holy baptismal festival; but Nureddin still knelt. "Holy father," said he, "I thirst for the water of life. Prithee withhold not longer from me what the first disciples of thy Saviour were wont to administer in the open air without pomp or ceremony."

"Be it done unto thee, my dear son, even as thou hast asked of me," returned the Pope; and perceiving a little spring of water as he turned round, trickling from a hill close by, he took of the same, chose Bertha, and after her all the warriors who had stood true to their posts, to be witnesses of the emir's baptism, and in the course of the sacred rite gave him the name of Christophorus, in memory of the good and mighty giant whose heroism, many centuries back, had been a bulwark to the Church. Then he kissed the newly-won disciple of the truth with fatherly fondness; but, turning to Bertha, he almost bowed his head in reverence to her, saying, "Thou art chosen to be a glorious instrument in the Lord's hand, lofty maiden: there dwelleth in thee that which even a priestly heart must do homage to. I beg of thee, in the name of lofty Rome, that thou wilt honour her by passing the coming winter within her walls, and thus vouchsafe her an opportunity of thanking her Heaven-sent preserver. Thy noble convert then will remain here as thy guard of honour, just as the noble lion strayed not from the saint who had tamed him."

In blushing meekness Bertha bowed her head in token of assent, and the noble Arab Christophorus vowed to do what God and his mistress demanded of him.

In the mean time a throng of people, of both sexes, old and young, that had been lured forth from Rome by the glad and wondrous tidings, were streaming towards-Ostia, bringing with them food and wine to celebrate the festival of deliverance. This began by the holy father gathering round him all his brothers spiritual, and passing with them through the ranks of the Arabs, when, aided by the silent prayers of the Romans, he administered baptism to the eager warriors, who now followed their emir to the portal of life with the same glad zeal that they were wont to show in confronting danger and death.

Then on the green level along the banks of the Tiber, and partly in garlanded barks that decked its yellow waves, began a merry carousal; and when Bertha pledged the emir in a cup of Falernian wine, and he for the first time drank the noble juice of the grape, earthly as well as heavenly inspiration coursed through the veins of the hero who had first seen light in the Cretan cave.

CHAPTER IX.

NOT so favourable as the sea-trip of the emir and the maiden had been that previous one of Folko's and the rescued ladies. The sea rose wildly against them as soon as they lost sight of Cartagena; and it was only with an arduous struggle that they could pass the straits between Africa and Spain; nay, when, near the high rocky pillar of Gibraltar, they sought to bear up for Gascony on the starboard tack, such a fell whirlwind arose, that Hernandez no longer had the bark under his command. She was driven far out on the foaming sea; and they at last found themselves obliged, partly from want of wood and water, but more especially for the sake of giving the ladies relief, to land on an island altogether untenanted, and unknown either to the passengers or the crew.

And now, whilst Folko and Hernandez, and even Vinciguerra himself, were bent on erecting a commodious shelter for the ladies, finding moss and coverlets for their couch, and, in short, doing every thing that knightly courtesy at such times suggests, Tebaldo's sole pleasure, for days together, was to play with the ring, and, by all kinds of strange tricks that he tried with it, to lure around him the monsters of the desert and the deep, forcing them to grotesque dances and positions, and often laughing aloud at their gambols. Folko and Hernandez were filled with indignation to see the merchant plying his silly frolics to the utter neglect of the noble ladies; and when he at last carried things so far as frequently to bring the wanton beasts, with their hateful howl close to Blancheflour and Gabriele, till the latter trembled and shrieked with fear, the two knights resolved, come what might of it, to endure the nuisance no longer.

After a display of the kind above mentioned, Montfaucon one day planted himself full in Tebaldo's front, and silently gazed on him with a penetrating and sparkling eye. The baron had again donned his knightly suit on board the bark, and looked so hero-like in his mail, that the merchant, with ill-concealed embarrassment, cast his eyes to the earth. "Well, what does all that mean?" said he at length. "Are you going to make a Roland's pillar of yourself, that you thus stand so stern and motionless before me?"

"Not exactly that," returned Montfaucon; "but I know very well what I shall do with you if you comport not yourself more modestly than you have hitherto done."

"Do with me!" cried Tebaldo, in a tone of bravado; "ask me rather what I shall do with you, and your whole company in the bargain!"

"Sir," rejoined Montfaucon, with undaunted coolness, "you have saved my life, and have done much towards the rescue of the ladies; the ring, too, has put you in possession of mighty enchantments; but fancy not, on that account, that you can play off your jests on a Frankish baron and banneret, and still less on ladies who have committed themselves to his guardianship. If you ever frighten them again with the mad gambols of those beasts of yours, you must look well to your life, unless your witchcraft can do better service than my good sword. You may rely upon it the thing will be tried."

"You look quite as if you would keep your word," said Tebaldo gravely; "and it is perhaps better for both of us if we battle not to see which is to be master. Set your mind at rest, and pardon me; it shall not happen so again." Whereupon Folko, with reconciled feelings, gave Tebaldo his hand; and the ladies were not frightened any more.

Soon after this the heavens brightened, and the anchor was weighed, that they might pursue their voyage. Every thing went on prosperously till they again reached the rock of Gibraltar; but scarcely were they on the point of sailing past it, and bearing up for France, when another terrible hurricane arose, forcing the ship back into the straits, driving her past Malaga and Cartagena, and ceasing only when they came within sight of the Genoese coast. The state of the vessel, and the exhausted condition of the ladies, left them no alternative. They resolved on making the rest of their way by land, and ran at once into the port of Genoa.

No sooner were the ladies furnished with all the comforts that a noble mansion could supply, and the most necessary stores of arms, apparel, and other movables, brought away from the ship, when, at a wink from the knight of Montfaucon, the merchant followed him into a remote quarter of the town.

"Tell me frankly," began the knight, "have you not been at your fool's play with us, wilfully calling up, by dint of your enchantments, the vexatious storms that always beset us at Gibraltar?"

"Why did you not ask me that on board the bark?" said Tebaldo. "Then, perhaps, there might have been time to repair my fault."

"I know not whether there is mockery or earnest in what you say," returned the baron; "one never can get at the real truth of what the like of you mean; and it is a matter of small account that one should: for my part, I answer you seriously. Look ye, your witchwork might have conjured up feller foes to our ship, and the ladies come to harm at the same time. Here it can only light on me; and in all knightly honour I call you to account. Did you make free thus to sport with us?"

"In all mercantile honour, I reply to you," said Tebaldo, "that I certainly did summon up the stormy clouds that drove our ship before them; not for the sake of making sport of you, but because I had once for all taken it into my head not to land in France, but in Genoa."

"Genoa, maybe, will bring you ill store of luck, if you have any honour and spirit in you," said the baron, looking down on his broad knightly blade.

"What you are exclusively pleased to call honour," quoth Tebaldo, "I know not, and do not care any so very great deal about it either; but I have proved my courage before now, and think of doing so again on more important occasions than the one to which you significantly hint."

"Sorry evasion!" cried Folko; "the resource of all cravens and runaways! Have the goodness, without further ado or palaver, to say at once whether you are minded to go with me into one of the gardens that lie before us, and there measure your sword with mine, till one or other of us have taken the measure with his body of the ground that he wants for a grave."

"With all my heart, my lord," retorted Tebaldo, laughing. "We will soon find a place: only follow me!"

The merchant strode lustily forwards, and the knight was no less quick to follow him. Then, of a sudden, it appeared to the latter as though Tebaldo were calling him from behind; and, looking round, he perceived not only one, but many Tebaldos, some peeping from the windows of the neighbouring cottages—some grinning and screaming at him over the low garden-walls, and all wanting to fight him at once. Sure bestead, Folko turned round and round in the circle; but when one of them at last cried out, "Ha! we are grown too many for you; it is all up with your fightfulness now," knightly anger got the better of the baron, and down went his drawn sword on the jeering crew. "My pots! my pots!" screamed an old woman; and of a sudden all the Tebaldos had vanished, and the baron stood alone, with an old stall-woman before him, whose stand of earthenware had been shattered by his sword. Chagrined at the saucy pranks of the wizard merchant, he threw the old crone a few gold pieces to make up for her loss; and, whilst her astonishment burst forth in a volley of thanks, he hastened back to the abode of the ladies.

CHAPTER X.

Close by the door of their dwelling he was met by Alessandro Vinciguerra, who saluted him with a sort of moody politeness, saying he had just taken leave of the ladies, and now availed himself of this opportunity to pay his parting respects to him. Folko looked on him for a moment in silence; and then, offering him his hand, "We part, however, in peace and friendship, sir count?" said he in a kindly tone.

With a noble, yet cool and estranged show of courtesy, Vinciguerra pressed his hand in his. "At your service, sir baron," he replied. "I feel a true respect for your prowess and knightly bearing; the which assurance, forsooth, were unnecessary; for, were it otherwise, I should as little be wanting in spirit as any one of my race to speak the plain blunt truth."

"Of course so," said Folko, withdrawing his hand with comely gravity; "and it is equally a matter of course, that no one else can or dare think otherwise of me than you have just expressed; but I hoped to say farewell to you in more friendly wise."

"Pardon me," replied Vinciguerra, with an almost sarcastic smile; "it would have been a source of honour and delight to me could such have been the case; but I always fancy you bear some resemblance to the young German knight who was once pleased to read me a lecture at your castle on the affair of young Messer Donatello and old Dimetri. I think you both of you have something of a turn for preaching and converting, whereof you gave me a sample or two on board our bark; and, that you may not begin it again at our parting, I beg to take my leave of you thus."

"Alack for the poor harried heart," said Folko, in true

tenderness of feeling, "that treasures up every cutting word like some rank and poisonous herb! Gladly would I have rooted out the weed with the words of kindness."

"Just so," said Vinciguerra, bowing to depart.

"God knows, I am truly sorry for you," quoth Montfaucon; and he said this with so little soreness or indignation, and with such a rich flow of sympathy, that the Italian was evidently taken by surprise; and instead of triumphing over the good-natured Frank, as he had expected, by dint of his blunt rudeness and raillery, he hurried in blushing embarrassment to the harbour.

In the apartment of the ladies Montfaucon met Hernandez, who likewise took a solemn farewell of him; for, having found a vessel in sailing trim, he had made an exchange of his own galley for it, and that very day intended to embark for Barcelona, to join the army of his brave countrymen against the Moors.

"Is this the day, then, for a general parting and separation?" said Montfaucon, with a mournful and half-discontented sigh.

"Of parting and separation, forsooth," returned Hernandez kindly; "but not of separation for ever, at least not for you and me, my noble knight of Frankland. I love you from the bottom of my soul; and well I know that if we Castilians ever need a worthy stay, there cannot be a better one for us than the mighty knight of Montfaucon, who hath made the Moorish brides to weep. If, however, we never see each other again, we shall at least hear from each other constantly as long as we both are living. Our duty and our destiny call each of us to his appointed place; and the golden bond of love and honour, that entwines itself round knighthood, unites the deeds of ourselves and our comrades in unbroken affection."

The two heroes embraced each other, and parted. Folko was not displeased to find that the ladies felt anxious to see beautiful Milano, and to leave Genoa on the morrow, as the autumnal gales were beginning to blow bleakly from the sea. Not only because he was in knightly duty bound to fulfil the wishes of the ladies, but also because he himself felt glad to quit a place where his sojourn had been rendered distasteful and sorrowful by untoward adventures, he made busy preparations for their journey, and rode forth soon afterwards through the Bocchetta, with his lovely companions, into the beautiful plains of Lombardy.

CHAPTER XI.

There had been an early fall of snow on the mountains to the north, and the roads had become either impassable or dangerous. The ladies, therefore, found themselves obliged to tarry the winter in Milano—a constraint which soon ceased to be a constraint to them, since in these happy regions the face of nature still was smiling; neither was there any lack of such diversions in that brilliant city as were worthy the noble ladies' regard.

Folko and Gabriele now lived delightful days, though not wholly unmingled with fear and misgiving. If the latter had been surprised, on the awful night of her deliverance, into that sweet confession of love, her beautiful lips had remained the more closely sealed on their sea-trip; partly from her feeling ashamed at her involuntary betrayal of regard—partly from a dread of the mockery of others, especially of Tebaldo and Vinciguerra. Thus it was that she and Folko had outwardly become almost like strangers to each other, though inwardly they were all the more closely and indissolubly united; so that Montfaucon, in his noble tenderness of feeling, would have been beyond measure happy, had not one terrible thought lain like a dead weight on his soul—namely, that he was betraying his friend, the good Sir Otto von Trautwangen. This prevented the smallest budding, and still less the blossoming, of any thing like true joy in the mind of the noble Frank; and it often happened that he would wend his steps away from Gabriele's bright glances to the stern stony eyes that gloated on the bewildered wanderer from the gravestones of the neighbouring churchyard. There his heart was more at ease; for he felt how death did away with differences, and how even the injured Otto himself could be angry with him no more, when a marble slab lay over his deep-sunk skeleton, and graven thereon should be—Cy oit Messire le tres haut et tres puissant Chevalier de Montfaucon.

As he was one day wandering in this mood over the grave-mounds of the churchyard, he found sitting on one of them, that was covered with weeds of tangled growth, an old hoar man. His eyebrows were white, as if glazed with frost; his eyes had almost lost their light; and his long gray beard floated down to his girdle. For the rest, the stranger looked very sad and thoughtful, and might even seem to have a cast of the terrible in his countenance, save that a deeply-rooted melancholy threw a gentle shade over his features.

Whilst now Folko stood respectfully before him, intently watching his movements, the old man put his hand in his bosom, and taking out a sparkling little thing, which Folko could not get a clear sight of, he described divers wondrous figures on the dusky evening air. Folko was still busied in pondering on the meaning of all this, and thinking, with a shudder, that the old man might perchance be going mad, when a lofty form, gorgeously arrayed in the equipments of knighthood, entered the churchyard by the northern gate. It seemed one that was familiar to the baron; and he was on the point of approaching it, when, with a wondrously severe and woe-begone mien, looking, moreover, nearly as old as the aged sire on the grave-mound, it strode several times to and fro before the latter, and then vanished among some of the neighbouring monuments.

"Enough, enough!" said the old man; "now I know thee, and I shall not easily fail thee. But thou," continued he, as he bent over the grave-mound, "sleep in peace. The victim of vengeance shall not escape thee, though I stake my soul's weal on the venture."

Then it seemed almost as though a low sobbing might be heard from the grave; and the old man said, "I know very well, mother, what thou wishest for. Thou art far too gentle-minded, and his approaching punishment gives thee pain: but vengeance there must be, or else wherefore have I the ring?"

For a moment the baron quivered with horror; and then, borne impetuously onwards, as is the wont of honour-loving and valiant souls, he rushed towards the old man, and, accosting him in a harsh tone, "What dost thou here, wizard mortal?" said he. "Why rufflest thou the repose of the tomb?"

"She who sleepeth here," replied the old man, raising his sorrowful glance, "was forced too early into her dark scant bed; and mortal fruits like these, that are shaken off ere they ripen, can seldom find rest in the grave. There is little fear of troubling *her*: but prithee, good sir, trouble not *me*. I will soon set matters right with the dead."

Montfaucon remained irresolutely still. He knew not whether he should reverentially obey the singular warning, or whether he might not be destined to set some knavish sorcery at naught. "Do you know her so well who sleepeth here?" said he to the stranger.

"How should I otherwise?" returned the latter: "she was my own true mother."

"And thou wilt now avenge her, old man," continued the knight; "or did I misunderstand thee just now? for he who did outrage to her must long since be dead and buried; and to visit vengeance on his offspring rests with the highest tribunal only, whose starry eyes are beginning to glimmer forth above us."

"The crime is not of such long standing as you think for," replied the old man. "The miscreant still lives, and will continue to live, I trow, till I light on him. It may perhaps go as hard with me as with him; but was not Brutus, as chroniclers tell us, the own fond son of the tyrant Cæsar, without his dagger thereby being made to quail? Many a man begetteth his own chastisement. As for you, you are a grievous trouble to me to-day; and herewith, as you seem unlikely to be the first to make a move, I will rather do so myself."

So saying, he strode with unexpected nimbleness of foot towards the churchyard-gate; and suddenly the thought flashed across Sir Folko's mind that it must have been Tebaldo in magic disguise; nay, on the hand with which the stranger waved him a somewhat scornful farewell, he thought he had clearly espied Gabriele's wonderful ring.

CHAPTER XII.

LATE in the evening, about this time, some knights in heavy armour came riding over the Hartz mountains, forming the obsequious escort of a noble lady. The deep-blue darkness of night contrasted strangely with the peaks of snow and the hoar-covered forests. The moon was full and bright in heaven, but murky clouds, with their raven pinions, swept hastily over her. The travellers soon saw that they must have gone astray, for every now and then one of them would separate from his party and trot to and fro in quest of a track; then he would wind a blast on his war-horn, till his charger recoiled in dismay from the precipices, or from the gigantic shadows thrown across the snow by the long arms of the leafless oak-trees. One of the horses only, whose spare and sinewy form, of the light-brown hue, showed as boldly and beautifully against the blue of the night sky as against the white plane of snow, bore his dark-harnessed rider stoutly this way and that, as often as he dashed forward—clambered up and down stone wall and precipice with gladsome spirit; and by his aid it was that they at length reached the valley uninjured, and there found a beaten track, along which the wonder-working light-brown trotted cheerily before the rest. Many of my readers, I ween, have recognised the noble horse to be Sir Otto von Trautwangen's charger; and they know that, besides the young knight himself, the lady Hilldiridur, the sea-king Arinbiorn, and Heerdegen von Lichtenried, came wending their way downwards from the northlands.

The beaten track and the hoof-marks on the snow led them on towards a little cot that was seen planted at the foot of a steep and dizzy precipice at a turn of the valley, and was surmounted by lofty pine-trees laden with snow. At the noise of their approach, a light was put forth from a little window; and its gleam glancing down the mountain, and falling athwart their path on to the frozen mirror of the brook in the vale, the horses took fright, and were well-nigh gliding down the steep; but the knights held them in powerful control; and, fully trusting to his faithful light-brown, without either bridle or spur, Otto caught lustily at the rein of his mother's palfrey.

"Fair welcome to you, ye noble guests!" said the sooty form of a charcoal-burner, who, in the mean time, had stepped forward to the door. "Ye will do well to put up with my cot for the night; for as ye get farther on, the road grows more slippery and unsafe. Besides, there is many an uncanny thing abroad in the mountains; and ye have a noble lady with you, I see, who most surely is used to be tenderly cared for."

They gladly closed with the offer of the hospitable man. Otto helped his mother from her palfrey, and led her into the cottage; whilst the rest, as well as they could, took thought for the weary steeds; for the light-brown, in case of need, would let himself be unbridled and tended by the sea-king only, to whom, on their long journeys, he had grown pretty well accustomed. Besides, he was now glad to see his old adversary the roan charger near him, and was wont to ward him bravely when danger threatened.

The fellow-travellers were now altogether in the charcoal-burner's cabin: and the lofty forms of the knights, in their magnificent harness, looked strangely between the narrow ungarnished walls, and beneath the lowly roof of the cottage. Their helmets, which they had piled up on a little table in the corner, threatened to crush the fragile woodwork forthwith, while their monstrous plumes almost touched the ceiling. Opposite to these stood the pile of sparkling swords; and the hearth flickered fitfully on their massive hilts of gold and brazen scabbards. Hilldiridur had taken her place, not far from these, beside the charcoal-burner's aged mother, who sat there, so grave and venerable, a poor deaf and blind solitary. A strange contrast to the lady's solemn, moonlike beauty was the snowy age of the decrepit old dame, whose loneliness seemed suddenly lit up by a conscious flash that some sweet apparition was at her side; for a smile, like the glow of evening in winter, came mantling over her worn and withered features. The charcoal-burner himself went to and fro with the true spirit of a kind and cheery host. He had a store of good wine, with which he catered to the knights' entertainment, and drank with them, in merry fellowship, at their invitation.

"You should tell us some fine old legend that will make our flesh creep again," said Heerdegen. "You charcoal-burners, miners, and the rest of you, are little used to be at a loss for the like praiseworthy wares."

"Ah, we need no old legends here," said the charcoal-burner; "we see strange things enough in the forest ourselves. But there is little rhyme or reason in talking of the like of them just now."

"Why so?" asked Heerdegen. "The wind is just beginning to pipe a hollow note against the windows, much as if the voices of men were at work outside; the stiff lank branches are creaking over the hut, as though giants were knocking about above us, and were ready to take the roof from over our heads, and come staring in upon us with their grisly faces. I cannot see that there can be a better time for such stories than this is."

"Yes, yes," replied the charcoal-burner; "when we want to make a jest of the like of it, and talk of things that have happened a thousand miles away from us, I would as lief choose this hour as any other. But in these parts it is quite a different matter. The goblins lie too close at home just now; and the end of it will be, that they'll worry us till they frighten the breath out of our bodies."

"What is it that rattles without? What hideous thing looks in upon us?" said the old dame, in a hoarse and hollow voice. "Children, children, my blood runs cold again."

"Ye see, sirs," said the charcoal-burner, caressing his mother, and striving to cheer her with a cup of wine, "this poor deaf and blind old woman is not proof to these horrible fears. She does not hear a single word I say, and not even the thunder; but if the goblin-creatures only rustle through the wood, or I begin to talk of such things, she notices that there is something unblest abroad, and trembles in all her limbs."

"Get your mother to bed," said Heerdegen, "and then tell us the whole matter from beginning to end. It is not only that we want to be amused; but, as true-hearted knights, it beseemeth us to seek out distress in every shape, that we may see whether it be in our power to lend a helping hand or not."

The two other warriors seconded what he said, and the charcoal-burner hastened to comply. So, after the old dame had retired to rest, he began to tell his tale as follows:

"On one of the heights of our hilly woodland stands an old heathen altar of gigantic size. The woodcutters seldom wander that way, because there are terrible stories told of the Runic Round being aforetime soddened with human blood. But I always thought in this sort of way: 'If there has luckily been an end put to every thing like heathenism hereabouts, what harm can the old weather-beaten stone do to me?' And so, at all times of the day and night, I used to clamber cheerily and trustingly up the mountain, picking out the best oaks, beeches, and pines for building and for burning, which grew there in great plenty, since they were untouched by the other folks in the valley. Now, it was not because I did not know that the troop of the Wild Huntsman swept ofteuer over this spot than over any other in the Hartz country; nor was it that I beheld without a shudder the half-burnt bones and pine-brands that lay on the top of the altar; but I put a check on every idle thought, and at length got quit of it all without fright or ill-fortune.

"Some weeks ago, I at length clambered up the stony slope at eventide; and as the snow glimmered so strangely in the dusk from the chasms of the rocks, I fancied I could see tall white men, or gigantic women, lurking in the clefts round about me. But I soon took courage, gave a keen look at every thing that appeared, and at last had a downright laugh at my own silly fears. When I got to the top of the hill, I saw something sitting on the altar that looked like a great heap of snow. 'How oddly,' thought I, 'the storm has blown it all up together!' I went no nearer, however, but set to work at once on a tall slim oak that I had long since marked out for felling. 'Charcoal-burner, charcoal-burner,' cried a voice from the altar, 'let the trees stand in the sacred Round. It is Freia's Round. Freia is again come to your groves: beware of Freia's curse and ban.' And as I turn to look, something rises on high over the altar in solemn length, stretches forth its arm to me with an air of command; and what I at first took to be a heap of snow changes to the tall veiled figure of a woman. Without rightly knowing what I am about, I take off my cap, let my hatchet fall, and bow very low to her. In the mean time the altar seems to open on either side; and two heavily-accoutred knights come forth, with their beavers down, in rattling and sparkling mail. They bring with them store of casting-spears and arrows, and lay them down on the altar at the feet of the veiled lady. Then they stand motionless before her, like two brazen statues, leaning on halberts that almost overtopped the trees. 'Are ye braced and ready,' saith she, 'for the chase with Freia?' The heroes bow their helmeted heads, and their iron gloves rattle among their arrowy store. 'There stands a weak fosterling of the forest,' cries she, and again stretches forth her hand towards me; 'he shall be a witness how I, the returning Freia, have power over all the beasts of the wood—nay, even over the goblins themselves. Then he may go and tell his mates in the valleys that he has seen me; and they shall sacrifice to me here on my time-olden altar.' Thereupon one of the knights stepped up to me; and seizing me with a mighty hand, till the icy chill of his iron glove crept through my every bone, he placed me close before the white lady, at the foot of the pile, and bade me keep where I was, in spite of all that might happen on earth or in the air. For a short time I remained upright, but at last fell trembling to the earth. The knights and the lady stood motionless on the spot.

"Then, sweeping over the mountains, and sounding from the clouds, came the frightful and deafening din of the wild chase. Being used of old to hide myself at the sight of it, I now too buried my face deeper in the tall rank grass, for so many years untrodden by the foot of man. But one of the knights dragged me up again: 'Look on!' said he. 'Thou must and canst do so, for this once, without danger to thyself.' Terrified by those who held me a prisoner, I forgot my fear of the wild crew that were sweeping along on high, and at once did as the knight commanded. Their thunder-clouds came rolling over us, fringed with red, and dappled with a thousand wondrous shapes—deer and huntsman, horse and hound. 'Hakelnberg, Hakelnberg!' shouted the knights and the lady, in disdainful mockery, from the altar; and as I knew that the Wild Huntsman had been called by his right name, I felt sore afraid that he would ride angrily down upon us, with his misty steeds, and destroy us. But, instead of this, the attack was made on our part. Bolt, javelin, and arrow, all with points of flame, were darted by the strange forms beside me at the spectres above; the dogs howled, the horses reared and plunged, the horsemen shrieked with pain. Many of them, severely wounded, rolled over in the clouds; and a rich shower of blood was rained down upon us.

"When, with the approach of morning, the knights at last let me go, and the wild chase, after many times returning as if to renew the fight, had at length ceased its din, I went back to my cabin, though I was often startled on my way thither by the legs of wounded horses or the bones of warriors coming rattling down before me from the flying troops overhead. In my dwelling here I found many an ugly spot of blood on my clothes; and I was fain to burn them, rather than set myself to the unblest and dangerous work of washing them. But since then, every part of our dell has been more frightfully haunted than ever. The new goddess Freia, with her two knights, sometimes dashes along over the country on uncouth steeds, and seeks to turn the Christian folk to her godless heathen worship. All the people quake and tremble at the thought of her. Sometimes, when they think that one of the good inmates of the house is with them, she, or one of her comrades, will suddenly be seen standing in the middle of the room, grinning so hideously, that every one goes crazed who looks at her. If things do not get better shortly, it is much to be feared that the true faith, in many of our dales, will give place to a slavish fear of her juggleries."

"God forbid!" cried the knights, with one voice. "Rather will we stake our blood and all we have, to our last mite, if needs be, and lose it all without wavering."

Whilst they were speaking thus, there came a quick knocking, like that of many fingers all at once, against the lattice of the little cot. At the same time, the deaf and blind woman in the next room began to scream with fear, and her son hastened in to comfort her. Still, the knocking against the lattice continued; and a busy whisper sounded fearfully through the darkness without, such as often fills the ear in the delirium of fever. Heerdegen stepped to the door, and called out loudly, "Who's there?" Then he came in again. "I see nothing," said he; "but there must be a horrid swarm of bats in the wood." And it really seemed to the others who sat there, that one of them had entangled itself in his clustering locks; for an ugly face glared on them from over his forehead. Otto and the sea-king made a rush at it; but it quickly disengaged itself, and glaring on them with a pair of sparkling eyes, it broke a pane of the glass, and flew out with a shrill whistle into the darkness. They thought it must have been an owl. Heerdegen, however, knew nothing about the grisly thing that had perched on his head, but looked about him quite unconcernedly; and Hilldiridur, when she saw this, began to sigh deeply, and grew full of anxious misgivings.

The charcoal-burner came into the room again. "The hell-brood is terribly rife in the forest again," said he. "Ye hear it yourselves, I trow, and feel it plain enough in your very life-blood. Even the poor old woman, with her sightless eyes, is not screened from the flash of the ghastly witchwork." But suddenly riveting his doubtful gaze upon Otto, he paused awhile. "Heaven defend us!" cried he at length; "there stands one of the knights from the Runic altar."

The sea-king and Heerdegen, with all these strange things happening around them, could not help casting a timid glance at their companion, as if they doubted whether Otto was still among them or not; but Hilldiridur, who seldom, forsooth, looked away from her beloved son, now rested her glance on him with trusting cheerfulness, whilst Otto, stepping forward to the charcoal-burner in friendly guise: "I know not," said he, "how all this witchcraft, and your own fears, may take your senses captive; but you may gather from my greeting that I am a true-born German knight;

'God's word for aye
Shall be our stay.'

Does my voice falter, or my eye grow giddy, when I call on the name of our God?"

"No; most surely not so, good knight," replied the charcoal-burner; "and I cannot at all make out how I could take such a heavenly smiling picture of St. George as thou art for an unholy spectre. My eye was fear-struck and bewildered by the cry of my poor blind mother, and by the raving sounds outside. Now I see clear enough, and rest my hopes most firmly thereon, that thou and thy noble companions are sent into these vales to bring us peace and deliverance."

"So, God help us, you are not wrong," returned Otto. "I trust in the Lord, am ready to fight, and feel the call powerfully within me. So I will out at once, whilst the saucy goblins are rampant; and, my brothers-in-arms, take my dear mother, in the mean while, under your care and protection."

"Thinkest thou we would let thee go forth on such an errand alone?" said Heerdegen and Arinbiorn. So they girded on their swords, donned their helms, and made the buckles tight.

"Who is to stay by my mother?" said Otto.

"Why," replied Heerdegen, "thyself, I ween, were best."

"Besides," added Arinbiorn, "Swerker is likely to follow in our track with the serving men and squires."

"Comrades-in-arms," said Otto, and his eye flamed again while he looked on them, "the plea ye make is all of no use; ye must feel that yourselves, I think. The charcoal-burner's voice hath called me most specially to this adventure. I myself am the man. No one can reckon on Swerker's coming up with our serving-men on such a witch-sped, goblin night as this; and little, I ween, on such a night would Sir Otto von Trautwangen confide the protection of his mother to a *likelihood.* One of you at least must remain behind with her."

The two knights looked on each other in silent hesitation, each of them hoping that the other might declare his purpose of standing guard that night beside the noble lady. Then Hilldiridur unsealed her beauteous lips: "Go, all three of you, young heroes, I pray you, in the name of God!" she cried. "A Prophetess and a Druda I am truly no more. The hand of my son hath lifted the dread crown from my brow; but the once familiar powers of augury still love their gentle ruler of bygone days, and flit past me with many an airy beck or warning, as nearly as the strict boundary-line of their realm allows. Thus have they hinted to me, that your errand is a very solemn one—perhaps the march of death to one of you; but still ye must all three take part in it. Set forth, then, and God be with you; and look not so questioningly at me, dear son, as regards my safety. I have found One here who never yet hath forsaken them who have trusted in Him."

So saying, she turned to the figure of the crucified Redeemer, that with a rude but masterly hand their host had traced on the wall above the hearth, and, making the sign of the holy cross over the heroes, she pointed towards the door. They found no power left in them for remonstrance, and strode forth into the darkness of night.

CHAPTER XIII.

PREPARATORY to their journey, the three brethren-in-arms had determined to leave their horses behind them; for, on the narrow slippery paths which, according to the report of the charcoal-burner, led up to the Runic altar, they felt they would be rather a hindrance to them than an aid: but Montfaucon's falcon, who had never left the knight of Trautwangen for a single hour since the evening they met in the Norwegian mountains, now too wound his flight round the heads of the wayfarers, resting every now and then on the crest of his master's helm. This was a cheering sight to them all. The noble creature hovered over them like a star of happy promise; and the ill-omened night-birds flew affrighted away. Through the tangled luxuriant growth of the bushes, over rugged stones and pathless rocks, the knights clambered on, whilst the storm swept howling adown the wooded precipice, and struggled in the fearful depths below with the waves of an impetuous mountain-torrent. At length the hoar-covered boughs of the beech, and the dark-green pine-trees with their burden of snow, opened out into an ample glade, which, the moment they set foot in it, they knew to be the one spoken of by the charcoal-burner: for, high in the middle of it, almost like a rocky cliff, the Runic altar was seen towering aloft; and the moon, suddenly breaking forth from behind a cloud, cast her pale, death-like gleam on the half-burned brands and whitened bones that were heaped up on the dread surface of the pile.

Still the knights stood in doubt before the stupendous altar, undetermined whether they should here await the miscreant spectres of idolatry, or at once set to work and search for the

FREIA'S HERDSMAN

p. 267

outlet, from which the charcoal-burner had aforetime seen the two figures in harness come forth; when suddenly they remarked, with a shudder of awe, that there were four of them. A shadowy man of gigantic stature stood beside them. "Ye mean well," said he, in a hollow, inarticulate voice; "but I would rather counsel you to leave off. The folks below are desperately strong; yet if ye are quite resolved not to give the matter up, ye must go to the north side of the altar, where entrance is easiest; strike thrice thereon with your sword-blades, and say,

'Ope anon, that we may pass,
Gritty stone and knotted grass.
Mighty strangers wait to see
What the weird abyss may be.'

It is best to be the assailants. All my life long I have liked better to fall on savage beasts myself than to be grappled first by them."

As the knights gazed on him in inquiring amazement, "I would fain wind you a note on my bugle," said he, "to cheer you up, and give you spirit for the fray; but I dare not do much to make myself heard just here. Good luck to ye, brave mountain folk!"

So saying, the strange shadowy forester was lost in the gloom of the wood; and the warriors resolved to follow his advice, because there was really something knightly and brave in it. They therefore struck their swords against the north side of the Runic altar, and Heerdegen uttered the charmed rhyme as he was best able to remember it.

Then there began a stirring and a rolling in the rock; and the mossy wall was sundered, so that they could see far down into a long, narrow, and precipitous passage. Little flames danced frowardly or shyly along the walls and adown the mouldering stair-way. "Here your mother's misgivings may lightly be fulfilled," said Arinbiorn to Otto, "and a grave be opened for one of us; for, in truth, this place looks altogether like one."

"Well," cried Heerdegen, "the whole world looks pretty much the same to a man who keeps his eye on the end of things. As long as we reach the goal by an honest path, we can scarce wish for any thing more; and an honest path is the one we are treading now. Why, then, need we scruple and hesitate?"

"Who says that I scruple or hesitate?" quoth the sea-king, in noble indignation, and strode hastily into the vault. Otto followed him, casting back a glance on the bright disc of the moon, that just then emerged from the clouds, looking to him like his dear mother's face; and then went Heerdegen, humming an old song about the mountain spirits. The falcon cowered timidly on Otto's breast, well knowing that between those narrow walls he dare not unfold his bold wings for flight. Soon, however, the path became wider. From a gallant wish not to be behind their brother-in-arms in encountering peril, Otto and Heerdegen pressed forwards at the sea-king's side, and the three adventurers pursued their way abreast, stretching out their long flashing swords like feelers into the darkness.

They met with nothing to bar their path; but the deeper they descended, the wider grew the cavern, and the more gentle the slope of the steps. Suddenly they stood on level ground. A stream of air blew over them as from the open country; and they were the more inclined to think they had really reached it, since far above them solitary stars were seen twinkling like those in the vault of heaven. They were still doubting and wondering how, at such immense depth underground, they could possibly have gained a glimpse of the firmament, when the falcon rose on Otto's breast, and, cheerily flapping his wings, he darted off into the unfettered space above him. But soon the mettlesome creature came fluttering down on dizzy and disappointed pinion: it was plain that he had been bent on the chase, and had lighted on some of the hideous things that now wantoned over the heads of the knights. They could not tell whether they were enormous birds of an unknown species, or cavern-vapours, stealing about that subterraneous realm in dense and threatening numbers; for it had become evident to the eyes of the wanderers, as they grew familiar with the darkness, that they were in a vault underground of stupendous height and structure, that might almost in itself be deemed a firmament, with a host of starry lamps dependent from the dizzy span of its cupola.

A vast lake lay at their feet, cheerlessly reflecting that pitchy vault and those starry lamps. The knights sought to feel its depth with their swords; and Arinbiorn did the same at last with his long halbert; but quite close to the bank there was no hope of finding bottom. It made them shudder to think of it—such a watery abyss, and so deep beneath the mountains! But they resolved to bring their adventure quickly to an end, and strode along the banks of the mighty pool. The falcon, in the mean while, sat on Otto's helmet.

They had wandered along the margin for more than a mile, when suddenly there arose before them a hilly steep, on which stood a turreted fortress. Whilst they were bent on approaching it, they remarked that the lake at this point received the waters of a turbulent river that wound along between them and the immediate spot they were journeying to. There could be no thought of wading or swimming through the terrible whirl of its foam: they therefore passed on up the stream, to see if they could find the means of crossing; and they soon reached a bridge with a sweeping arch of massive brass, which rung beneath the footsteps of the harnessed wayfarers to the tune of a frightful march. On reaching the other side, they beheld before them a wide and level plain—it might have been called a blooming mead, for there was the glittering of many flowers upon it, that, on a nearer approach, were seen to be pale little flames of wondrous shape, exhaling a sulphurous steam; and yet it seemed as if strange little animals fed upon them; for, as they went straggling alone, or trotting in a body over the plain, half like horses and half like bulls in form, they would often crop up a little flame here and there, and then spring merrily away.

"Shall we catch us a steed or two, and ride up to the castle?" said Heerdegen, with a hearty laugh, hoping thereby to stifle horror in his own and his companions' breasts. But the gay offspring of dismay awoke dismay anew. They all three shuddered till their harness rattled again. At the same time a little ugly dwarf came hopping along on one leg. "Covet not these animals," said he; "they are the goddess Freia's enchanted steeds: she rides on them through the wood, and chases the Wild Huntsman, and all the people who will not sacrifice to her. I am the herdsman of the noble horses." So saying, he blew a blast on a monstrous horn, with such a shrill and thundering tone that the knights could scarcely keep from recoiling.

"Does that frighten you?" quoth the dwarf, with a laugh. "I am only playing a little on the shalm, as is the way and wont of herdsmen. If you please, I can let you see our rustic dances. I have many a mate at hand." The knights signed him away with their mailed hands, and went silently towards the castle. The laugh of the dwarfish herdsman sounded shrilly after them, and the enchanted steeds leaped with many a wild neigh about the meadow of flames.

Over cloven chasm and rocky steep led the way to the subterraneous castle. Heerdegen and Arinbiorn, who had travelled far in southern lands, thought there were just the same sort of things there, and that it arose from the bubbling up of fiery springs from the very centre of the earth, which at one time made the mountains so curiously smooth, and at another time rent them asunder.

The three knights passed drawbridges and gates, as if they were entering a regular baronial castle. Men in brazen harness seemed to be keeping guard at the different approaches. They bowed to them as they passed in, strictly giving the salute of arms; yet it was hard to decide whether they were not merely cunningly-wrought statues that made such a singular rattling, bowing, and then flying up to their full height, and planting themselves motionless at their posts.

They then had to thread their way through empty chambers and galleries, their footsteps sounding fearfully again in this seemingly deserted pile. Flickering lamps hung here and there on the walls, lighting the wanderers with the lurid gleam of funeral tapers. At length they reached a chamber richly garnished, though strangely set out with painted spectral forms and death's-heads. Here a knight was sitting at a large round table, reading in a book thrown wide open before him, in which the faint outlines of ghastly figures might be seen intermixed with Runic characters. Otto felt as though he had aforetime seen something of the sort in a dream. Whilst he was trying to recollect himself, the knight closed his book, and springing to his feet, he said, as he went out, "Ye would have done wiser to have kept away; but as, once for all, ye are here, I will announce your arrival." And as he passed on he cast a look of compassion on Otto, who, at the same moment, thought he beheld in the stranger his half-brother Ottur. Most likely he was right, for his two brothers-in-arms called out with one voice, "If we did not see thee standing before us, Otto, with real flesh and bones, we should be inclined to say thou hadst just gone out at the door there."

They were speaking thus, when a womanly form of wondrous beauty stood before them, which they all three, at the first glance, knew to be the young Norwegian enchantress, Gerda. Though they bent low before her, with true knightly courtesy, yet they stood for a long while speechless in wonderment and doubt, and were quite at a loss to know how to open the conference with her.

Gerda looked on them, one by one, with a smile. "Why are ye, then, so sorely bewildered, noble sirs?" said she at length. "Was it by mere chance that ye went astray, and arrived at my castle? and if so, what is that to the point?"

"It is somewhat to the point," replied Heerdegen, with a frown, "that we are deep beneath the surface of the earth."

"And the wild dancing of your charmed steeds outside," added Otto, "and the dwarf that tends them: can mortal senses help being bewildered by such sights as those?"

"But, in the first place," said Arinbiorn sternly, "inform us whether thou art she who is worshiped in these mountains as the goddess Freia?"

"You seem to fancy, sir sea-king," retorted Gerda, "that

it beseemeth you to assume a lordly tone towards me; but ye are wrong. I am no longer in your train; and if I formerly loved you better than you deserved, all that is long since at an end. I have now other and much better things at heart. But as to all of you," continued she, looking round on them with a laugh, "I must, forsooth, take you to be arrant madmen. Ye visit me in my castle, with its sun-bright morning beam, and talk of subterranean realms, enchanted steeds, and all sorts of crazy nonsense. Above all else, I beseech ye, set your senses right again in the light of the sun." She drew aside a purple curtain, and pointed through a large bright window to the blooming landscape beyond. In one bright arch of blue, over which the rising sun threw its crimson tints, heaven rose before them. A vale, bespangled with tasteful mansions, already smiling at the early touch of spring, opened on the gaze of the wondering warriors. Shepherds, in gay attire, and with shalms in their hands, again drove their flocks afield; while the maidens in the meadows were seeking snowdrops and violets.

"Good heavens!" cried Heerdegen, "it is as though we were in Italy!"

"Who told you," returned Gerda, with an enchanting smile, "that ye were not there? If ye take the view ye now have before you for an illusive dream, why not also your earlier wanderings about the snowy mountains of the Hartz? Or, if they were really something palpable and true, think ye ye can measure time and space, since ye have given yourselves over to the Runic altar, and to the wondrous paths that lead to it?"

The knights knew not what to make of the scene before them, but continued gazing still more eagerly through the large bright window of glass. Then, while heath and field became brighter and brighter, they beheld three noble forms, in friendly converse, strolling down from a beautiful mansion on the gentle slope of a hill. They were a knight and two high-born dames. Riveting his glance on them more intently than before, Otto at last turned to Heerdegen. "Ah!" cried he, with a sigh, "methinks I see Folko, Gabriele, and Blancheflour; but thy sister is not with them. Heavens! where can she be?"

"Let us ask the three that are there!" cried Heerdegen passionately; and he sprang forward to the glass, in order to open the casement, when Gerda put herself threateningly in his way.

"Brothers! brothers!" said Otto, "a monstrous cheat is revealed to me here: that is not a window at all; it is a mirror—a wizard-mirror—such as my mother formerly had in her Swedish watch-tower; and who knows on what distant plains Folko is now strolling with the beautiful ladies? I will shiver the wizard gear in pieces, as I formerly succeeded in doing by its fellow."

The good sword, called Ottur, glistened in young Sir Otto von Trautwangen's hand; but before he had brandished it fairly for the blow, Gerda snatched a spray of the medlar-tree from a vase that stood near them, and, muttering a few mystic words, she waved it over her head. The three knights fell to the earth in a giddy swoon, benumbed and powerless.

CHAPTER XIV.

MEN that are bewitched, say the olden legends, seem to lie in a sort of feverish slumber, that leaves their senses only sufficiently free to make them feel that they are bound. The spell-work of illness has made many of us familiar with a similar state; and those of us who know it, will the better be able to understand the half-conscious stupor of the three hapless knights.

They lay side by side on the floor of the curiously-bedizened hall for a long, long time, moving sometimes as though they wished to rise; and then falling back as before, with a half-smiling, half-sullen murmur. The one who could remember things best, and at times so clearly as to see every thing around him, and almost to gain his feet, was Otto; for in falling he had murmured a little prayer that he once learnt of Bertha when they both were children. This too he always kept well in his mind during his enchanted slumber; and when he once succeeded in giving it free utterance, or in even running it over in his thoughts, his sight became strong and clear.

At such times he sometimes saw his half-brother Ottur standing before him at Gerda's side. These two always appeared to be holding earnest and mysterious parley; and Otto could anon catch a few words of what they said. "No!" said Ottur; "once for all, I cannot lay hands on a helpless and spell-bound man. Besides, you can see yourself that the features of the middle one are just those of my own face. We have made a league with one another; his sword is called after me, and mine after him. Leave me alone with your entreaties. Though the golden apples of Iduna should blossom forth for me from the blood of the sleeper, I would never so much as raise the skin of a man in his state."

Then Gerda stamped her foot and turned away, beckoning the poor brain-sick knight to follow her, to whom Otto vainly strove to call out that he was his half-brother. Both lip and tongue were held in bondage, as it were, by the terrors of his dream; and when these vain endeavours were at an end, stupor sat all the heavier on his weary eyelids. As vainly too did he often strive to rouse his two companions. They mostly lay stark and lifeless at his side; and their deathlike look filled his soul with chilly horror. He even thought at times they all three were slain, and lying in one large vaulted tomb; and that life, in him alone, was still struggling ingloriously with death. Yet when he turned his half-closed eyes on Heerdegen, who lay at his left, a very spring-tide of tender sorrow seemed to open in his heart. The resemblance to Bertha, which he before remarked in the stripling's features during his still swoon on the banks of the Main, was soothingly and softly shed over them now. Otto thought he was allowed to wrestle with his stupor simply that he might keep watch over Bertha's brother.

"If I could but be the victim in his stead!" he would sometimes murmur. "For Bertha's sake, it must be so sweet to become a sacrifice." For that one out of the three was chosen to meet that fate he thought he felt sure of, and that the other two must forthwith be completely overcome; since the adventure could only be victoriously ended so long as there were three of them. Then, again, it seemed as if the safety of the rest depended on the death of one of them. Whence all these thoughts arose in him he knew not: sometimes he fancied he had heard them in the hubbub of the mountain-goblins' song, booming up from the pits and hollows. "The men in the fiery furnace were all saved," thought he. "But we are not saints; and so one of the three, I ween, must perish. Oh, let it not be Bertha's brother!" And again he began, with all the strength that fever left him master of, to fill his post as watchman near the beloved countenance, that brightened on him in the semblance of the pure being he loved.

Then the wizard maiden drew near once more, but another voice than Ottur's gave answer to hers; and whilst Otto exerted himself to listen, he remarked that it was young Kolbein.

"Prithee, ask me not to slay my kinsman the sea-king," said he. "And it would go sore against me to smite the young German. Yet, if you command me, my enchanting mistress, it shall be done."

"Strike whom thou wilt," replied Gerda; "it is enough for me if the triple bond of the champions be broken, for then I can make sure of the other two. Thank Odin that thou art at last returned from thine errand; for Ottur grows every day more brain-sick and visionary."

"Oh, mark me!" cried Kolbein: "I shall at last root every other mortal child from your heart, and dwell therein like a god for ever."

"Dazzle not thyself with such lofty conceits," said Gerda

"Thou art not the man whom my every dream and thought and feeling point out to me as the future mountain-king of the Hartz, locked in whose embrace I shall truly raise us both to be gods."

"Is it Arinbiorn?" murmured Kolbein. "Then my battle-axe shall smite him, though he were ten times my kinsman—and ah! ere now my beloved leader."

"No, Arinbiorn it is not," said Gerda, with a chilly smile. "The folly with which I clave to him hath vanished before the beauteous silvery vision of the mirror. But strike him if thou wilt: it is enough if my dangerous foes are overcome."

"Then the stranger rather," said Kolbein; and he whirled his battle-axe over Heerdegen's head.

In indescribable alarm, and having long foreseen the result, Otto had listened to the conference throughout. Now the fervour of his fidelity and his prayer so far availed to break the wizard spell, that he was able to raise himself on his shield, and to cover with his own body the brother of his beauteous friend. But ere he could throw himself over him, Kolbein's battle-axe came rattling down. Heerdegen fetched a deep groan, and a rich jet of blood gushed from his helmet. Still, in the hope of saving him, Otto hove his shield across him; and lodging the rim of it against the ground, he flourished the good sword called Ottur, though with a palsied arm, and offered his own mailed breast to the blows of the battle-axe. Thick as hail they fell, in mockery of his helpless resistance, shivering Otto's gorget in pieces, and drawing forth his blood in a bubbling torrent, till, uniting with that which Heerdegen had lost, it spread a coverlet of purple over the spot where they lay.

CHAPTER XV.

Rushing through the door of the chamber, which flew open with a loud crash, a knight stepped in in flashing silver mail.

"Strike at him, Kolbein; kill him!" cried the young enchantress; "Heerdegen may be nearly dead, but still with the stranger there would be three of them again."

Brandishing his battle-axe, Kolbein strode towards the door. The stranger raised his shield to guard his head, and lowered his sword-blade for a manful underhanded cut, as soon as the foe should have made his first false stroke. Whilst they stood confronting each other thus, Gerda trembled at the sight of the new-comer's silver mail, and quivered in every limb as she gazed on the visage that flamed on her so boldly from forth his open beaver; then suddenly thrusting herself between the two combatants, "Halt," she cried. Accustomed to tender his mistress implicit obedience, Kolbein dropped the dreadful weapon. The stranger was still standing in hesitating and distrustful mood, when Gerda bent the knee before him. "Oh, is it thou thyself, thou mighty hero! Thou who art chosen to be the mountain-king of the Hartz, and to rule like a god at my side! For if I am Freia, thou art of a surety the young valorous god Tyr. Or what we are not yet, we doubtlessly soon shall become."

"Lady," said the stranger, drawing himself up with true knightly grace, "I know not what you desire of me. Avaunt with your gods of heathen name; for I, as a good Christian, will have nothing to do with them. Neither can I nor will I ever be made king of the Hartz, for I acknowledge the ruler of the holy German realm as my feudal lord, and myself as his vassal. Thus have my forefathers ever done, and I, who bear the name of Archimbald von Walbek, will far sooner abide steadfastly by this honoured title than be made any such idol-ruler by your wizard jugglery."

"Oh, thou knowest naught of the true glory of the Hartz-king," cried Gerda; "high on the peak of the Brocken will we plant our throne, and build us a castle, that with the vast sweep of its arches, its bold watch-towers, its solemn portals and sounding halls, shall not find its equal in the whole inhabited world. Then we shall gaze far over German hill and vale from its airy windows and giddy battlements, and far as our glances roam, our vassals shall pay us feudal service. All the best and fairest they have they shall bring hitherward to the mountains of the Hartz, and send their noblest sons and daughters to be our dutiful knights and handmaidens; or if not, we will harry them with storm and hail, hurl their little dwellings to the earth, and gallop on fiery steeds over the ruins. Below, at the foot of the mountains, grim giants and dragons shall be our body-guard, fashioned indeed only from the poisonous fog, but fraught with death, and dissolving in unfathomable hollows, at the approach of the unlicensed intruder. But he whom we summon to us and receive in our hall, oh, he shall fare delightfully, and live like the gods on Asgard's sunny heights. Love and war shall speed in happy alternation through our vales. Sun, moon, and stars, and the host of the welkin, must yield us service, and grace our festivals; and when yearly, at spring-tide, we hold our grand court on the Brocken,—when the people come thronging up to us with rich offerings in their hands, and the flame of our worship rises in our castle-halls, and flashes forth at the same time over every mountain-height and dwelling,—then above all—"

"In the name of Heaven, hold!" cried Archimbald; "how

can a woman look so like an angel and give vent to such demon like words? Alas, by your own language I can tell that you are she who causeth the whole country to mourn; of whom people say, that you seek to overthrow the gentle creed of Christendom, and to wring from them divine worship as the haughty Freia. I am heartily sorry for you, for in this way you will become an arrant witch at last, and in all truth and equity we must bring you to the stake."

Kolbein gnashed his teeth, and strode forward towards the count; but Gerda said to him, "Oh, stay thy hand, I command thee; the words of his lips, though they be angry as the thunder, are far sweeter to me than all your silly pleadings for love."

Then Kolbein stood sorrowfully still; and Archimbald, without paying very great heed to what the maiden said, continued as follows:

"I will not conceal from you that I sought you in these horrible depths as a foe, and that I am come to put an end to all your abominations, but at the same time either to save or to avenge the three knights who, a long time back, disappeared in your cavern. Now be equally frank with me, and tell me how you came to take me to be the destined king of the Hartz, and the ruling idol of this wondrous land. For neither I nor any of my race have ever had dealings with paganism and witchcraft."

"Who stands pledged to thee for that, my bold warrior?" returned the enchantress, with the sweetest smile. "*Thy* forefathers, too, in time-olden days, were wont to worship the glorious Odin, the father of the gods; and if they afterwards fell away from him, he nevertheless remains their friend, and the golden guerdon of promise will rest for evermore on the sunny locks of thy brow. In that magic mirror did I summon to me the form of the fairest scion of the olden hero-race, and just as thou appearedest there in thy silver mail, shining in the battle, the race, and the tourney, my heart was thine at once. Then, mighty hero, command thy handmaid."

Kolbein struck his battle-axe on the ground; and while the scorching tears glistened in his eyes, "Father of gods and men," cried he, "must a man hear this and be still?" Then, at an angry sign from Gerda, he stood as if petrified before her.

"Things here seem very different to what one might have expected," said Archimbald. "And since they are really thus, I will do hurt neither to yourself nor your liegemen; but prove not less obedient than you have promised to be."

"I know they used to call me the wild Gerda," said the wizard maiden in a softened tone. "Before thee, great Saxon hero, I am a gentle roe. Ah, would that it were not too late!

would that thou wouldst receive at my hands the sparkling crown of the mountain-king!"

"Trouble not thyself any more," replied the count. "Wert thou less of a witch and more of a Christian, there might indeed be crowns which I would sue for at thy hands. But that is nothing to the purpose now; and I have only to talk with thee on a point of strict justice. Where, then, are the noble knights of whom I spoke with thee before?" And at the very same moment, casting his glance round the chamber, he descried the three mailed warriors on the floor.

"Have ye murdered them?" said he, with a look of wrath. "Then the whole subterranean haunt of robbers shall rue their death, and above all that of the one in the silver-black eagle mail; for I know both knight and harness well, and am dearly attached to them."

"My lord and master," returned the trembling wizard-maiden, "he whom you speak of is still alive, and may be easily restored; though over him who lieth beneath him Death hath truly spread his chilly pinions."

"Give life quickly to those who still may live," cried Archimbald; and Gerda obediently took the medlar-spray in her hand, waved it over the prostrate bodies of the knights, and murmured thereto her mystic charm. Then Arinbiorn and Otto raised their eyelids; and the falcon, that had hitherto shared its master's stupor, and had sat perched like a lifeless ornament on his helm, now began to move at the sound of the spell. The sea-king looked in amazement around him, grasped the arms that had fallen from his hands, and, rising to his feet, he swung his limbs boldly about him, as if to try them anew. Otto, on the other hand, seemed to have recovered his full strength only the more keenly to feel the poignant sorrow caused by Heerdegen's death. Bending over the pale face of his friend, he wept a warm but silent flood of tears, and at the same time his blood gushed freely down from his shattered gorget. But the moment it touched the dead man's face, Otto wiped it gently and carefully away with his sash. "O Bertha," said he, with a sigh, "thou pure angel-child! in this mute slumber, how like he is to thee!"

Arinbiorn and Archimbald, who in the mean while had explained matters, stepped up to comfort their friend. "Leave me," he answered; "I know it is not Bertha, and that I am not as ill-fated as the mighty Hugur, who slew his innocent mate. No; I fought for the poor youth with the best strength I had. But see, he is dead for all that; and he was so good and true-hearted; and, as he lies so peacefully here, he must remind every one of Bertha: must he not, Arinbiorn?" Then too the tears gushed forth from the sea-king's hero eyes; and

Otto wept more freely, though much more calmly than before.

The sea-king and the count now unbuckled his gorget and looked at his wound. Gerda also drew towards him with healing herbs. But Otto brandished his sword threateningly on high. "Avaunt from me, ye hell-brood, one and all!" cried he, "if ye wish me not at once to become the avenger of murder beside the corpse of my friend."

Gerda stepped meekly back. A sign from her removed Kolbein from the chamber; and the two noble comrades-in-arms bound the knight of Trautwangen's breast-wound with their sashes. This being done, they lifted the body of Heerdegen. Otto would not be prevented helping to bear it, and forsooth at the head. "I am free to look on thee now," said he, as the face of the dead man hung over on his side; and he passed his hand kindly over the chilly cheeks. "To-day we understand each other better than we did then on the banks of the Main."

By command of Archimbald, Gerda had kindled a long torch of pine-wood, with which she lit the solemn train on its way. Thus they passed out of the castle, over the flaming meadows, the brazen bridge, and along the lake, and again took the ascending path to the upper world.

CHAPTER XVI.

Coolly and refreshingly the gentle gleam of the moon fell on their faces, as they stepped forth at the outlet of the Runic altar. Arinbiorn and Otto too were astonished to hear the whispering of the tall leafy shoots of May that had sprung up in the neighbourhood of the altar.

"What is all this?" said the sea-king. "When we went into the cavern last night, all was covered with a hard case of ice and snow, and now the moonbeams are playing on the grassy ground and fresh green branches."

"Ah, my friends," returned Archimbald, "whole weeks have flown over your heads since you first lay spell-bound in the halls below, and now the bright glance of spring wanders anew over the landscape."

But Otto, who gazed on the disc of the moon as on his dear mother's face, started back with affright. "O heavens!" cried he, "and has she been all this time in the charcoal-burner's cot, at the mercy of all these juggling goblins?"

"He is asking about his mother," said the sea-king to the count.

"I know that," replied the latter. "She is in my castle. I found her in the charcoal-burner's cot on my return from war, a few days after ye had disappeared, and conveyed her away with me, that she might be more worthily tended. Good heavens! she is a very picture of the blessed mother of God, whose heart openeth itself unto us all. Her stilly tears and sighs drove me forth to this adventure. Swerker and your serving-men have joined us, and they, with my castle-warriors, have remained behind as Hilldiridur's body-guard; for, of a truth, so heavenly a jewel cannot be cherished too tenderly."

Kindly and joyfully Otto pressed his hand; but as the exhaustion caused by his wound now began to gain power over him, he tottered to the earth beside the pale Sir Heerdegen, whom they had laid on the fresh green moss. Archimbald blew his horn, and serving-men hastened up with his steed, in which Otto speedily recognised the foaming black charger with the silver chain-rein that had figured on the mead near Castle Trautwangen; so that strange feelings came over him in his uncertain swoon, as though he were dreaming the visions of long-past days. Archimbald, in the mean while, bade the serving-men prepare two litters—one for the dead man, and another for the wounded one; at the same time he despatched a messenger to Castle Walbek, to bear the anxious mother tidings of the safety of her son.

All this time Gerda had stood timidly on one side, cowering closely back in the thicket. Now she lifted up her voice in a plaintive tone: "Ah! may I not go with you?" she said.

"With all my heart," quoth Archimbald; "but I must impose upon thee three necessary conditions, which thou either wilt not or canst not fulfil."

"Oh, say on!" cried Gerda; "I can do much for the love of thee."

"Well," cried the count, "first of all, thou shalt vow to me that neither by word nor deed thou wilt ever work witchery in our good Saxon land again."

"That I gladly vow to thee," returned the maiden, laying her wondrously beautiful hand fondly on Archimbald's gauntlet.

"Ah!" said he, "thou promisest too sweetly; but who can say whether we may trust thee?"

Then Gerda unbound her rich flaxen tresses till they floated around her like a vesture of gold; and Otto was almost on the point of asking the sea-king whether it were not Aslauga, the wondrous daughter of Sigurd; for this northern legend, which the smith Asmundur had aforetime inwoven with his song of Sigurd, rang deceptively in his fevered ear, as the maiden stood before him in the mantle of her flaxen locks. However, there was no time for questions; for the young enchantress turned round in the circle with strange and solemn gesture; then snapping her medlar-wand, she cried aloud.

"Fly ye, flee ye,
Spirits, free ye!
From the wave,
And darkling cave;
With the searing
Lightning veering:
Freer now than it, and faster,
Seek ye all another master!"

And as the parted wand flew away on the four winds of heaven, a strange murmur was heard in earth and air, as of warrior-hosts disbanding. When this had ceased, Gerda said to Archimbald, in a kindly tone: "Now I must be careful how I think of playing the sorceress again. My liberated slaves would twist my neck for me if I sought to lay new bonds upon them. Thou hast now as powerless a maiden before thee as any in the world."

"There thou hast been too hasty," said Archimbald. "Now thou canst not compass my second condition: that was, the demolition of the heathen altar, and the filling up of the whole magic-pit beneath it."

"Oh, fear not," replied Gerda; "that will all take its own course. My sorcery alone held it together, for it is rotten in its basements; and if Kolbein has but found the outlet by the brook,—Ottur being on a distant quest,—the whole pile will fall to pieces with the breath of the last man who leaves it. Do ye see? It begins already."

And truly there was heard a cracking and a rending below, as though gigantic immemorial pillars were giving way; and so awful was the sound, that the knights gazed on each other in doubt, and Otto started up in affright from his feverish slumber.

"Fear not," said Gerda; "the surface of the mountains here is Hertha's choice and favourite stay, and will remain unshaken, whilst my beautiful vaults below are crumbling into their olden ugliness. The one falls, the others rise; the foundation of the whole remains the same. But let no one go too near to the altar; for the ground it standeth upon is not of the firmest."

And, ere very long, the stones of the Runic altar began rolling one over the other, as though some fearful impulse had awoke them to life. At length they all tumbled in a heap into the yawning pit beneath them. Little blue flames leaped flickering and sighing over them, and vanished at last in the depths below. "Those," said the maiden, "are the souls of such as were sacrificed here without being able to meet death with brave resignation;" and then, meekly pleading her own innocence, "I cannot be blamed for that," she added; "I never caused any one to be sacrificed. It is many hundred years ago that the blood of these poor things was shed."

"Neither do I blame thee," said Archimbald in a kindly tone. "Who could for a moment suppose, to look on that lovely form of thine, that thou couldst have done such horrid deeds? Thou shalt go with me. Only do this for me, and I resign all further conditions. Look now!"—he drew his broad falchion, and planted it before her on the ground—"that is the holy symbol of the Cross. Kneel to it and adore it."

Gerda recoiled in affright, and vanished without a word into the neighbouring thicket.

Archimbald sighed from his inmost soul. "A real pity it is," said he, as he plucked out his sword and dropped it into the scabbard again. Then he bade the serving-men raise the litters; made a soft couch for the knight of Trautwangen, and covered him carefully with his mantle; had a horse brought for the sea-king; and forthwith the train wound slowly down the hills towards the plain, where stood Castle Walbek.

CHAPTER XVII

They had just descended a rugged slope, when an abrupt, unforeseen turn of the path brought them to an opening in the wood. Pointing to a cross-road that divided the glade, "Look, sirs," said Archimbald, "we are among the signs of habitation again. From this spot we have something less than a league to a village, where there is a good hostelry; and there we will make halt, and give the wounded man a day to recruit his strength; for it will take us more than one day to reach my fortress."

Now the mists began to rise from the valleys, and came curling through the trees; and as the knights approached the cross-road their horses became restive, till, by the uncertain gleam of the moon, they descried a body of horsemen, who seemed forming a meeting there in the forest, and ever and anon increasing in number as single riders came trotting out of the wood. A half-timorous, half-impatient yelling showed that there were dogs, too, among them. "They must be huntsmen," quoth Archimbald; "yet we must ask them whence and whither they are bound. There are too many of them together for us to gallop through them at random." So saying, he made the bearers halt, drew up his serving-men in front of the litters, and placing himself and Arinbiorn at their head, he sent forth a horseman with a courteous message of inquiry to the strangers.

The horseman rode on and on, and the glade seemed to grow longer beneath the hoofs of his steed; for, although he might be seen trotting cheerily forward, yet it was just as plain that he was unable to get any nearer to the hunting-troop. The latter were stationed, in motionless array, a little distance in front of the knights, while the baying of dogs and an indistinct murmuring were heard incessantly in their ranks.

Now, all of a sudden, a gigantic rider, on a horse equally above the common size, made halt betwixt Archimbald and Arinbiorn. "Your henchman cannot ride," said he in a hollow, laughing voice that seemed almost chafed away by the night-storm. "He would let morning dawn, and not be a whit the farther on his way; so I thought it was best to come to you myself, and thank you for driving Gerda and her spirits out of the forests of the Hartz. Take, then, I pray ye, the game that I will send you to-morrow as the first-fruits of my sport in my enfranchised preserves. Hakelnberg is your friend." And so saying, he rose in his stirrups. "Hark-a-way, hark-a-way!" he cried, and flew up into the air; while the knights fancied, as they gazed after him, that they could see whole droves of flying deer scouring along overhead. The horsemen, too, at the cross-roads, dashed aloft; cheerily bayed the dogs; wildly rose the huntsmen's cry; but the sound was soon lost in the distance, till it passed only like a hollow storm over the woods. The startled game cowered closely in their lairs, or sped in terrified haste through the bushes; and hart and roe plunged anon into the train of knights and serving-men, without one of them daring to open their lips anent this wondrous adventure. And yet, as they ambled forward along the narrow riding, the mysterious hurly-burly of air still kept pace with them.

Morning dawned; and with the last dying echo of that airy hunt, the train entered the village where the wounded man was to repose. They found every one up and stirring in the hostelry; and whilst the host hurried busily to and fro, anxiously catering to the wants of his guests, Count Archimbald asked him whether the halloo of the Wild Huntsman, Hakelnberg, had frightened him and the rest of his household so early from their beds?

"Sir count," replied the landlord, as he handed the sea-king and Archimbald a morning-cup, "most assuredly the chase in the clouds called us all from our cribs; but—frightened us? No, no; not exactly that. On the contrary, we have rendered our thanks to God, be it frankly confessed, in many a prayer and hymn, that old Hakelnberg, who, in days of yore, used to appear to our fathers, is again sweeping, with his bugle-note and hounds in full cry, over the mountain-forests of the Hartz and the blooming plains at their feet. Master, what has once taken root in us, and grown up with us, though it be of itself something fearful and uncanny, becomes as dear to us at last as though it were a necessary part of ourselves, and as though one of the ties of life were broken when the wonted phantom comes no more. Besides, what harm has Hakelnberg ever done to a Christian soul? The worst that can be said of him is, that this or that saucy wight has been frightened by him. But the wizard-maiden, with her two grim accomplices—when they dashed about on their great, ugly steeds, what were they not ready for? What threats did not they hold out? All this time our good old Hakelnberg was bound to keep silence, and to pine away his life in his lonely castle in the air. Thank God that he has now begun to ride over the woods again; for, of a surety, it is all over with those other witcheries."

"That it is," said Archimbald; "ye may take my word for it."

The landlord clapped his hand in the proffered one of his guest, and cried aloud, with true-hearted jollity, "Long live Count Walbek, and long live Hakelnberg!"

At this moment a noise in the road drew the attention of the speakers. They stepped to the window, and lo! a stately stag came bounding, in hot haste, out of the wood, as though huntsman and hound were on his traces; and yet there was no vestige of any one in pursuit. The wakeful shepherds and labourers tried to turn him and take him; but he dashed impetuously through them, and made directly for the hostelry, where he ran his breast against the count's lance, as it jutted from the fence, and died at once of his knightly wound.

"A wager upon it," said Arinbiorn, "that this is the game which Hakelnberg promised us!" The count was of the same opinion. Setting to work at once, in true sportsmanlike sort, they cut up the stately stag of fourteen points; and at noon-day they sat down, with their host, his household, and their own serving-men, to the noble repast, and drank to Hakelnberg's merry hunting-sport. Otto, too, had tasted of the wondrous quarry; and it seemed to have endued him with such wizard strength that, in the evening, the silver-black gorget, that had been cloven by the blow of Kolbein's battle-axe, needed restoration far more than himself; for neither in his colour, gait, nor bearing, were there many signs left of the terrible wound.

The sun was darting its farewell beam of crimson into the chamber, when Otto rose from the couch upon which he had just lain down. Stepping gravely up to his comrades, "A sacred duty craves fulfilment at our hands," said he. "It appears to me, that we none of us should take rest so long as the dead body of our friend is on the unquiet face of earth; and this little village, with its linden-trees and fountains, looks just as if it would afford him a peaceful grave. The only question is, whether there is hallowed church-ground to be found here."

The landlord offered to show them the way to a little chapel, within whose precincts many pious Christians had been buried, and the whole of the ground around which had been consecrated by priestly hands. They therefore set forth at once, covering their friend's bier, for want of a coffin, with costly kerchiefs and store of weapons. As they clomb the hill, the little lamp that burnt night and day in the chapel shone mildly on them through the green webwork of the leaves, and the now darker gray of evening. Otto wept in silence, and would not be supplanted in his office of bearer to his departed friend. Round the chapel above was a solemn circlet of green, formed by the over-arching boughs of the elm and the beech, and towering on high, as it were, like a second and a loftier shrine. The stars now glimmered in heaven, and peeped in through the vault of its dome. The knights themselves took shovel in hand, and in triple bond of union they dug Heerdegen von Lichtenried's grave, lowered him into it, and covered the mound with turf. Then they remained awhile on their knees in silent prayer, Otto at his head, the others at either side; and afterwards, in mute and solemn thought, they returned to the village.

The next morning they set forth again. Otto was so far recovered as to be able to mount a serving-man's steed, and continue the journey side by side with his friends. One evening, when it was growing late, Archimbald told them they were now near Castle Walbek, and that very night would be sitting beside the lady Hilldiridur in his native hero-hall, with the wine-cups before them. Then the branches and brushwood in the thicket were heard to snap and crackle again; and something sprang suddenly forth from it, reared itself on high like a giant, and, in rampant posture, rushed angrily towards them. All were at a loss what to make of it; but Otto at once recognised his light-brown; and the moment he called out to him, "Still, my good fellow!" the menacing animal dropped his feet with a joyful neigh, trotted lightly forwards, and, meekly taking his station by his master, he bent his proud head lower than the saddle-tree of the borrowed steed. Then Otto dismounted, kissed his faithful charger, and vaulted on him at once, uusaddled as he was; whereupon, with the same cheery neigh, and more gentle seeming, though he still poured forth the evening air from his wide, snorting nostrils as if thirsting for the fight, he took his way with the rest. Like the call of the clarion, or the trumpet-blast of the herald, the glad neigh of the light-brown was heard in Castle Walbek. Swerker threw himself into his saddle, and galloped out to meet his friends; then was there right knightly greeting, full of heartiness and brotherly love: and when the first inquiries and communications were over, and they rode on more quietly at each other's side, Otto asked how the light-brown was thus at large without either saddle or bridle. "Master," replied Swerker, "all the time you have been away, no one has been able to keep the warrior-steed in check. He has never seen a stable, nor eaten fodder from a rack. Wherever the lady Hilldiridur might be—whether in the charcoal-burner's hut, as she aforetime was, or in the castle where she is now—the faithful fellow has always taken his rouuds in warlike wise, as though he were the noble lady's appointed guard."

The knight of Trautwangen patted the neck of his light-brown still more kindly than before; and the gallant creature turned round his head as if to answer his master's caress.

They now rode iuto the courtyard of Castle Walbck. Hilldiridur stood at the portal, her moonlike eyes glistening with tears of joy. Otto flew into her arms; and his wailings over the death of his comrade seemed sounds of gentle solace, now that he was permited to pour them forth on his fond mother's breast.

CHAPTER XVIII.

For some weeks they sojourned in Count Archimbald's fortress before they set forth on their journey to Castle Trautwangen, whither, as a friendly brotherhood of warriors, they had resolved to travel together. They looked forward with joy to the prospect of becoming Otto's guests; and it was only the time necessary for his full recovery, and the due welding together of his silver-black gorget, that caused any delay. In the mean while they passed the time in the recital of sundry adventures, which either Hilldiridur remembered to have read in old books of mystic lore, or the knights themselves had encountered in their wanderings. Thus it was impossible but that the subject of Folko and Gabriele's struggles for the ring, and Otto's conclusive combat, should be set forth at length.

Hilldiridur had been a grave and attentive listener. At the end of the story she made special inquiry of her son concerning the ring; what embellishments there were about it, and with what jewels it was set. Otto described it exactly; and the noble lady fetched a deep-drawn sigh. "There can be no further doubt of it," said she. "The great Messire Huguenin, in France, was one and the same person with the mighty Hugur in the Northlands; as also with thy father, Sir Hugh von Trautwangen. My sister, Fair Astrid, received the magic ring from our wizard kinswoman, the Icelander; and this was the way it happened:—When she had chosen me to be her helpmate, and heiress to her wonderful lore, she cast a compassionate look on Fair Astrid, who stood so meek and childlike and merry-hearted at my side. 'Thou lookest too sweetly, pretty child,' said the Druda, 'for me to think of going away without giving thee some right beautiful keepsake. Come, now, take this;' and she placed the magic ring in Fair Astrid's lovely hand. 'I entrust it to thy innocent simplicity; but take care what thou dost with it, for it hath store of mighty virtues. Never mayest thou give it away, save to the man to whom thou givest thine own self.' In this way it passed into the mighty Hugur's hands; and God grant that it be not now in less worthy keeping; for I know very well that most wonderful things may be done with it."

"Set your mind at rest, mother," replied Otto: "either Blancheflour or Gabriele hath it, and they both are paragons of all that is beautiful and good; even though," added he in a faltering tone, "Gabriele plights her troth too hastily, and is too laggard in remembering it."

"Thou knowest not who has the ring," said Hilldiridur: "once let it pass out of thy hands, and it is as little in thy power, or within the reach of thy conjecture, as the lark, there, that, ebriate with spring, now soars up to heaven over the roof of the castle. Thus it is with poor though richly-endowed man. All lies within his power so long as action is at rest within him—nothing is in his power the moment action has displayed itself, even by the lifting up of a finger on the immeasurable world."

When they separated for the night, the sea-king went with Otto to his chamber, and, seating himself on his couch, "Hast thou felt the fulness of thy joy, happy man?" cried he, as soon as they were alone; "hast thou fully felt the unheard-of happiness of Blancheflour being thy sister?" Otto answered him by a friendly nod.

"Well, then," said the sea-king, "thou wilt of a surety bethink thee of the promise that thou gavest me thy hand upon, in the Swedish frontier mountains, when we, for the first time, rode up to thy mother's watch-tower. Dost thou remember—Blancheflour was to be my bride, if she were but thy sister?"

"Like knighthood's mail is knighthood's word," said Otto; and he gave Arinbiorn's hand a cheery grasp: "besides, I should be at a loss to tell to what hero the whole world over I would rather betroth my sister than to thee, saving and excepting she be already the promised bride of her equal in birth."

"Of course," said the sea-king; "but I can scarcely think that Heaven can have so great a woe in store for me." And thereupon, with heartfelt joy, and an increased sense of affection, the two brethren-in-arms wished each other good night.

CHAPTER XIX.

Now the corn-fields waved in glad luxuriance; the fruit-trees were hung with blossom, and here and there with budding fruit; the flocks and herds moved cheerily afield, and the deer glanced anon through the forest-glades—when the travellers set out for Castle Trautwangen, on Danube's banks. All around them looked so full of promise, that each thought he was soon to be blest with that which his heart had long harboured as its dearest wish: yet the most frequent matter of discourse, when they spoke aloud, was the common concern of the whole knightly estate of Europe—the king of the Lion-heart's captivity, and the disheartening disappearance, as it seemed for ever, of that inspiring star of honour and gallantry. "God will give us news of him," Arinbiorn would say. "Think with what replenished splendour he brings the sun again over our icy northlands, that for so many long months hath vanished, and then what a long bright day we have."

"If the magic of a few stoutly-dealt sword-strokes would do any good," said Otto, "I would fain my whole war-suit, on such a battle-field, were as fairly besprinkled with blows as my gorget is now." For it was easy to see that the welding-hammer of a common smithy, and not the weird Asmundur's cunning master-strokes, had botched up flaw after flaw, as it best was able, without availing to remove the blemishes.

Then Hilldiridur would often say, "God will summon forth the chosen arm,—and shame to the craven who loiters at the call! but the casting one's self wilfully between the millstones of time is hair-brained folly, and sorry and mangled corpses are the result."

Thus, with every step that they took, the glory of our German South opened anew on the knights in all the fulness of its ravishment, while their brave breasts swelled with gentle hope, chastened, at the same time, by the prescient wisdom of Hilldiridur. Montfaucon's falcon was seen hovering on gladsome wing over the train. The merry zest of travel, which cheers us all in bright and happy days, now, too, wrought powerfully with Count Archimbald, as he noticed a Benedictine monk sitting a little apart from the road, closely shrouded in his long black weeds. "Up, brother!" said he to him; "those bare feet must be growing painful. Try a horse for once, and come along with us. This very evening we shall quarter ourselves in the best of hostelries."

"On horseback or on foot, on foot or on horseback," returned the Benedictine, with a hollow murmur, "shod in mail, or bare of foot, we all shall reach our hostelry. Know ye what is written over the doorway? The little sign has a double facing: the one tallies well, though somewhat strangely, with the other. On one side are the words, 'Endless Joy!' on the other, 'Endless Woe!'"

These solemn words told dismally on the cheerful mood of the travellers. They halted involuntarily, and gazed on the dark form of the speaker. Then, still shrouded as before, the monk rose from the bench of stone, and, drawing towards them, "I should know you," quoth he. "The way I am faring ye acknowledge to be the best and the safest; at least ye have often enough said so. Why, then, do ye drift about so madly and venturesomely in the alluring world? Off with the mailed shoon and golden spurs, and put the poor sandals in the place of them! Or will ye not do thus? Then I understand you not. What I do, I do thoroughly." So saying, he turned aside into the gloom of the adjoining wood, where, peeping over the tree-tops, might be seen the turrets of a lonely cloister. A fearful shudder crept over the travellers, especially as the voice of the monk, despite the closeness of his garb, seemed familiar to some of them.

On leaving the inn the next morning, which stood at no great distance from the spot, a noble page, of tall and tender growth, was seen busily employed about the baggage. No questions were put to him, from a notion that he perhaps belonged to another party, and made himself so useful from a knightly sense of courtesy. After tendering him their thanks, they set forth at once through the dewy mists of the twilight, and had already left the hostelry far behind them, ere they remarked that the stripling still kept pace with those in the rear of the train, and eagerly lent a helping hand in ordering this or that, wherever there had been any oversight, at the moment of departure, with regard to the arrangement of the baggage or the furniture of the horses. There was something solemn in the whole bearing of the stranger, as though he belonged to the world of spirits; and the squires and serving-men felt a seal upon their lips whilst that noble form strode on so mutely beside them in the fresh breeze of morning. Some of them thought to themselves, he must be a troublesome sprite, that would soon display itself in its own mischievous shape: others took him to be a kindly elf, escorting the train in lovelier guise. But these and other conjectures could only find vent in a furtive whisper, that at last spread through the train, and reached the ears of Archimbald and his knightly colleagues. After inquiring what was the matter, the count ordered the party to halt, and bade the mysterious stripling appear instantly before him. He hastened up with a graceful show of obedience to do the will of his lord, and was presently standing in the circle which the knights and Hilldiridur had formed about Archimbald.

Just then the earliest beam of morning came darting through the fir-wood on the tresses of the fancied page, discovering Gerda's lovely face, to which her present meekness of mood lent an indescribable charm. "Look not thus amazed on me," said she to the bystanders: "only one here has a right to upbraid me; but he is good and gentle as a child, with all his bravery; and assuredly he sorely compassionates me, instead of being angry with me. Is it not so, Otto?"

The young Sir Otto von Trautwangen bent to her in friendly guise. "I am not a whit otherwise than what you suppose me to be," said he. "God forgive you the death of my beloved Heerdegen: the harm you have here and there done me shall be counted as empty air, and be thought no more about."

"Now, Archimbald," resumed the maiden, turning round to the count, "thou surely hast naught to complain of in me. I force thee not to be king of the Hartz, if thou art determined not to be so. Ah! let me go with thee, then. I mean most truly well by thee."

"Thou art a most lovely creature!" quoth Archimbald; "and I might as lief dislike the brightness of the sun, the beauty of the flowers, and the nightingale's song, as refuse to have *thee* near me. But the cross, remember, the cross! Thou knowest it all depends upon that."

"Archimbald," returned the maiden, "in the warmth of my devotion, I even wished to do that for thee; but it cannot —in truth, it cannot be. Check for a single moment thine upbraiding tongue, and the thundering words of ban that again hover on thy darkly-bearded lip. Hear, now, what hath happened; and if thou art wise, thou wilt deem me right.

"In the dark wood there, beneath us, stands a stately pile, with strong walls, narrow casements, and a bell that rings dolefully from its highest tower. They call it a minster, and aver that the happy faith ye boast of dwells peculiarly there. Dear Archimbald, my foot trembled not at the damp, hollow-resounding pavement of its courtyard and corridors—my eye turned not away from the dark, complex span of its arches. I entered it, and sought to learn how I might approach thy God, and thereby draw near to thee: but they understood me not, and as little did I understand their strange questions and threats: so at last they all came towards me in a body, a pallid group, closely shrouded in black, sprinkling water about them, and making solemn signs and passes; and as I well knew that, by such things as those, one may easily be bewitched, I fled back in dismay across the threshold. I stood still outside, and began to weep bitterly, because I now could think of no way of ever becoming one with thee. Then one of the black men was touched with pity for me; and, calling out to me over the walls, he bade me go and ask for Brother Zelotes. He had not long since been a heathen himself, he said, and had made his way among them almost by main force; but the heroic sternness of his will had overcome every obstacle in a wondrously short time; so that, in a few months, he was not only on an equal footing with them, but, as a signal instrument of victory in the hands of the Christian God, had been despatched on a mission, of which himself only and the superior of the cloister knew the purpose. If he could not help me, no one could.

"I set off at once, and made inquiry for Brother Zelotes, as the poor wretch, smitten by a poisonous arrow, seeks for him who is to suck the venom from the wound. They told me where to find him; and not far from this spot I fell in with him. Ah! listen now how it fared with me.

"Towering gauntly on high, with his long weeds mantling round him, he met me, like a cowled giant, in a narrow dell, over whose crisp and quivering bushes the bloody disk of the full moon just came forth on its way. 'Art thou Zelotes?'—'Yes.'—'Lead me to Christ.'—'Most gladly: follow me.'—'Whither?'—'Unfitting question for him who is bent on finding the Lord. He knows the goal he seeks, and the road must be all one to him.'

"A fearful shudder crept over me—a dreader fear than I had ever felt when I stood on the thrice-charmed perilous witch-ring, with the hideous phantoms of the grave and the powers of night around me: at the same time the voice of the speaker sounded so awfully familiar to me. 'Yes, yes!' he cried, 'I know thee well too, and I was once a renowned warrior; but a horror of thy fearful sorceries it was, and thy urgent entreaties that I should murder the sleeping knights, that revealed to me the ghastliness of hell, and drove me forth to seek the blessedness of Christians. From thy enchanted mountain-fastness I tore myself away as though sallying forth to war; but my pathway led me to a goodly minster, and there, in the course of a few months, I have won the divine gift of faith with the prowess that once nerved my arm to worldly victory.' He threw back the black cowl from his face, and, haggard and altered as he was, stern and ghostlike as were his features, I could not entertain a moment's doubt that, in the garb of Zelotes, Ottur really stood before me. Then I had to tell him every thing that had happened to myself and you since his flight from the mountain. He listened to me with sorrowful attention, and for a long time shook his fearfully transformed head in silence. 'Only follow me,' he began at last; 'thou knowest in my earthly wanderings I held thee very dear to my heart; and thou mayst believe that I shall fondly guide thee, to the best of my power, on thy heavenward way.' 'Whither wilt thou lead me?' said I again, my limbs quivering the while with horror. And Zelotes began a tale at which the hair of my head stood on end:—how he would convey me to a cloister of maidens, to endless and increasing penance—how he would cut away the golden hair from my temples—and how I should never see thee, Archimbald, again. I staggered back in bewilderment, as though tottering on the brink of a living grave: he made a grasp at me. I thought, beneath his shadowy garments, I could hear the rattle of the scissors that threatened ruin to my locks, and, fleeter than the hunted roe, I bounded up the mountain-steep. Wilt thou have me near thee, Archimbald? Oh! let it be without the cross, for *that*, thou seest, is death."

Hilldiridur was just opening her gentle lips to frame some soft reply, when Archimbald cried aloud, with half-stern, half-terrified air, "Avaunt, seducing spirit! or adore the holy cross at once!" And, flaming up in all her olden fury, Gerda frowned threateningly on her regardless lover and his comrades; and then, as if borne on her fluttering locks of gold, she flew with the swiftness of an arrow into the neighbouring thicket of firs.

Severally busied with their own thoughts, but Archimbald more so than all of them, the travellers continued their journey.

CHAPTER XX.

One day they were reposing under shady elm-trees at the foot of a hill, on the summit of which stood a church of rich and beautiful structure, forming the solitary centre of devotion to the many large villages around it. Near it was the little house of a chaplain only; so that there was always somebody at hand to keep the building open for all true believers, and at the same time to take care that it was neat and clean.

A pretty sight it was to see the noble travellers sitting under the trees, with their chargers and sumpter-horses grazing around them, and their bright shields sparkling on the boughs. The cups circled coolly and refreshingly in the sultry noon-day, and squires and serving-men began many a merry carol; but the usually sociable and cheerful Otto now sat enrapt in silent thought. The austere cloister-life of his half-brother weighed heavily on his heart—sometimes as a painful and oppressive burden, and then again as a peerless treasure that he never thought to have won; so little could he make up his mind as to whether Ottur's renouncement of the world were the more sorrowful, or his quick and heroic conversion the more cheering. With all this, the beautiful arches and tall, slender pillars of the church on the hill seemed to lure him towards them with magnetic power. He could not take his eyes off them; and when Hilldiridur noticed this—"In the name of Heaven, go up, my dear son," she said. "Me thinks thou feelest thyself inwardly called to pray alone on holy ground; and thy great Lord paramount will gladly receive thee in His castle. In the mean while we will wait for thee beneath the cool shade of the trees."

Otto bowed low in thankful silence, and bent his way up to the beautiful building. As he entered its solemn aisles, he seemed filled with the spirit of prescient joy. All that troubled and oppressed him seemed to have been left behind him; and through the hospitable portals, that stood open to all quarters of the world, and the glowing crimson of the windows, the summer light seemed to stream in upon him in beauteous promise. For a long time he walked along among the pictures and holy relics, continuing in glad and childlike prayer. In all his life he had never felt happier, though he was at a loss to know what good fortune had so very lately befallen him. Still, whatever might be his thoughts, Ottur's conversion and transformation into Brother Zelotes, the journey he was bent on, and the nearness of his home,—all lay before him suffused, as it were, with the rose-light of heaven.

In the indescribable keenness of his joy, he raised his eyes to a part of the church where, among its more distant glories, he descried a richly-garnished faldstool, shut in with trellis-work of gold and bright glass casements. Such he at first took it to be; but he soon became aware that it was a quaintly ornamented shrine, the accustomed repository of the costly effigy of a saint; for, brightening on him through the glass windows, came the angel beauty of a maiden, whose equal he seemed never to have beheld before. There was a refreshing gentleness in her features, blent with the awe-inspiring solemnity of an angel's glance; a lofty and at the same time childlike loveliness, in the pure tone of the early days of spring, when they descend so softly on this nether world, and breathe upon our souls the first faint whispers of paradise. The beauteous eyes of the figure were but partly open; for, in calm maiden devotion, they had fallen on a large book, on which her hands were folded in all the faultlessness of their moulding; yet even from her drooping eyelashes peeped forth anon the sweet blue heaven beneath them, as our heaven often does, forsooth, when morning clouds and shady woods obscure its festal dome. Rich braids of pearls were enwoven with her light-brown hair; a high lace ruff stood out from her fair, swanlike neck; while her dark-velvet vesture shone with spangles, and pearls, and glittering jewels.

Whilst Otto was gazing on the lofty vision with increased tenderness and delight, and striving to compass its goodly magnificence, he suddenly perceived, what he must first have overlooked, that a man much older than herself, but in equally handsome array, was standing behind the lady. He wore a grave and foreign air; his eyebrows were arched and royal-looking; while his eyes, sparkling like stars, were steadfastly riveted on the beautiful maiden; and his whole mien pointed him out as her chosen guard and protector.

"This, perhaps, is to represent St. Joseph," thought Otto; and without further contemplation of the man's splendid costume, which in that country there could be little chance of seeing, he again turned his glance to the woudrously beautiful lady. Then, like lightning, the thought flashed upon his mind, that the features he beheld were no other than those of his lovely kinswoman Bertha, though hallowed and illumined with such a flood of glory as latterly he might have guessed of in his dreams, yet never could have hoped to look on when awake. He closed his dazzled eyes, and remained thus, for some time, in a state of half-consciousness. On again looking round, he found that the space behind the glass-work was empty. Neither the maiden nor her protector was to be seen; and Otto left the church in as sad a mood as his feelings, but a short time before, had been joyous; for he could not help thinking that Bertha must have died at that very hour, and have revealed herself to him in the heavenly form in which she had been arrayed as an angel of glory.

When he returned to his companions, he found them in anxious surprise and commotion. Even Hilldiridur cast many an eager glance along a horse-road on the other side of the hill, on which, drawing nearer and nearer, was heard the pleasant sound of a number of instruments. Soon afterwards horsemen appeared, in gaudy and foreign-looking attire, with Turkish turbans and lofty heron-plumes on their heads, and divers sorts of musical instruments in their hands—flutes, shalms, trumpets, and oboes. Some beat the golden cymbals; and others struck splendid kettle-drums of silver, with a rich purple fringe. The clang of the instruments was altogether lovely and joyous. It rose in no warlike strain, but in one that seemed irresistibly inviting, luring them forth, as it were, to pleasant journeys through a country all splendour and beauty. Round the musicians came many mounted men in glistening armour, who, with their golden corslets and their broad sweeping sabres, were like people of another world to look upon. But the eye could not rest upon them long; for, on a stately steed, all black and brilliant, that ambled lightly onward in its encasement of steel, appeared an elderly knight of heroic mien, arrayed, like the rest of his retinue, in the peerless magnificence of the East. Hanging on his breast, over his raiment of purple, was a large gold cross, richly studded with jewels. On a snow-white palfrey, at the side of the knight, keenly contrasting with his own shadowy charger, rode a lady in black-velvet vesture, embroidered with pearls, at sight of whom the knights uttered a faint cry of astonishment, and then stood petrified and spell-bound to the spot. We need not say that Otto was quick in recognising her to be the angelic maiden of the shrine in the church, and in discovering in her companion the fancied vision of St. Joseph.

The beautiful lady cast a significant glance at the silver mail worn by Count Archimbald von Walhek; but as she suddenly turned her astonished gaze on Otto's darker war-suit, and caught a glimpse of his features, a faint gleam, like the early blush of morning, suffused her countenance with an unspeakable charm. Then she turned hastily away, fell into earnest discourse with her companion, and the cavalcade was soon lost to view in a blooming hollow in the vale beneath.

"We must follow them!" cried Otto, as though awaking from a prophetic slumber; and Archimbald and the sea-king, while they showed themselves ready as ever to fulfil the wishes of their brother-in-arms, might this time perhaps be incited by glad curiosity on their own part. Moreover, the wondrous cavalcade seemed to have taken the very road which they intended to follow on their way to Castle Trautwangen.

To survey its windings more freely for the present, Archimbald mounted the fragment of a rock, that lay, like a ponderous die, hurled into the middle of the valley. In the mean while,

Ariubiorn, Otto, and Swerker lent a ready hand to the saddling of the chargers and the loading of the sumpter-horses. Truly, Hilldiridur sought more than once to warn them that such headlong haste might be fraught with little good; but that faint and gentle call seemed quite overruled by the hardy impatience of her friends.

CHAPTER XXI.

A LOUD clashing of arms, proceeding from the stone on which Archimbald von Walbek was standing, rose above all the noise and bustle of departure. Looking upward, they beheld the count in unexpected combat with a tall and sinewy foe, saw him reel at the same moment beneath the overwhelming shock with which the stranger brought his ponderous shield to bear against his breast and brow; and now the pitiless battle-axe of the conqueror seemed to whistle on high ere it descended for the last time on his fallen antagonist. Scarcely could they tell whether it were not an illusion; and still more were they at a loss to know how any one could climb the lofty crag in time to save the count. But Swerker, with true Northland nimbleness of limb, was soon at the top of it; and turning aside the weapon of the conqueror, with such a sweeping blow that his own blade and the battle-axe were shivered with the shock, he manfully clutched the body of the stranger, and wrestled with him for the throw. Before the count could rise, the two impetuous combatants had lost their footing; and now, with limb enwreathed in limb, they rolled down from the crag. Whether from superior adroitness, or the mere fortune of the headlong fall, the stranger was uppermost when they reached the bottom; and with the fury of a lion whose prey has been torn from him, he drew forth his dagger, and felt for the seams of the harness betwixt his foe's gorget and cuirass. But Swerker too had drawn the same deadly weapon as promptly from his girdle; and now the little glittering knives flashed, like salient serpents, in their nervous grasp. Suddenly the stranger gave a deep groan, his arm grew slack; and as Swerker struggled manfully to his feet, his foe grew giddy with the drench of blood, and swaying himself hither and thither on his hands, he at last lay stretched at his length on the crimsoned grass.

The knights gathered round him and unbuckled his fallen vizor. Hilldiridur kneeled down at his side; and as the ghastly wound yawned on her from the loosened gorget, "He is smitten unto death," said she, with a piteous sigh. "Neither charm nor simple can save him now."

"That I readily believe—most readily," gurgled forth the

bleeding warrior, whilst a gentle smile flitted athwart his livid lips; and Otto and Arinbiorn beheld in him the once hale and blooming Kolbein.

The circle that had formed round the fallen young hero was now darkened throughout with sorrow. "A woful hap is this, thou fair mettlesome champion," said Archimbald, with his hand before his eyes, "that for my sake thou must meet thy death so early. But what had I done to thee that thou shouldst fall on me so unawares, and with such bloodthirsty rancour, on the rock?"

"Thou hadst taken from me more than the whole happiness of my life," said Kolbein, with a painful smile; "but naught more than thy life did I wish to take from thee. Without Gerda I could not live.—Dost thou remember," continued he, as he turned his glance on the sea-king, "how my little ship was set on flames with those Greek fire-shafts of thine? Even so Gerda's beauty has wasted my being. Oh, ye cannot at all tell how ruinous are such things to a poor bark."

Arinbiorn shed a flood of bitter tears over this flower of his hero-race thus early doomed to fade.

Hilldiridur, still kneeling beside the dying man, warbled like a nightingale in his ear, "Think on God, think on our loving God, who receives into His gracious favour even him who comes so late."

"That I feel most keenly," said Kolbein, with a still happier smile. "To him who hath loved much, shall much be forgiven; God is the very sun of love, and the light of His liberty breaks through all the night-clouds of idolatry."

"Ah, kinsman," said Arinbiorn, with a sigh, "how wert thou so stubborn-hearted in thy lifetime, and what a heavenly beam bursts on thee now! Canst thou not still put away death from thee, and abide like a bright light with us for a time?"

"Alas, not so," said the stripling; "did not my little ship flash fairest just as she was burning her last?" And with these words his eyes were lit up with a passing ray, and then they closed for ever. He lay on the blooming meadow-land a beautiful and peaceful corpse.

When, a short time after this, as if asking for mutual tears and other solace, they stood gazing on each other, a man in white vestments appeared among them. It was the chaplain of the church on the hill. They commended the dead to him, that he might receive Christian burial, and told him of the last goodly words he had uttered.

"I am fain to believe you," said the churchman; "the heavenly peace depicted on this death-pale face is undeniable testimony to one who is versed in these matters. In the name of Heaven, continue your journey. The dead man will remain behind, in the care of God and His servant; and you will never get so far from him as may perhaps seem to you hereafter, when ye are fairly mingling with the world again. Now, mark me what I say." With an earnest smile, he made the sign of the cross over them; and when he had given them his blessing, they went in silence to take their horses. Yet Otto could not help turning back to him once more, and saying to him, "Good father, think not ill of me if in this solemn hour I put a question to you that almost seems to savour of curiosity. But it is something better than curiosity, and much more urgent. My earthly happiness and the peace of my soul are closely allied to it. Was it a mere phantom that just now wound round the hill in such wondrous brightness? or were they really men? And has the angelic lady who rode by the strange lord of the train really been praying in your church, in the high shrine with the golden grating up above there?"

The good old chaplain moved his hoary head to and fro with a gentle smile. "It seemeth strange to one of our order," said he, "when the long-forgotten life of this world peeps all at once inquiringly into our seclusion. But I tender thee answer with all my heart. The little birds even, that are made to flit far and wide over the earth, have a sort of innocent curiosity in them; and why not man, when wedded to a similar calling? Know then, good sir, that the pious lady about whom thou askest was really praying in our church a short time ago, and up above too, in the most costly shrine in the whole building, for such was the one that her companion engaged for her. On the other side of the church, beneath a gorgeous tent, they rested on their way; and sooth, no spectral cavalcade was it, but a truly royal one, that passed before thine eyes along the causeway."

"And who is this noble lady? Who is her princely escort?"

"Thereof I can give thee no tidings. On cloisters, on places of pilgrimage, and on the poor, they lavish gifts such as no emperor ever distributed within the memory of man. The hearts of all men are delighted with their sage discourse and gentle words of solace; wheresoever they set foot, discord is hushed, and peace begins to smile: but what name we are to give them, neither I nor any other in these parts can tell, far and gloriously as their fame flies before them. Many think the cavalcade is come from India, and that its leader is the renowned priest John, whose Christian power and splendour is told of by some who have travelled so far. The lady of angel beauty is thought to be his daughter or niece, and people will have it that her hand is already given by solemn betrothal to one of the greatest of our European princes. Neither lords, churchmen, nor people, I assure thee, hold the lofty pair in less account than this."

Otto thankfully dropped a gold piece into the casket which the chaplain carried with him to make collections in for the poor of the parish; but when the lid of it was lifted, he felt ashamed to see the rich treasure of gold and pearls that already lay within it—the bountiful largess of the mysterious travellers.

As he was mounting his horse, Swerker rode up to him and whispered in his ear: "Farewell to thee, my brave conqueror and converter. The Swedish eagle is flying up to his native eyrie again." Otto gazed on him with inquiring astonishment. "Look now," he continued; "Arinbiorn, you know, can never look on me with pleasure, now that I have slain his blooming kinsman. A Christian, I know, wreaketh not bloody revenge on a fellow-man; but this I know, that the like thought is very deeply rooted in us Northlanders, and becomes fatal to our own lives where satisfaction is impossible. The sea-king, believe me, would pine to death if he had me much longer before him. Besides, what can come of it if we, who feel ourselves valiant Christians and cheery warriors, are to carouse and make merry in thy halls without a spark of the common fire within us ever flashing on the night-gloom that needs cheering and illumining? Fare thee well. I will tell the noble race of Swerker how dear thou art to me, and, above all, how dear to me is Christ."

Thus, after hanging on his friend's neck, with many a hearty kiss and embrace, he put spurs to his horse, and vanished with the speed of the wind behind the hill; and before Otto could tell his mother and comrades of the impulse that hurried the noble Swede onward, the latter was far away from them for ever.

CHAPTER XXII.

"There have been mournful barriers to your headlong haste," said Hilldiridur, as she rode on with the knights; "death and parting are their names. Do not ye now see that I did well to warn you against your reckless impatience? And will ye now dash with the same uncontrollable eagerness after the wondrous cavalcade?"

For a time they remained in silent thought, till at last Otto, with a glowing cheek, began to say, "But, mother, dear mother, if it really was Bertha! The resemblance—nay, the striking likeness, save that the maiden seemed to move in such a halo of glory—must surely have spoken to your heart as it did to mine."

"Thinkest thou not that my whole soul is in a glow at the thought of my dear foster-child?" said Hilldiridur, with a smile. "But who is to say whether the royal apparition be really Bertha? and if so, whether, amid the brightness of her glory, she be pleased any longer to acknowledge thee?"

"Then her companion is a sorcerer and seducer," quoth Otto, in the ill-repressed wrath of his sorrow; "and I will talk to him in such wise as shall be almost as little to his mind as Bertha's estrangement is to mine."

The mother shook her head and looked silently on her son. "Who has given thee a right—thee above all men, Otto—to lay down the law so peremptorily with regard to Bertha's behaviour? Who hath empowered thee to threaten a noble cavalier whom the innocent forsaken one hath chosen for her protector? Besides, young knight of Trautwangen, ye are travelling to your vassals, who have been left without a master by your father's death; and it little becometh you to entangle yourself in any new adventure till they have been cheered and comforted by you."

A deep blush of shame succeeded the glow of impatient longing on Otto's cheek; and bending reverently to Hilldiridur, "Mother," said he, "let all be ordered by your loftier and better wisdom; I bow to you in every thing. Besides, I now see too plainly, that if it had been Bertha, and she had thought fit to recognise me, she would not have ridden past us all without a word of greeting. I bear the penalty of my own folly; and perhaps I am no longer worthy to raise my glance to this heavenly envoy."

With a kindly smile, Hilldiridur patted him gently on the shoulder. "O youth's stormy heart! youth's stormy heart!" said she; "in an approved hero even, how like it is to the billowy sea—now foaming up to the stars in its arrogance, now sinking in despair to the fathomless abyss! No, my dear son, thou must not quite give up the thought of pride. A right glorious and goodly knight art thou, who may be bold to cast a tender glance on any fair lady in the world." And so saying, the well-pleased mother looked with a smile full of tenderness on her comely young hero.

During this discourse something had every now and then been seen to glisten in a copse of alder-trees on the side of the road; it was almost like the flash of the evening sky through the green leaves of the thicket, and had been taken to be such by some of the party. But on looking steadfastly at it, it was easy to see that it moved continually onward, and eagerly strove to keep pace with the travellers; nay, a little lawn that opened amid the bushes showed the phantom to be the lady Gerda, who, with her golden tresses floating on the breeze, and arrayed in female attire, now held on her course along a foot-path. Just at this moment she was close to the causeway; and Archimbald cried aloud, as he turned his horse's head towards her, "Begone from me, thou sweet allurer, or kneel at once to the cross! I say this in good part to thee for the last time."

Gerda stood still; and putting back the tresses that had fallen over her brow as she bent forward on her hurried course, half sullenly, half tearfully, she fixed her large blue eyes on the count. "I may surely go along the footpath," said she, in the tone of a froward child, whose little melting heart is ready every moment to burst forth into tears. "What is my travelling to you? The roads are broad, and they are not yours either. But if ye seek to kill me because I am so very troublesome to you, in the name of all the gods strike home at once. But thus much I tell you—I shall often meet you in the way, and nothing shall prevent me doing so but death." So saying, she again drew her rich golden tresses over her face, and began to weep bitterly.

"God knows what will be the end of this," said Archimbald, with a deep-drawn sigh; then swaying his horse violently round, he let down his rattling beaver over his face.

But Hilldiridur turned the head of her light palfrey towards Gerda, and soothingly she parted the thick veil of her tresses. Like a flower-bed in the dew of morning, that beauteous face looked brightly forth on the gentle harbinger of solace.

"Weep not, oh, weep not so, sweet maiden," said Hilldiridur. "There are other ways to Christ than those which the stern Zelotes would lead thee, and such as bear thee not across the charnel-vault and the wrecks of earth's perished pleasures. Look at me; I am she who held such stubborn contest with thee on the Swedish boundary-line in the name of Christ, and baffled thy sorceries. Dost thou remember it all?—my watch-tower and thy winding hell-cave? how they stood confronting each other, and enchantment on either side struggled felly with enchantment?"

The maiden looked on Hilldiridur with bewilderment, and a gleam of hope mantled over her tear-stained loveliness. "Now thou knowest," continued the latter, "that I mean truly by Christ, and yet I hope to frame a gentler path for thee than the rough warrior Zelotes could guess of. Christ is found by His people in many different ways. Wilt thou ride with us now, and be Hilldiridur's disciple?"

"O heavens, how gladly will I do so!" cried Gerda. "But

he with the silver-bright harness there and the helmeted head will not let me."

With the utmost despatch Count Walbek had chosen a beautiful palfrey from among those which the grooms were holding by the bridle-rein; and now leading it towards the maiden, he craved the favour of being allowed to lift her into the saddle. With a sweet smile she bowed to him, and the boon was granted. Then Archimbald again raised his beaver, and reverently kissing Hilldiridur's hand, "You beam upon us, noble lady, like a saving angel," said he.

"Ah!" returned Hilldiridur meekly, with a sigh of earnest misgiving; "assuredly another bright angel is needed, ere the happiness of us all is secured."

Otto thought he had already seen the saving angel, and in every town and hamlet he made anxious inquiry for the train of the supposed priest John. For a time he always lighted on the track of his soul's envied mistress; but he soon gained tidings of both herself and her retinue having turned out of the high road to Castle Trautwangen, and having made towards a famous and somewhat distant place of pilgrimage. Far more sadly and thoughtfully than ever he now rode forward on his way.

CHAPTER XXIII.

MEANWHILE, like merry singing-birds returning with a fairer sky, Folko, Gabriele, and Blancheflour were holding their homeward course in the bright summer-tide across the mountains that sever Italy from Germany. In the beautiful plains of our native land, that tell so richly of the toil of the husbandman, the three light-hearted travellers found many a varied trip to lure them onward; up the vales or down the vales, over the lakes and rivulets, and then as fleetly back again—now following the course of the streams, and now seeking to stem them—they pursued their gladsome path. For from whatsoever country strangers may come, our land seems to them to be the garden of gladness and faithful true-heartedness; and most European wanderers are very fond of it, from its being the common mother of them all. Folko and Gabriele might feel especially averse to think of the end of their journey, because then a solemn parting awaited them, which, as the Frankish knight was aware of his friend's claim to Gabriele, he could never seek to prevent by forming any indissoluble tie. But thus they travelled onward, closely knit with one another, as it were, in the whirl of the dance, the streamlets of their lives flowing side by side from one day to another;

and the gentle, kind-hearted Blancheflour, long since accustomed to let the wishes of her own heart go unheeded and unspoken, could scarcely think of any thing more delightful than thus lightly rambling over wood and vale at the side of her brother and her friend. One day it happened that they came in sight of a stream that went sparkling on its way between meadow-lands, corn-fields, and gardens; and on inquiring, they found that they were on the banks of the Danube. Rejoicing at the sight of the far-famed river, and of the favoured land of Suabia, which it waters, they seated themselves, towards noonday, not far from the bank, in the shade of some tall, leafy elm-trees, and made a cheerful repast of the viands and other stores that they had with them.

But now all of a sudden a swarthy man, in the garb of a gipsy, stood before them. Folko threw him some money, and bid him be off, that his somewhat grotesque appearance might not alarm the ladies. But in the mean while the gipsy had deftly unshouldered a box; and throwing it quickly open, he displayed such a sparkling store of jewels, so daintily set, and in such tasteful array, that the beautiful ladies could not take their eyes off them.

Now the baron began a very different parley with the gipsy. Whatever the ladies seemed to be pleased with, he bade him put on one side, and then he at last asked the price of all the pretty things that had specially taken their fancy. The gipsy set an extravagant price upon them; but the baron, little accustomed to haggle with any one, and at all times full of knightly generosity, immediately ordered a squire to fetch the required gold pieces. Then the swarthy pedlar gave a jeering smile, pretended to have made a mistake in his reckoning, ran over every item again, as if busily engaged in calculation, and then demanded double the amount for his wares. This too the baron bade them give him, when, with the coolest effrontery, "The things are not for sale at all," cried the gipsy, "and there is no price that I will part with them for."

"But I will have them, be the price what it may," retorted the angered baron. "It would serve thee right, thou miscreant fellow, that darest to tamper with noble ladies, were I to rid thee of thy whole stock by way of easy penance for thee, and give the value of it to some cloister or hospital, instead of to thee."

"Oh, yes!" said the pedlar, with a laugh and a grin; "there have been robber knights before now, and some too that have afterwards given the stolen beeves to the poor. It rests wholly and solely with you whether you will make their number full or not."

The noble Montfaucon blushed, and turned away from him.

"Quick, fellow, and be off!" said he; "and if thou hast aught of Christian faith in thee, thank God thou hast fallen into gentle knightly hands with thy saucy speech and dealing."

The gipsy went his way, slinging his box upon his back; but before he had gone far, he stopped again, looked round, and pointing to a castle on a lofty eminence, "Only be up there," said he, "in a few hours' time, sir knight, and I will come to terms with you for what you like; nay, you shall have many a curious unheard-of sight into the bargain. It were not at all amiss if the ladies were to come with you, for my performances concern you all in some measure, each in his own way." And so saying, he vanished of a sudden among the bushes.

The three travellers looked up in silence at the eminence he had directed them to. Sternly and solemnly, and full of the promise of peace, the time-olden castle-wall peeped forth from amid the shade of its immemorial oaks, the moss-grown gables of its watch-towers rose festally into the blue vault of heaven, while a gigantic gilded cross flashed on the main tower of the fortress, looking like a thing of glory in the sunbeams.

"We must betake us thither," said Gabriele in a faint but resolute tone. "Whatever cast of messenger may have invited us, something tells me the fate of all of us must be decided there." Blancheflour bowed her little ringleted head in grave token of assent; and Montfaucon, full of momentous expectation, bade the grooms hold themselves ready to set forth.

Just then a peasant happened to go past, and the baron asked him the name of the fortress.

"It is Castle Trautwangen," said he.

Folko and Gabriele looked at each other and trembled; then, as if with one voice, they murmured again, "We must go thither; we must go thither. There must the fate of all of us be decided."

CHAPTER XXIV.

Sir Hugh was once more sitting all alone in his bannered hall, with the huge wine-cup formed of silver medals on the round table before him. He was anxiously looking for the arrival of the old minstrel Walther, and was thinking to himself, "I stand pretty much in need of him with his wondrous time-olden legends, for my own life in the Northlands and in France, as also in the parts about Italy and Greece, that was once so rife of joy and sorrow and never-heard-of encounters, now shrinks back into the every-day nothingness of a childless old man, and shrivels up as other frozen leaves do. I shall never live to see any thing great again, uaught of fear nor of transport. How beautiful, then, it would be if the hero-deeds of our olden forefathers were ceaselessly riuging on my slumberiug ear! Walther, my laggard Walther, where lingerest thou?"

With a face all pale, a serving-man entered the hall. "Your noble son is returned, noble sir," said he.

"And must thou wear the aspect of death, with the errand of life ou thy lips?" cried old Sir Hugh, in joyful indignation. "Lead him in to me, the young bright star of blessing."

The serviug-man murmured a few unintelligible words, and threw open the large oaken doors. Sir Hugh had already risen from the great arm-chair, in his eagerness to welcome the best joy of his heart.

Loug draggling robes came rustling onward. A tall man, in deep black attire, strode firmly and heavily across the threshold, while his brawny right hand was waved threateningly over his head. The oaken valves again closed behiud him, and the terrified serving-man was heard bounding down the stairway. "Where is my son?" said old Sir Hugh; then his eye grew dizzy, and he reeled back into his chair.

"Thy son stands before thee," said the spectre; and on the old man's failing vision, the features of Otto glared forth too plainly from the haggard face of the stranger.

"Art thou turned monk, then?" murmured the former,—"a black-robed Benedictine monk?" And instantly recoveriug himself, "Who has given thee grace," cried he, with the stern mien of a judge, and the sturdy spirit of an olden hero,—"who has given thee grace to do this? I shall speak roughly with the cloister that has had the effrontery to put a cowl on the young Sir Otto von Trautwangen without his father's good-will."

"I am not young Sir Otto von Trautwangen," cried the monk in a shrilly tone. "In the world I was called Ottur, the son of Fair Astrid and the mighty Hugur, and now I am Brother Zelotes."

The old man sat motionless in his arm-chair. His new access of strength was not so easily to be shaken, yet he fixed his gaze in icy stupefaction on his fearful and unexpectedly risen son.

"Thou art a branch beloved of the Lord," continued the latter, "but one that is well-nigh lost. Therefore did I obtain grace from my abbot that I might wander forth to thy conversion, ere death should have drawn the black mantle over thee that he fetches up from hell for dying impenitent sinners." So saying, he seated himself opposite old Sir Hugh, and began an exhortation to penauce, that curdled up the marrow in his limbs, and flashed like consuming fire on his sight. He still went on; his heroic voice, and the burning words that gave it power, rose above the merry uproar that now came sounding from the courtyard and the halls below. Otto, who had gained tidings of old Sir Hugh's recovery, and had hastened on in advance of his mother and her party, that he might be the first to announce their approach, had now entered the castle. There he learned of the ghastly apparition of his monkish counterpart, and, guessing the true state of the case, he darted up the stairway.

"Ottur, Ottur, what dost thou here?" he cried, as he rushed into the hall. "Thou art my half-brother, and old Sir Hugh is the father of us both." So saying, he threw his mailed arms round the old man's neck, who seemed to feel a new life within him at the clang of Otto's harness; for, stroking the cheek of his knightly son, he now turned a threatening gaze on the monk.

But the priestly hero said to his brother, "I learned all that long ago in the cloister and on my way hither, where we met, by the by. Dreams, too, have often set me right about it. But my name is no longer Ottur. Ottur is as good as dead and buried. The man before you must be called Zelotes." And again, as if true to the stern name, which in the Greek means a zealot, he began his fearful homily of penance, so that Otto stretched forth his gauntleted hand towards him, as if to warn him off. "Why revilest thou thy father," he cried, "though thou knowest all the while that he *is* thy father?"

"That is my very reason," retorted Zelotes. "The mighty Hugur, once for all, shall not go to hell so long as there is breath in this bosom."

"Hear me," said Otto. "He will know well enough how to keep himself from hell without that horrible rant of thine. Still! I say, and ruffle not the hallowed repose of the old man, nor outrage thus rudely the solemn gladness of our meeting. Besides, I have such sweet tidings to bring him as will much more surely lead to heaven than the threatenings of all the monks in the world."

"Have it as thou wilt," said Zelotes composedly; and then he continued his terrific exhortation. Otto, on the other hand, raised his voice and shouted forth his message of joy, telling how his mother was still living, and was now bending her way, full of love and peace, to the long-wished-for castle of Trautwangen. Rapt in thought sat old Sir Hugh between the two young men; and while they beset him with embassies of such a different cast, he looked like the tower of a sunken castle rising above the conflicting ebb and flow of the waters.

Suddenly breaking on the confused medley of their discourse, a loud cry was heard in the courtyard of the castle. "Uguccione! Uguccione! thou murderer of Lisberta, come down. Uguccione! Uguccione! The avenger of Lisberta calls thee!"

Old Sir Hugh looked round him several times in the bannered hall. The voices of the youths were hushed. "All seems firm and strong," said he at last. "The day of general doom can scarcely be come, but mine of a surety is here. Follow me, my children, and pray for me." Then he rose slowly to his feet, leaned on Otto's shoulder, and moved towards the door. The young men durst not ask their grave, gigantic sire what was the matter, but in answer to their looks of wonderment, "I know not," said he, "what fearful power calls me to the courtyard, but its summons is irresistible. I hear names, at the very sound of which my heart's blood leaps again, as though it would bubble forth in atonement of my past iniquitous doings. But never, so long as he lives, shall old Sir Hugh of Trautwangen be found a coward. Forwards, my children, to meet my terrible doom." Still leaning on Otto, he passed down the stair-way, and, humming a death-song, Zelotes followed them. It was almost as if old Sir Hugh were already going to his grave.

They found a concourse of people in the courtyard. Not only the whole serving-train of the castle, but the country-folk also from the surrounding villages, who had easily gained entrance to a stronghold that at all times was open, were there assembled round a man who stood in Eastern costume in the centre of the area, uttering without ceasing that frightful cry that had been heard above every other sound in the bannered hall. At the same time he held in his right hand a glittering ring, which he kept twirling round and round. Old Sir Hugh recognised the jewel, and in valorous mood took his seat under a lofty lime-tree in the middle of the court. "That man there has Fair Astrid's ring, the mighty magic ring," said he; "and Heaven therewith hath given him power over my life. He is doubtlessly come to put an end to me."

"Seest thou aught, thou over-ripe offshoot of sin?" cried the stranger,—in whom, at the same moment, Otto recognised his olden friend and squire.

"Diephold!" cried he, using the German name which had once united them in such a close bond of affection,—"Diephold! It is my father thou art speaking to."

"Thy father?" cried Tebaldo in bewilderment. "Then we are brothers; for I am the son of poor Lisberta and Uguccione, and Uguccione and this old Sir Hugh are one and the same. But that matters not now. Down into his grave must my father go; for I swore to revenge Lisberta on hers."

"Never!" cried Otto, planting himself with his drawn sword before his parent. "Here I take my stand for victory or for death."

And "Never!" cried Zelotes also, enveloping the old man in his shadowy robes. "My father shall live and do penance. He who seeks to harm him must first rend these sacred garments."

"Thou canst never veil him so closely," cried Tebaldo, with a scornful laugh, "but what my spirits will glare on his inward eye, and force him to confession." So saying, he seated himself on the ground, and wrote strange characters with the ring in the grass.

Then a faint breathing and rustling arose in the deep vaults beneath the castle; cold, invisible arms seemed to sweep through the gathered throng, till many a man thought the likeness of himself was standing, like a grisly skeleton, beside him; and then it passed aloft into the tops of the linden-trees and the immemorial elms, revealing itself in wordless murmurings and the clapping of mysterious wings.

Every limb trembled, every lip was still. Old Sir Hugh alone raised his sonorous voice, that sounded more fearfully from forth the swathing robes with which the guardian Zelotes enwound him. Fair Astrid, he cried aloud, his own slaughtered love, came, all dappled in blood, before him; the drooping Lisberta made his heart her chilly grave; with store of other ladies and maidens to whom he had plighted his troth, and had afterwards forsaken them; so that in this terrible hour of witchcraft their avenging phantoms came staylessly careering through his anguished soul. Yet old Sir Hugh's words were those of a stout-hearted hero, who suffered unspeakably for his crimes, but nevertheless rose manfully above himself and his pain.

Then Tebaldo sprang from the ground, and called aloud to the bystanders: "Do judgment, ye people, on this abandoned sinner, who still brings down the vengeance of Heaven with his unchastened arrogance. Abominably as he deserted my mother and me, I shrink from being a parricide. But if the safety of your towns and villages be dear to you, the safety even of the very ground on which ye stand, then destroy him from among the living. Neither heaven nor earth can bear him longer. Hark! behold!" He cast his magic ring on high, and a sudden clap of thunder shook the cloudless heaven, covering them in a moment with a baleful sulphureous smoke. At the same time the earth trembled, little lambent flames of blue leaped forth from it; and, in the wild frenzy of dismay, serving-men, vassals, and all, ran with deadly purpose on old Sir Hugh. Otto warded his father manfully, as he sat encircled with the robes of the monk; while Zelotes, reviving the Northland strain anew, kept continually crying: "Strike well home, my valiant brother!

Spare them not, the coward minions! Had I here at hand the falchion after thee surnamed Otto, fiercely would I fall upon them; do so thou, thy sword is Ottur!"

CHAPTER XXV.

Already had Otto's sword drunk the blood of many of the shameless assailants, while others were quivering in every limb at the terrible sound of Zelotes' war-cry; and had not their senses been clouded by Tebaldo's sorcery, and they themselves been continually driven forward by a fear of grisly danger behind them, the crowd would long since have dispersed. Thunder-clap on thunder-clap rent the air: the fires of earth rose hissing on high, fashioned almost in the semblance of fiery cobolds; round the fortress was heard a roaring and a rustling, and the heavy pattering of rain and hail; but not a single drop fell within the precincts of the courtyard, as though the whole of it were changed to a charmed round, inaccessible to the gentle waters of the sky. Through all this thundering and roaring, howling and shouting, Tebaldo's yell-like laugh might at times be heard mingling with the mystic spell-words with which he conjured the firmament.

In the mean while Hilldiridur and her fellow-travellers had reached the castle; and the anxiety she felt for those whom she knew to be within it amid the tempests of heaven and the wild uproar of the people urged her to quicken her pace; till, under the protection of the sea-king, Archimbald, and her serving-band, she gained the linden-tree where sat old Sir Hugh, defended by Otto's almost fainting arm. Hilldiridur clung to him with words of peace and reconciliation. Gerda, obedient to her noble mistress in every thing, stationed herself meekly and watchfully at her side, ready to lend a helping hand wherever it was needed; while Archimbald and Arinbiorn fought their way to their brother-in-arms, and called out to their serving-men to hew down the rebels, and clear the castle of the miscreant mob.

Folko and the two ladies, with an escort of squires, had by this time arrived in the court. Entering at the side-port which terminated his path, he had passed on almost without bar or hindrance to the old lime-tree round which the war was raging; and, partly that be might the more amply secure protection to the ladies, partly because he saw the knights pitted against their inferiors in birth, he flew, with his sword drawn, to their rescue, and bid his squires do the same.

Just at this moment rose the cry of old Sir Hugh amid the press of the grim phantoms that haunted him: "Woe is me! Wittib rises before me, the mother of Folko, Baron of Montfaucon, and upbraids me with having forsaken her and Blancheflour her poor child. And of a truth she is right, for I was the great Messire Huguenin; and, by the word and honour of knighthood, that was a fair wreath of fame!"

No sooner did Blancheflour hear this than she fell down on her knees before her veiled sire, and covered him with her caresses, shouting through the close weeds that enveloped him, "I am thy daughter, thou venerable hero who art still shrouded from my view." Then turning again to Folko, "Fight cheerily, my brother, fight and conquer," she cried; "for the safety of thy father, the great Messire Huguenin, is at stake." And cheerily did the noble Baron de Montfaucon fight; and manfully did Arinbiorn, Walbek, and their serving-men support him. But the lurid darkness of the storm wound its wizard pall round their heads. The thunder and rain grew still more deafening, and Tebaldo's cry seemed to harry their senses. The retainers knew each other no longer, but in disastrous frenzy fell to blows with their comrades; and to such a pitch rose the fury of infatuation, that they at last turned their arms on their lords. Even *they* could not at all times hold delusion aloof; so that Arinbiorn, just as he thought to deliver some decisive blow, would remark with dismay that it had fallen on the gold helm of his kinsman Montfaucon; or when the count and the sea-king were making their firmest stand against the maddening rabble, Folko would rive them asunder with the shock of his shield. Then Archimbald would make fierce play upon them both, till they reeled and staggered again; when all three would discover their fearful error, lock themselves together once more in close array, raise the cry of war, and then, in a renewed fit of madness, fall foul upon their comrade Otto. He alone remained fresh and hale, and free from the clouds of that malignant sorcery. He kept repeating in an undertone the little prayer that he had learned in his childhood of Bertha, and which had stood him in such good stead in the mountains of the Hartz; and, like a radiant cherub hurling the lightning of wrath, he maintained his post before his perilled father. Yet he would scarcely have made good his position amid that tumultuous din, had not his light-brown, breaking loose from the grooms outside, come plunging and neighing through the press of the combatants. Stationing himself at his master's side, as though no magic on earth could cloud his faithful instinct, he brought his fore-hoofs down thunderingly, with their plates of iron, on the heads of the insensate foe, fastened his teeth furiously on their breasts and shoulders, and hurled them, stunned and stupefied, one over the other.

In the mean while the old minstrel Walther, with undaunted spirit, had made his way through the turmoil to his friend. "Wild work is going on without," said old Sir Hugh, growing aware of his approach. "But the voices of wife and children sound soothingly on mine ear. Would that the long slow train would pass away that winds along before mine inward eye! Still I hope for the best; for what says thy rhyme, good, faithful Walther—thy rhyme about night and sun?"

Walther sang, and roused the strings of his zittar:

"Night flies away before the sun,
And fear doth into transport run,
And grim death into life."

"I cannot hear aright," said old Sir Hugh, "for the wild uproar and the black robes that defend me. Sing louder, old minstrel! sing louder!" And again, in a bolder note, he began his song; but old Sir Hugh never ceased calling out, "Louder! louder still! much louder!" Then, fondly alarmed for the weal of his hoary companion, Walther smote his zittar with such tyrannic violence, that not only the strings, but also the framework of the gentle instrument flew asunder with a woful cry.

Then too rose the cry of old Sir Hugh: "Woe is me! woe is me! the lute is riven with my terrible misdeeds! Now all is lost!" And, half fainting with affright, he sank senseless on his seat. Zelotes murmured a prayer over him. But once more in manful defiance the renowned old hero started to his feet, and cried aloud, with a voice like the shrill blast of the trumpet, "Who would read mass over me, as over an outcast from the knightly order? Good heavens! am I, then, an outcast from knighthood?" And he fell back motionless into the arms of his son.

"Ah, lady, ah, mistress!" said Gerda to Hilldiridur, with a sigh, "Why did we give up our enchantments? Now we might protect, we might save him. Shall we to the work?"

"Away with all such idle thoughts!" returned the weeping Hilldiridur: "feelest thou not the power of this grisly magician? Feelest thou not that it is beyond all that we availed to do in our palmiest days? The strength to save is ours no more."

But Otto had heard the fearful plaint of his fainting father, and had felt his own limbs quail at the sound of it. Frenzy, wilder than ever, enthralled the senses of his comrades; Tebaldo rent the air with his savage huzzas; the mob pressed forward; and witchcraft, hovering hideously over the castle-court, began to change it to a place of judgment and death.

CHAPTER XXVI.

"Hold!" cried an angel-voice, that seemed wafted from some sweet paradise; and in a moment the horrible uproar was hushed. Those soft yet powerful tones had thrilled through every breast. All were obliged to obey them without demur; and every one stood motionless before his neighbour—not brought into subjection by petrifying fear, but by the heavenly solvent of reconciling love. When, in those of wilder mood, some unchastened outburst of anger sought to show itself, glittering warriors in foreign costume would gallop up to the refractory souls, and, brandishing their double-pointed javelins and flashing sabres, would restore their distempered minds to peace and order. Tebaldo in silence passed his hand across his eyes, and raised his dazzled glance as if to the sun.

And, sooth, a very sun, dazzling indeed to the guilty, but shedding a refreshing balm on all beside, was the gentle lady who but just before had bidden the combatants be still, and who, with a smile that spake alike of lofty sternness and child-like innocence, now made halt in the middle of the courtyard on a snow-white palfrey. Her gorgeous barbaric train ranged itself heedfully around her: at her side was a glorious and awe-inspiring warrior in floating raiment of purple, from which a cross of gold hung down over his breast. In faint peals of thunder the storm rolled away westward, and the pattering hail and rain were hushed.

Then it seemed as though Tebaldo sought to nerve himself anew to the deadly war. Wrathfully he waved the magic ring over his head; but again the angel-voice of the lady cried, "Hold! Against such foes as thee the holy father hath furnished me with this sainted water." And from a phial of gold she sprinkled a drizzling rain on Tebaldo, that glistered brightly in the evening sun, till the mighty magician trembled and fell upon his knees.

"That is not enough," said the lady, with a severity that gave a strange cast of awfulness to her lovely features. "The ring! deliver up the ring!" And as Tebaldo seemed sullenly to hesitate, she raised her phial: "Shall I again sprinkle thee with the rain of disenchantment?" said she; "I will not answer for the event if I do." Tebaldo drew near with trembling, and with a downcast glance he laid the magic ring in the wondrous lady's hand.

Then begging her companion to assist her to alight, she led him up to the linden-tree, where old Sir Hugh, as if reanimated by the presence of the beautiful apparition, had just disengaged himself from Zelotes' dark weeds, and now again raised his eye to the cheering blue of heaven. Truly, as his first glance chanced to alight on Arinbiorn's helm, a shudder of misgiving came over him. "Good God! the Avenger with the vulture-wings, too, is here!" said he. "But he must be come as a peacemaker, I trow; for an angel in woman's form sweeps past him, whose hallowed mien is right well familiar to me."

"Yes, as a peacemaker! All is peacemaking to-day!" Such were the heavenly tones that fell from the lady's angel-tongue. Then she led her curiously-arrayed companion, who looked half an Arabian, half a Christian, to the old man's embrace. "As truly," said she, "as thou wert Sir Hygies on the isle of Creta, so truly is this the son that was born to thee and the Damascene maiden in the cave of the Thunderer Zeus—formerly the great Emir Nureddin, but now graced with the nobler name of Christophorus."

Father and son looked long on each other in silent emotion. For a whole lifetime they could scarcely be said to have seen each other; and now the one sat by the linden-tree, an old hoary-headed sire, while the other stood before him, with his sun already on the decline. Then Christophorus felt touched with a deep sense of veneration; and, forgetting all former grounds of complaint, he was on the point of falling on his knees in meek devotion, when his father caught him in his arms, and cried aloud, "O thou bright Damascene sword-blade, how gloriously hast thou budded forth from the rose of Damascus!" And, locked in each other's embrace, the tears coursed freely down their cheeks; whilst Blancheflour, looking on old Sir Hugh with a smile of thrilling sweetness, "Gracious Heaven!" said she, "what a kind and venerable father hast Thou given me!" The old man laid the hand of blessing on her little ringleted head; and Montfaucon stepped forward, and told his olden master-in-arms how he had hitherto cherished for him his beauteous child, and how it was the fortune of war, and not his own fault, that she no longer had the magic ring on her finger. "But no one, I ween," he added, "would have wrested it so easily from me, had not your own valiant son entered the lists, and the scholar been forced to yield the palm to the lineal offspring of the hero." Otto bent over Sir Hugh, and embraced the knightly baron, on the plumes of whose helmet the falcon had again found a perch, and now sat clapping its wings for joy at the sight of its newly-restored lord. "The falcon brought me this, but only by mistake," said Otto, as he placed in the baron's hand the rose-coloured slip of parchment on which Gabriele had avowed her love in Cartagena. A faint flush mantled on Folko's cheek, and Gabriele veiled her crimson blushes.

"In right of that former tourney," continued Otto, clasping Gabriele's hand, "I must still claim some little power, I trow, over this snow-white little tablet. May I exert it now?" And so saying, he joined the hands of herself and Montfaucon, who had almost fallen on their knees before their friend, but who now, as he hastily drew back and vanished amid the crowd, were fain to mingle their embraces. Archimbald approached Gerda, and cast an inquiring glance at Hilldiridur. "She has shown herself to be a Christian," said he, "and I stand pledged for her truth." Then, bending over the beautiful hand of this maiden of the North, he uttered the solemn words of betrothal, Gerda glowing brightly the while like a tall festal taper.

In the mean time the lofty lady, in gentle speech, but with words of potent meaning, had gravely reprimanded Zelotes for having sought to terrify his father, and drive him to a severe course of penance. "Knowest thou not," said she, "that the Saviour draweth sinners unto Him by looks of gentleness? But where fiery terror is needed to cleanse them throughly, ah! good friend, our Father Himself taketh thought for that, and oftentimes by means of unconscious instruments." Zelotes stood in still humility before the lofty apparition, and, bending mutely low, he acknowledged her heaven-sent and transcendent power. But poor Otto steadfastly fixed his longing gaze on her. He could not feel sure whether it was Bertha or not; but this he knew, that in either case it would only be the most unexampled display of favour on her part that could entitle him to approach her with the faintest expression of his wishes.

But a kindly beam fell on him from the blue heaven of her eyes. "Knight of Trautwangen," said she, with a crimson smile, "why thus disguised in that black coat of mail? Methinks thou wouldst do better to don the sliver war-suit again, which is at present worn by Count Archimbald von Walbek. Well I know that ye both are bound by something like a vow; but thou, sir count, didst away with thine when, from their grave in the Hartz mountains, near to the centre of the earth, thou again broughtest up both knight and harness to the fair light of heaven. Neither shalt thou, Sir Otto, be any longer disquieted by the blood-spot on thy mail, for thou hast redeemed it by the scar that thy dark gorget received in defence of poor Heerdegen. I met Zelotes on my way hither, and he told me every thing. Oh, my good, faithful Heerdegen!" The tears glistened brightly beneath the dark shade of her eyelashes; but, suddenly bending low, she touched the silver-black gorget with her beautiful lips. "Thus, ye knights," said she, "doth a pure virgin release ye from your vows. Haste ye, then, and exchange your war-suits." The two gallant warriors bent in lowly obedience, and with an escort of squires they entered the castle.

In the mean time the wondrous maiden bade the menials kindle a bright flame on the hearth, and soon it was seen blazing up in the vaulted hall, while, through the open door of the chamber, it flickered in hospitable cheer on the green leaves that shaded the threshold.

By this time the two knights had returned in their new change of armour—Archimbald in the shadowy pride of his quaintly-formed mail, and Otto in the silvery sheen of his glistening war-suit, in the same youthful array as when he bade adieu to his little kinswoman Bertha.

Now, the lofty lady went forward to the hearth, and, besprinkling it with the holy water of her golden phial, she took her stand on the further side of the flame, folded her beautiful hands, and, in a voice as sweet as it was solemn, she cried aloud to the bystanders, "Hold evil thoughts aloof!"

And who could for a moment have cherished any at the sight of that beauteous image, so brightly illumed by the sportive flame, and with a sainted meekness in her every feature? She prayed awhile in silence; and then she cast the weird ring into the midst of the fire, describing over it the sign of the cross; and, while she again made her mute yet fervent appeal to God, the melted gold might be seen trickling over the stones, and the magic cement of jewels flying asunder in the heat.

The solemn work was over. With a light and buoyant step the beautiful maiden issued forth from behind the hearth; and at that moment Otto could not help feeling certain that his little kinswoman Bertha was before him. Yet there was a glory round the smiling girl like that of some radiant cloud of morning; and when she at last stood still before old Sir Hugh, and gave him friendly greeting, he involuntarily bent low the hoary head that was wont to look so proud in its wreaths of victory.

"Oh, pardon me, dear uncle," said she, "for not approaching you sooner with a due show of reverence, and for speaking to you like a strange lady, and not as your dutiful foster-child, Bertha von Lichtenried. However, up to this very moment I really was not such, but, more properly speaking, the ambassadress of the holy father. In a mighty vision—for he condescended to invoke the holy Virgin for my sake—there appeared to him all those monsters of evil with which the magic ring threatened you and your house: therefore I hastened hither with Christophorus by the straightest roads we could find; save that, hearing of my dear brother Heerdegen's death by the way, I went a little out of the direct road towards a place of pilgrimage, that I might there offer up more efficacious prayers for the peace of the faithful warrior's soul: but not till the magic ring was destroyed—such was the holy father's bidding—dare I discover myself by word or sign to those even whom I held dearest in the world, lest the ambassadress should be changed to a fond, meek-spirited maiden; and that was why I passed you so silently as you lay encamped near the chapel—you, I mean, my mother, Hilldiridur." And, sinking into the arms of her former beauteous hostess, she hid a face bright as the blush of morning in the green folds of the veil, for with the last words she uttered she had involuntarily turned towards Otto.

Christophorus now stepped up to the latter, and, grasping his hand, "Welcome, brother!" said he; "I rejoice in being able to call a youth by this name, the fame of whose valiant deeds brightens from pole to pole; but since I always had the character, as the great Emir Nureddin, of bestowing guerdons more lustrous than those of any other prince on earth, thou, my brave German kinsman, shalt be convinced, at this first meeting of ours, that it is so. Thou mayest sue for the hand of this heavenly creation; her angel-heart beats for thee." So saying, he led him up to Bertha, whilst she still lay enveloped in Hilldiridur's veil; and as Otto fell on his knee before a mistress who inspired him with veneration for her, "O mother! mother!" said he, "do thou speak the word for me; I am all unworthy of such blessed forgiveness." Then Hilldiridur placed the consenting hand of the maiden in Otto's; and as Bertha kneeled beside the stripling, she said, "But thy father will bless us, dear Otto!" Shedding tears of joy, old Sir Hugh laid his hands on the heads of that blooming pair, as they knelt before him in the full springtide of life and love.

CHAPTER XXVII.

With a dark and sorrowful countenance, a man entered the circle of the blessing and the blessed. It was Tebaldo. Bowing very low before the lady Bertha, that fair harbinger of peace, "For me, I ween," said he, "every possible hope of earthly joy is fled. Ye have destroyed the enchanted power on which I staked my whole perishable existence; and for what is called happiness in the arms of a father, brother, or sisters, I have given my own self the final death-blow. What, then, am I to do? Forsooth, I know not: but take my leave of you I will, and seek out the cave that is fitting for me. If I find it not, I shall all the more surely light on some precipice down which to dash myself."

"That is not at all my meaning," returned Bertha, with kindly earnestness; "neither does our good God mean any thing like that. Ye must do penance, and be reclaimed in that way; but not a word was said about your being lost. It were well, I think, for ye to undertake a pilgrimage to Jerusalem, and to struggle stoutly against the Evil One on your lonely way thither, cherishing pious thoughts and manly hopes; then must ye confess your sins at the holy grave, and return a reconciled offender among us. Speed ye, my pilgrim! The shepherd calls his stray lamb lovingly." At the same time, brothers and sisters, father and stepmother, all stretched out their arms fondly towards him, as though he were really coming back purified to his ancestral halls.

"Oh, truly, Bertha!" cried Tebaldo, "thou hast not ceased to be the ambassadress of the holy father, although thou art changed to a happy bride, all love and smiles. Yes, to Jerusalem! to Jerusalem! From the very first I felt impelled thither, as though presaging the sins that I should have to atone for on holy ground. But first obtain for me the pardon of the venerable old man, whom I am scarcely worthy to call my father any more; gain for me Hilldiridur's gentle favour; and plead for me with Otto, Christophorus, Blancheflour, and even the stern Zelotes, that they may fold me in a sisterly and brotherly embrace, and not merely in the cold forgiving way that golden apples are thrown to a poor culprit, as a last token of compassion, while he wends him to the place of punishment."

Bertha looked on him with a trust-inspiring smile. "Here I am not needed as an ambassadress," said she; "a kind-hearted maiden shall make all things right again." And gently she drew the repentant sinner towards his father, who folded him in a close embrace: Hilldiridur did the same; brother and sister wreathed their arms over him like a bower; while Otto cried aloud, in the melancholy outpourings of love, "Ah, Diephold! poor Diephold! this it was that, from the very first, made thee so unspeakably dear to me."

At length, with gentle violence, Tebaldo disengaged himself from their embraces. "Ye have now given me fresh store of strength," said he, "not only for my journey, but for my whole life beside. Farewell. I part from ye in gentle, peaceful mood, and full of hope. The star of your love shines brightly on the path before me; and when another year is past, and a pilgrim, with staff and cockle-hat, knocks at the gate of your castle, there will be a new festival of rejoicing in my father's halls."

Waving his greeting, he now strode slowly out. For some time they all remained silent, and followed him with weeping eyes. It was the bitter drop in the earthly cup of joy that ever and anon reminds us of its perishableness and ours.

"My son will come again," said old Sir Hugh at length; "and God, of His great goodness, will grant me once more in this life to press him to my breast. It seems as though a winged messenger were sweeping past me with these blessed tidings; and if Lisberta is changed to an angel of glory, she herself, perhaps, is the kindly envoy of peace."

The brothers and sisters wove their embrace still closer over their father, as he sat peacefully smiling beneath the mimic shade of those lovely boughs, till, breathing more freely from the depth of his bosom, "Thou art right, Bertha," said he: "all is reconciliation and peace. I will now no longer be the lone, inactive guardian of the castle. Come along with me to the meadow beside the Danube, ye dear ones, one and all. On Hilldiridur's hand, and amid the blessed throng of my children, I may again make the free bright creation my home, as in earlier, happier days."

As though the magic ring were changed to a living wreath of bloom, the just now solitary old Sir Hugh passed out of the castle-gate, with wife, children, and friends, into the crimson glow of the evening landscape. A beautiful rainbow was seen sparkling through the trees; and, folding their hands in silent prayer, the glad rout greeted the blessed token that now spake to them so significantly of heavenly peace.

CHAPTER XXVIII.

As they wound slowly down the castle-road, with the joyful and thoughtful old man, like a banner in the midst of them, the sun cast his last farewell rays on the green, bright mirror of the Danube, and the full moon rose in cool and dewy glory on the cloudless sky. The old minstrel Walther had meanwhile been busy in setting out a rich evening repast on the meadow; and round the circle that glistened with the flagon and the cup rose the merry blaze of the torches, parting off its green limit from the darker shades around it. The happy party now seated themselves within it.

"Ah! how much more refreshing and delightful it is," said old Sir Hugh, "on this green and blooming table, than it used to be up above there, in the stony precincts of my lonely fortress!" And Hilldiridur pledged him in the large beaker formed of silver medals; and two warm tears of pensive joy fell from the old hero's eyes into the wine. But Bertha and Otto, as also Folko and Gabriele, remembered the evening when the like blaze of torches had marked out the rounds of combat on the mead; and the sense of this enhanced the sweetness of their present good fortune. The Count von Walbek felt a passing touch of chagrin, because on that very spot the flare of the torches had played upon his silver-black mail; but Gerda stroked his frowning visage with a hand soft as the down of the swan; and that inglorious hour was at once forgotten amid the entrancing gleam of the north-star of his love.

Now, some one patted Otto gently on the shoulder; and, turning round, he met the sea-king's flaming eye, who immediately whispered in his ear, "How was it when we rode up together to Hilldiridur's watch-tower? Blancheflour has acknowledged thee as her brother; and the sheen of the torches, at no great distance from us, is making enchanting play on her beautiful face." Otto pressed the sea-king's hand in trusty joy, and rose to take his place beside his lovely sister, who, lost as she was in thought, looked like a lonely floweret of the mead; while, in the glowing ecstasy of hope and doubt, Arinbiorn remained at a short distance apart from them.

In the confidence of elegant discourse, the brother had soon drawn sufficiently near to his newly-won sister to be able to ask her whether she was the betrothed bride of her equal in birth?

"I will venture to answer 'No' for her," replied Folko, with some little warmth of tone, as he sat on the other side of her. And like a listless echo resounded the obedient "No" from Blancheflour's beautiful lips. Then came the sorrowful accord of a zittar from the throng of the bystanders. Blancheflour looked round in affright; until, in a louder but more plaintive voice, "God knows," she added, "that I am the betrothed bride of no man on earth."

Thereupon Otto beckoned the sea-king towards them, and made suit for him with his sister. Folko pressed them earnestly to unite themselves thus in closer kinship with his house; whilst Arinbiorn, with a crimsoned cheek, stood silently expecting, in lowly heroism, the end and aim of all his hopes. Like the tendril of some white flower in the breath of evening, Blancheflour seemed to waver to and fro; till at length, in silent resignation, she bowed her gentle brow to a "Yes." Taking her and Arinbiorn by the hand, Otto led them before his father; and as old Sir Hugh gave the two kneeling suitors his blessing, "Young image of the Avenger with the vulture-wings," said he, "take this pale flower of mine; and now all thought of vengeance is blotted out for ever."

"Vengeance is blotted out for ever," replied the sea-king, bowing his head still more lowly before his father. Blancheflour wept in silence.

Scarcely had the betrothed pair risen again to their feet, when the accord of the zittar sounded still more distinctly, and Master Aleard stepped, like a flower of the spring, into the beaming circle. The azure mantle of the singer floated around him; his bright lute rested on his arm, and he sang to its minstrelsy the following song:

"In summer's glow
How fast the flow
Of love's rich tide returning,
By morning gray,
Or bright noon-day,
Or when the stars are burning:
And if the dear moon shines above,
More heavenly then, and deeper,
Joy steals upon the weeper,
And parting speaks of hope to love.

If, when we choose
Awhile to cruise,
Round Love's green island sailing,
Our bark be hurled
On this rude world
Of ice—away with wailing.
The sailor sinks to rise no more,
The moon shines o'er him sweetly,
And where his tears fell fleetly,
Bright roses bloom upon the shore.

Bloom, roses, bloom;
Sweet moonbeam, come,
In thy bright maze enwind them;
They've 'scaped whole
From rock and shoal,
And cast dull care behind them.
Some love there is so pure and fair,
That, from his watery pillow,
Beneath the struggling billow,
The sailor hails the happy pair!"

Blancheflour held both her hands to her eyes; and her tears flowed so gently beneath that alabaster veil, that Arinbiorn only, who stood close beside her, and never once looked away from her, could discover a few drops of the burning shower that came trickling in silver flow from between her beautiful fingers. Otto immediately recognised Aleard to be the singer who, beneath the shady beech-trees, near Gabriele's castle in Gascony, had sung of Abelard and Heloisa with Blancheflour; and being told by Bertha that he belonged to the retinue of herself and Christophorus, he hastened up to greet him, and to thank him for gracing their general festival of betrothal with his noble minstrel-strain. But Aleard had at once vanished among the crowd; and whilst busied in searching and inquiring for him, Otto suddenly found his way barred by an apparition that powerfully arrested his notice and that of every one present.

On the other side of the torches was heard the tramp of mailed chargers, and the rattling of their harnessed riders; and as all eyes were turned that way, a tall knight, on a high, snow-white steed, became visible. He wore a war-suit edged with ermine, and carried a monstrous shield of solid gold, on which the torches flashed like lightning; in his other hand he held a lance of unusual length, resting it on his harnessed thigh, and lowering it as he drew near to the ladies with a puissant and graceful dexterity. But as he now too bowed low his helmeted head, richly glittering with gems, and surmounted by his waving plumes, and advanced at the same time into the torch-lit circle, some thought they could see a beaming coronet of jewels enwreathed round the splendid head-gear of war.

But before they could exchange a word on the matter, the kingly hero had swept past with his train, and they could soon hear the horses dashing forward at a gallop, and flying over the meadow with shrill neigh and thundering hoof.

"Was that not—" said Gabriele, in astonishment, as she fixed her glance on Folko.

"I think not the knight can have his equal on earth," replied the noble Montfaucon. "The Lion it was, and no other denizen of the forest."

Every eye hung questioningly on his; and he was just opening his lips to speak, when, from the same side on which the hero-knight had first appeared, came the sound of a zittar, so sweetly wafted that lady and knight, squire and serving-man, all seemed held in enchanted thrall. No one ventured to stir; but every ear, athirst with transport, drank in the delicious sound that now floated nearer and nearer through the night-air of summer, and at last caught new sweetness from the strain of the angel-voice that accompanied it

"And to the castle wending,
So high, so far,
In strain of saddened feeling,
Through chilly night-gloom stealing,

The minstrel sang the vanished star,
The pride of war.

In dungeon high enthralled
The Lion lay;
But as the song rose o'er him,
Bright visions passed before him
Of tented field and proud array,
On victory's day.

Thus only one can warble
Through night and gloom!
Song, spread abroad thy pinion;
The minstrel claims dominion
To stay the kingly captive's doom,
And rend his tomb.

The minstrel proved his power,
And death gave place.
'Twas Blondel's lay of wonder
That rove the tomb asunder:
Now lies the king of lion race
In love's embrace."

Singing this lay, a minstrel-form had drawn near to them on a pretty white palfrey, that seemed to be the younger and tenderer brother of that high, snow-white war-horse. A green mantle of velvet encompassed the figure of the beauteous stripling, whose countenance, unspeakably fair, beamed forth with an almost feminine loveliness from his thick ruffle of lace, save that a trim little beard fringed his upper lip. He stayed his dainty palfrey, looked pleasantly on the bright circle of torches, and at the same time continued striking the zittar that hung by a rich chain of gold on his breast.

Otto recognised the lovely apparition to be Master Blondel, who had formerly appeared to him in the blooming woods of Frankland; and the closing lines of the song had at once given the whole company to know what a noble star of love and minstrelsy had just risen upon him.

"O thou thrice-noble Master Blondel," cried the ladies and the knights; "then the great King of the Lion-heart is really saved? And was he, perchance, the glorious knight that just rode past us?"

Blondel confirmed all this in a friendly tone; and in true minstrel fashion was easily prevailed upon by the beautiful dames and noble knights to tarry awhile at their banquet, and recount to them how he had saved his beloved king, hero, and friend, seeking at every keep and castle the echo of his lute and song; an adventure whose beauty and true-heartedness, my courteous reader, will already have become endeared to thee by many a lay and legend.

The knights raised their voices aloud and lauded the minstrel and his whole order as glorious and blessed, who had achieved that which so many mighty warriors had in vain sought to compass by dint of their renowned blades. The ladies rained down a shower of flowers on the victorious troubadour.

Then Arinbiorn stepped up to Otto, leading by one hand Blancheflour, by the other Master Aleard, whom, with a keen and rapid glance, he had singled out of the throng.

"Dear brother," said the sea-king, "here is the stripling whom I before told thee I saw in the magic mirror at Blancheflour's feet when I gave the name of Rosalind to the virgin star of my life."

Otto changed colour; he darted glances of flame at the minstrel, and Folko pressed towards them with a wrathful look. But Arinbiorn continued: "Wherefore all this anger, ye magnificent knights? Have ye not just now felt that the minstrel on his airy path can often do more than we glistening men of steel? Master Aleard is of a noble house. Franks, Spaniards, Englishmen, and Germans praise his lays. Otto, why tarriest thou? Or shall we trample the zittar at once under our mailed heels, just as it has given us a proof, in Blondel's victorious emprise, of its superior power and glory?"

Otto and Montfaucon blushed deeply. The former took the minstrel, the latter the lovely Blancheflour in his arm, and in this way they drew near to old Sir Hugh. Arinbiorn strode before them as their deputed herald. The hoary hero joyfully gave his consent. It seemed as though an inspiring ray from the after-life on which he verged were sent to remind him how much more beautifully his white flower would entwine itself round the rose-tree of song, than round the bloody spear of battle. Or was it the soothing, moonlike gaze of the heavenly Hilldiridur that enlightened him? He blessed the beauteous lovers, whose blush at the first long-wished-for kiss seemed to mantle each tender cheek with the brightest tints of morning.

"And thou, Arinbiorn?" said Otto pensively, as he grasped the right hand of his brother-in-arms.

"God has dealt graciously with me," replied the latter. "Had Blancheflour in strict justice been the betrothed bride of another, I should scarcely, I ween, have been able to endure my misery. But now it has been so sweet to me to be allowed to resign my claims; and such resignation as this nerves every royal soul to joy. Come, then; I hear the summons of the sea, with all its green, impetuous billows. Hope is wafted on the sound—the hope of fame, at least, if not of love; and Rosalind remains for ever the war-cry that shall lead me to fortune and to victory."

"All is so good and fair," said Bertha, with a peaceful smile; "how can any one find room for doubt?"

And every heart that had felt anger or ill-will was lulled to rest by the word and gesture of the spotless maiden.

The aged hero looked wistfully on Zelotes and Christophorus. "Then two of old Sir Hugh's sons," said he, "shall pass through life without the bridal-garland."

"I weave them for others," returned Zelotes. "Rejoicing in my sacred gift of priesthood, these several pairs will I unite; and it shall be to me no unworthy source of pride, that in this matter also the house of old Sir Hugh is raised and held together by its own independent virtues."

"But I," said Christophorus, "am bent on extending the glory of my noble house by the renown of victory and noble lore. The heart of no one woman, I ween, is formed to satisfy the cravings of my love. Be earth my bride, in all the bloom and splendour of its enchantments!"

With a warm and manly grasp, old Sir Hugh pressed the hands of his two sons, and darted a look of keen delight on Otto as he stood opposite to him, with his arm enwound in blissful pride round Bertha's high angelic form.

Then Master Blondel, who had been told by his fellow-minstrel what wondrous things had happened there, drew near with a lovely obeisance to Bertha; and taking from beneath his mantle a tastefully-wreathed little chaplet of gold, that glistened with jewels red and green—

"Ah, would that in thy lofty beauty," said he, "thou wouldst for this once deign to accept a crown at the hands of poesy! Thou must often have granted a boon such as this."

Then sweetly blushing, and yet with a consciousness of her dignity, Bertha bowed her angel-brow, and the brilliant circlet soon glistened on her light-brown hair, pointing her out, even to uninitiated eyes, as the inspiring spirit of all these bright achievements, and the beautiful queen of that festal hour.

But Blondel had again vaulted on his little white palfrey; and as he trotted along in the moonlight, he sang them thus his parting lay:

"Loving, longing, sea-ward sailing,
With the sword or song prevailing,
All the strife is ended now

'Neath the golden lustres gleaming
Stands the lady in her pride;
Brightest she where all is beaming,
Knights and minstrels grace her side.
Scenes of hero-life and light
Wait her glance;—good night,
Good night."

His song died away among the shades of the dewy wood, as now too this whole story hath sounded in your ears its last GOOD NIGHT.

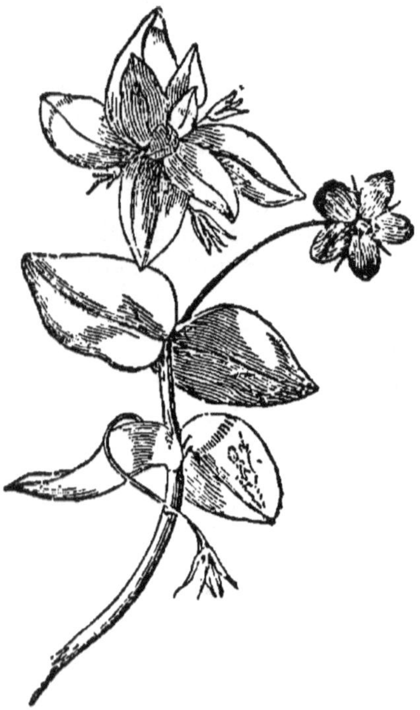

NOTES BY THE TRANSLATOR.

"*Zittar.*"

This foreign word frequently occurs in the course of the translation. I have ventured to introduce it, because the instrument alluded to is entirely distinct from any thing I have ever seen in the musical world of England. It is at present peculiar to the Tyrol, where many of the peasantry play upon it the light dances and love-strains of their country, varying their song occasionally with that guttural yet pleasing note which they call the Jodel (yodle). It in some measure resembles a guitar without a neck, square at the end where the pegs for the strings are fitted, yet rounded in the usual way at the other. Those now in vogue have cross-pieces of wood at the back of them, so that they may stand upon a table; and thus, from their being slightly raised, the sound receives a freer vibration. The air is played on three tinkling wires running along a finger-board that extends lengthways on either side of the orifice of sound, while the accompaniment, or bass (if bass it may be termed), is produced on seven or eight strings of the ordinary kind, each affording one solitary note. It is needless to add, that the manner of tuning it is peculiar.

P. 39. "*The clang of the ringing pledge-cup.*"

The ceremony of drinking healths in Germany on convivial occasions is not performed as in England; but the glasses are rung against each other once, twice, or three times, as the enthusiasm of friendship or joviality may require. The true knack of eliciting the silvery chime is not acquired at once. This custom is, no doubt, of very ancient date.

P. 82. "*Don Gayferos, Don Gayferos.*"

We do not find this kind of verse in the body of English poetry; neither, as far as I know, have we any distinct name for it. We should probably call it the ballad. And the Germans might possibly call it so too. But it seems rather to be the blending of two kinds of verse, termed in Germany the "Romanze" and the "Ballade." The former is probably of Spanish origin, and love was its privileged theme and object. The "Ballade" is of Italian extraction; and in the Middle Ages, though love too was the burden of its strain, it was set to music and made the accompaniment of the dance. No species of verse, perhaps, are more purely lyrical than these. Their form and measure, however, admit of more variety than it would be in place to notice here. From the exact correspondence of its stanzas in the first two parts, the above poem lays claim to the title of "Ballade;" but the third part, with its recurring rhyme, trenches more upon the "Romanze."

But we must not suppose that either the "Romanze" or "Ballade" are now to be found in their original purity. In Britain they assumed the form of a narrative poem, liable to a roughness and irregularity which was greatly at variance with their olden cast; and both in Britain and Germany the two distinct forms of verse soon merged into one. In the former country, indeed, the "Romanze" must have been wholly unknown. Weisse, Loewen, Gleim, and Schiebler, who flourished during the latter half of the eighteenth century, were the first to revive this kind of poem among the Germans. But they were not fortunate in the cultivation of it, and deviated considerably from the chasteness of its original form. Herder, however, who was born twenty years later than the first three of the above-mentioned poets (although he may rightly be styled their contemporary), produced the "Romanze" and "Ballade" in their genuine character. He was materially seconded by Bürger, the Counts Stolberg, Voss, Hoelty, and others. Like Goethe, he often took English and Scotch ballads as the groundwork of his productions, without endeavouring, like his great contemporary, to infuse into them a strictly German character. But as I am rather hinting at the propriety of adhering to the form of the original poem, than writing a history of this sort of verse, I will content myself with merely referring the reader to what has been called the "Romantic School" of Germany, where in the works of the Schlegels, Uhland, Schwab, Justinus Kerner, Gustavus Pfitzer, and others, many beautiful specimens of the "Romanze" and "Ballade," in one form or other, may be found.

P. 110. "*Thy conquest-bringing Wallkura.*"

The idea of the beautiful houris with which the crafty Mahomet peopled the paradise of the faithful seems to bear a close resemblance to that of the Wallkuras, or Valkyriæ, alluded to here. The whole system of the Gothic mythology is too intricate to allow us to form any very exact conception of the attributes of the latter. The subjoined notice, however, may be welcome to those who have not time or opportunity for more abstruse inquiry.

Valhalla, in the mythology of the ancient Celts, Scandinavians, or Goths, signifies an abode of delight, promised by Woden (or Odin) to those of his followers who should perish in battle. It was the abode of the god Odin himself, and the pleasures to be enjoyed there were conformable to the warlike notions of those martial hordes. The chief happiness shared by the inmates of Valhalla was supposed to be that of arming themselves, of passing in review, of ranging themselves in the order of battle, and, strange to say, of cutting one another in pieces! But soon as the more festal hour arrived, the warriors returned to Odin's hall, perfectly healed of their wounds. There they resigned themselves to the pleasures of the banquet, and quaffed in the skulls of their enemies the delicious mead poured out for them by nymphs called *Valkyriæ*. A warlike death was the only title of admission into Valhalla; every other end was regarded as ignominious; and those who died of sickness or old age were banished to the Niflheim, or the hell of cowards and villains.

The more curious reader may consult Bishop Svensen's translation of the "First Edda or Runic Chronicle," 3 vols. 4to, 1643; Svensen's "Dictionary of the Northern Mythology;" and Creuzer's "Symbolik."

P. 251. "*Roland's pillar.*"

"In many of the towns of Saxony and other parts of Germany, columns with a sculptured sword upon them may be seen in the market-places or public squares; or in some places these columns are surmounted by a man armed with a sword, the symbol of supreme justice. These monuments have been thought to represent Roland, nephew of Charlemagne, the far-famed hero of romance; but this is a mistake; and it is supposed that the name they bear comes from the ancient Saxon word *ruegen* ('to denounce in a court of law, to punish'), or perhaps from the words *ruhe* ('rest'), and *lund* ('land'), as though these monuments were the symbols of the tranquillity consequent upon the due administration of justice."—(*Encyclopédie de Didérot et D'Alembert.*)

P. 273. "*Live like the gods on Asgard's sunny heights.*"

Odin, king of the Asæ, dwelt at Asgard, between the Euxine and Caspian seas, where anciently there was a city called, by Strabo,

Aspurgia, the metropolis of a province denominated Asia. Etymologists will see at once that Asgard and Aspurgia are one and the same word. But how this city of Odin's earthly sojourn came to give name to one of his more beatified abodes, it is difficult to determine. For it was not till this wondrous young Celt, or Scythian, had passed to the Baltic, had taken his downward course through Saxony, Westphalia, and Franconia, and then reascended to Jutland—whence he crossed to Sweden, and brought that country under his sway—that he died and was worshiped as a god. Yet when we consider that learned Danes of old refer the conquests of Woden to the year 1100 B.C., the Saxon chroniclers to some very different period, and most other writers to the year 66 B.C.—nay, that those who place the expedition of Odin in the year 66 B.C. confound it with that of Pompey against Mithridates,—our astonishment at any minor difficulty may cease. Plain it is, that had some of the aforesaid chroniclers cast an intuitive glance forward, they might almost have identified the brilliant Woden with William the Conqueror, merely altering the B.C. into A.C. For common purposes, however, it will be sufficient to know that Woden flourished within the ages of Mercury and Augustus Cæsar, inclusive.

THE END.

www.ingramcontent.com/pod-product-compliance
Lightning Source LLC
Chambersburg PA
CBHW031341070726
47496CB00017B/1394
* 9 7 8 3 3 3 7 3 1 0 2 3 3 *